LIMP DICKS & SAGGY TITS

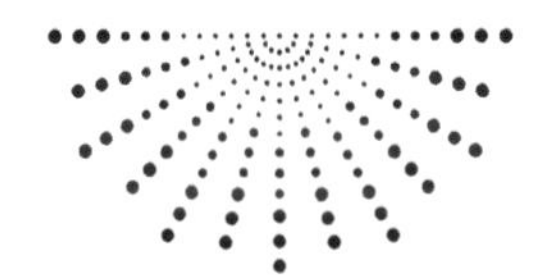

TRACIE PODGER

For my mum, my greatest supporter – even if she has been the cause of my premature grey hair!

Limp Dicks & Saggy Tits

By

Tracie Podger

This is a work of fiction. Characters, names, places and incidents, either, are products of the author's imagination or they are used fictitiously. Any reference to actual locales, or persons, living or dead, is entirely coincidental.

CHAPTER ONE

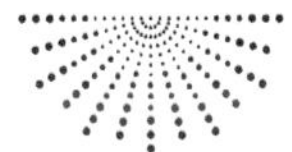

Fifty and single was not a great place to be. Especially when I had no desire to be either. But, against my wishes, I found myself to be *exactly* at that point.

Why should meeting a man be so difficult at my age? Why couldn't I walk into a bar and not look like a cougar on the prowl or a nearly-OAP being patronised by the youth? Why couldn't I still have a healthy sex life even if I didn't have a husband anymore?

Too many whys, and after my third glass of wine, I guessed I could continue to add more but…what the fuck good would it do?

"Lizzie, are you listening to me?" I heard.

"No," I replied, draining the glass I held in my hand. "I'm thinking about what the nurse said to me."

"What did the nurse say?"

"That I might need to consider lubricant." I was aware of the slur to my voice. "She said I have vaginal atrophy. Fucking vaginal–"

"What's vaginal atrophy?" he asked, interrupting.

"A shrinking fanny, Joe!" I replied.

"Let's just call it a return to virgin fanny, it sounds better. So, did you hear what I said earlier?"

I was lying on the sofa. There was a romcom playing on the TV that I had absolutely no interest in—had probably seen twenty years ago—while my best friend, Joe, was sitting in the chair opposite me.

"No, what did you say?" I asked, shuffling up a little so I at least looked interested in what he had to offer.

"I said, I think we need a little weekend break away," Joe repeated.

"I like the sound of that."

"I might have a look online tomorrow."

Maybe he told me more, I had no idea. I awoke the following morning with a banging headache and a mouth tasting like a sewer.

"Who filled their mouth with sewer…*stuff*, to even come up with that phrase?" I said aloud as I climbed from the sofa in need of water.

The kitchen was spotless, and I gave an imaginary thumbs up to Joe who had obviously cleared away our takeout containers. I smiled at the small box of empty wine bottles he'd left on the counter, ready for recycling.

I scratched my head, feeling the tangles in my hair from sleeping on a sofa at a strange angle, and probably tossing and turning at that. On sniffing my armpit, I tried to decide on the urgency of a shower, or whether I could fit a cup of coffee in first. However, since I was alone, it didn't matter if there was a slight sweaty smell; coffee was needed.

The only time I drank instant coffee, from the jar, was when I was hung-over. I hated the stuff normally, but I couldn't be arsed to make fresh. I unscrewed a jar, banged it on the counter to loosen up the granules, and plunged in a teaspoon. Once deposited in a mug, boiled water added, and a splash of milk, I piled in some sugar and sipped. On hung-over mornings it was nectar for the brain.

Flashes of conversations filled my mind as I walked through to the bathroom. I was sure Joe mentioned a weekend break at some point the previous evening. I hoped it involved a spa, and wine, and maybe a nice restaurant, and a bar, and maybe more wine.

My singleton life since…*him*, revolved around too much alcohol, and not enough self-love, of any kind so yes, a nice spa would be perfect. It was time to kick myself and my alcohol-fuelled body back into shape. I was that buoyed in that precise moment, I showered quickly, drank down the rest of the coffee, and then had the bright idea to hit the gym, a place I hadn't ventured to in months.

I pulled on some leggings and accompanied them with a long t-shirt to hide the rolls of fat. I found my trainers and a gym bag with a towel and toiletries and before I could change my mind—or sanity returned—I left the flat and walked up the road.

I'd made it halfway before my body started to sway and a small wave of nausea washed over me. I could have very easily turned around and headed back home. I was determined, however. I *was* going to the gym; I was sick of myself, and I was sure everyone else was too.

Many a time I'd made the decision that I didn't want/need a man in my life and every time, I knew I was kidding myself. I also knew it was the fallout from being cheated on and left to pick up the pieces while he swanned around town with a bloody drag queen.

Maybe if she'd been tall, blonde, slim and well spoken with a high profile job in the city I might not have been so bitter. If she had been the typical just-out-of–her-teens bimbo with no aspirations other than wanting a sugar daddy, I could have understood, *sort of.* But a drag queen? Now, I have nothing against drag queens, per se. I have *everything* against my husband running off with one.

I had no idea why the situation seemed worse, I mean, it was pretty laughable. He was short, balding, with a paunch forming, and heading for his sixties. 'She' was over six feet in height and that was without the five-inch heels, muscles, tattoos down one arm from days in the navy, of disputable age, and with one false eye! I mean, for fuck's sake, why?

I shook my head, as if that would actually rid me of the images, and walked on. I wasn't going to dwell on him. Our divorce was due any day soon, and according to Joe, the font of all gossip, Harry and…*her*, were going to get married. My eyes stung as tears formed. I wasn't sure what was worse, to discover your husband was having an affair with another person, or to discover your whole marriage had been a sham; a cover for some twisted sense of respectability on his part when in actual fact he had been gay from birth but refused to acknowledge it. That was the part that hurt the most. He had denied his true self for fear of… God knows what. His parents were more liberal than the Liberals. In the meantime, I was the one who got hurt.

Joe had joked once, years ago, about Harry being in the closet. I guessed he'd seen something in either Harry's face or mine, as he never mentioned it again. I didn't want to think about it anymore.

I powered on to the gym, despite the headache. Taking a deep breath, I pushed through the heavy glass doors and then got stuck at the turnstile. I fumbled around for my membership card. I'd been a gym bunny for years; I would have kept my card in my gym bag, somewhere. By the time I'd emptied the bloody thing out, wrinkling my nose at the stale smell of a bag that hadn't been opened in a while, the smirking receptionist had handed me a temporary one. I snatched it from her and barrelled through.

I took a corner locker in the changing room and stuffed my bag in an equally smelly wooden closet. I put my fifty pence in the mechanism and locked the door, slipping the elastic band that held the key on my wrist. I ran up the stairs to the gym floor, desperately hiding the lack of breath by the time I'd reached the top. I could feel my cheeks redden with that little exertion, and realised I was in *bad* shape.

I nodded to the personal trainer as I passed; I doubted he knew who I was, but it made me feel good when he smiled back. Then I walked to the warm-up mats and started my stretching.

I wasn't concentrating when I decided to stretch my inner thigh. I slid my leg out to the side, not realising the twit on the mat before me had placed their *condensing* water bottle there. My trainer connected with the droplets of water and what should have been a gentle stretch as I crouched ended up a half-split and a torn muscle (self-diagnosed, so who really knew what damage I'd done?) and my hooha screaming with the reverse wedgy that had occurred as my leggings were pulled not just tight, but *upwards*.

I gritted my teeth, hissed out an expletive and gently slid my leg back to a more natural position. The burn in my inner thigh suggested I wouldn't be walking straight. Shame the swagger was from a muscle strain and not a night of rampant sex.

Deciding the walking machine—or as I called it, the gentle stroll machine—was probably out of the question for the time being, I hobbled to the bike

I pedalled slowly, realising how out of shape I was and watched MTV, or whatever it was, on the huge screen in front of me. I couldn't hear anything and had to lip-read as I'd forgotten to bring the earphones I'd need to plug in at each machine for sound.

I was glad, though; I was sick of watching *girls* with big tits and perfect teeth prancing around the stage wailing about a lost love they'd never experienced.

Be fucking fifty and dumped before you scream about your heart-break, I shouted, in my head.

I pedalled faster. "Harness the anger," I whispered to myself and then chuckled.

The anger lasted all of about thirty seconds; it coincided with the agonising pain that shot up my dodgy knee from pedalling so fast. With one torn (self-diagnosed) inner thigh muscle and one dodgy knee, I slid off the bike and limped to the wind-down mats. I used the excuse of a post-exercise stretch to lie down and rest from such an arduous workout.

Maybe I'll book Pilates, I thought, as I just lay there like a limpet and looked at the ceiling. Lying around wasn't hard work, probably something I could do very well.

Yes, Pilates, that would be next on my list.

CHAPTER TWO

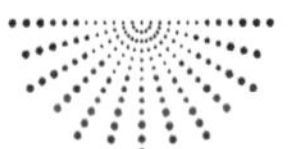

After a shower and a cringe in the mirror at my discoloured bra and non-matching, greyish, Tena Lady knickers (think period knickers—wide gusset to hold a pad that soaked up…not the substance that reminded women they were all woman, despite their moans about it, but *pee*), I dressed, cursing myself for not actually having a clean outfit to change into. I stuffed my towel in my bag and scraped back my wet hair into a ponytail. Sighing, I dragged my fingers under my eyes, annoyed at the bags and dark circles that hadn't been there prior to *him* running off.

I'd always been one for manicures, for regular appointments at the hairdressers, nice clothes, and a spacious house. Harry earned well, although I wasn't the trophy or the freeloading wife I seemed to have been so-called throughout our divorce. I took all the menial jobs I could to support him while he worked the shit jobs and did the training to become the broker he ended up as. It seemed to have been forgotten that *he* was the one that said I shouldn't work when he 'made it'. But I still kept house, I still cooked and cleaned, and made sure his friends and colleagues were always well entertained during the many, *many* dinner parties I hosted. I was the perfect wife, and when he had decided to embrace his *gayness*, all that was forgotten.

In my grief I'd let myself go. I wanted to get back to me; the one I liked or thought I had. I just wasn't sure who that *me* was. I needed to start with my diet and lose the break-up chocolate, the wine, and the many take-outs. I was going to get healthy.

I rang Joe. "I'm just leaving the gym, do you want to meet for some shopping and lunch?" I asked.

"Lunch, yes, shopping, no. I have two viewings this morning and then a waxing later."

Joe was an estate agent, but not just any old estate agent. If I remembered correctly, the cheapest property deal he'd done had been in the low millions. He was also addicted to a sack and crack wax. I doubted he allowed the hair to grow back before he made the next appointment. I'd told him many a time to join a BDSM club and get his pain kicks there instead of ripping his skin to shreds. But perhaps, having never experienced a BDSM club, it was the same thing.

"Okay, Carlo's at twelve?" I asked.

It was our favourite restaurant. "Perfect," he replied.

"Oh, and I want to talk about BDSM clubs," I said, just before I disconnected the call. I heard him splutter as if he'd choked on a drink.

I browsed the rails of a department store concession and sighed. When Harry left, he'd also closed down our joint bank account and cleared off with the money. When I realised I couldn't keep the house, not only was it in his name but I couldn't afford it anyway, I had moved into an apartment that Joe owned. It was meant to be a temporary move; when my divorce was finalised, and the money I believed I was owed was released to me, I could buy my own place and purchase the nice clothes my fingers fondled. I wasn't bitter—well, not much—but I was still angry. Angry with Harry for his deceit and angry at the way he thought he could walk away and leave me with nothing. He was the one in the wrong, he was the liar, the…

"Ma'am?" I heard. My eyes came back into focus, and I realised I had screwed up the silk, thousand-pound garment in my angry little fist.

"I don't like the colour," I said and stalked off.

I decided to head to Carlo's and grab a spritzer before Joe arrived. It wasn't beyond the realm for him to be late if his client wanted a second tour of the thirty-something roomed property he was likely showing that morning. He had offered me a job with his agency but being nice to people wasn't on my list of things to do at that time, and it didn't change for quite a while. Instead of showing people around, he had me doing his paperwork. It was charity. It *felt* like charity, but I wasn't so proud that I turned it down.

I pushed through the door to Carlo's.

"Lizzie, it's good to see you, you look…" Paul, the owner, said as we embraced and air kissed.

"I look?"

"Shit, my darling. Is that prick still hurting you?" he asked as he stepped back and held me at arm's length so he could *study* me.

"Thank you, you're too kind, and no. I'm hurting me by letting him hurt me still."

He chuckled as he showed me to my favourite table. I settled in, kicking my gym bag into the corner and wishing I'd left it in the locker to be collected later.

"Usual?" he asked.

"White wine spritzer with lemonade, not soda," I replied.

"Mmm, okay. Eating alone?" he asked as he placed a menu on the table.

"No, Joe should be here shortly."

"Ah, the delectable Joe. I wonder when he'll succumb to my charms," he said, licking his finger and wiping it across his eyebrow.

"Never, my darling, but we can fuck just the once if you like," we heard.

Joe had arrived earlier than I expected. He kissed Paul on the cheek and then pulled out the chair opposite me to sit. I watched Paul flush and felt sorry for him. They would make a great couple, but Joe was too much of a slut, and Paul was too nice for it to work. I sighed.

"I'll have what she's having," Joe said, and then placed his palms down on the table. "You will never believe who my last viewing was with?"

"Who?"

"No, you have to guess," he said, pouting with displeasure that I wasn't playing.

I sighed dramatically. "Joe, it could be one of a million names. Who?"

He rolled his eyes. "Dave Thompson," he said, then sat back with a triumphant smile on his face.

I stared at him.

I stared a little longer and took a sip of my wine.

I stared some more.

Eventually I had to ask. "Who the fuck is Dave Thompson?"

He gasped. "Lizzie, Dave Thompson is the brother of *you know who*."

I continued to stare. "I have no idea who '*you know who'* is."

"Jesus Christ. I'm trying to be subtle here," he hissed through clenched teeth. "Dave Thompson is the brother of Saucy Sally. He's a darts player."

I stared just a little longer but blinked when Joe slammed his palm on the table causing the cutlery to jump about. "Sally! Shagging your husband," he said slowly in an overly-dramatic theatre whisper.

"Her name is Pete," I said.

"That may be the case, but when she is a *she*, she's called Saucy Sally."

"Like I would know that. Who is a darts player?" I replied with a scrunch of my brow.

"Dave," Joe said, with a voice raised in exasperation and followed with a sigh.

"How do you know he's Pete's brother?"

"Because that's who is buying the house."

It dawned on me what Joe meant then. My tight-fisted husband had argued that he was *oh so poor* was buying a multi-million-pound property with Pete/Sally. I doubted being a professional drag queen earned enough for that type of a mortgage.

"Are you sure *she's* buying the house and not Dave?"

"Who's buying a house?" I heard. Paul had returned to place Joe's wine on the table and wait for our order. Joe and I had spoken at the exact same time.

"Saucy Sally."

"Pete the husband snatcher."

"Oh! Awkward," Paul replied. "Now, lunch?"

I ordered a pasta dish; Joe opted for pizza. I'd never known anyone who could eat as much as he did and stay as thin. I looked at food and the weight piled on.

"How much is this house?" I asked.

"One point five, but I think the owner will take one and a quarter."

"She can't afford that!" I shouted, then choked on the mouthful of bread I'd taken to soak up some of the alcohol. I noticed other diners looking our way. "So I'm guessing Harry is buying it. Why not look himself?" I whispered, not wishing my dirty laundry to be aired so publically.

"He's hardly going to ring *me* and arrange a viewing, is he? Dave said he was viewing on behalf of his brother, and then dropped the name in a later conversation."

I sat back and took a large gulp of wine. "What a wanker." The eavesdroppers on the next table sniggered.

Harry had argued over every penny I'd won in our divorce. I hadn't even wanted *half* of everything, just enough to start life again at fifty bloody years old. I'd given him my life; we'd been together since I was sixteen (that was a lie, I was fifteen, but I buried the first year for the sake of legality). I deserved what I was after, and if he could afford a million and whatnot pound property, he hadn't suffered that much.

I swallowed another gulp of wine to wash away the anger. "Do you think they'll buy it?" I asked as Paul placed our dishes on the table.

"I don't know to be honest. I get agents looking at property on behalf of clients all the time, but they're usually the investment types or an Arab wanting a holiday home near Harrods. I guess if we see them for a viewing themselves, they're serious."

"Well, I don't want to know," I said, knowing full well that I did.

We ate and chatted about some of Joe's other wealthy clients and their unbelievable demands where property was concerned. After Joe drank his coffee and I finished my tea, he checked his watch, blew me a kiss, and rushed off for his fortnightly waxing. I gathered my gym bag and headed back to my flat.

I'd accompanied Joe to some of his properties; we'd pranced around pretending we owned them, and I specifically remember one time where we spent the day using the pool and spa. I'm sure he would have lost that client had they realised, but most lived abroad and trusted their investment portfolio with him.

As I put the key in the lock and opened the flat door, I chuckled over how unprofessional he'd been. I bent to pick up the post, wincing at a twinge in my lower back before placing my hand over my heart to…I wasn't sure why my hand was there; it should have been over my mouth to stem the belch from lunch.

I heard a laugh and before I could turn, the vacant flat door that was opposite mine closed and obviously not vacant anymore. With cheeks flushed, I quickly closed my door, thanking the Lord I hadn't farted.

I'd just about placed my gym bag in front of the washing machine and the post on the kitchen table when there was a knock on the door. I walked and pulled it open.

"I thought I'd introduce myself. I'm your new neighbour and wondered if you needed these," he said, holding out a packet of Rennie.

I opened my mouth to speak but closed it again and reached out for the Rennie even though I didn't need them, and eventually looked up and smiled. Standing at my front door was a man, probably about my age, greying at the temples with dark hair and startling blue eyes.

"I'm not really in need of them, but who knows? I might keep them for when I do. Lizzie," I said, offering my name.

"Danny, I moved in yesterday."

"Well, if you ever need a cup of sugar, I'm probably not the one to ask. I'm crap at food shopping," I said.

He laughed, and the sound brought another smile to my lips. He had a lovely laugh, a genuine laugh, if there ever was such a thing.

"It's nice to meet you, Lizzie. I'm new to the area so, if you don't mind, I might be asking your advice since you're the first person I've spoken to since I got here."

I stepped back at little. "Well, come on in for a cuppa, and you can ask away."

Danny told me that he worked for an engineering company that was relocating; the precise details went over my head. He was newly single after a long-term relationship had broken down. He liked cats over dogs, and was fond of the cinema and dining out.

"That's your Tinder profile sorted," I said, raising my cup of tea as a salute.

"I can't be bothered with all that. I mean, I want to date, but all this online crap isn't for me," he said. We clinked cups in solidarity at that.

I told him, "Once I tried an online site, something to do with aquatic life, it was about the funniest, and worst experience of my life." I laughed, reminding myself that I hadn't checked in a while. I stood and rinsed our mugs under the tap.

As I showed him to the door, he said, "Well, it was nice to chat to you, maybe we can do it again."

"Sure. I'd like that." I closed the door behind me and sighed.

Nice guy, way too much baggage, scary eyes—I got in all the reasons I didn't like him in *that* way as a defence, ready for when he said he'd just like to be friends because I was sure that's what he'd say at some point.

The slightly sour smell reminded me I needed to wash the items in my gym bag. I debated on another shower, although it wasn't like I'd actually worked out at all, but it gave me something to do.

CHAPTER THREE

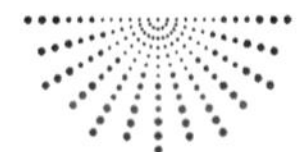

Gone were the *friends* that like to lunch, although the term 'friend' was probably an overstatement. They really were just the wives of *his* colleagues that I was forced to entertain. It was as if there was something contagious about separations. And there was clearly something distasteful about a single woman. I'd watch them clutch at their husband's arm as if I was going to swipe him away from under their beady, careful watch. Once the gossip was extracted—I mean, it wasn't often a high earning member of the London brokerage club ran off with a drag queen—I never heard from them again. Although some of the women were more than interested in what divorce settlement I'd agreed on, of course.

I was bored. I didn't *do* single. I had no clothes to iron or washing to collect from the dry cleaners. I had no diary to coordinate with dinners and events. I had no meals to prepare, and table plans to worry over. I didn't miss all *that*; I missed doing *something*; being busy, albeit, when I sat and thought, it was a pretty shallow life that I'd led.

Pilates. I remembered that I was going to take up Pilates. I'd put on some weight since my break-up, not that I worried about my roundness; I just didn't feel healthy. I picked up the gym booklet from the bottom of the now-clean bag and flicked through.

There were several classes, so I circled an intermediate one. It couldn't be that hard to do, I'd seen a couple of DVD's, and it was all about stretching and tying one's self in knots.

I repacked my gym bag in anticipation of my new Pilates class.

❧

"You have to come and view this house with me. Lizzie, it's in Knightsbridge and has a wine cellar accessed through a glass trap door." Joe oozed enthusiasm as I answered my phone. I hadn't even wished him a good morning.

"Okay, when?"

"Now, come now! Jump on the tube, and I'll text you the address."

"I can't come now. I'm going to Pilates."

He snorted. "Pilates? Have you ever done that shit before? I dated a Pilates teacher once. Boy, could he get to places I'd never imagined," he said, dreamily.

"I'd rather not know where he got, thank you. Anyway, I watched a DVD, and it's not that hard. I don't think so, anyway."

"Well, when you're done with Pilates, call me. I doubt I'll be here but come round and I'll show you the pictures."

We said goodbye, and I left the flat at the same time as Danny left his. He was suited and booted, and I had to admit to a slight fluttering in the nether regions. He looked rather hot, a little like the model on the cover of a book I was reading.

"Hi, where are you off to?" I asked as we walked to the stairwell together.

“I have a meeting in town, nothing exciting. Another new office block to be built and they want my input,” he said, as he opened the door.

The building we lived in was listed and had been a very exclusive private school back in Victorian times, I believed. It was now plush apartments. Joe would scowl every time I called it a flat. *Flats were high-rise, and for council tenants,* he’d say, and then I’d remind him he was once a council tenant, and his mum still lived in one of those high-rises because she refused to leave her mates in Bethnal Green. No amount of, ‘let me buy you a nice bungalow,’ from Joe would persuade her to move, and I loved her for it.

“If it was good enough for your farva (as she’d pronounce it), *and it was good enough for the Krays, then it’s good enough for me,”* she’d say before reminiscing about the good old days when the Krays ruled the streets, and everything was just lovely. She’d hold up her hand as if to dismiss the words: gangsters, bloodshed, murder, and fights when Joe would remind her of the *good* old days.

Danny and I parted at the front door; he went left, and I turned right, then doubled back because I was meant to go left as well.

“Lost already?” he asked, noticing me behind him.

“No, forgot where I was going for a moment. I’m off to Pilates,” I said, with an air of someone who did that on a regular basis.

“Pilates, huh? Well, have fun,” he said as he crossed the road towards the underground.

I carried on to the gym. That time I had my card ready, in fact, I waved it at the *smirker* behind the counter who was so rude to me the last time I visited. I waltzed through the turnstile with my nose in the air and my eyelids half shut.

As before, I inserted my fifty pence into the mechanism to extract my key and locked away my bag, then I walked, gently that time, up the stairs to the gym and crossed the floor. I saw a small group of women waiting, and I held back. Whereas I wore my usual leggings and a baggy t-shirt, these women had matching top and bottoms that wouldn't have looked out of place on an Olympic athlete. In fact, I was sure I remembered what-shername Ennis wearing the same outfit.

It was the *foot coverings* that stood out the most. They weren't wearing the latest fashion trainers but things that looked like slip-ons, something between a ballerina shoe and socks. One woman turned to me I gave her a smile.

Thankfully, she smiled back. "First time?" she asked.

"To this class, yes," I replied.

I was saved from a full-on conversation when the doors opened and what resembled a hippy-ballerina-come-extra-from-Fame stood there. He was tall and very skinny, with a cropped top, tight Lycra pants that left absolutely nothing to the imagination, not a hair on his legs, and the same slipper type shoes.

He introduced himself as I walked in. "Ah, you're new. I'm Casper like the ghost," he said, with a laugh. I looked blankly at him. "Never mind, come on in."

I walked into the middle of a very blue room and came to an abrupt halt. The walls were painted one shade of blue, the floor was another, but it was the contraption in the corner that had me stunned.

"Oh. My. If it isn't the Christian Grey of Pilates." I laughed. The woman I'd met outside laughed with me, a fellow reader I assumed.

In front of me was a large bed, for want of a better word. It had four metal poles rising from each corner creating a frame from which hooks, pulleys, and God knows what, hung. I spied what could have well been fluffy handcuffs at one end.

It wasn't quite the introduction to Pilates I was expecting. In fact,

Pilates wasn't quite what I was expecting full stop, and bore no resemblance to the old DVD I'd found and watched.

We were shown to mats, and I was expected to contort my body into positions it hadn't been in since I was a rampant teenager with a penchant for experimental sex positions. It was the slight leakage from a weak bladder and the pain from holding in a fart that had me pretending to remember a very important appointment and leaving the class early.

I hobbled from the room with a chorus of, "See you next week!" from Casper and his *blue room of torture* playmates following me. I raised my hand in a wave.

Yeah, like fuck you will, I thought with a smile. Although the bed with the trapeze type contraptions made me smile, so maybe I'd return for a one-on-one session.

As I stood under the shower—not because I needed to wash from exertion but to see if I could ease the muscle cramps—I thought back. Harry had always been quite adventurous in the bedroom, but when I remembered, penetrative sex wasn't often something we did. I never thought too much about it at the time, now though, it was obvious. He liked a little anal…*he* did, not me. He liked a little tying up and blindfolding, and we had a range of toys to play with. I thought it was all quite exciting at first and how cool we were; women were only just reading about that, and we'd been doing it for years. I stepped out of the shower and wished I hadn't. I felt a tear as it rolled down my cheek. The shower could have masked that; instead, I raised my towel, pretending to wipe away a droplet of water.

I walked briskly back to the flat, I mean *apartment*, and managed an even brisker walk up the stairs. Although it felt like the crepitus in my knee was echoing up the stairwell, I pushed on. I laughed as that held in fart decided to creep out in time with my climbing the last three steps. Three little toots that bounced off the bare white walls and rolled down the stairwell. Secret farting was a pleasure of mine, and I guessed it went back to the days of not feeling like I should do it in front of Harry. For years, I'd held all bodily functions in check—not that he had reciprocated, of course. Perhaps it was a woman thing. At just over fifty and newly single, it was fast becoming a favourite pastime.

I waved my hand around to disperse the smell before opening the hallway door and trying to slam the door closed quickly. Danny stood there with his arm outstretched as if he was about to open it from his side. I saw him through the small glass window and smiled, while I frantically—and out of sight obviously—waving my arms around.

Eventually, he pushed the door gently towards me. "Everything okay?" he asked.

"Yes, sorry. I dropped my bag just as I was pulling the door open. I didn't want the door to drag against it," I lied, raising said bag as evidence of its existence.

The gym bag had once been cream, I think. It was now cracked and a light brown colour from age, being dragged or kicked around on the floor, and living most of the past two years unused on top of a wardrobe.

"Yeah, looks brand new, I can imagine you wouldn't want to scuff it up," he said, laughing as he walked through the door and down the stairs.

Cheeky sod. I began to walk through into the hallway.

"Oh, Lizzie? You stink," he said, and followed the statement with more laughter.

"Oh…fuck off," I whispered, as my cheeks bloomed with embarrassment.

I decided that I didn't particularly like Danny after all. I might have, when we shared a cuppa and he was polite, but then I thought about our interactions. He had heard me belch and decided to mention it with a packet of Rennie's. Any decent fella would have ignored that to save my shame. He had heard me fart and decided to mention it. Like I said, any decent…I didn't even know him, but I'd made my mind up; he was rude.

❧

"Did you know I had a neighbour? He's very rude," I said, after hearing Joe answer my call.

"I did, and is he?"

"Have you met him?" I asked.

"No, a colleague interviewed him for the apartment."

"You don't own that flat, do you?"

"No, but I manage it for the owner. He's a Saudi, owns most of that block and the next-door one, too," Joe answered.

"Anyway, he's rude. He was rude to me twice."

"Didn't you say you thought he was *nice* when you invited him in for tea?"

"I don't recall saying that, but he might have been then; now I think he's rude. I went to Pilates today; you have got to let me tell you about this bed," I said, excitedly.

I then proceeded to tell Joe all about my day.

"Do you want to come to a new bar with me tonight?" he asked.

"Sure, why not. But will you do me a favour? Make sure you look super gay. I don't want any nice single men thinking we're an item."

"Sure, I'll wear my 'I find pussy repulsive' t-shirt, and you can have a neon sign with the word, 'desperate' on it."

"I'm not desperate at all!" I replied, feeling indignant.

Joe laughed. "You are, and seriously, a friend is opening the bar. I only intend to stay for a couple of drinks then leave. I have a very early start tomorrow. I doubt you'll get an opportunity to ensnare your next victim." He added a manic laugh as if it would soften his words, but I frowned.

Joe often took the piss out of me; I did the same to him. We had been friends since school days and had the kind of relationship where we could rib each other, but his words stung a little. Maybe I wasn't as hard and tough and 'over it' as I led everyone to believe. Instead of telling him that, I laughed.

"I'll see you later, call for me when you're ready," I said.

Joe lived a few doors up from the block in a beautiful town-house. Instead of selling property, he should have been either an architect or an interior designer. His eye for detail was like nothing I'd seen before. We would take a walk, and he'd point out the minute details on the façade of a building that would have otherwise gone unnoticed. His talent was wasted with simply *selling* the properties. But then, his love of buildings and architecture was what made him as successful. He didn't sell the interior alone; he sold the bricks, the mortar, the idea, and the dream of a building, not just a home.

❧

I mused on Joe's words the rest of the day and when he finally came calling at gone eight o'clock–so much for an early night–I had decided I would speak to him about it.

"Hey, you look lovely," he said, kissing my cheek as I met him at the block's front door.

"So do you, very dapper indeed." We linked arms and walked towards a waiting taxi.

Joe gave an address, and we settled back into the leather seats.

"Who is this friend, and I thought you wanted an early night?" I asked.

"He's actually a client that I'm hoping might be interested in something a little more. And this *is* an early night for me. Seriously, we'll grab a couple of drinks, and then I need to be home by eleven. I have a call coming in from my Saudi prince about some property he wants me to look at for him."

"Oh, a prince, huh?" I hadn't come across a Saudi prince in any paperwork Joe had asked me to sort out for him.

"Yes, he's been a client on and off for years. Owns a lot of property in London. I don't think he has ever visited one of them. Shame." He sat back and sighed. "I really don't get why people own all these beautiful buildings and don't live in them."

"Can I ask you something? Earlier you made a joke about me looking for my next victim, what did you mean by that?" I decided to ask and muse no more.

His eyes widened with genuine surprise. "Did I? I doubt I meant anything by it, just one of those cougar type jokes I guess."

"Cougar? Do you think I'm desperate for a man?"

"Aren't you? I don't mean this horribly, but now your divorce is nearly finalised you seem to be anxious to get back out there and date."

"Is there something wrong with that?" I asked, twisting in my seat to face him and realising the level of defensiveness was obvious in my voice.

"No, of course not. I didn't mean anything by it. Honestly, I can't even remember what I said. Have I upset you?" he asked, and the question came with all sincerity.

"Yes. No, not really. I just didn't really like the comment. Joe, I've never been on my own, and I don't like it. I don't think there's anything wrong in that. I just want company. I want to be able to go out for a meal with someone, or the pictures, or whatever. I've lost most of my friends because they don't want a single woman around and they've got all the gossip they're going to get from me. I'm lonely."

The taxi driver interjected, "We're a bit late for Sunday Love Songs on the radio, love. And Simon Bates', Our Tune, finished in the eighties."

Joe laughed, but I muttered expletives under my breath.

It didn't deter the driver's unwelcome input. "Seriously, love, you want a man, you go get one. You're a pretty bird, you shouldn't be on your own, and if your friend here thinks otherwise, you wanna be looking to trade him in as well," he added, looking at me in his rear view mirror.

I raised my eyebrows and smirked at Joe. "See, someone agrees with me," I said, although I thought the old man driving the car—who was now running his tongue over his lips in a really not very sexy way—was looking for a little lovin' from someone he deemed as desperate.

"No chance," I said, smiling back at him as he waggled his tongue at me. What the fuck he thought he was doing was beyond me.

He pulled the car over a little way from our destination, embarrassed, I hoped. We climbed out, and I left Joe to pay as I buttoned up my jacket. I shuddered.

"Eeww. Just…eeww," Joe said as he joined me.

We walked the short distance to the wine bar and were waved through the door. It wasn't usual to have a doorman on such an establishment, but I guessed, what with it being opening night, the trays of free champagne being waltzed around could attract the wrong crowd.

Joe pulled two glasses from the tray of a passing waitress and handed me one. We chinked before sipping the cold, fizzing liquid.

Joe turned to face me, and with a stern expression, he said, “Remember, don’t take any drinks from any strangers. And don’t take anything from the barman unless it’s been opened or poured in front of you. Don’t leave your drink on the bar, either.”

Like an errant teenager being lectured, I rolled my eyes. “I know, you’ve said this a thousand times already. I have been out on my own, during *and* after my marriage. And I haven’t been drugged as of yet,” I said.

“Just a reminder,” he said, with a smile.

“Did you check these?” I said, raising my half-empty glass of champagne.

“I doubt the whole tray would be drugged, and I doubt the waitress would be interested in doing either of us,” he replied with a laugh.

I shook my head and looked around the room. The bar had been decorated nicely; fresh colours adorned the walls that held abstract art. I tried to remember what the venue had been before.

“Ah, Joe, my friend,” I heard.

I turned to see a couple walk towards us. A woman hung from the man’s arm, and by the way she clung on, I would have thought she had been surgically attached to him. The man didn't introduce her at all and struggled to straighten his arm to shake both mine and Joe’s hands.

“Welcome,” he said. “I see you have a drink. Please let the barman know if there’s anything else you need.”

“We will, thanks, Rich,” Joe said. I finally got to know the ‘friend’s’ name.

“I like the décor,” I added.

Rich turned to me and smiled. “Thank you, Joe had a hand in what not to do, of course,” he said.

I thought he had a lovely voice and wondered how Joe knew him. I believed I knew most of Joe's closest friends but neither Rich, nor his name, had ever come up. He walked away still without introducing the woman on his arm.

I heard a gentle sound to my side. "What was that sigh for, Joe?"

"Nothing, shall we grab that table?" he said, a clear diversion but a necessary one as my feet had already started to hurt, and I'd only been standing a few minutes.

I sat on what resembled a perching stool at a high bistro-style table and kicked off my heels. "I swear I'm getting bunions," I said, subtly rubbing the side of my foot.

"Old lady feet," Joe replied, with a laugh.

I whacked him playfully. "No, feet that have been wedged into high heels for too many years." I pulled some flip-flops from my handbag and slipped those on instead. "So, that sigh…" I asked.

"Rich can't decide if monogamy is for him. We dated a little, then he just disappeared for a while, came back, we fucked a few times, but I have no idea where I am with him."

I cocked my head to one side and frowned. "That doesn't sound like a nice thing for him to do. Regardless if he's still trying to figure out his preferences, he shouldn't string you along, Joe."

"I know. I guess we're all getting on a bit now and, like you, I want to settle down with someone."

"We should make a pact. If we're still single and sixty we marry each other," I said with a laugh while raising my champagne glass to my lips.

Joe had never given any indication that he wanted to settle down. He was the same age as me but I didn't see myself as fifty at all, and I certainly didn't see Joe as fifty either. Fair enough, he had a little grey in his designer stubble, a little grey winging over the tips of his ears but that was it. He was fit, fun, and no different to the teenager I'd met all those years ago.

"When did we get old?" Joe asked, quietly.

"Fifty isn't old. We're still in our prime. Look, we're at the opening of a bar, drinking champagne. We need more, of course, but most fifty-year-olds would be sitting at home with Corrie or some soap on the TV, and wearing slippers while having a cup of tea."

Joe's statement had thrown me. He was the life and soul normally; the one to grow old disgracefully.

He performed the perfect dramatic stage shudder, complete with a 'brrrr' from the lips. "I have no idea where that came from," he said, grabbing another two glasses of bubbly from a passing waiter.

I smiled as he handed me a glass, not for one minute, fooled.

I heard someone say, "Hi, I'm Ronan, silent partner I guess, in this place." I turned to see a man standing beside me.

I slid from my stool and regretted removing my shoes. Ronan must have been nearly a foot taller than I was.

I held out my hand. "Lizzie and this is my friend, Joe," I said.

I watched Ronan smile at Joe and the smile was different to the one I'd been given. Was he gay? Did he like what he saw with Joe?

"We've met, although I'm not sure you'll remember. You visited with Rich one time. I'm his older brother," he said.

Joe shook his hand vigorously. "Of course, it's nice to meet you again."

"Rich speaks very highly of your eye for design, and I wondered if you'd have a little time this week to talk about a project I have coming up," Ronan said.

I shuffled slightly to one side, aware I wasn't part of the conversation. I sipped on my drink and, in one way, was quite glad not to be included in the chat. Ronan was a very attractive man. His dark hair had streaks of grey, his dark brown eyes had a sparkle and his *designer stubble*, as Joe would call it, matched his hair in colour, but it was more than that. Ronan had presence. He was quietly confident.

"Lizzie, I saw you from across the room. I wondered if I could buy you a drink? You, too, Joe," he said.

I blinked a few times with surprise. I had been quite busy coming up with as many adjectives to use for his looks and demeanour that I hadn't realised he had spoken to me. "Oh, I'm happy with this," I said holding my glass aloft.

"An empty glass? I'm sure that can be arranged, but how about a top up?" He smiled, the laughter lines around his eyes just added to the attractiveness.

"Ah, okay, yes…you won't put drugs in it, will you? Joe informs me that a man buying a woman a drink in a bar is after one thing only, and will drug the woman to get it," I rambled until I felt the subtle punch to my side.

He smirked and raised one eyebrow in question and rather sexily, I'd thought. "Joe is a wise man, but no, I won't drug your drink. In fact, I'll ask a waiter to bring a bottle and open it in front of us, deal?"

I watched Ronan as he pulled up another perching stool, although he managed to keep one foot on the floor while the other rested on the bar as he caught the eye of a waiter. He spoke quietly, placing his order and then smiled at us.

"So?" I said.

"So, here we are," he replied.

"So, this is awkward, and I really do need to pee. Lizzie, don't make a fool of yourself," Joe said, with a wink and slid from his stool. "I'll be right back."

"I feel I ought to apologise for him. He does say the most bizarre things every now and again," I said, my cheeks aflame with embarrassment.

A waiter appeared beside us.

"Lizzie, watch carefully. In fact…" Ronan slid off his jacket. He undid the cuffs of his crisp white shirt, and I saw tattoos, lots of them, snake from his wrists upwards as he rolled up each sleeve. He showed me first, his palms, and then the back of his hands, like a magician would while the waiter poured. I tried to suppress the smirk.

"No drugs, see?" he said, as a glass was slid in front of me.

"Listen, Ronan, I haven't been single in over thirty years. I have no idea of all the rules Joe keeps forcing me to listen to, but I do believe that he must keep the most god awful company, or frequent the most god awful places if all he worries about is being drugged and assaulted." I raised my glass and just before I took a sip, I glanced in, just to make sure there wasn't a little white pill lurking in there.

"He's looking out for you, and so he should."

"I'm quite capable of looking out for my—" I hadn't finished my sentence before I half slid from my perching stool and sloshed champagne down my front. "Oh fuck it," I said, and Ronan laughed. "These are stupid chairs unless you're eight feet tall or can 'perch' in high heels for a whole evening," I continued with a grumble.

"Yes, they are stupid stools," he agreed.

Joe returned, and I caught the subtle wink to me. "You have a project you want to discuss, Ronan?" Joe asked.

"I do, perhaps we can arrange to meet. I have something I'd like design input with."

"I'm not an interior designer. I sell property," Joe said quite matter-of-factly.

"But you love architecture. The very fabric of the building is as important as the interior, in my opinion. I've struggled to find a designer that will appreciate the bricks, the wood, the flaws and cracks as well as what colour carpet should go down."

Joe held up his hand. "I can't do carpet," he said, dramatically.

"Perfect. Perhaps we should exchange numbers, and you can call me when you've had a chance to check your diary," Ronan said.

They did, and as I was about to take another sip of my champagne, Ronan interrupted me. "Lizzie, maybe I could call you for lunch or dinner one day next week?" he asked.

"Oh, yes, that would be nice. Except I have no idea of my mobile number," I said, suddenly nervous about the prospect. I fussed with the clutch in my hands in an effort to divert the attention away from me.

Joe recited my number, and I both thanked and cursed him.

Ronan tapped my number into his handset. "I'll send a text, that way you can decide whether to reply or not," he said.

He slid from his stool and rolled down his sleeves, covering deliciously muscular forearms. Forearms did a thing to me, a tingling type of thing. That thing was happening, and I found myself licking my lips as if I'd spotted a piece of KFC.

With a broad smile that lit up his face and caused my stomach to flip, he left.

Joe nudged me. "Well, fuck me. If you don't, I am."

"You're *what*? Oh, don't answer. He's not gay…is he?"

"No, *that* I doubt, which is a shame," he said.

"Can't you tell? I've always wanted to know that. Do you have like, *gaydar*, or something?"

"Gaydar? No. How do you know someone fancies you?" he asked.

"I don't, which is why, two years on, I'm still single. Someone could smack me in the face with a frying pan embossed with *I fancy you* and I wouldn't know." I bent down to pick up my shoes.

"Well I don't have a gaydar; sometimes I know, and sometimes, like just then, I don't. But I do know a man who does," Joe said, cryptically.

I followed his gaze towards Rich, who still had the limpet stuck to his side. I wondered if someone would need to pour salt over her to release him. I chuckled at my inner sarcasm—I did amuse myself sometimes.

While I tried to wedge my high-heeled shoes into my small clutch bag, Joe said goodbye to Rich. I gave a smile and a wave as Joe returned, and we walked to the door. Joe really did mean an early night; I think we'd been in the place no more than an hour and a half.

As we left the building, Joe informed me, "Single, has been for a few years. Likes to renovate property, spends a lot of time outdoors, hence the tan I guess. Wealthy, successful, and his brother is insanely jealous of him." He steered me to a taxi rank.

I gasped. "How the fuck do you know all that?"

"Because Rich told me some and then proceeded to tell me everything that was wrong with his brother. Jealous," he said in a singsong voice, tapping the side of his nose.

There was no question, Ronan was the better-looking one of the two, for sure. But I didn't know either, and as much as it had been a little fun, I doubted I'd hear from him again. He was too good looking for me. I'd be competing for mirror time, I thought, giving myself those reasons to confirm my thoughts…

❧

Hey, Ronan here. I said I'd text instead of calling so here I am. I wondered if you'd like to meet for lunch this week.

I stared at the text for about half an hour. It had been a week since Joe and I had been to the opening of Rich's bar and I hadn't really thought any more about Ronan. Joe hadn't heard from him about the 'project', otherwise, I was sure he would have said.

What to reply? I thought. I didn't want to immediately say yes, although I wanted to immediately say yes.

I typed a reply three times before I was satisfied.

Hi, Ronan. That would be lovely, thank you. I'm afraid, though, I'm only free on Wednesday through to the end of the week. Look forward to hearing back.

My heart beat a tattoo in my chest as I pressed send. I was free every hour of every day of that week for that man, but I didn't want to seem too eager. I'd play it cool, that was what we women did wasn't it?

I watched the phone for an hour before getting cross and turning it to mute and placing it face down. That lasted all of about five minutes, and I sighed as I said, "Someone might need me, urgently," aloud to an empty kitchen.

My parents lived in Spain; I swear they moved there when their swinging lifestyle became public, and Dad's job in the local council offices was *ended*. He was beyond retirement age then, if I remembered. I loved my parents; in their eighties but still partying and having the kind of social life I'd never managed.

I spoke to them every week, and they constantly asked me to visit. I always put that visit off. It wasn't that I didn't like Spain; I didn't like Spanish swingers who thought everyone was game including their friend's daughter. Mum and Dad thought it hilarious, of course, and that I ought to *lighten up a little.*

Never.

I decided I needed to do a food shop. I pulled my hair into a messy ponytail, not because it was a sexy thing to do but simply because it needed a wash, and I couldn't be bothered to even brush it that morning. I dragged my fingertips under my eyes to rid my skin of the black smudges from mascara and pinched my cheeks to add a little colour.

I pulled a sweatshirt over the tank top I'd normally sleep in (I hadn't gotten to shower or dress properly, I'd been distracted by the text) and slipped on a pair of jeans.

It wasn't like I was about to bump into anyone, now, was it?

I picked up a basket as I entered the supermarket. I didn't have a pound coin for a bloody trolley even though I wanted enough shopping to overfill a basket. Still, I slid my arm through the handles and walked to the wine aisle. I wanted a couple of bottles for when Joe came for our weekly romcom night. It was as I was peering at the label of a bottle, not realising my reading glasses were on top of my head when I heard my name being called.

I cringed and closed my eyes for a moment; I wanted to curl up and slide under the display counter. I cursed, pretended I hadn't heard, and wished I'd thought to put some earbuds or headphones, or whatever, in, to cover my ears. My heart rate increased, and I wiped my sweaty palms over my thighs as I took a deep breath ready to face her.

"I thought that was you," she said. Penny Frankenstein sidled up beside me. Of course, that wasn't her real name, but I'd been calling her that for so many years I couldn't remember what it was. "I heard you got divorced." She pouted in feigned pity. "You should come and join my club. It's disguised as a book club, but we have so much fun, share dating tips and giggle over the online dating apps. We meet every Thursday evening, do come," she said, eyeing me up and down. She placed her hand on my arm as she continued, "It's hit you real hard, hasn't it?" Her eyes with the coloured contacts brimmed with tears.

I looked at a hand that gave away her age; it had baggy skin and sunspots. And then to her face that was pulled so tight from multiple facelifts that her eyes were stretched nearer to the side of her head and her lips were pulled so far across her cheeks she looked like the Joker. It always amazed me that she could actually speak. She made Jocelyn Wildenstein look normal.

I plastered on a smile and clutched my basket tighter to stop the shake to my hands. "Penny, it's nice to see you. You'll have to excuse my dress this morning," I leaned in conspiratorially and whispered, "I'm actually doing the walk of shame," and then laughed out loud. I was impressed I'd remembered the term from a book I'd read.

I had no idea if she understood because her plastic face was so moulded she couldn't show any emotion.

"I think I have a date on Thursday. I'm undecided whether to go or not, so I'll have to take a rain check if that's okay," I added.

"Of course, and how exciting for you. It must be a relief to date a *real* man," she quipped.

"Oh, I don't know, Penny. There is something to be said about living with a gay man, my closet is amazing, all my underwear matches, and my vagina, my dear, is as tight as a nun's," I said. I placed the wine in my basket where it clanked against another and with a wave I walked off.

I muttered, giving the impression I was someone with mental health issues as I walked around. I needed bread, and I hated supermarket loaves, especially when I had the most amazing artisan bakery near home. I needed milk and tea bags. I needed food, but I just could not be arsed to cook or decide what to eat. I cursed the lawyers for not getting me some sort of allowance to live on while my divorce was being finalised, then I could've just dined out and not done this supermarket thing.

I loved shopping in the French market that came once a month; the little deli's that had popped up. I hated the commercial conglomerates that sucked dry the suppliers while pandering to the consumer with ever cheaper, poor quality products wrapped in endless acres of plastic.

By the time I'd got to the checkout, I was grumpy. Not grumpy enough to not take care of the bottles of wine on the…what was it actually called? A conveyor belt? Or was there an official term? I shook my head, not wanting to care. I stood the bottles up, tutting as the checkout lady jolted the conveyor belt along instead of letting it run smoothly.

"Those will fall over and break," I said, grabbing a bottle before it did just that.

"Most people just lay them down," she said with a smile.

I sighed. I wasn't *most* people. When my items were rolled without much care to bounce off the metal surround in the collection area—was there an official term for *that*?—I realised I didn't have a bag for life with me. I patted my pocket, as one did, in the hope a bag for life would miraculously appear. I should have relented and bought one of those tiny fold-up nylon bags with a clip to secure it to your keys. The kind of thing old aged pensioners used and bought from the magazine in the Sunday supplement. Yes, those OAP's actually had some sense.

"I need a bag," I said, watching my wine roll around.

She grabbed a bag and rung it up. By that point, all my items were piled high, the bag was on the top and she was telling me how much I had to pay. There was a queue a mile long, which was probably an exaggeration, and I was put under such immense pressure that I could feel my armpits leaking panic.

I fumbled around in my bag for my purse, and my heart rate increased the longer it took. I pulled out wads of old receipts, Tena Ladies, pens with no lids that had leaked ink, a set of keys I had no idea what they opened, a packet of very old mints, and a piece of tissue paper that felt like it had a chewed piece of gum in the middle of it. Eventually, I found my purse, not before the lady waiting behind me had tapped her toes enough times that I wanted to impale something through them to keep her foot still. I grabbed my card and handed it to the checkout lady. She looked at me, then the card machine. "Do you have a Nectar card?" she asked.

"No, I don't," I said, knowing full well she could see the purple loyalty card poking out of my purse, but it was too late for me to produce it, and I didn't want the distraction while I was trying to remember my pin number.

Purchases paid for, I began to fill my carrier bag while the checkout lady started to scan the waiting foot tapper's food. In protest, I picked up her packet of condoms that had the free lube attached to it and loudly asked if they were hers since the checkout girl appeared to be mixing up our shopping.

"Yes, and I need those for the weekend," Foot Tapper said, giving me a wink. "You should try the lube, it's flavoured," she added.

I grabbed the carrier bag, my handbag after shoving all the debris back in, and walked away, still muttering to myself.

Danny was at the front door of the block when I arrived. "You look like a bag lady," he said. "And I bet that's alcohol in there," he added, as he tried to take my carrier bag from me.

"I look like a *what*?" I asked, shocked by his statement.

He raised the carrier he had prised from my hand. “Your bag, m’lady. I’ll carry it for you.”

“Nice recovery,” I muttered, as I held open the door for him.

“I haven’t seen you around much,” he said, as we climbed the stairs to our floor.

“I’ve been busy, you?” I asked, wanting to be polite.

“Same. I have to be in Birmingham for a few days, I was going to ask if you’d check in on Pat for me?”

“Pat?” I frowned at the unfamiliar name.

“Pat the cat. He’s elderly so doesn’t go out, doesn’t want to, so you’ve no fear he’ll leg it as soon as you open the door. He just needs feeding twice a day, and his litter basket changed.”

Danny handed me back my carrier bag as we approached our front doors. I quite liked cats and missed having a pet, so I nodded. “Okay, you’ll have to let me know exactly when and give me a key, of course,” I said.

“That’s great, thank you. I know I can be a twit sometimes, I never really know what to say to people. Pat’s so easy to take care of; you probably won’t even see him. He sleeps on my bed most of the time. His litter basket is in the bathroom, and his food bowls are in the kitchen. Why don’t you come in now, and I can show you?”

It seemed a sensible thing to do, so I left my carrier bag outside my door and followed him.

Danny showed me where the cat food was stored, the bowls, and the plastic fork with the cat on the handle to identify it. I mean, who knew that large grey plastic fork completely unsuitable for human hands or food, would be a pet food one? He showed me where the litter tray was, and I was pleased to see it was one of those covered up, little house types, and he used a plastic bag over the tray before he put the litter in. That would make it nice and easy to clean. I didn't see Pat, though. I left Danny and he promised to drop his key off in the morning.

The following day I woke and as I padded, bleary-eyed, towards the kitchen, I saw a piece of paper and a key that had been posted through my letterbox.

Thanks for looking after Pat. I'll be home Friday at some point so no need to feed him that evening – Danny

Maybe he wasn't as bad as I made him out to be, that was a nice gesture. I put the kettle on to boil and picked up my phone. I noticed a text message.

Thursday? How about I call for you at 7 pm? If you're happy to, text me your address or we could meet at the restaurant? Ronan

There was no apology for the delay in replying, but I'd ignore that. I typed.

You can meet me here, that's fine… Words from Joe seeped into my mind. I deleted the text before I sent it and started again.

If you'd like to give me the address of the restaurant, I'll take a taxi and meet you there. Lizzie.

He quickly replied that time, and I smiled as I heard the kettle click off. I made myself some tea and sat on a stool at the kitchen counter. I read the text again, and a little giddy feeling washed over me. I laughed.

I shook my head. "Oh, for fuck sake," I said, aloud, rolling my eyes. I was fifty, getting giddy was for teenagers over pop stars.

I liked the giddy feeling, though. I texted Joe to remind him it was romcom night and to tell him I had a date. His reply wasn't what I was expecting.

Need to cry off tonight. Mum's not well, going to see her. I'll

call later, sorry, my lovely. Glad to hear about the date, though. You didn't invite him to your apartment, did you?"

I replied. **What's wrong with your mum, and no, I told him I'd take a taxi and meet him. Call me when you have five minutes.**

Instead of a reply, I got a thumbs up. I suspected he was busy and couldn't talk right then. I worried about his mum, though. Joe was trying to talk her into moving into a home. She had recently been diagnosed with dementia and Joe had been called out a few times during the evening when she'd gone for a walk. It was heartbreaking to see and many a night I'd held Joe while he sobbed at the injustice of the disease, wondering at what point she'd forget who he was.

I decided on a shower. I might be spending the night alone, other than a minute or two with Pat the cat, but I ought to start to make an effort.

CHAPTER FOUR

I sat with a glass of wine, wondering what time Pat the cat wanted dinner. Danny hadn't said a specific time. I'd eaten my pizza, leaving the crusts because, my whole life, I'd had that irrational thought that crusts made your hair curly. I placed the wine on the coffee table and paused the movie I'd been watching, then slid from the sofa, grabbed my keys and Danny's, and made my way to his flat.

I knocked before I inserted the key, not knowing why, then slowly pushed open the door and called out, "Pat, here puss puss."

I'd been in the flat once before and knew it was empty, but I still tiptoed around. I pursed my lips and sucked in air to make a squeak—cats liked that noise I believed. I picked up the bowl that had been used from the morning and gave it a quick wash then opened a tin of food and nearly gagged at the smell. I looked at the label. Salmon and tuna. It smelled like old ladies.

"Urgh." I spooned some into the newly washed bowl, trying not to throw up.

I topped up his biscuits and refreshed the water then looked around for some washing up gloves and, not finding any, decided I'd bring my own next time. I headed for the bathroom to the litter box and lifted the lid expecting to see some poop or clumped granules where the cat had peed and instead found nothing but clean litter. I replaced the lid assuming Danny had cleaned it before he left, and Pat the cat hadn't needed to use the loo. I pursed my lips and sucked in to make a squeak again.

Danny had said that Pat was old and slept most of the time so I decided to leave him to his evening. I'd left his food, and was sure he'd eat it when he was ready.

The following morning I decided to venture to Danny's before I'd showered or even had my cup of tea. I opened his door and called out to Pat. When I walked into the kitchen, I frowned. The food bowl was full of hardening and smelly food.

"Pat," I called out as I walked to the bathroom. I lifted the litter lid and once again it was clean.

Danny had said that Pat often slept on his bed, so I pushed open one of the doors that led to a small bedroom, which had a work-bench along one wall. I stared at the numerous certificates that hung above the bench; I guessed Danny was staying around for a while. I couldn't imagine a reason to hang educational certificates in a temporary location. I backed out of the room and widened the slightly-open door to the other.

A large bed dominated the room and my attention was drawn to the iron headboard, specifically the handcuffs hanging from them.

"Oh," I whispered as I took a step forward. The footboard played host to more cuffs at the corners. "Oh," I said again. "Pat?" Nestled in the pillows was a curled up bundle of fur, it didn't move. "Pat, come on puss," I said, louder that time. Still no movement. I walked to the side of the bed, feeling very conscious that I was invading Danny's personal, and maybe erotic, space. I reached out to stroke the cat. He was very cold to the touch. Not just cold but stiff as well. And he didn't make a peep, not a movement, or a purr.

"Oh…" I added a 'fuck' to that one as I backed from the room, not sure why, and when I was clear of the bedroom, I grabbed the keys and ran for my flat.

"Joe, phone me back, urgently," I said into my mobile at the prompt of Joe's voicemail. I laid the mobile on the kitchen counter and paced. "Oh no, poor Pat," I mumbled. "Danny is going to be so sad."

I wondered how long it took for rigor mortis to take hold of a cat, at what point would…fluid escape cavities. That *would* happen, wouldn't it?

"Oh fuck."

At some point he'd disintegrate, surely? I wondered if I should bag him up; double bag him just in case. Would Danny want to bury him? Should I call a vet? Maybe I ought to report his death or at least get some advice. I would have to move him; I couldn't leave him to *weep* on Danny's bed. I decided I needed a cup of tea and to think. While the kettle boiled, I brought up the Internet. I needed to know how long I had. I could hardly leave him nestled among the pillows until Danny came back. Not that it was summer, but I was sure we'd still have flies, and if we had flies, we'd have…Oh, fuck. I was about to scroll around when my phone vibrated in my hand; I'd received a text message.

Just checking in, hope Pat is okay – Danny

There was no way I could reply, so I tried Joe again. I sighed when he didn't answer and then remembered I hadn't heard back after he'd told me his mum was poorly. I felt awful.

Another thought came to me. I dialled.

"Hello?" I heard.

"Ronan, it's Lizzie. I'm sorry to call you, and this is really strange, but I need some advice, urgently."

"Lizzie, it's good to hear from you. You're not about to cry off our meal, are you?" he asked, and then laughed.

"No, but I have a problem. I've tried Joe, but I can't get hold of him."

"Oh, he's at a venue of mine checking it out for me before I refurb. Do you want me to call him? I doubt he has any mobile signal, but I can ring the landline," he said.

"That's okay. I have you now. Right…here we go…I'm supposed to be looking after Pat, but I think he's dead on Danny's bed. And on his bed he has handcuffs, and foot cuffs, is that what they're called? They're leather and metal, and I really don't want Pat to leak, or whatever they do when they…"

"Lizzie? Lizzie! Slow down, take a breath. Who is Pat, where is he? Did you call the police?"

"No, I haven't called the police, should I?"

"Yes, if he's dead, then you need to call the police, they'll call an ambulance and whatever. Is he attached to the handcuffs? You haven't disturbed any evidence, have you? Oh, fuck, Lizzie. Get off the phone and text me your address. I'm on my way."

With that, he cut off the call, and I stared at the phone. Why would we need an ambulance?

I texted the address, and then it dawned on me. I tried to call him, but his phone went straight to answerphone.

"Pat is a *cat*, not a person," I said, hoping he'd listen to his voicemail before he called the coroner or whoever one calls for the dead.

I tried his phone again and got no reply. I started to giggle. Ronan thought I was talking about a dead *person*.

I groaned. “Oh, God, he’s going to think I’m such an idiot.”

I decided to be proactive. I reached into the cupboard under the sink to find some rubber gloves. I grabbed some plastic carrier bags and doubled them up. I also grabbed the kitchen roll, a bottle of bleach and a sponge, just in case Pat deposited something whilst being bagged up.

By the time I’d gathered my phone and the keys, I heard the main block door open. Footsteps pounded up the stairs, and the fire safety door swung open from the stairwell.

“Ronan, I think—”

His eyes widened, and he gripped his hair in his fingers. “What are you doing, Lizzie?” he asked, coming to an abrupt halt.

“I’m going to bag him up. I thought the bleach would get rid of any…you know.”

“Lizzie, what have you done?” he asked, quite slowly.

I held up my hands. “Oh, oh, Ronan…Pat is a *cat*. You didn’t give me a chance to tell you.”

“Pat is a *cat*?”

“Yes, a cat. A *dead* cat.”

He visibly relaxed. “You’re kidding me, I thought…”

“I know, and I rang you back to tell you.”

“Holy shit, Lizzie. I thought…” For the second time, he didn’t finish his sentence.

I scowled at him. “You thought…? Oh, you thought I'd *murdered* someone, and I was about to clean up the evidence? I’d hardly call you to help, would I? Now, what do I do about the cat?”

Ronan started to laugh. I stared at him—it wasn’t remotely funny really.

I folded my arms across my chest and glared at him. "Danny is going to be so upset. He might want to bury him, or something. But I can't leave him on the bed with the handcuffs," I said.

Ronan ran his hand through his greying hair, and as he did, his white t-shirt rose a little, exposing a tanned stomach. A dark trail of hair headed south under the waistband of his jeans. I wanted to twirl my fingers in that hair, but I had shocking pink rubber gloves with fur around the wrists and a fake plastic engagement ring, and I was holding bleach.

Instead, I groaned. "What am I going to do about the cat?"

"Okay, show me," he said. I handed him the key, as the gloves were three times larger than my hands and the fingers were doubling over, such was their length.

I showed Ronan to the bedroom, and I watched as he ran his fingers over the foot cuffs. "Ankle cuffs," he said matter-of-factly.

"That they may be, now…Pat?" I said, hoping to bring him back to the situation.

He chuckled as he moved up the bed. I heard the clank of metal as he played with the handcuffs, and before I could comment again, he leaned over to look at the cat.

"How long do you think he's been dead?" I asked.

At first there was no reply. "I'd say a few years," he finally answered.

I was in the process of frowning when he picked the cat up; I leapt forward with my carrier bags and bleach spray. When he turned, he held Pat on a wooden plaque.

The smile on his lips grew wider until he started to howl with laughter.

"What?" I asked, feeling rather bemused.

"He's stuffed. I think your friend was having a joke with you," he said.

I widened my eyes and shook my head in disbelief. "No way."

I reached forward, and as Ronan had said, the cat was stuffed and mounted on a wooden plaque.

"Oh my God, look at his eyes," I said, covering my mouth with my gloved hands.

The cat had fake amber eyes, obviously, but he was boss-eyed.

Ronan was laughing so much at this point he had to sit on the bed, which made the metal headboard clank further against the handcuffs.

I held in the mirth for as long as I could. I crossed my legs in the hope my bladder might not embarrass me and, with tears streaming down my face, I joined in the laughter.

That was until I realised something.

"That prick had me feeding his stuffed cat!"

Ronan laughed harder, fell backwards onto the bed and started holding his stomach.

"He asked me to clean the litter tray," I said, my voice no more than a squeak with a combination of mirth and anger.

Ronan was screeching. It wasn't manly at all.

"This isn't funny," I said, in spite of my contorted face and aching stomach muscles.

"Oh, Lizzie. It is, for sure it is. It's the funniest thing that has happened in ages," he replied.

"Well, I'm going to bag up the bloody cat and tell Danny it died, and I've shoved it down the rubbish shoot."

Ronan laughed some more. I grabbed Pat from where he'd fallen onto the bed, boss-eyed and with his tongue hanging out, and I shoved him into the carrier bag.

Before I could make my way out, Ronan stood and grabbed my wrist. “Sorry, I know, it’s not funny. It’s a shitty thing your friend has done,” he said.

I squinted, studying him closely. The laughter lines around his eyes had softened, but his lips still twitched enough for me to think he was trying to pacify me.

“Look around. I think your friend is an amateur taxidermist.”

On the windowsill was a small glass case with what looked like a mouse, I think, in it. There was a second glass case on the bedside cabinet. A small bird was perched on a branch in that one.

“That’s grim,” I said, looking at the bird’s face. It was as distorted as Pat.

“Do you think this might have been his cat?” Ronan asked.

I shrugged my shoulders. “I have no idea. But I know what I’m going to do.”

I removed Pat from the plastic bags and put him back between the pillows before I left the room and grabbed the cat food tins. I scraped the contents into my carrier bags and deposited the tins, after rinsing them out, in Danny’s recycling bucket. I then walked to the bathroom, lifted the lid of the litter tray and scooped out a handful of sawdust, sprinkling that in the waste bin, making sure to drop a little on the floor. I wanted Danny to think I had scooped poop from the litter tray. Ronan followed me from the flat.

“Coffee?” I asked.

“That might be nice.”

Ronan and I walked into my flat, and it was only as I passed the mirror in the hallway that I realised what a state I looked. I had bed hair, no makeup, my PJs still on, furry slippers, and the pink washing up gloves.

"I might need to get dressed," I said, wrapping my arms around myself as if it would conceal my outfit. I jutted out my chin, however, brazening it out.

Ronan nodded. "How about I make the coffee, or tea for you if you'd prefer, and you get dressed. As much as those fleecy cow PJs are endearing, they don't match the gloves."

I dumped my carrier bag in the bin, placed the bleach and sponge next to the sink, and then peeled off the gloves. My hands smelled of rubber and were coated in a white 'fur' from the interior. I sniffed them and then screwed up my nose.

I pointed to a cupboard, sure that Ronan would be able to figure out how to boil the kettle and make the tea without further instruction. Once alone in my room, I decided I didn't feel comfortable having a shower and leaving Ronan in my flat. He could easily snoop around without my knowledge and the noise of the shower pump, which was akin to a jet engine I might add, would cover up any noise he made.

I dragged a brush through my hair and scrunched it into a topknot. I had a quick wash—a pits and bits wash—then cleaned my teeth and dressed quickly before joining Ronan in the kitchen. He was lounging against the countertop, and before he'd seen me, he was chuckling as he held his drink.

"It was funny, I guess," I said, picking up the tea from beside him.

He bit down on his lower lip, and those laughter lines were back in full force. He nodded.

"What a shitty thing for Danny to do, though," I said, contradicting myself.

Ronan nodded some more. He sipped his drink, and I pulled out a stool to sit.

"I'm sorry for calling you. I panicked because I thought he loved that cat. I just didn't know what to do. Had it been mine, I'd have just buried it in the garden, or maybe not, the foxes might get it, but anyway…I didn't know what to do," I repeated.

He smiled gently at me. "I'm glad you called. It's been an interesting morning in what was meant to be an otherwise mundane day. I had a couple of meetings planned, but this has been way better than those would have."

"Oh, no, you should have said."

He shrugged. "My team can take care of it."

"What do you actually do?" I asked. I thought it a good time to get all those 'introduction' questions out of the way before our date; we could concentrate on dinner that way.

"I invest in businesses, own property, a bit of this and that, really," he answered, vaguely.

"Mmm, okay, another time for the answer to that one."

He looked at his watch and then placed his mug in the sink. He reached for the tap.

"Lizzie, it's been enjoyable, and I think your friend has a little kink going on over there," he said. "I'll meet you at the restaurant on Thursday unless you'd like me to collect you on the way?"

"Collect me, please. I was trying to be safe and not let you know my address in case you ended up being a stalker or a murderer, or worse."

"Or *worse*? What could be worse than a murderer?" he asked with a grin and a glint in his eye.

I walked him to the door. "I don't know—figure of speech, I guess." *A liar and a cheat could be worse*, I thought.

Ronan paused after he'd walked over the threshold. He turned to face me—a little too close, not that I was complaining—and he leaned down to kiss my cheek. "I look forward to Thursday," he said, and then he walked away.

I closed the door and rested my back against it. I really did like him. It was only as I walked back down the hallway and passed that blasted mirror again that I realised I had my t-shirt on, not only inside out, but back to front. The size fourteen label was hanging out for all to see, displaying the garment's washing instructions.

I dragged it over my head and righted it while cursing myself. I never used to be this way. Divorce can do awful things to a woman in her fifties, I decided.

It pleased me to know that, unlike Danny probably would, Ronan hadn't mentioned my pathetic dress sense at all.

I picked up the mobile and scrolled to my text messages. I replied to one.

All is good. Haven't seen Pat yet but he's eating and toileting well, so I guess he's happy

I left him to ponder on that, the prick. I had half a mind to invoice him for my time.

❧

"The cat was what?" Joe asked, aghast. We were sitting in my kitchen eating a Chinese takeaway and had already consumed a bottle and a half of wine.

"Dead. Not just dead but stuffed and mounted on a wooden plaque," I said, trying to stop my chopsticks from crossing and flipping my food across the room. Joe slid a fork towards me, but I was determined to master the chopsticks one time in my life.

"Stuffed?"

"Yes, like taxidermy stuffed," I said, throwing the chopsticks on the table with a huff and picking up the fork.

"And handcuffs?"

"Yes, although Ronan said the ones on the footboard were ankle cuffs, which is obvious when you think about it."

"Did Ronan happen to tell you how he knew?" Joe asked with a wink.

I stared, open-mouthed, but closed it before the chow mein could fall out. "He didn't, what a crafty…Oh, I'm going to dinner with him tomorrow," I said.

"Well, let's hope he doesn't bring any restraints to the restaurant. Now, can we go and see the cat?" Joe's eyes had that sparkle of mischief.

I placed my fork on the counter and slid from my stool. Joe and I crept, although I had no idea why, to Danny's. I opened the door and led him to the bedroom.

"Oh, they are real, like proper, not Ann Summer's handcuffs," Joe said, jangling them.

"Like police ones?" I asked.

"No, like full on kink ones."

I wondered how Joe would know the difference, if, in fact, there really was any. Handcuffs were handcuffs, surely?

I watched as he reached over to pick up the cat. Instead of holding him by the plaque as Ronan had done, he picked him up under the belly. All of a sudden a noise echoed around the room. I stared at Joe; Joe stared first at me and then we both stared at the cat. It made the noise again. Joe dropped him, and Pat bounced on the bed before throwing himself off. I reached forwards to catch him, all the time the fucking cat was meowing. I didn't get to Pat in time, and he hit the wooden floor, his plaque bounced one way, and one eye bounced the other.

"Oh, my God," I said. Joe just stood with his hands over his mouth.

"Get his eye," I shouted, I wasn't sure why I shouted. It wasn't like it was a real emergency.

"I'm not picking up his eye," Joe said, finally taking his hands away from his mouth.

"It's not real," I said, assuming that to be the case.

Pat had an orb in the side of his face with a glob of dried glue that had been unsuccessful in holding in the glass eye, or marble, or whatever it was. Joe picked up the eye and held it at arm's length with his head turned away, as if it was the most offensive item he'd held in his palm. I giggled at the thought of the *other* offensive items he could have touched.

"We need to fix this. He loved this cat," I said, grabbing the eye and the plaque.

I placed the still meowing Pat under my arm and hoped to God he had a thing inside him, like the teddies at Build-A-Bear. In fact, how had Danny got a recording and then…? I didn't want to dwell on it.

I walked into the kitchen and placed the bits on a small dining table he had pushed against one wall. "We need glue," I said, more to myself as Joe was trying hard to stifle the laughter.

I rifled through the cupboards but couldn't find anything. I remembered the office and walked to the door, pushed it open and stepped in. I'd looked in the room before but other than the certificates on the wall I hadn't taken too much notice. Lying on the bench were trays of implements.

“Joe, can you come here?” I asked as I stepped closer. I lifted the tea towel off one tray and quickly dropped it.

“Oh my God,” I said. That was fast becoming my favourite phrase and was being used *way* too often.

“What is it?” Joe replied as he walked in. I pointed to the tray with the towel. Joe lifted it. “Eeww, eeww, what is it?”

“A dead animal, obviously.”

Lying on the tray was a squirrel. A very flat squirrel that had obviously had its innards removed and was awaiting stuffing.

“You did vet this guy, didn’t you?” I asked.

“Lizzie, he didn’t tell me one of his hobbies was stuffing dead animals for fun.”

Joe started to pull open drawers of a unit. I heard more mutterings of “eeww” and didn’t want to look. Eventually, I heard, “Ah ha.” He turned around with a tube of glue in his hand.

We left the bedroom and returned to the kitchen. I picked up Pat and saw underneath the row of stitching where the pelt met. I could also feel the lump where I imagined that little recording device sat. When Joe had picked him up, he’d activated it.

“We need to glue his paws,” I said, holding him upside down while Joe uncapped the glue.

“Why don’t we just leave it where it was?”

“Because I’m pretending I haven’t seen this. If Danny comes home and it’s all broken, he’ll know I’m lying.”

“Why are you pretending?”

“Because that prick asked me to feed his cat, Joe. *This* cat,” I said, waving Pat around.

“That wasn’t nice. In fact, it’s a little odd.”

I nodded as Joe deposited a blob of glue on each paw. I could see where the cat had been positioned before and while Joe held the plaque still, I stood Pat in place. We held on for a few minutes until I thought the glue had taken and then slowly I released my hands. It wasn't until then that I realised—Pat stank.

"Now the eye. If I don't make him boss-eyed, he's going to look like he's looking left," I said, as I studied the piece of amber glass.

"Looking left is a little better than boss-eyed," Joe said. I nodded.

Excess glue had stuck the eye onto my finger, and by the time I managed to get it off and into the socket, I began to agree with Joe.

I put Pat in between the pillows on Danny's bed and placed the glue back in the drawer. "It is odd, isn't it? Maybe I should keep my distance…in fact, Danny texted me, and I don't recall giving him my number at all," I said.

"Block him. Let's lock up, leave the keys through the letterbox and see what happens."

As I closed the door and lifted the letterbox, I said, "To go to the extremes of a litter box is…" I looked at Joe.

"Oh no, you don't think…" I said, as I opened the door again.

We scoured the flat for a cat, a *real* one. We found a couple of toys but no live pet. We called out, opened the closets and drawers just to check he hadn't got stuck. When we were completely satisfied there was no live cat in the flat I finally shut the door and left the keys through the letterbox. I'd already left a large bowel of biscuits; should it materialise there was a real cat, at least it had something to eat.

"Maybe Pat only just died," Joe said, as he refreshed our wine glasses.

"Maybe Danny is a dick who thinks that was funny," I replied, accepting my glass and taking a sip of my wine.

"So, tell me again what happened when Ronan came over."

We laughed at the misunderstanding, and I found my smile getting wider the more I talked or thought about him.

Joe told me, "He has a spa that he's hoping to open soon. You know I said about a weekend away? I've snagged us a discount. It's going to be a very exclusive place. I'm going to help with some finishing touches."

"That sounds great; I could do with a spa weekend. We could time it for when my divorce is finalised. That should be some point next month according to my lawyer. It can be one of those divorce parties that seem to be popular nowadays."

"Yes! Do you still have your wedding dress? We can do a *trash the dress* photo shoot." Joe seemed very excited about that.

"I doubt I'd fit in it now, and I imagine it's in storage somewhere. Which reminds me, I really need to sort out somewhere to live soon. Maybe you'll keep your eye open for a fairly cheap flat or house for me?"

Joe spluttered, and I suspected it was the word 'cheap' that had been the cause. I laughed as he recovered himself. "I need to get going. When is Danny back?" he asked.

"Friday, I'm not sure what time. I thought I might be out all day, I really don't want to bump into him. That stuff with the cat has creeped me out, to be honest. I don't know him well enough for pranks like that."

"I agree. Maybe I could keep my eye out for something suitable for you. I'll ask a few friends; see what's on the market. I'll then rent this place out to someone really awful, a convict maybe."

"I don't think convicts—who wouldn't be convicts if they were out of prison by the way—are going to afford *this* apartment in *this* plush part of London."

"Well, we'll just have to find someone else that we think Danny will dislike then. When is your date with Ronan?" Joe asked, as he gave me a hug goodbye.

"Tomorrow."

"You make sure to ring me before you meet up, at least once during, and as soon as you've left him, okay?"

"Why?"

"Security, Lizzie." He sighed. "He might murder you, this way I'll know he hasn't. If you don't call, I can ring the police."

"What if I forget to call?"

"Put a reminder in your phone. And dress in layers, much harder to get through."

I pushed him from the threshold and slammed the door. "Layers, murderer…" I mumbled to myself. "No wonder you're single," I shouted, knowing he wouldn't hear.

I sat and nursed the remnants of the wine as unease settled in my stomach. What if he was a murderer? I grabbed my phone and set three alerts to ring throughout the evening. As for layers, by the time anyone got my Tena Lady pants off, my tights, my body sculpture corset thingy that was supposed to give me back the shape I had twenty years ago according to the saleswoman, they would be too exhausted to do anything awful!

Yes, I was safe from being attacked, I decided, I just had to make sure not to be murdered.

CHAPTER FIVE

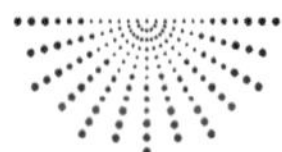

Thursday morning meant a hair appointment. While I sat with my head being massaged, which was really just an excuse to charge another twenty quid while the conditioner had time to soak into my brittle split ends, I had my nails painted a bright coral colour.

"Are you going anywhere special this evening?" the nail girl asked.

I didn't know her, and I wasn't about to chat with her about my date. I hated that she cracked gum and blew bubbles. I hated more that her nails were awful, bitten down and dirty. She really wasn't a great advertisement for a nail technician.

"No, I just like to get my hair and nails done regularly," I replied. I hadn't opened my eyes; I was enjoying the head rub.

I heard her crack the gum and sighed.

"Is that nice?" Kelly, the young girl who washed my hair, asked.

"It is, thank you. What's not is listening to gum chewing and bubble blowing."

There was no reply, and although there was no more noise, I did wonder if, once I opened my eyes, I was going to find polish all over my cuticles or fingertips.

As the day wore on, so my nerves increased. After soaking in the bath, I sat in my robe with a glass of wine. I had an hour before Ronan was due to collect me. I checked my alarm settings to cover the, 'I haven't been murdered' thing, and I double, and then triple checked the text message from Ronan to be sure I had the correct date.

I tried to remember the last time I'd been on a date. Of course, I was early teens, and it would have been with Harry. I still struggled when I thought of his name. My stomach knotted, and I took a deep breath in to relax myself. It had been nearly two years. I had to move on, and my first date was going to be the start of it.

I carefully applied my makeup and then dressed. When I was done, I stood in front of the mirror and smiled. I looked, and felt, a little like my old self. Although I wished the jowls weren't there—and the few lines across my brow and around my eyes. I didn't look as haggard as I had the previous couple of months. Yep, I was looking good.

I emptied my 'day time' handbag and then loaded my 'night time' handbag with a few panty liners, my lipstick, phone, my purse, a pen and small notepad, my keys, a packet of tissues, and some headache pills. Before I slipped on my shoes, I added a spare pair of knickers in case of accidents. And flip flops.

I texted Joe that Ronan was due in a few minutes and this was the first of my check-ins. Then I waited.

I sipped some more wine, and I watched the clock. When it was time, I pulled my handbag closer to me and kept my phone in my hand. I watched the clock some more.

I'd refreshed my wine glass while the hands on the clock moved past the time Ronan was due and continued to move until it was half an hour, then three quarters, and then an hour later. At that point, I emptied my night time handbag and gently placed the items back in my day time bag. I stood and walked into the bedroom, placed the bag back in the wardrobe, and kicked off my shoes. I picked them up and put them back in their protective cloth bag before storing them away. I unzipped the dress and hung it back up. I slipped off the panties and bra and walked to the shower.

I stood under the jets of water and let a couple of tears leak and mingle with the droplets before soaping a sponge and washing the makeup, the perfume, body lotion, the 'date' from my skin.

With my wet hair piled on top of my head and my fleecy jammies on, I walked back into the kitchen. I wasn't so low that I resorted to Horlicks, but I did scour the cupboard to see if I had any hot chocolate. When I didn't find any, I made myself a cup of tea and then panicked.

I picked up my phone to see a missed text and then a missed call. I replied:

Nothing to panic over, he didn't show. I took a shower, and now I'm sitting with a cup of tea xx

My phone vibrated with an incoming call, and Joe's name appeared. I wasn't up for talking, so I held it while I walked to the sofa. I pulled a comforter around my shoulders, curled up, and turned on the TV.

I wasn't angry. I was disappointed, and I was sad. I had been looking forward to my date. I liked Ronan, and the thought that someone liked me, and wanted to take me to dinner had boosted my bruised ego no end. I sighed. It obviously wasn't to be, but I didn't think that Ronan was the kind to make a plan and then just not show. Something had kept him away, but a call or a text could have saved me from sitting clock watching and wondering.

A text arrived from Joe:

Honey, I'm so sorry. I tried to call. Do you fancy some company?

I smiled as my best friend was offering up his Thursday card night with his friends for me:

No, it's okay. I'm sure there's a reasonable explanation. I can't imagine he'd be someone who just doesn't show. I'm going to have an early night xx

Joe was quick to reply:

I think you're right. I tried to call, his phone is off, and I texted. He might be caught up somewhere with a dead battery – sleep well, my lovely xx

I didn't respond; there was no need. I sipped on my tea, and I watched some trashy reality show. I hated them, but they were compulsive viewing sometimes. I pitied the 'stars', having to be on show constantly. Just layering that amount of makeup on my skin every day would be tiring enough without tottering about in heels made for inhuman beings and wearing daft outfits in the middle of the wrong season. Car crash TV, perfect for my non-date night.

❧

I woke with a stiff neck and a chill. Although I still had the comforter wrapped around me, I'd fallen asleep on the sofa, and the timer had kicked the heating off at ten o'clock. I glanced at my watch; it was closing in on midnight. I rose and stretched my arms above my head, deciding on another cup of tea and the comfort of a mattress. It was as I was standing, waiting for the kettle to boil that I heard laughter from the hallway.

I crept to the door and placed the side of my head against the wood. I could hear a female. I looked through the spy hole to see Danny with a blonde teetering in impossibly high heels, a skirt that was probably no more than a belt, and a tank top. It was way too cold for that kind of attire normally, let alone this time of year. I did notice her Michael Kors handbag, of course. There was something about the way she swayed around that made me suspect she wasn't completely sober. It was the first time I'd seen Danny since his trip and the dead cat episode, and there was something about him that had me on alert. He was home a day earlier than I was expecting and he hadn't thought to notify me of that. He looked a little inebriated as well, but he also looked unkempt—something that wasn't the case on the previous times we'd met. His hair was greasy; he had stubble around his chin and not the designer kind. It was the type that meant the owner of the stubble hadn't had access to a razor.

Although he wore a suit, his tie was skewed, and the front of his white shirt looked dirty and very crumpled. I watched as he inserted his key, and his companion giggled some more as the door was opened. They walked in, and I saw him kick it closed. I mentally wished them a good night with the handcuffs and whatnots.

I had just settled into bed an hour later when I heard doors banging and stage whispers. It was the first time I'd noticed how thin the walls were and how much noise could filter from the hallway. Obviously, Danny's guest was leaving, and she wasn't going quietly. I thought it very inconsiderate and although I didn't want to be *that neighbour*, I was here first, and I was going to mention it in the morning. I picked up my phone to check the time, and while I was there, I thought I might as well check any messages.

"Bollocks to you, Ronan," I said out loud when I saw nothing from him.

Although I was of the same mind as Joe in that something must have happened—fifty-year-olds didn't just fail to turn up for a date—I was still pissed off.

Other than a death, there was no reason I'd accept for the lack of communication.

❧

Unusually, I woke late the following morning. No matter what time I go to bed on an evening, I'm normally an early bird. I took a quick shower and dressed before grabbing my phone and heading for the kitchen.

I was munching on a piece of toast when I thought to check my messages.

Hun, I heard from Rich that his mum died. I guess that's why Ronan didn't make your date. I think their mum lives in Scotland somewhere.

Joe finished his text with a sad emoji.

I replied:

How come Rich can find the time to tell you yet Ronan can't tell me?

Then I regretted the words.

Joe's replay came:

I don't know, sorry xx

I shook my head as guilt niggled at me:

Don't apologise. I feel terribly sorry for them both.

I immediately wracked my brain for any mean thoughts in case I'd hexed Ronan with them. While I continued to munch on my toast, I toyed with the idea of texting him my condolences. I didn't want to disturb him, and I certainly didn't want my text to remind him about our missed date and for him to feel bad. Before I could make a decision, I heard Danny's front door open and then slam shut.

I rushed from my seat. "Danny, do you have a minute?" I asked as I opened my front door.

He wore a black t-shirt and jeans with dark glasses on a dull morning. He smiled but didn't speak.

"I'd like you to be a little more considerate when you bring your guests home. The walls aren't as thick as they should be in this building." I placed a hand on my hip to indicate I meant business.

"Ah, I'm sorry. She's a bit loud," he replied, pushing his glasses up to his forehead.

I was little confused by his reply. "I'm sorry?"

"She's so loud. I mean, she even gives me a headache sometimes. I end up gagging her."

I know I let my mouth flap open, but I quickly shut when he winked at me, slid his glasses back over his bloodshot eyes, and turned to walk away.

"What a prick," I said, as I closed my front door.

I heard him laugh as he entered the stairwell. He hadn't even mentioned his prank with the cat and that annoyed me too.

The more I thought about Danny, the more I wondered why he was such an arsehole. There was no excuse for his comments or his behaviour. He didn't know me. We could have been friends, and we were neighbours. I'd have thought that fact alone would have warranted some form of respect. Still, I'd be leaving soon enough, and he'd have to start all over again with a new neighbour and an unsavoury one from what Joe had been planning.

❧

A few weeks had passed when I received a call arranging a meeting with my solicitor. I guessed the final day of being married was here. I was both pleased to wrap up that period of my life, and sad that period of my life was wrapped up. It hadn't been the case that my husband had fallen out of love with me. It was simply that he couldn't find it in himself to hide any more, and I respected that, to a degree. What hurt was the speed and method he'd embraced his new identity. I made a decision that I wasn't going to dwell on it; I wasn't going to let it make me a bitter and twisted woman. I fought that, sometimes, but I was trying, and with the final appointment, I'd be able to take that deep breath in and let it all go.

I hadn't heard a word from Ronan, and I hadn't seen Danny, either. I was sad about one, happy for the other. Joe had discovered that Ronan's mum had been poorly for some time; it wasn't an unexpected death, although it had happened quicker than they were prepared for. Right or wrong, a little niggle formed that he could have sent a quick text message—I would have done so, had it been me.

Later that day, as I left the flat to head to the solicitors, I decided I would send Ronan a text message. I would be the bigger person. I sat in the back of the taxi and typed:

I'm sorry to hear about your mum. I would have messaged earlier but thought you'd be so busy. Just wanted to let you know I'm thinking of you and your family right now – Lizzie

I switched my phone to silent and placed it back in my handbag. Of all my friends, I was probably one of the last to own a mobile phone, and I still had the iPhone 5s that I'd bought as new and had caused me all sorts of headaches to learn. There was no way I was going to upgrade, despite the constant bombardment from my network provider and the ever-slowing apps and fast-depleting battery.

It was with a deep breath that I pulled open the door to the solicitor's and was shown through to a waiting area. I was told Mr Thompson would be with me shortly and I hoped that to be the case. The man was charging me enough, and on the previous meeting, he'd been nearly an hour late.

"Lizzie, it's good to see you," he said, holding out both hands as if I was a child about to be swung around.

I ignored the outstretched hands and rose from a particularly low grey uncomfortable sofa. "It's good to see you, too, and on time," I replied with a smile.

He laughed, but it was tinged with awkward embarrassment rather than genuine mirth.

"Please, follow me."

We walked to his office, and I was shown to a chair and offered coffee or tea, which I declined. I was keen to get the meeting underway and could see the bulging folder with a smart white envelope on top, which I suspected that contained his invoice.

Since it was payday, for both of us, I guess any tardiness went out the window.

He cleared his throat as if about to make a monumental statement, perhaps something as profound as Martin Luther King since he had a framed poster of the great man on his wall.

"It's done," he said, then beamed a smile at me.

"I gathered that, but maybe you'd like to be more specific?"

"Oh, yes. He agreed to everything, as you know. He has deposited the money with us, so if you're happy, you just need to sign off this invoice, and you're finally free."

He gently slid the white envelope across the desk to me, and I opened it. It contained their invoice, and I tried not to baulk at the fee.

"This is a little higher than expected or quoted even. Can you explain?" I asked, pointing at a forty-five-pound figure.

"That's a bank transfer fee. Standard amount," he answered with a dismissive wave of his hand.

I really didn't have much choice but to sign off the document since the money was already sitting in their account. It pissed me off when solicitors, or lawyers, or estate agents even, demanded a fee to transfer money when there certainly wasn't any bloody cost at their end. And if he even tried to quote the Money Laundering Act at me, I'd smack him one.

I slid the document and his pen back to him, and it was rather disconcerting to see him pick that pen up and roll it over his upper lip as if sniffing it.

I shuddered. "When will my money be transferred to me?"

"It takes three working days."

"And those are all the documents?" I asked since he hadn't actually given me my divorce papers.

"Oh, yes, of course. Will you be celebrating?"

"Celebrating? What a strange choice of words to offer someone who has just dissolved over thirty years of marriage," I said. I gathered the documents and stood.

"I didn't mean to offend," he said.

"Well, you did. Now, if you'll excuse me, I'll be off to *celebrate!*"

I left his office a single woman with a million and a half pounds in the bank. Technically not in *my* bank, but it would be. And technically, it would be minus their fee and the blasted bank transfer.

It sounded a lot of money, especially when I whispered the amount as I walked along the road towards a taxi rank. Living in London, though, meant that extra half a million would just about buy me a small apartment. If I moved out of town, I'd get more for my money, and I did long to move away.

I'd lived in London my whole life, and there had been a time when I'd loved the hustle and bustle, the fumes and the honks of car horns at all hours. I'd loved to be able to walk to a deli or coffee shop.

Over the past month or so, though, I had begun to long for some fresh air, some quietness, and open space.

I opened the door to a waiting taxi and gave my address. As I settled back, I pulled out my mobile and saw a missed call from Joe, and a text wishing me luck with my appointment. I texted him:

I am officially a single woman as of this moment.

He replied:

That's a great thing, isn't it?

I didn't reply immediately. I wasn't sure it *was* great. It certainly wasn't where I expected to find myself at fifty-years-old. I placed my phone in my bag and stared out of the window. Terraced housing lined either side of the street; cars were parked, causing bottlenecks in places. We passed black bags of rubbish sitting at the kerb, waiting to be collected. Some of those bags had been ripped open, probably by the many urban foxes that had been lured in by good-willed homeowners who thought they needed feeding, and the loss of their natural environment, of course.

I sighed. For the first time, I saw the grime and the greyness of unkempt houses and cars that needed a wash. I saw what was once bohemian, simply masking run down. I wasn't sure when it all happened. Yesterday, I was in love with the area.

The taxi pulled over outside my address, and I sat and looked up at the Victorian building. Although at the nicer end of the street, it was still a terraced house, albeit double width, among a hundred similar properties with no real character.

"Are you getting out?" I heard. The taxi driver, who gave me a kind smile, brought me out of my thoughts.

“I'm sorry. I was just thinking how miserable everything looks today when it hadn’t yesterday.”

I rifled around my purse for the fare, and I placed it on the little tray built into the partition separating me from the driver. I thought it a stupid place to have to leave the fare; the poor guy was going to need a chiropractor after reaching behind to retrieve it.

“Doesn’t look too bad, gotta have a fair bit of money to afford one of these places nowadays. My sister just moved out into Kent, got a house three times the size for the same she would have paid for two-up two-down here,” he said.

I smiled in return and reached for the door. I stood on the pavement for a moment while he drove away. I looked up at what was once a grand house, now four flats, or apartments as Joe insisted I call them.

I’d never taken the time to get to know the neighbours who lived on the ground floor. I knew them both to be elderly, but that was it. I decided that I’d at least knock and see if they wanted to join me one day for a cup of tea. I didn’t get that chance, though.

“Lizzie?” Ronan’s usual smooth tone of voice seemed slightly broken with grief. I turned to face him. He continued, “I’m so sorry not to have called. I lost my phone. My mum died that day and…” He looked very different to when I’d last seen him. Dark circles framed his eyes, emphasising how pale his skin was, and I wondered when he’d last had a decent night’s sleep. The whites of his eyes were tinged with red and unshed tears.

I smiled sadly at him. “Rich told Joe. I’m so sorry to hear that, Ronan. I did send a text of condolence, but I guess you didn’t see it.”

“I left my phone in the taxi, I think. I got to the airport to grab a flight to Scotland and then realised it was missing. I didn’t have time to go back home and check. I had to buy a new one.

Leaving it in the taxi is all I can think I did. Stupidly, I didn't save your number."

"Would you like a cup of tea?" I asked.

"That would be nice." He shrugged his shoulders as if feeling awkward. "I wanted to see you, to apologise—"

I held up my hand to cut him off. "There's no need to apologise, Ronan. Your mum died."

"I could have gotten your number if I'd tried, I didn't. I got caught up in arrangements." I noticed the lack of eye contact.

I opened the door into the building, and we slowly climbed the stairs to my floor. Ronan rushed past me to open the landing door, and I stopped and looked up at him. The sparkle of mischief that I'd noticed before in his eyes was missing and deep lines fanned out either side.

"You look tired," I said quietly, placing my hand on his arm.

He nodded. "I am. I hired a car and drove back late last night."

As we walked to my apartment, I heard him sigh. I opened the door and let him walk in first and through to the kitchen. He lifted the kettle to test its weight before deciding it needed a little more water then he opened a cupboard and retrieved two mugs. As he placed them on the counter, he turned to me, and his smile, although sad, was genuine.

"I'm sorry. I'm taking over, and this is your house, not mine," he said, and then laughed.

I replied with a smirk, "The last time you were here we had *Patgate,* and you had to make the tea."

His eyes brightened. "Patgate! Oh, Lizzie. I don't think I'd laughed as much in years as I did that day. I still chuckle when I think about it. What did your neighbour say when he returned?"

I continued to make the tea while Ronan sat on a stool at the counter. “He hasn’t mentioned it at all, which I find not only strange but a little scary as well. He texted me, but I don’t recall giving him my number. He came home with some real tart the other night. He was drunk, I imagine, and then dismissed my complaint about their noise the following morning. I don’t know…something isn’t right with him at all.”

“I can’t say that having you feed a stuffed cat was the best prank to play on a neighbour you’ve only just met. The litter tray was seriously odd, though.”

“I know. Who goes to all that trouble just for a laugh? I don’t get it, but I’m damned if I’m going to ask him about it.”

I made the teas and slid one mug towards him. I watched as he cupped both hands around the ceramic as if to warm himself.

“When do you need to travel back to Scotland?” I asked.

“Today, unfortunately. I came back to pick up some clean clothes, check on work, and to see you. I didn’t want to ask Rich to pass on a message. I can’t trust that bastard to get anything right,” he said, and I noticed the bitterness in his voice.

“It’s all up to you, is it?” I asked, gently.

Ronan nodded. “Rich fell out with my mum a long time ago. He’ll want his share of the inheritance, I imagine, but he won’t want to help sort it all out.”

“Well, if there’s anything I can help you with, please just ask.” It was a statement we all make, one that we don’t ever expect to be taken up on.

“Come back with me,” he said.

CHAPTER SIX

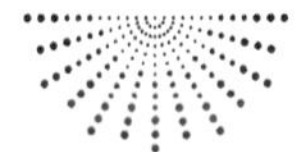

I blinked a few times before I raised the mug to my lips, then squealed as I gulped a mouthful of scalding hot tea.

Ronan continued, "Seriously, come back with me. I mean, I still have to sort out my mum's affairs, of course, but, it's a stunning part of the country."

"I'd be in the way, I'd…" I tried to think of every reason why heading to Scotland to sort out a dead woman's house, with a man I'd met for less than a couple of hours in total, was a terrible idea. "Okay," I said.

"Okay?" I couldn't tell if the edge to his voice was shock, joy, or a combination of the two.

I still couldn't quite believe it myself. "Yes, okay. I can be of use, Ronan. I can help pack your mum's house. I'm only sitting here getting bored anyway. I need to find somewhere permanent to live, and I can do that from anywhere."

I had totally surprised myself. It was about the most random thing I'd ever done—but, what the fuck, why not?

"I thought this was your home," he said.

"No, this actually belongs to Joe. My divorce is finalised, done, dusted—just waiting on the money to be transferred. I'd just come back from my solicitors when I saw you. I want to buy myself a little cottage somewhere, maybe in Kent or Surrey. Somewhere outside of London. I'm hankering for some quiet countryside."

Ronan took a step towards me. He took the cup from my hand and placed it on the countertop and then pulled me into an embrace. "Then I'm glad you're coming with me. The first weeks, months, are the strangest. I felt in limbo, not knowing what to do or how to start again." He stepped back and smiled at me.

I hadn't realised he'd been through divorce. We hadn't gotten that far in our conversations.

"Thank you. I felt odd earlier today but, well, maybe we can share our stories on the journey up."

I picked up my tea and continued to sip. Doubt started to creep in my mind. Did I have enough layers for the trip?

"How long do you think we'll be in Scotland?" I asked, mentally calculating how many days the corset could go before it needed a wash. No one was getting past that.

"A week, I guess, longer if you want to. I have to pack up mum's things. There's a lot to sort out," he replied. "You can help as much as you like or sightsee, I really don't mind. Just come, it's a big old house, and I'd enjoy the company. I know we don't actually know each other; in fact, we haven't shared surnames even, but so what? It's time for an adventure, for both of us."

I placed my mug on the countertop. "I guess I better go pack," I said. "What's the weather like in Scotland at the moment?"

"Cold, and wet, and muddy. The house is in the middle of nowhere," Ronan said, as I walked towards my bedroom.

I pulled a small case from the top of one wardrobe and filled it with clothes I thought suitable. I packed shoes, underwear, and toiletries. I grabbed my Kindle, a paperback I was keen to start, and a coat. As an afterthought, I grabbed a scarf.

"Do I need wellies? I don't know where they would be," I said, dragging the case to the kitchen.

"I'm sure there'll be wellies at the house that will fit. The boot room is full of them."

Boot room. I was liking the sound of this house.

"This is about the most spontaneous thing I've ever done but…I need the address to give to Joe. You know, just in case you murder me, or something," I said.

Ronan laughed as I slid a pad and pen towards him. He wrote down an address, an email, and a landline number. He tapped the pen against his teeth as he thought, then wrote a series of numbers.

"What's that?" I asked, pointing to them.

"Coordinates. He can give those to the SAS so they can organise a midnight raid to release you from my dungeon."

I laughed, although I was more than aware, and I suspected he was as well, of the hitch that had been caused by nerves. It was completely reckless, but a bubble of excitement burst in my stomach.

"Lizzie, they aren't really coordinates, that was a joke," he said. I was mildly disappointed that he didn't know them. "I also had to get a new mobile number because the service from my provider in Scotland was shit. I don't know it off the top of my head and the phone is in the car. You can text him that later."

I picked up the pad and my mobile and texted Joe:

I am doing something completely mad. I'm going to Scotland with Ronan to help him pack up his mum's house. This is the address, just in case he kills me, or puts me in his dungeon.

I added the address and pressed send. I chuckled as, seconds later, my phone vibrated in my hand. I pondered for a second on whether to answer or not but did.

"Don't you think you should get to know him a little first?" Joe said before I'd even greeted him.

"Maybe, but how exciting is this?"

"It's a…oh, fuck it. Yes, it's exciting. Do you know how large that house is? Rich was telling me…"

"Joe, I don't want to know any more. We're leaving shortly, and I'll call you when we arrive. I'll check in regularly," I added.

I wasn't interested in what Rich had to say after the comment Ronan had made. I said my goodbye to Joe and gathered my handbag.

"How are we getting there?" I asked.

"Driving. It's about an eleven-hour drive but a nice one once we get off the motorways."

"I guess that gives us plenty of time to get to know each other then," I said.

Ronan collected my luggage, and I picked up my coat and handbag. I took one look around the apartment, not entirely sure what I was looking for, but it was one of those things I'd always done. I switched off the lights and then stepped into the hall. As I double locked the front door, the one opposite opened.

"Oh, Lizzie, I forgot to thank you for feeding Pat. He was super happy to have you take care of him. Seemed to have doubled in weight," Danny said. There was not a smirk or wrinkle on his face to suggest he was joking or thought himself funny.

"That's okay, mate. We had some fun in your apartment if you know what I mean," Ronan said, giving Danny a wink while my cheeks flamed.

I had to hold back the smile when I saw Danny blanch a little.

As we walked away, Ronan turned to me. "You did change the sheets, didn't you?"

"No, I thought you had," I replied. We pushed through the fire door into the stairwell, not knowing if there was a response or not.

I chuckled as we descended the stairs; the bouncing suitcase on the wood masking any of those chuckles reaching Danny.

Ronan walked towards a Range Rover, pressed for the boot to open and loaded my bags. I placed my coat over the top and walked to the passenger door. I was about to open it when a hand reached to grab the handle before I could.

"Allow me," he said, as he swung the door wide.

"Why, thank you, kind sir," I replied with a laugh.

Once Ronan was settled in the driver's seat, and we had pulled out into the traffic, I felt my shoulders start to relax. "I thought you said you hired a car?" I asked, looking around the plush interior.

"I did. I hired this one. I'm not doing that journey in a beat up ex-Uber," he said. "I wonder what Danny thought about our comment?"

"I find it very odd that he hasn't mentioned the cat until now. I've seen him a couple of times since. I half expected him to keep the joke going by leaving me a bottle of wine or chocolates as a thank you," I said.

"It is strange, for sure. Very odd."

I watched Ronan as he negotiated the city traffic. He was a confident driver, way more than I was a confident passenger. I closed my eyes as we nearly sideswiped a black taxi. He cursed under his breath, and it was only then that I noticed the accent.

"I haven't noticed your Scottish accent before," I said.

"I haven't lived there for so many years. I guess I slip back into it every now and again."

"Were you born there?"

"Yes, so was Rich, obviously. My parents separated when we were small and to be honest we were shipped back and forth between Mum and Dad for a few years. It's amazing we don't have a mix of American, English, and Scottish."

"Your dad was American?"

"He was…*is*. He's still alive. Haven't seen him in years though. He's remarried with a new family as far as I'm aware."

"And you've never been curious to get to know them?" I wondered if my line of questioning was a little too prying considering we barely knew each other.

"No, to be honest, I haven't. Imagine their surprise if I turned up, and he hadn't mentioned me before. He might write or send a card, rarely, but he'll only sign it from himself as if he wants complete separation. That suits me, if I'm honest."

Ronan stopped chatting to concentrate on joining the motorway. For a little while, we drove in silence, and it didn't feel uncomfortable at all. He hummed along to a song on the radio, and I let my seat back just a little and closed my eyes. I was notorious for 'car mode'. As soon as I hit a motorway or any smooth travel, I could close my eyes and drift off. My mum used to say that when I was a kid and wouldn't stop crying, she'd load me into the old car she had and drive around the block, within minutes, I'd be asleep. I guessed my 'car mode' came from there.

❧

I felt a nudge to my arm, and I jolted awake. Ronan was smiling and, strangely, holding out a tissue. He fluttered it at me, towards my face. It took me a moment until I embarrassingly realised he meant for me to wipe the drool from the side of my mouth.

"You super snore when you sleep in that position," he said, with a laugh.

"I do not! Do I? Oh, God, do I? I'm so sorry," I stammered.

"It's okay. Super snore is probably an exaggeration. You snuffle. It's quite endearing."

I wasn't sure, at fifty-years-old, I wanted to snuffle *or* be endearing. I wiped my mouth, checked myself in the mirror and then realised we'd pulled into the motorway services.

"I thought we could grab a drink, toilet break if you need one. Are you hungry?" he asked.

As if on cue, my stomach grumbled. I raised my eyebrows and laughed.

"Let's grab a dirty burger or some other junk food," he said, and he unclipped his seat belt.

We walked into the service station, and while Ronan queued at a burger outlet, I headed for the loos. I didn't need to pee but sat and tried to squeeze one out anyway. My fifty-year-old bladder had decided, lately, it would play games with me. I sat and… nothing. Not a drip. I stood and flushed, and then the bastard bladder decided to leak. As quick as I could pull my knickers back down, I was nearly at full flow.

I muttered under my breath as I wiped, dabbed at the crotch of my knickers and rifled around in my bag wondering if I'd put a clean pair in. I thanked my foresight not to trust my bladder and changed, depositing the worn ones in the bin.

After washing my hands and checking my makeup and hair, I joined Ronan at a table with fixed, very uncomfortable plastic seats. He slid my burger and fries and my diet Coke over to me, and I chuckled at the irony. I wondered how many calories and fat I was about to consume and whether that small saving in the diet Coke really was worth the effort.

“Mmm, you know, there is nothing like a little junk food every now and again,” Ronan said.

“I think my hips might disagree with you on that one.”

“Your hips are damn fine,” he replied, mimicking an American accent.

“You do that accent well,” I said, taking a bite of my burger.

I was conscious of sauce dripping down my chin or settling at the corner of my lips. It took forever to eat as I wiped my mouth after every bite. When we’d finished, and I’d visited the bathroom again to wash my hands and double check I didn’t have a slab of gherkin on my cheek, we headed back to the car.

“Do you want me to drive for a while?” I asked.

“You won’t be insured, I don’t think, but I can get you added once we get to the house if you like.”

“As I spoke, I was trying to think of the last time I actually drove a car.”

“I guess there’s no need since you live in London. Do you like it?”

“I did, and then for some reason, I got an urge to move away. I think it was a taxi driver that planted the idea. I need to buy a house or rent somewhere, and I was thinking about Kent.”

“There are some lovely parts, some not too lovely, but you’ll get that anywhere. I live in Kent. I’ll take you to the village my cottage is in.”

I had a mental checklist in my mind of all the things I ought to learn on a first date. Where someone lived was obviously high up on that list. I ticked it off.

"How about we do that thing…that questionnaire thing we would have done had we made our date?" I asked with a laugh.

"Okay, you get five questions, then I get five. Deal?"

"Deal. Number one. How old are you? No…wait…that's a lame…" I stuttered through my first question.

"It is lame, do you want to change your question?" he asked with a grin.

"Erm, what star sign are you?" I could have kicked myself, that was an even lamer question.

"Leo, now I get to ask a question." He paused, pursed his lips and narrowed his eyes as if thinking hard. "Does your husband's betrayal still hurt?"

I stared at him. "Wow, I ask something as benign as your star sign, and you go for the killer question."

He shrugged his shoulders. "I never said there were any rules on what type of question could be asked. You don't have to answer, take a pass," he said, giving me a smile.

We had left the car park and were back on the motorway, and I guessed a minute or two had passed since he asked his question.

"You know, it certainly doesn't hurt anywhere near as much it did. It wasn't the betrayal that hurt the most, it was the lie we…*he*…had been living. My husband is gay, Ronan. He knew, I didn't. He felt the need to have a 'conventional' relationship, for want of a better word. Then one day, he couldn't do it anymore. I feel sorry for him, that he has wasted his life living the lie, although I understand why he did, and I feel sorry for the wasted years we…*I*…had."

He cringed. "I'm sorry, I didn't know. Maybe that was too much of a killer question for our first date," he said.

"So this is our first date? A dirty burger while driving up the motorway. Gee, you take a girl to all the best places," I replied, with a laugh.

"I love your humour—it was the first thing that attracted me to you in that bar."

I was stunned into silence. I hadn't expected Ronan to be so forthright, so honest. Of course, there was a small part of me that started to tingle, and that tingle travelled south to my girly bits. It wasn't just my ego that was inflating.

"My turn, killer question to you. Why did you get divorced and how long ago?"

"That's technically two questions. She believes I cheated, and it was ten years ago, could be more."

"Oh." It was such a blunt confession, and I was confused at his lack of a definitive answer for how long ago it happened. The date I filed for divorce, and the decree absolute date will forever be imprinted in my brain.

"I'll let you have an extra question because I'm sure you want to know why she believes I cheated," he said. He hadn't taken his gaze from the road ahead.

"It's okay, I'm sure that's private," I said.

"So, is it my turn now?"

"Erm, yes, I guess so."

He ran his palm over his chin and I could hear the slight scratch as his skin caught his stubble. That sound added to the tingle.

"Let's go safe…How long have you known Joe?"

"From schooldays. He was part of my circle of friends. You

know, I can't actually remember how we became friends, we just always have been. There was a little period of time where we didn't see so much of each other. He went off to uni, moved away and then came back, and we picked up our friendship where we'd left off."

As if on cue, my mobile vibrated in my bag. I could hear it clink against a set of keys. I pulled it up. "And as if by magic," I said, as I answered. "I was just talking about you."

"I hope it was all good. Where are you?" Joe asked.

"On a motorway."

"Okay, and he hasn't killed or done something nasty to you yet?"

"Since you're speaking to me, I guess we can assume the first hasn't happened, and as for the second, no. All's fine in that department," I answered, cryptically.

"Okay, I was just checking in. After your call this morning, I began to think. This is very out of character for you."

"I know, and isn't that wonderful. I'll call you when we arrive, just so you know, I haven't been murdered, or…"

Joe laughed, and I didn't finish my sentence. I turned to look at Ronan, who was smirking while still concentrating on the road ahead.

"So, where were we?" I asked as I disconnected the call. "I think it's my turn. What do you do for a living?"

"That's easy. A little of this and a lot of that," he said with a laugh.

"Not a good enough answer."

"We never agreed on the quality of the answers. I get involved in fledgling businesses and help them get off the ground. I own property that I rent out. I have a couple of clubs, a bar that others manage because I like to stay in the background, and I renovate property to sell on."

"Sounds...interesting," I replied.

"What do you intend to do with the rest of your life?" he asked, I guessed the answer to my question was over.

"I have no idea. I've been a wife for the majority of it, and now I'm not, and although I don't want to be married, I don't want to be on my own all the time either. Joe seems to think that makes me a cougar; as if I'm always on the lookout for the next..." I shut up, quickly. I didn't want Ronan to think I was desperate, which I bloody well wasn't.

There was a very awkward pause.

"You know, it's okay not to want to be on your own. You've done it already for what—a couple of years now? So what if it's not your thing. Joe flits, from what I can see, from relationship to relationship, clinging on to the hope that my wretch of a brother might be the one, which he isn't by the way, so I don't think he has room to give advice."

Had it been anyone else to criticise Joe, I might have snapped back a response. Although I bristled, it felt good to have someone actually understand where I was coming from. Of course, Ronan was absolutely correct.

"I don't think I enjoy my own company for too long and thank you for understanding," I said. "I think it might be my turn but why don't we save the remainder for later, over a glass of wine?" I didn't want to expose myself any further.

"That sounds like a plan."

❧

It was dark when we weaved through the narrow lanes of a village and out the other side. There were no streetlights, no pavements; just fields either side until we came to a set of gates attached to ornately carved brick pillars. They were open, and we drove through what I could only describe as a park. Past mowed lawns, perfectly shaped bushes and trees until something akin to Buckingham Palace came into view.

"What the…?" I whispered, thankful the crunch of gravel under the tyres covered my words, or at least I hoped so.

We came to a stop. Ronan hadn't looked at me as he turned off the engine. He sat with his hands on the steering wheel and his face staring ahead.

"Ronan?" I asked gently.

He took in a deep breath, exhaling slowly. I saw his features soften a little as he looked towards the house and at the person who had opened the front door. I followed his gaze to see an elderly couple.

"Ronan?" I asked, again.

He turned to me and smiled. "Welcome to my home, Lizzie."

The couple walked down the stone steps from the front door. The gentleman went straight to the boot and pulled out our bags, and the woman opened the passenger door.

"Lizzie, I'd like to introduce Maggie," Ronan said. I noticed the soft tone to his voice, the fondness contained within the words. I smiled.

"Let's get you inside. I have some tea ready for you. You must be exhausted," Maggie said with a heavy Scottish accent.

"It's been a long journey," I said. I took her hand as she helped me from the car, not that it was needed.

She embraced Ronan, and I watched her wipe a tear. The gentleman nodded to me as he walked past with my bags.

I looked at the house, the manor, or stately home. I had no idea what it was officially called other than huge.

"When the sun comes up, and you can see the loch, it's an amazing location," I heard. I turned to Ronan who held out his hand, and I took it.

As I stepped through the front door, I was immediately reminded of a TV series that I'd loved. I struggled to remember the name, an English family that owned an estate in Scotland. Gilly was the gamekeeper, or maybe that was his job title, I couldn't remember. Whatever programme it was, this house had to be the set. I was in total awe and instantly in love with the property.

CHAPTER SEVEN

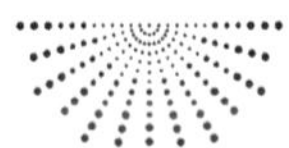

I had been shown to a bedroom that was the size of my flat. My bags had been placed on a small table beside a wooden wardrobe. A dressing table contained a silver hairbrush and mirror set, a couple of vintage glass bottles that I imagined once held perfume, and a glass vase with small, heavily scented flowers.

I walked to the side of an enormous bed. It wasn't that it was super king sized, but so high I would have to hop a little to get on the mattress. I ran my hand over a silver velvet comforter that was draped across the bottom of the bed. I loved the way the material changed colour as the fibres were reversed.

Heavy, floor-to-ceiling embroidered curtains were pulled across one wall. I doubted there was any point in looking out the window, it would be too dark, but I looked forward to the morning when I could see outside.

I was disturbed by a knock on the door.

"Come in," I called out.

Ronan stepped into the room. "Everything okay?" he asked.

I nodded. "This is an unbelievable house, Ronan. It's…"

"Really something, isn't it? It's been in my mother's family for centuries. Tomorrow we can do the grand tour, and I'll tell you all about my ancestry. For now, Maggie has set out some tea for us."

I followed him along a wide corridor and back down the sweeping staircase. We crossed a vast hall to one of many doors, down another corridor and eventually found ourselves in an industrial-sized kitchen.

Copper pots hung over an Aga that looked as if it hadn't been used for many years. The layer of dust and rust was a shame. On the opposite side of the room was a modern range, and the ping of a microwave seemed to dissolve the charisma instantly. Maggie retrieved a jug and, wincing at the burn to her fingers, she placed it on a scrubbed wooden table. Around the table were mismatched chairs; one or two had woollen throws over the back.

Maggie handed me a throw. "Here, take this. It gets cold in here at night. The cheapskates couldn't extend the heating down here, and that old thing gave up on us years ago," she said, nodding at Ronan and then diverting her gaze to the Aga.

"Maggie, half the house has no heating. At least you have windows that shut!" Ronan replied.

I heard a chuckle from behind. The elderly gentleman came into the room; he removed his gloves and scarf and took a seat. He smiled at me, a toothless smile that showed an expanse of gum.

"Where are your teeth, you old fool?" Maggie scolded.

He replied, in a deep-toned voice, something totally foreign, alien even, unrecognisable by only me. Maggie answered him, and Ronan laughed.

I didn't want to be rude and ask for a translation, of course. Whatever language it was he spoke, I was impressed that Ronan understood. Learning another language had always been one of those things on my list.

“Charlie is Maggie’s husband. I’m not sure I introduced you earlier,” Ronan said.

Charlie grinned again and my hand itched to point out something that appeared to be stuck to his gum, a piece of greenery.

He spoke, and I did that thing. That thing that every foreign person hates; that thing that most British people do as if all foreign people are stupid and if we just speak louder and very, very slow, they’ll understand us.

“Thank. You. For. Taking. My. Bag. Upstairs,” I said, slowly and loudly. I was pleased not to have added, unconsciously, the obligatory hand gestures as well.

Charlie spoke and then cackled. Whatever the sound was, it could hardly be called a laugh. Maggie poured the hot milk from the jug into a mug half filled with chocolate and slid it towards me.

“His accent is a little heavy, dear. You’ll get used to it,” she said.

“Where is he from?” I asked, aware that I was being obnoxious in not addressing him.

Ronan chuckled. “Third farm up the lane. Obviously, that was many years ago. He’s worked here since he was a child, so he’ll have us believe,” he said.

I was a little confused.

“Yous think I’m a foreigner do yous? I was speaking Gaelic, lassie,” Charlie said, as slowly and loudly as I’d addressed him. He did, thankfully, have a mischievous smile.

“Yes…No…Sorry. I have a hearing problem,” I blurted out. “No, I don’t have a hearing problem as such, I…”

Maggie laughed. “It took me until I was in my mid-thirties to understand a word he said. I'm sure he does it deliberately. He spent way too many years out on the hills with nothing but the cattle, not another human in sight. Ignore him and drink your chocolate," she said, giving my shoulder a squeeze as she passed. She punched Charlie on the arm.

While I sipped on my hot chocolate—something I hadn't drunk in years—Maggie placed some sandwiches, cakes, and biscuits on the table. It was like an afternoon tea, only without the tea, and, I checked my watch, it was heading towards midnight.

I stifled a yawn at the sight of those little gold hands on my Breitling. I imagined Ronan must have been exhausted as he'd driven all the way.

"Do you want to take a plate up with you?" Maggie asked.

"That might be nice," Ronan said, assuming the question was directed at him, *or* he was answering for me.

Maggie plated up two 'midnight snacks' I think Charlie called them and handed them to us. Ronan and I left the kitchen, and I followed back through the maze of hallways to the main stairs.

As we climbed to the first floor, Ronan said, "There's another set of stairs from the kitchen, but I haven't used those in ages. They would have been for the staff back in the day."

"This is an amazing house. It must have been truly something to have lived here as a child." I could imagine the hours of hide and seek.

"It was very lonely. We'll do the grand tour tomorrow. You might be in for some rather interesting surprises. My mother was…bohemian I guess is the right term."

He chuckled and that *thing*, that tingle happened again. I smiled at him as we stood at the top of the stairs.

"Did anyone show you your bathroom?" he asked.

"No, I literally stroked the bed lovingly, and you called for me," I replied.

"Okay, follow me."

I followed him back to the bedroom I'd been allocated. I placed my plate of goodies on the bedside table with my mug. One wall was panelled with dark oak, and it blended so well that I hadn't noticed a door with a wooden handle. Through that door was a large bathroom, but what caught my breath was the bath. Standing beside floor to ceiling leaded windows was a claw-footed, enamel tub. I could immediately picture myself lying there and looking out over the lawns to the rear of the property, and then the woods beyond.

"This is wonderful," I said.

"There is the shower, obviously, and the sink and whatnot. Just be careful, the water runs cold for a while before the boiler gets up enough steam to push hot water up this end of the house," he said, with a laugh.

"You know, I really didn't expect this. When you said you had to pack up your mum's house, I thought she lived in a semi somewhere in a town."

"I'll own this house now, as the oldest son, but when I said pack up my mum's house, I guess I meant her personal things. You'll see what I mean tomorrow."

I watched as he covered his mouth to hide a yawn, and I told him, "Get some sleep, you must be exhausted. I'll find my way to the kitchen in the morning."

"I'll just be across the corridor," he replied.

Ronan left, and I stood in the middle of the room, once again sipping on the chocolate. I longed for a tea but had no desire to navigate to the kitchen on my own, despite my earlier statement that's where I'd head in the morning.

I finished my drink and decided to unpack my bags, and then take a shower. Ronan was correct. I sucked in a deep breath and clenched my jaws tight to stop the squeal as ice-cold water hit my skin. I leapt from the shower, sliding on a thin towelling mat on the wooden floor, and wrapped my arms around myself. I turned around, reaching for the robe I'd left over the back of a chair when I realised anyone outside could see straight into the bathroom *and* my naked form.

I reached out to grab the curtains to close them when I saw—not that far below where I stood—naked, full frontal, and arms outstretched as if crucified—the embers of a cigarette light up as the smoker inhaled. It was too dark to see the face, and I wasn't about to hang around to see if I could make out who it was. I pulled the curtains closed so fast, one half of the left one came away from the rail, and a layer of dust floated down, causing me to cough.

"Oh, for fuck's sake," I whispered, pulling the chair close. I stood on it and rethreaded the curtain rings on the pole.

By that point, steam was starting to swirl from the shower cubical, so I assumed I finally had hot water. I took a quick shower, deciding that from then I'd only be using the bath. The shower controls appeared to have two settings, ice cold or scalding hot.

With my PJs on, my book, and the plate of snacks beside me, I sunk into what had to be the most comfortable bed I'd ever laid on. I wasn't sure I managed a chapter before I could feel my eyelids drooping. I turned the corner of the page to mark my spot—laughing at the amount of fellow readers who would think that an act worthy of a fast track to hell—and then placed it on the bedside cabinet. I wriggled lower under the duvet and sighed.

❧

"Good morning," I heard, or thought I heard. It could have been a dream until it was repeated.

I sat bolt upright, totally disorientated as the bed dipped with an unwanted visitor.

"Oh, erm, morning," I said, as Maggie smiled at me.

"I made you some tea. I heard you talking, maybe on your mobile, so thought you were awake," she said.

I frowned at her. "I was asleep…I think."

"I'm sorry, I must have startled you then. This looks interesting," she said picking up my book. "*The Facilitator*, strange name for a novel." She scowled at the title.

I blinked a few times as she thumbed through my book. *I* might be allowed to crack the spine, dog-ear the corners, and flick through pages so they crease, but no one else was. I itched to reach out and take it from her. Her disregard for my literature riled me.

"The title makes sense when you read the book," I said.

She paused mid-flick and started to read. "Oh…oh…that's rather naughty," she said and then chuckled.

I leaned forwards a little, conspiratorial and whispered, "It's an erotic romance. Seriously naughty," hoping that might put her off.

She smiled some more. "I like a good erotic romance. Perhaps I could read it when you're done?"

Thankfully, she placed the book back on the bedside cabinet and stood. I wasn't a bookworm as such, and I would gladly give her the book when I was done but…When. I. Was. Done.

"I'll leave your tea there, there's a plate of biscuits beside it," she said, smiling as she walked to the door.

"Thank you. I appreciate that."

I hadn't, but I was a grumpy mare in the mornings sometimes, especially when woken suddenly by a stranger sitting on the edge of my bed, rifling through my possessions. I was sure that was a *slight* exaggeration, but I didn't care at that point. I picked *The Facilitator* back up, wondering what page she had read that had so fascinated her. I laughed. I had nearly finished with the story, and I would hand it to her. If she liked a little—or a lot in the case of *The Facilitator*—erotica I thought she would enjoy the story.

I reached for my tea and sipped, pondering on Maggie's comment that she thought she'd heard me talking. Had I spoken in my sleep? If I had, what on earth had I said? I had an irrational fear, or perhaps it was rational, of speaking all those thoughts that shouldn't leave my mouth when I wasn't conscious enough to control them.

I could have stayed put all morning. Instead, I placed the tea back on the cabinet and slid from the bed. It was a little jump to reach the floor, but once I had, I wished I hadn't. The wood was freezing. I stood hopping from foot to foot until I ran on tiptoes to a rug in front of the dressing table.

"Bloody hell," I said, realising the whole room was cold. The duvet had been so sumptuous that I hadn't noticed.

I slid my feet, one at a time, towards the curtains. This ensured my feet stayed on the rug, and the rug came with me. I pulled back the curtains, and whatever cold I felt disappeared with the beauty of the view in front of me.

An expanse of lawn, the same view from the bathroom, but that time, the grass shimmered with icy dew. In the distance, I could see deer; one raised its head and a puff of steam left its nose as the exhaled breath froze in the cold air. All I needed now was to see a majestic stag standing there, and for it to raise one leg, or hoof, or whatever it was called, like a view in an oil painting and this would be the epitome of a Scottish stately home. I would have to find out if that was, indeed, what it would be called. I'd be rather disappointed to learn it was nothing more than a large house on a venison farm.

No matter what the official term, the view was simply stunning, and I worried that I hadn't brought the correct type of clothing. I slid towards the wardrobe and opened the oak door. I pulled out a pair of jeans, a shirt, and a woollen jumper. It might be that those items would need constant washing or Ronan could run me into town to buy more. There had to be a department store somewhere, perhaps a John Lewis, or a Harvey Nicks.

I hadn't taken much notice of our journey up, as the majority had been spent on the motorway and the last few hours in the dark. We hadn't passed through a town large enough for a Lidl, let alone a John Lewis. I placed the clothes on the bed and grabbed knickers, a bra, and one of only two pairs of socks. I then slid towards the bathroom.

I remembered the shock of cold water from the previous night and decided on a bath. I turned on the hot tap only, assuming it would run cold for a while then warm up. I hadn't brought bubble bath but grabbed a bottle from a shelf close by. I hadn't read the label but caught the last half of the word, *shampoo*. By that point, I'd already poured a capful under the running water. It smelled nice enough, so I let the bath fill while I stripped off.

With the cold water added to give the right temperature, I sank under the bubbles. I gripped the sides as the bath was way longer than I, my feet wouldn't reach the end to hold me in place. The enamel was slippery, and after the second time of sliding under and waterboarding myself, I climbed out.

I grabbed a towel for my wet hair and wrapped another around my body. As I released the plug, I caught a glance of the *bubble bath.*

Delicious Derry's Dog Shampoo was scrawled on the label.

"Dog shampoo?" I said, picking it up. It promised a shiny, tangle-free coat, with a built-in flea and tic treatment.

My head started to immediately itch.

I dragged the towel from my scalp, scrubbing at my hair as I did. Thankfully, my hair was fairly short and a few minutes of vigorous rubbing had it, not only standing in every direction, but mostly dry and, I hoped, flea and tic free.

I sniffed the towel. What hadn't been an unpleasant smell in the bottle was like wet mutts when…well, wet!

I padded to the bedroom, still with the rug beneath my feet and vowed to purchase some slippers. I dressed quickly, forgoing any makeup or hairdryers and left the room.

One wrong turn later, I found the kitchen. "I forgot to bring down my cup, Maggie. I'll grab it later and wash it up," I said to her back.

She was mumbling at the hob. "That's okay, dear. I'm making pancakes, but the blooming hob is playing up. Honestly, this house needs a lottery win thrown at it. Did you have hot water this morning?" she asked.

"I did, just no heating."

She hummed. "Yes, we seem to have only one or the other. What with winter on its way, if that doesn't get sorted, we'll be in trouble in a month."

"I saw a deer in the distance. The grounds look amazing," I said.

"I'll give Verity that credit, she did love the grounds," she chuckled as if I should have known, one, who Verity was, and two, why she loved the grounds so much.

"Did I hear my mother's name mentioned?" The low tone of voice didn't need a face for me to know who had entered the room. I felt his hand on my shoulder as he passed behind me, and I smiled up at him when he took the seat beside me. "It's bloody freezing upstairs," he said, pulling a teapot towards him. He lifted the lid and looked in.

"Yep, I said to Lizzie, it's either hot water or heating at the moment. Until you get the blooming boiler sorted, that is."

Ronan took the teapot to the kettle and topped it up. He poured three mugs, sliding one towards me, while we waited for the pancakes. A few minutes or so later, Maggie placed a platter of perfectly round pancakes in the middle of the table. She added pots of jam and bowls of sugar, plates, and cutlery. My stomach rumbled at the aroma.

"We'll save the Scottish cliché for tomorrow and have stodgy porridge," she said, as she joined us.

"I happen to like porridge. It's healthy," Ronan said.

"You won't be getting any of that healthy crap from this kitchen," Maggie answered, stuffing a whole pancake in her mouth.

She was a little round, with ruddy cheeks and grey hair cut short, pixy style. I guessed her to be well into her seventies, or it could be the harsh Scottish weather. Didn't all the Scots look a little rugged? A thought popped into my mind—Ronan in a kilt.

It was decided that Ronan would take me for a walk around, first the house, and then the grounds. It proved to be an eye-opener of epic proportions!

CHAPTER EIGHT

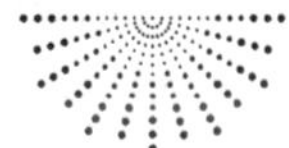

The house tour was really interesting. Ronan knew everything there was to know, which, I guessed, was to be expected. He knew how old the wood panelling was, where it came from, who carved a door. He was able to detail the first edition books in a library that housed a layer of dust everywhere. He recounted who every single person was in the paintings and photographs. Some were immediate family, some distant. It appeared that his mother, Verity, had been the sole heir to the family home when her brother had been killed at war. Ronan was a little vague on that, as it appeared Verity was very young when her older brother had died and it had been so devastating to her parents, his grandparents, they seemed to wipe all memory of him away. Ronan remembered his grandparents and referred to them as fearsome.

There was an air of neglect about the place that seemed to sadden Ronan. He would sigh as he ran his hand over a broken piece of wooden doorframe or a torn brocade curtain. He would tut at cracked glass panels in lead divided windows.

"We need a lot of money to get this place back to its former glory. Or I need to make a decision to sell it," he said, as we walked from room to room.

"Could you use it as a wedding or party venue, generate a little income that way?" I asked.

"We …sort of…already do that. You'll soon see. Not that it generates an income," he answered cryptically.

We had toured one half of the house, the more traditional and less used side, I guessed. We crossed the hall on the lower floor, and Ronan paused by a closed door.

"This is my mother's…art collection is about the best description. She was an *artist,* and I'm using the word loosely. She dabbled in…Well, let's just take a look. Are you ready?"

He looked at me as if whatever was behind that door was going to cause me to run. There was a pleading in his eyes to be calm, rational even. He opened the door and then allowed me to walk in before him. On the walls, leaning against the same walls, on easels, lying flat on the floor, in piles, balanced on chairs and sofas were huge canvases of… I had no idea, although it was colourful.

I took a step closer to one. "I'm not sure what I'm looking at," I said, trying to find something to say other than, '*that's the biggest pile of crap that's been called art since a condom on the floor next to an unmade bed'*.

Ronan laughed. "You're absolutely right. It's abstract to the point it's a bloody mess. Look at the ones on the wall—the photographs, not the paintings," he said.

I walked to the other side of the room and as I approached, all I could see, as I had before, was splodges of multi-coloured paint. But then something stood out. There was something that seemed out of place, and when I looked closer, I realised it was a head with hair fanning out. I was able to track the head down to a naked body covered in paint and then I realised what I was looking at. The naked woman appeared to be rolling on the canvas, spreading the paint, covering herself. I frowned.

"That's my mother," Ronan said.

"Okay, it's…*interesting*." I squinted as I stared closer, to the point I was sure I'd created a monobrow.

I heard a soft chuckle. "I told you she was bohemian, hippy even. She had a whole greenhouse of cannabis out back one time. I'm surprised she was never arrested. I don't remember the last time the woman wore fucking clothes!"

I studied his face to see if he was joking or not. "She must have. It's flipping freezing in here!"

He shrugged his shoulders. I wasn't sure what to say, but I was more surprised at Ronan. Perhaps I had misinterpreted the *face* he'd given me before we walked into the room. So his mother rolled around in paint, in the nude. It was…odd, maybe, but it wasn't the worst thing I'd heard. My husband, correction, *ex*-husband, ran off with a drag queen. I was sure that might outrank in oddness if there were such a list.

"Well, if that was her art, then good luck to her," I said, with a smile. "What do you intend to do with them?"

He raised his hands and then let them fall by his side. "I have absolutely no idea. Maggie can't bring herself to help me clear them away, or do anything with them. I was hoping you could."

"So you only invited me to clear some naked pics of your mother?" I teased.

His cheeks reddened and my heart sunk a little. He had! "Can I be honest with you?" he asked as he perched on the arm of a chair, knocking some of the canvases over. "Richard isn't interested; our mother embarrassed him, so he says, to the point that he stopped having anything to do with her years ago. I think she might have had some mental health issues in her life. That might have been a reason my father left, we don't know. Anyway, I'm rambling. Honestly, Lizzie, I don't have anyone to help me deal with this, to make decisions, and to do… I like you—we connected, even if just for that short period of time, I think. You're the perfect person to help me."

I wasn't sure I was, but I was flattered that he thought so. The pause, the lack of completion of one sentence hadn't escaped me but at that moment, that man looked a little vulnerable.

I rolled my sleeves up. "There's no better time than now. I suggest we actually pile these up in size order, then we can order picture crates. Let's at least clear them from the room, box them up, and you can decide what to do with them another time. I don't think you should destroy them. That's your mother there," I said.

It took less than half an hour to pile the paintings and remove the photographs and canvases from the wall. I wasn't sure how old Verity was, in some images she looked lithe and toned, in others older and slightly rounded. I guessed she'd been painting for many years. It was, obviously, hard to pick out any distinguishing features as she was covered in paint.

"You know, I bet that's quite liberating," I said as I placed the last painting on the pile.

Ronan stood and looked around the room clapping his hands to rid them of the dust. "It was," he replied.

"Not clearing the room. I mean that," I said, pointing to the painting on the top of the nearest pile.

"I have no idea. I know it used to freak me out. I remember as a child coming home from school on a Friday and seeing her standing in the middle of the lawn, covered in paint, with no clothes on, obviously. I was mortified." His eyes widened in shock as he recalled the memory.

"Do you have children?" I asked. He looked at me, clearly surprised by my change in subject.

"No, I never wanted them. I wouldn't know how to be a parent, Lizzie, if the truth be known."

I could relate to that. I'd decided many years ago not to have children. *Or* maybe I'd decided that to mask the hurt I felt when it was discovered the cheating ex was infertile, and adoption, or even fostering, was totally off the table, according to him.

"Do you have Wi-Fi here?" I asked as I pulled my mobile from my jeans pocket.

"Surprisingly, we do, although the signal can be hit and miss. You're better off using it from the office, though."

"You have an office?"

"No, we have an estate manager, and *he* has an office."

"Is that Charlie?"

Ronan laughed, but I didn't understand the reason for his humour. "No. Charlie is Maggie's husband. I guess he's a handyman of sorts. Totally useless at everything, but if we need Maggie, we have no choice but to have Charlie."

We decided on a break for lunch and made a plan to get online and order some picture crates afterwards.

❧

We left the house and crossed a small courtyard to one of many outbuildings. I could hear dogs barking, and my skin prickled a little at the sound. They didn't sound like the *pet* type of dog.

I didn't get to meet the estate manager, as the office was empty when we arrived. I winced at the mess. A desk was covered with paperwork, and an ancient computer sat beside a shotgun. The stone floor was muddy; a pair of wellies sat in one corner next to a bucket of walking sticks. While Ronan rifled around the desk, scattering paper, I looked at the photographs on the wall. A remarkably handsome man held the reins of show horses displaying coloured rosettes. He was the type of man who could grace the cover of a magazine, or a star in a movie.

"Who's this?" I asked.

Ronan looked up. "That is the great Felix Carter-Windford. My father."

"Gosh, you don't look like him," I said, then quickly closed my lips to stop any further insults erupting.

Ronan shuddered as if the thought of looking like his father repulsed him. "No, I don't, thankfully, and whether he is *actually* my biological father is questionable. I think he knows the answer, and I imagine my mother knew the answer, but no one felt it necessary to tell me. Still, water under the bridge now. I was looking for the Wi-Fi code," he said.

I walked over to the router and picked it up. On the back was a label with the code that I punched into my phone to connect to the Internet. I had no intention of trying to navigate what looked like one of Lord Sugar's early Amstrads.

"There's a company here that make wooden crates for fragile items, and they claim to deliver all over the UK. I think they would be perfect for the pictures. We don't want standard cardboard boxes. You never know, in a few years, you could be sitting on art worth a fortune," I said with a chuckle.

Ronan handed me a credit card, which I thought very trusting.

I took the card but told him, "I'll shop around for some more prices first; we don't want to just buy from the first place we find." I bookmarked the page and handed back his card.

We left the office and crossed back over the courtyard to another outbuilding. It held a series of dog kennels. "Oh, how sweet. What lovely dogs," I said, crouching to stroke a puppy through the bars.

“Working dogs. We breed sheepdogs and sell the puppies, and those others there are our gundogs.”

I gasped before I could stop myself. “Do you shoot things?”

He shrugged. “Sometimes we have to. We have a lot of deer in the grounds. They’re not pets or for decoration.”

I thought it a slightly condescending comment but chose to ignore it. I was a city girl, I didn’t do the ‘shooting things’ thing. Not that I was against it, of course. Each to their own and all that.

“You said you lived in Kent, do you have land there?”

Ronan laughed. “No, just a bloody large garden and some woodland. I’ll take you there. You said you wanted to look in Kent for a cottage. There are some stunners in my village, and the one over.”

We strolled across the courtyard and down some steps to a manicured lawn. I could see someone on a ride on mower and assumed it to be Charlie. As he raised his arm to give us a wave, the lawnmower wobbled.

I heard Ronan sigh. “That lawn looks like a pissed man mowed it most of the time,” he said.

I laughed. “That’s not a kind thing to say. Although, maybe he is pissed.”

“It wouldn’t surprise me. Come on, I have something else to show you. Might as well get all the ‘mother was very strange’ things out of the way.”

We climbed into an old Range Rover and drove through the woods. I could see a pathway that snaked through trees and what looked like a glamping site. Cream canvas was pulled taut over wooden poles, and guy ropes were strung from the top. As we approached, I could see the sea of neglect that mirrored parts of the house. The tops of the canvas tents were green with age and dampness. The area between the tents, in front, was unkempt. There were patches of earth, slightly dug out holes and then, in contrast, there were areas of woodland flowers that, even at the end of autumn, still bloomed.

Bunting hung from trees, glass jars, which I imagined had once held candles, and strips of colourful material were wrapped around tree trunks. It was easy to see the *hippy* here. In the centre of a circle were the remains of a large fire.

"So, camping…" I said.

"Sort of. I have no idea how to explain this area of my mother's life, her…*friends*, I guess we'll call them."

"Try to explain," I encouraged.

Ronan tapped his chin in mock thoughtfulness as if he was thinking of the correct term but his smirk gave him away. "Let's go with extreme earth lovers."

I had no idea what that meant and was a little sad to leave the area. Ronan didn't appear to want to stay too long. I wrapped my arms around myself. The chill had started to seep through my jumper and shirt, and the vehicle was redundant of something as modern as a heater.

Ronan cringed. "Shit, I should have offered you a coat. I guess I've lived here for so long I don't tend to feel the cold. Anyway, tomorrow, if we continue down this path, we'll end up on a beach. Our own private beach."

I smiled at the thought. "That sounds idyllic. So, what happens here? Do you rent these out to holidaymakers?"

"My mother ran art retreats if that's what you could call them. There's one starting tomorrow for the weekend. I didn't have the heart to cancel it—those people loved my mother as much as I did, but after that, I don't know what to do with the place."

"Does it make any money for you?" I wasn't so dumb that I

didn't know places like this cost tens of thousands of pounds to maintain.

"It did, for a while, and then it didn't. My mother was very much, as you can probably guess, at one with nature and didn't believe in charging people a fee to share this place with her." There was a slight bitterness to his voice when he spoke.

"And I guess you don't have the money to get it back to spec, or is that too personal a question?"

"Not too personal at all. I do, but Rich wants it sold. My options are: I either have to buy him out and then pay for all this myself, convince him that there could be a thriving business here which, long term, would be better and keep him as a partner, or sell up completely."

We had started the drive back to the house. "Could you…sell up?" I asked as the magnificent house came into view and all at once I couldn't imagine letting it go if it were mine.

Forget the cracked windows and the fallen down chimneystack. Ignore the peeling paint of the doorframes and the moss-covered stone window casements; the building that stood before me was unique, and breathtaking. As we climbed the steps from the lawn to the terrace, gargoyles silently snarled down at us from their perches. Strangely, there was nothing fierce about them. They were rather cute and comical.

I followed Ronan into the kitchen. He sat at the table, and his shoulders slumped. "I just don't know where to start, Lizzie. I can't make head or tail of any of the paperwork; everything's just in a complete mess. We might have an estate manager, but he hasn't been managing the estate at all. The accounts are in disarray too; I dread to think what the bank balances are like. Thank God Mum actually had some money, but none of it got spent here. When I left here, ten years ago I think, this place was thriving. I took my eye off the ball and in that time, it's all become a little overwhelming to deal with on my own."

I leaned forward and placed my hand on his. "You don't have to. I can help. I've been doing admin stuff for Joe for ages now. It's not hard to file papers; all I need to remind myself of is the alphabet." I grinned in encouragement. "And, believe it or not, organising events is something I'm bloody great at. A few fundraising events could bring in some money."

He brightened. "This is why I thought you'd be just the one to help me."

I wasn't sure how to respond to that. I was both flattered, and a little disappointed. Had he returned specifically to *recruit* me to help him? Or had he returned, as he'd said, to apologise for standing me up? I filed it away for the moment.

"Why don't we start with a meeting with the estate manager? You can't know what state it's in if you're guessing. If you ask him for a complete breakdown of all activities and costs, you can make a decision on what needs to go and what gets to stay."

Ronan scoffed. "Did you see his desk? I don't think he has that information anymore."

"You have to start somewhere, and if it all happens in that office, then that is where we start. The first thing to do is tidy the place up. I don't see how anyone can work in such a mess."

He nodded his agreement. "Tomorrow. I'll let him know, and tonight I'm taking you out for a meal. The local pub has an amazing new chef."

I smiled in thanks. "So, we finally get that date?"

"We finally get that date," he replied.

CHAPTER NINE

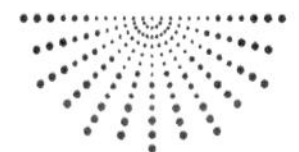

Ronan opened the door and allowed me to walk into the pub in front of him. It was a wonderful, traditional-looking place with a roaring fire, dogs resting on a wooden floor or rugs, a few tables and chairs dotted around and stools standing along an oak bar. I was used to the trendy cocktail bars or the faux pubs that mixed the traditional, the old, with the stainless steel modern. The pub was most certainly authentic. Even I, at one point, had to duck under a wooden beam that crossed the room and had the year, fourteen-sixty, engraved, or rather branded, on it.

"What a wonderful place," I said, as Ronan guided me to a table.

Although the pub was mostly empty, the patrons all smiled, offered a nod or a word to Ronan as we had passed. It was the type of country pub that I'd seen in an episode of *Midsomer Murders,* but I prayed we wouldn't have any dead people to contend with. Ronan headed to the bar after taking my order for a glass of wine. He returned with a bottle in an ice bucket and two glasses. He poured, and as I raised my glass to him, a shadow fell over us.

"Ronan, I'm surprised to see you back so quickly," she said.

The look on his face as he slowly sipped his wine and ignored her, suggested this wasn't going to be a pleasant meeting.

He finally turned to her. "I have things to do, obviously."

The woman glanced my way with a sickly sweet smile. "Aren't you going to introduce us?"

"Carol, this is Lizzie. Lizzie, this is Carol."

I noticed the lack of 'relationship' that should have accompanied her name. However, by the stiffening of his back and the smirk on her lips, I had a half idea *Carol* might be his ex-wife.

I rose from my chair. "It's a pleasure to meet you, Carol," I said, holding out my hand. She looked at it and then promptly ignored me. Ronan sighed.

"This is a wonderful pub, Carol, do you come here often?" I asked.

She laughed bitterly. "I used to own this pub, *Lizzie*, until my husband had an affair and we divorced. I lost it in the battle that followed."

Ronan sighed again but didn't reply. He didn't even look at her, keeping his gaze on me. There was a slight roll to his eyes and a gentle shake of his head as if he'd heard that line many times.

"Well, it was nice to meet you." I turned my attention away from her and back to my date. "Ronan, did you find a menu?" I asked as I sat again.

Carol huffed indignantly and walked away, and for a moment, we sat in silence.

"I'm sorry," he said.

"No need to be. I don't know your history, but I'm guessing she's still very upset with you."

"We've been divorced fucking years, but as soon as I'm in the area, she makes a point to seek me out. She's remarried. It can't be nice for Jim to have to watch her do that," he said.

"No, I doubt it is."

"Do you want to know why she thinks I cheated on her?" Ronan asked.

His question threw me. "I'm not sure it's my place to know, but if you want to tell me, that's up to you."

"Our relationship was over years ago. We married because she told me she was pregnant and she wasn't, she lied. We stayed together because she told me she had cancer and she hadn't, she lied. To be honest, she was so unstable I was too scared to leave. I had an assistant, a female, that Carol constantly accused me of sleeping with. I did, on occasions, stay at her house when it became too much at home, or Carol had locked me out, but not *once* did we share a bed, have sex, *kiss* even. We were friends, nothing more, but she wouldn't believe that, and I couldn't be bothered trying to convince her otherwise anymore. Carol, however, blames me for *her* affairs. She tells me that had I not cheated on her, she wouldn't have *fucked other men in revenge*. Her words, not mine."

She sounded a real charmer, not that I voiced my opinion. "What made you finally leave?"

"She ran off with Jim, who happened to be the therapist I'd spent a fortune with trying to help her. To save her blushes and to enable a quick divorce, I stated that *I* was the one to have committed adultery." Ronan laughed at the irony, and eventually, I had no choice but to join in. As awful as the situation was, his laugh was infectious.

He shook his head. "I'm sorry. I really don't know why I'm laughing. She might be remarried, but she hasn't forgiven me for things that were actually out of my control. My mother's trust owns this pub—not me, and *never* her. We lived here, and yes, she ran the pub. She loved it, and it must be a killer to come in here with new management, but she couldn't run a business, she was too ill."

I wish I hadn't been a witness to his ex-wife's hostility. It was time to change the subject, ostrich style. "So tell me about the house. What plans do you actually have?"

Ronan, I believed, seemed mighty relieved to have the conversation back on safe ground as well. "I can't sell the house; it's been in our family for hundreds of years. I intend to pay off Rich, bring the house back up to date, and try to have it earn its keep. I just need the time and energy, neither of which I have, to analyse what is the priority and where it's failing."

He smiled, cocked his head to one side and placed his palms together in an 'this is where you come in' way. I found it hadn't irritated me as much as it did the first time. In fact, it was nice to actually be wanted, or needed.

I smiled eagerly. "I have nothing to hold me in London. I'll be happy to spend a month or so to help you go through the house and decide what to do," I said. I thought Joe would be super proud of my decision, as daft as it was. "You know, I've never, in my life, done something so spontaneous. We don't even know each other, yet here I am, hundreds of miles from home with you, deciding on what to do with a big old manor house. At least you're not a mass murderer," I said, raising my glass in a toast.

He leaned forward. "How do you know I'm not a mass murderer?" he asked, faking a spooky and ridiculously unconvincing 'mass murderer' type voice.

I leaned towards him in response. "Because the odds of *two* mass murderers being in the same big old manor house would be worse than the odds of winning the lottery."

He laughed, and that tingle at his deep tones travelled from my neck to my navel. Only the crossing of my legs blocked it getting any further.

"Are you hungry?" he asked.

"Yes, and I don't do well with drinking on an empty stomach. A sandwich and a bowl of chips would do if they have that."

He left the table, and I scanned the room. It hadn't occurred to me before then how many people were staring at me. I was hoping it was just curiosity, a new-girl-in-town-with-the-laird type thing. Or maybe they loved Carol, and I was the husband-stealing whore that broke them up and brought in new management. I sighed. I had a tendency to overthink, and the new me wasn't going there anymore. Who gave a fuck what these people thought? I wasn't about to. I smiled at one, raised my glass in a salute before taking a sip. Thankfully, I received a smile and a gentle nod in return.

"Art is on tomorrow is it, Ronan?" I heard someone call out.

I watched as Ronan looked to the other end of the bar. "Yes, I guess so," he replied.

I watched him walk back to the table, and for a moment, he really did look lost.

"Art? That's a start. We can look at lots of activities to hold in the grounds or some of those outbuildings. Maybe one or two can be used as a studio and gallery," I said.

He nodded slowly, and I could hear a very slow exhale of breath. "Yes. Art. Maybe we need to remind ourselves of my…" He didn't finish his sentence. Instead, he picked up his glass and took a couple of large gulps.

After we'd eaten our sandwiches and chips, finished the bottle of wine, and had a coffee, we took a slow walk back to the house. It was dark and I held on to Ronan's arm as he swept a small torch in front of us to light the way.

"Next time, we must try something from the menu. That chef is bloody expensive," he said, with a chuckle.

I hadn't wanted a full-on meal after our encounter with Carol, but I decided I'd take him up on that offer another time.

We didn't meet another person or a car on the short journey back, but I wished I had a thicker coat. The nip in the air had started to permeate my bones. I'd wrapped my arms around myself to hold off the cold by the time we started the walk up the drive.

"Jesus, Lizzie, you're shivering," Ronan said, ever the observant one. He whipped off his coat and placed it around my shoulders.

The warmth from his body heat immediately chased off those shivers. I pulled it tight around me. "I think I might need to buy some warmer clothes."

He wrapped an arm around my shoulders, causing me to stumble a little. I tried to walk in sync, but his long-legged stride meant in order to stay in his embrace I walked like a Geisha, shuffling as if my feet were bound.

Joe and I could walk in sync; we could even do that silly walk from *The Monkees*. But Ronan and me? No chance. I guess the height difference was a major factor. By the time I'd shuffled to the point of scuffing a shoe, I slid out from under his arm and walked at my own pace. Ronan slowed slightly. The front door was opened as we approached, and two mugs of hot chocolate were ready and waiting.

I grabbed one and wrapped both hands around it. "Thank you. I need this," I said with a laugh. I don't think I'd drunk as much hot chocolate since I was a child.

"I have some papers to go through, work calls, unfortunately," Ronan said.

"And bed calls me. I know it's early, but I think a nice hot bath and a read under the duvet is what I want."

I took my mug and climbed the stairs to my bedroom. I'd mastered the hot water system, I thought, as I ran the one tap knowing it would go cold at a point where I would normally add some. It rattled and creaked, the pipes objected to having water forced through from a distance and after a spluttering in protest, it started to flow.

I sighed as I sunk into the deep, enamelled tub with my hot chocolate on one side and a book on the other. Unfortunately, once again, I'd forgotten to take into account the length of the bath and the fact my feet didn't reach the end, and I slid under the scalding water that rushed up my nose. I sat up spluttering and reaching for the towel, knocking the hot chocolate to the floor in my haste.

"Fucking hell," I cursed, as I wiped soapsuds from my eyes.

So much for a long soak and what a waste of the limited hot water. I climbed out, unable to leave the hot chocolate spreading over the wooden floorboards and soaking into the one small bath mat. With a towel wrapped around me, I cleaned up as best I could. I had visions of the drink seeping between the floorboards and dripping on anyone unfortunate enough to be sitting below.

I scrubbed a towel over my head to dry my hair as much as possible, and with it standing in all directions I pulled on my PJs. I collected the towel I'd used to mop up the drink, along with the mat and my empty mug, and took them down to the kitchen.

"That was a quick soak," Maggie said. She was sitting, darning a hole in a woollen jumper.

"It was. I knocked my hot chocolate over when I forgot I couldn't reach the end of the bath and sank under the bubbles."

She chuckled as she laid the jumper on the table. "Let me make you another one, and dump that washing over there. See the basket? There's a pile to go in tomorrow."

"Thank you. I can make the drink. I think I'd prefer a cup of tea, to be honest."

"Tea it is. I forget that Ronan is an adult now. Hot chocolate and ham and crisp sandwiches was all he'd eat and drink when he was young. Breakfast, lunch, or dinner, it was the same thing. Amazing he grew to be such a strapping lad," she said, as she made tea.

"I think he's a little older than the typical strapping lad," I replied with a laugh.

"Yes," she said, with a nostalgic sigh.

"You're very fond of him, aren't you?"

"I am. I don't know what he's told you about his family and no doubt this is out of turn but being *in turn* was never my thing. His parents were total arseholes, the pair of them."

I wasn't sure how to respond so just reached out to take the tea being offered to me.

She continued, "They were totally neglected, those boys," as if to justify her statement.

"I don't know anything about them, other than the hippy and the American." I gave an embarrassed laugh.

"No doubt Ronan will tell you himself, but as soon as he could, he was out of here. It's why Rich is a mean bugger. He never forgave Ronan for actually moving on. But then Rich just upped and went as soon as he could, and Ronan had to come back and sort out the mess."

"I met his ex-wife tonight, she's a classy lady," I said.

Maggie snorted. "Oh, she's a fine one is that…" she struggled to come up with an adjective that was suitable, I guessed.

I laughed. "I'm going to salvage my book from the bathroom floor and hope it isn't covered in chocolate and then climb into bed."

"You have a good sleep. We have a busy day tomorrow, some visitors you can help me with."

"Will do, and thanks, Maggie, for making me feel welcome."

"It's nice to have someone around who wants to sort this old monstrosity out."

I didn't tell her that I'd only just learned what was expected of me. Obviously, Ronan had told her before asking me. I'd gone from bristling to feeling wanted, to bristling again.

I said goodnight and left Maggie repairing a jumper that really should've ended up as a dog bed. I climbed the stairs again, and as I made to turn left to my room, I could hear Ronan's raised voice.

"I don't care what you think," he said, spitting out the words.

I stood where I was, resisting the temptation to creep to the right and earwig at his door.

"She has offered to help with this place. I'll thank you to keep your fucking nose out of my business, do you hear?"

The level of aggression wasn't what I expected from the usually quietly spoken Ronan but then, I didn't really know him. I walked to my room wondering who he was talking to, and assuming it was a discussion about me.

As I climbed into bed, I had to remind myself I was doing something out of character. I was being spontaneous, and it prompted me to check in with Joe. I sent him a quick text to let him know I hadn't been murdered yet and would call him in the morning. I sipped on my tea and sighed as I dived into my book, *The Facilitator,* and made a mental note to hand it over to Maggie when I was done. But the way the story was shaping up, I'd either be embarrassed that she'd know I'd read it, or I'd want to read it for a second time before I dared to part with it. Mackenzie Miller was to die for!

CHAPTER TEN

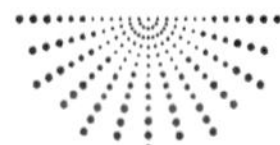

After falling asleep on my book and a night of erotic dreams, I woke to find the imprint of a page on my cheek. I decided to forego waiting for the shower to heat up or the bath to fill. Instead, I strip washed at the sink. I could make out a couple of words on my face and scrubbed until my skin was red. I chuckled, knowing the scene I had been reading before I fell asleep.

With a little makeup on, I dressed and ventured downstairs. I found a note in the kitchen to help myself to breakfast. Maggie had gone out for provisions (her words), and Ronan was chasing up the estate manager for a meeting and to gather paperwork. It seemed odd to me to have such an errant estate manager, and I wondered if there was a little bad blood between them; hence, the reason Ronan was forever hunting him down.

I made some tea and uncovered a dish of homemade biscuits. I placed a couple on the side of my saucer and decided to take my cup to the library.

The room was dusty, unused, and it was a shame. I decided this would be where I'd work, should I get an office as such. Once the drapes were pulled and if the windows were cleaned, the view was spectacular. It needed some love and attention. I perched on the edge of an antique chaise. Its brocade was stripped bare in places and what were once such vibrant yellows and reds were dulled with neglect and age. I had a feeling it would scrub up well under the right hands, though.

The house was eerily quiet, even the usual racket of the plumbing had decided to take a break that morning. Perhaps everything was on shut down when Maggie was out. The chill in the air told me the heating hadn't kicked in, especially in this room, and I worried about all the books. Dampness settled around me. I shivered and decided that I wanted to investigate the outside a little more.

I remembered the piles of Wellington boots and padded jackets hanging in one of the outhouses. I was sure I'd find something that would fit and be a little more suitable for the walk.

I thought I could see Charlie darting from outhouse to outhouse as I crossed the courtyard. I found some wellies that fit and tried on a couple of jackets. They were all too large, of course, so I picked the one that didn't smell the worst. The scent of wet dog permeated the air. At the thought of the dogs, I could hear them bark, the slam of metal doors and then excited yapping. Either it was walk time or breakfast.

Before I got pounced on by a pack of dogs, I scuttled across the courtyard and back towards the woodland Ronan and I had driven the previous day. I wanted to take a good look at the camping area. If there was access from the road, avoiding the main house, a camping site could bring in much-needed funds. Perhaps we could look at holding a festival where local bands and comedians could entertain. Plans started to run through my mind as I walked.

I wasn't aware of how long I'd walked, but I could hear voices. I tried to follow but found myself disorientated and off track a little. I thought I knew the way back, but I was curious as to who had spoken. I stood for a while listening, but not hearing anything more. Maybe it had been Ronan and his estate manager?

As I walked towards where I believed the campsite had been, I could hear rustling. I quickened my pace. It might have been the middle of the morning, in bright but cold sunshine, but eeriness descended on me. I could be murdered and no one was around to help. I should have brought a walking stick with me; at least it would have given me a weapon. I turned on to a well-trodden path and could see the tents in the distance. The rustling continued, as well as a man's voice. I wasn't able to pick out the words, just the tone, and I knew it wasn't Ronan.

I paused—I was being silly. It was highly unlikely there was a murderer following me; it was more likely to be the estate manager that had probably spoken with Ronan. Or at least it could have been Charlie. Just in front of me, I saw a bush move a little as if someone was forcing their way through. I stared. My jaw clicked open at the sight I was greeted with.

Shuffling towards me through the undergrowth was an elderly woman. In fact, she was a *naked* elderly woman with scratches up her shins from the whipping bushes she'd barged through. Her eighty-odd-year-old pendulous, sagging tits swung from left to right in sync with the stomp of her swollen legs and boot-clad feet. The slapping sound was the poor breasts hitting the sides of her Zimmer frame as she crouched over it. I covered my mouth with both hands. I wasn't sure if I wanted to laugh, scream, piss myself, or throw up. However, her beaming smile and twinkling eyes made me shake my head in disbelief. She called out over her shoulder, and an equally-aged gentleman, also naked, soon joined her. No matter how hard I tried to keep my gaze focused over their shoulders, without it being obvious, I failed. I slowly tracked down his hairless, white, and freckled chest with nipples the size of saucers, to his paunchy soft belly that didn't quite hide the lack of penis. I say lack of penis. There was a mass of skin, and I guessed the chill in the air had ensured his penis was safely tucked up warm and snug inside him. However, it was his balls. *Huge* balls housed in a hairy sac that contrasted his hairless body and slapped against his thighs. I wanted to wince for him but the smile he also had suggested he had either been nerve blocked and couldn't feel any pain or quite enjoyed it.

"I think I just found myself in the middle of a *Carry On* movie," I whispered to myself.

"Morning, dearie. We're off to art," Saggy Tits said. "Are you joining us? Ronan said he had a guest this week."

I raised my eyebrows at the discovery that Ronan was aware he had naked people in his woods. "Erm, I don't think so. I was heading for the campsite," I said.

"So are we. I like to take a stroll, get with nature, before we start art but we got a little lost, didn't we, dear?" She giggled as she raised her voice so the gentleman could hear her.

"Well, the tents are that way, is that where art normally is?"

"It is. We have such a lovely couple of days. Painting, a bonfire, and barbeque. Good old Charlie always does the cooking for us. Doesn't do to be standing too close to a metal container full of hot coals in this outfit," she said, waving her hand across her body.

I had no idea what to say. "I imagine it could be a problem."

"We best get on. It takes Eric a while to walk with me nowadays, doesn't it, Eric?" she shouted. Eric nodded, still holding that broad smile.

I wasn't sure which view I preferred. The limp dick and saggy tits or the wobbly arses with a little tuft of grey hair sprouting from his butt crack.

I winced with every step Eric took, his ball sack swinging in time with his wife's tits. I started to giggle. Fair play to them both, I'd never have the confidence to stroll naked around woodland on a chilly day.

As we approached the campsite, I could see a nice bonfire already lit and a group of people sitting in a circle. Some were on the ground, some on tree stumps and one or two on shooting sticks, which I could not imagine, was a comfortable seat at all.

Smiles and greetings were thrown my way. I apologised for intruding, explaining that I wasn't aware they had their art meeting. There didn't appear to be one of them under sixty, and with a wave, I left them to it. I laughed all the way back to the house.

"What has you so amused?" I heard. Ronan strolled across the courtyard.

"I happened to stumble across some naked art lovers in your campsite."

"Ah, yes, I did try to warn you, didn't I?" he said, knowing full well he hadn't.

"I think I was shocked into silence to start with. But what a perfect location for a nudist camp," I said. My mind had whirled with the possibilities all the way back.

"A nudist camp?" His eyes widened, and his grin spread at what he probably thought was an absurd idea.

I nodded enthusiastically. "Absolutely. I have no idea how many there are in this part of the world, but you have total privacy, it could be glamping if we tidied up a little. All we have to do is offer activities. And I know just the man to help." I pulled my phone from my pocket and dialled Joe.

"You met what?" he screeched down the phone. I repeated my discovery. He laughed. "Limp dicks and saggy tits? Oh my god. I have to get the next train up. Are there any hot men under, say, fifty?"

"No, but there could be. I think we could turn this into a *To The Manor Born* nudist holiday camp!"

"Do you remember Dick and Dinner?"

I started to laugh. "Oh yes, we could do Dick and Dinner," I said, and I watched Ronan frown. "Anyway," I continued, "I just wanted to tell you and for you to get your thinking cap on. What would a campsite need to accommodate nudes, or nudists, or whatever they are called?"

"I'll come up with some ideas," he said.

We chatted a little more, and he told me that it appeared my ex was about to buy the million and whatnot property with Pete or Saucy Sally, or whatever her name was. I shrugged my shoulders. It didn't seem to be so painful anymore, and there was a part of me that was happy for him. Perhaps, when I returned home, I would take them a bottle of something as a moving in gift. Or, maybe not.

When I returned my mobile to my pocket. Ronan asked, "Dick and Dinner?"

I felt my cheeks heating. "It was a daft idea of mine. I decided that I wanted to open a nightclub, a high-class one with male pole dancers and a gourmet menu. *Dick and Dinner*, see?" I said with a laugh. "Anyway, I thought we should do a little research. How many nudist camps are in Scotland?" I asked.

As we walked back into the kitchen, Ronan answered. "Bearing in mind the average weather temperatures we have up here, probably not that many."

"I don't doubt that. But for the weeks that there is nice weather, why not? I mean, those guys are out there, and it's not exactly summer right now."

"They're ardent naturists," Maggie said, as she bowled backwards through the door.

Ronan raced towards her to catch the shopping bags that were about to fall from her hands.

“See, Maggie agrees,” I said, giving her a wink.

Maggie chuckled. “I can’t agree to whatever it is because I didn’t hear most of it,” she replied, placing her remaining bags on the table.

“We could open up a nudist camp. See if it will bring in some money for the estate,” I said.

“Trouble is, those guys have never paid, so it might be a shock to ask them to do so now.”

“*They* don’t have to; they’re only here for art. But what about a proper facility; a spa or something?”

“The Naked Spa,” Ronan said, slowly while grinning. “I quite like that; it’s unique, and a little more upmarket than a load of oldies running naked through the woods.”

“All natural ingredients, yoga or some other…stuff. We could be on to something here. I need a pad and pen,” I said, excitement starting to build.

“Just dinnae have those extreme earthers, or whatever they’re called,” I heard. I turned to see Charlie behind me. “We don’t want no shagging the trees or the ground,” he added.

“Huh?” I replied.

Charlie waved his hands around as if to assist his point. “The earthers, they love the earth, shag the trees an’ aw’ that,” he said, nonchalantly as he reached for one of the biscuits left over from the morning.

I shuddered at the thought and looked towards Ronan who shrugged his shoulders.

“Anyway, I think the idea of a spa is a great one, but we have one complication. We’d need a building,” Ronan said.

"The outbuildings? Or are they too close to the house?"

"A little too close to be honest. However…grab your coat; I've got something to show you."

I followed Ronan to one of the outbuildings and watched him sit astride a quad bike. "Hop on," he said.

I did as I was asked and wrapped my arms around his waist as he backed it out. As we passed one outbuilding, I finally got to see who I thought was the estate manager. A seriously handsome man with jet-black hair and piercing blue eyes stared at us as we drove slowly across the courtyard.

"Off to the old gatehouse. I have an idea," Ronan said.

The man spoke, and by his accent he most certainly wasn't Scottish. Spanish perhaps? I didn't get the chance to ask. Ronan drove us out of the courtyard and onto a large track through the woods. It was at least half an hour before we came to an area that was grassed but lined with trees, like an avenue. Ahead I could see two buildings and a rusting old gate between them.

"That used to be the old entrance," Ronan shouted over his shoulder.

We pulled up outside one of the gatehouses. I expected a smallish building, something perhaps a sentry would be posted at, if they had such thing back in the day.

"This is a two bedroomed cottage, same the other side. Staff would live here, hundreds of years ago, I imagine. They've been shut off for years. I remember my granny living in one before she died, and my father would have one of his mistresses in the other."

"His…?"

"Yeah, a right regular *Marquis of Bath* was my father," he said, disdain dripped from his words.

I frowned at him. "Marquis… Ah, Longleat, the Lord and is concubines, or whatever he called them. How awful for your mum," I said.

"She didn't seem to care, to be honest. Anyway, spa," he said, waving his hands from one building to the other.

"Can you extend them?"

"No idea, we'd have to speak to the planning department at the local council for that, and I suspect the answer would be no, but, if we're doing this all *au naturel* then what's to say we don't have some posh yurts or similar as treatment rooms?"

"I like that."

I peered through the window of one of the gatehouses while Ronan fumbled with a bunch of keys. He managed to open the door, and it was like stepping into a museum. Antique furniture crowded the cosy rooms. It was obvious they were good quality pieces but way too large for the gatehouse, and I guessed had been appropriated from the manor house.

"Your gran's house, I take it?"

"Yeah. She lived in the main house until Mum married and since she couldn't stand my father, she moved here. She didn't want to be too far away from my mum and she would drive an old Land Rover every day up to the main house, stay the whole day just to piss off my dad and then come home in the evening. I think that's why Dad put one of his mistresses opposite, just to piss Gran off."

"It can't have been a nice environment for you and Rich," I said, as I walked through one door and into a deceivingly large kitchen diner.

"Rich idolises his father, which is why he also emulates him. He spends his life shagging anything that walks, no offence to Joe, of course, but *that* Rich learned from Dad."

"It's a shame because Joe really likes him. I've told him time and time again, Rich is nothing but a player," I said.

"I've told Joe that myself, but he won't listen, and since there's bad blood between Rich and me, I guess he thinks it's just sour grapes."

"Why did you invest in the bar if there's bad blood?"

"Because Rich blew his money on some Ponzi scheme years ago, and I guess I feel guilty since I invested mine and it's grown substantially."

We walked around the gatehouse. It had two bedrooms, one of which was a decent size, a bathroom that certainly needed an update, but as I fiddled with the tap, I screeched at how hot the water was.

Ronan laughed. "Better plumbing than the main house."

"This is lovely, Ronan, and I can certainly see potential here. We need to upgrade the bathroom and keep one kitchen for making lunches or afternoon tea, but other than that, it's perfect, don't you think?"

He nodded. "I do, and I can't believe I'm even considering a naturist's spa!"

We left the gatehouse laughing.

Ronan drove us back to the main house a little slower. He pointed out certain trees, and it impressed me when he could name the type and even the age. He certainly seemed to know all there was to know about the estate, and he spoke with such fondness, I imagined it would be a real wrench for him to sell it.

"How much is the estate worth?" I asked as we parked up in the outbuilding.

Ronan took a long breath in and released it in a huff. "Honestly?

I don't really know. I should have had it valued ages ago, but I've been delaying it. A few million, for sure."

"I know this is a personal question, but can you afford to buy Rich out?" I asked.

"I can, but I think by doing so it would limit what I have readily available to invest. It might be that I have to liquidate some of my assets, and that would take time. I want to be fair to him, of course. It might be that he's happy to take a smaller lump sum then a cut of the profits if we can get the estate profitable, of course."

I liked the sound of 'we.' "What about opening up the house as a hotel or a wedding venue?" I asked.

"It's not a simple as that. We'd need a permit, and planning applications on historical buildings are a pain in the arse. Scottish Heritage would be all over us if we made the slightest modification or change. I think I'd like to keep the business element outside the house."

"Okay, what about opening the gardens though?"

He rubbed at his chin. "We'd need to create something worth visiting. Right now, there are no 'formal' gardens. Mum let everything *go to seed* as she'd say, revert back to nature. She didn't want formal—she wanted bees and butterflies, rustic and natural."

"Surely that would be attractive to someone? What about butterfly conservation people, there must be an organisation that might like to come visit and document how many butterflies there are? You could then… I don't know …sell tickets to butterfly enthusiasts to come and photograph them."

Ronan stopped walking; he turned to me and placed his hands on my upper arms then smiled. "I love your enthusiasm, Lizzie. When Joe suggested I ask you to help me, I wasn't sure it would be your thing. I'm glad I did. This could be the project we both need to take our minds off our shitty love lives."

I stared back at him aghast. "I wasn't aware that Joe had *suggested* me."

"Oh, he told me that he'd speak to you about it. I just assumed he had, which was why you agreed to come back here with me."

"No, I…" I shook my head. "Never mind. Let's get in and start to plan."

I wanted out of his touch, away from his stare, and his slightly crooked smile made by full lips that I would've loved to kiss. I wanted time to think and maybe curse Joe for not being honest with me.

CHAPTER ELEVEN

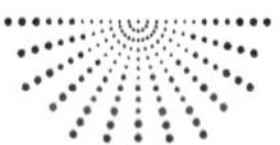

Ronan and I spent the next day in the library making notes. He fired up a laptop so I could do some research on what the local area offered, what other manor houses did to bring in that extra income, and we made lists. We argued the film set idea; Ronan didn't think the house historic enough for that. I disagreed—it didn't have to be the location of a period drama, and I made a list of agencies that we could register the house with. We laughed, talked about our childhoods and what aspirations we had growing up. We had fun. It felt so natural, even talking about our childhood fears.

That evening, Ronan decided that we'd visit a different pub for dinner. It was half an hour drive away, and he was greeted warmly as we entered. He explained that landlords generally supported each other in the pub industry, but I thought it was more because Ronan was a nice guy, friendly, and personable. He had a kind word for everyone, a smile at the ready. I enjoyed watching him as we made our way to the bar where he gave a wink to an elderly lady and her cheeks coloured.

We ordered our drinks, and Ronan handed me a menu. "I can

seriously recommend the burgers. They use buffalo meat, and it's about the best beef you'll taste," he said.

"Buffalo burger it is then. Will you order for me? I need the ladies."

I left him at the bar and made my way to the toilets. I was still smiling as I looked in the mirror while I washed my hands. I enjoyed his company, and I thought he enjoyed mine. It seemed we had grown a little closer the past few days and although that tingle was still present, I was happy we were developing a friendship. I touched up my makeup, and as I prepared to leave the bathroom, a thought hit me.

I was falling for Ronan, and I wasn't sure what to do about that.

I wasn't sure that the feeling would be reciprocated, either.

I placed a piece of tissue to my lips to take off the shine of newly applied lipstick and chuckled. I didn't think Ronan would have invited me to join him, even though recommended by Joe, if he wasn't mildly fond of me.

By the time I re-joined him, he had found a table and poured me a glass of wine. His smile was broad as I took a sip and sighed. "This is a nice wine," I said, turning the bottle to face me.

"It's one of my favourites."

"You know, I can't imagine how you can choose to live down south and not here full time. The house, the area, this pub even, is just stunning."

"It is hard, but I think I need that time away on occasions so that I can really appreciate it when I come back."

"Other than investing in Rich, what's the main thing that you do?" I knew he'd told me, but it had seemed vague and varied.

He tilted his head. "Property renovation, mainly. I buy old buildings, do them up and sell them on. Rich brought Joe to my house once, to see if we'd benefit from knowing each other."

"Do you think Rich will ever stop pissing my friend around?" I asked.

Ronan laughed. "I like that term, and no. No, he won't stop while Joe allows it. If Joe lets Rich walk all over him, he'll continue to do so. Rich is like my mum, he wants the hedonistic lifestyle, but he's sixty years too late."

I laughed at his comment. Although it appeared Ronan and Rich weren't necessarily best buddies or at least friendly brothers, I did detect a quiet note of affection in his voice when he spoke about him. I wondered, from a previous comment, what guilt Ronan felt where Rich was concerned, not that I would ask.

The evening wore on and, like the day, we laughed and chatted. It felt a little like a date, especially when it was time to leave and Ronan held open my jacket for me, and then placed his hand on my back to guide me through the pub to the door. He jumped in front to open it and again, to open the car door.

"I've really enjoyed today, and tonight," I said, as he started the car.

"It's a little like that date we never really got to," he replied.

In the dark, I smiled at him. I watched as he focused on the road ahead. Of all the days I had spent with Ronan, and I knew it wasn't many, that day had been the best. I believed we could have a great working relationship, although I still wasn't sure what my role was, exactly.

Ronan's mobile started to ring, and on the dashboard, I saw the name 'Carol' appear. I heard him sigh and watched as he clicked to decline the call. Within seconds it rang again. He ignored it that time and after four rings the call ended, going to voicemail.

"You don't want to answer that?" I asked.

It took a few seconds before he replied. "Not really. She only wants to row."

"Why? You've been divorced a long time now."

He sighed. "She feels that she should be entitled to part of the estate. We settled our finances when we divorced, so she's entitled to fuck all, but she won't let it be. She knows the estate will come to me and Rich, and I guess she's pissed off she's not entitled to any of it."

There wasn't really an answer I could give for that. We continued the journey in silence, although I did wonder why he had added her contact to his new phone. It wasn't a question I felt I could ask, however.

❧

Something had disturbed me—a voice or a noise. I had fallen asleep pretty quickly after returning from the pub, but as I lay in bed, I could hear talking. I peeled back the duvet and, using just my toes, felt for the pair of slippers Maggie had given me, not wanting my feet to touch the cold wooden floor. I shivered as I stood and reached for my robe.

First, I crept to the window and peered through the tiny gap in the curtains. Many a time I'd spotted Charlie on the lawn. That evening, however, there was no one visible, and by the quietness of the voice, I knew it was in the other direction.

I walked to the door and stood with my ear close to the wood. I could hear Ronan and although he wasn't necessarily shouting, his voice was loud enough to carry along the corridor. I guessed he had left his bedroom door open.

I wasn't generally the snooping type, but I gently opened the bedroom door and peeped out. The corridor was empty, and the raised voice wasn't coming from along the way, it was from downstairs. I tiptoed to where the wall ended, and the staircase opened up.

Ronan was standing in the hallway, hands on his hips, and Carol was there too, mimicking his pose while at the doorway. He hadn't invited her in. I guessed it wasn't so much shouting that I'd heard but the echo of his voice in that vast hall that had floated up to my bedroom above.

"I only wanted to know who she is," Carol said.

"No one that you need to be concerned about. I've told you to stay out of my life," Ronan replied, a little aggressively, I thought.

"You have left me with nothing, Ronan, after everything I've done for you; supported you, stayed up night after night while you were out partying," she said.

Ronan laughed. "You really need to give this a rest. It's fucking boring, Carol. We're divorced, you're remarried, there's nothing about me that you need to know, and I would appreciate you not turning up here demanding answers to questions you have no right to ask."

"Does she know you can't be faithful even if you tried? Does she know of all your affairs?"

"She. Is. Staff. Nothing more, okay? Lizzie *works* for me, I have no feelings towards her at all. Satisfied?"

I reeled backwards, white noise filled my head until that cleared, and all I heard were his words. I spun around and despite my earlier caution, stepped on the creakiest floorboard in the whole house.

"Lizzie?" I heard. I didn't reply.

By the time the footsteps echoed down the corridor towards my bedroom, I was in the bathroom. I heard the knock on the door and, when I didn't answer, I heard it creak open.

"Lizzie?" Ronan called out.

"Sorry, I'm in the bathroom. Are you okay?" I replied, forcing a jolly tone to my voice.

"I thought I heard you by the stairs."

I opened the bathroom door. "Did you need to speak to me? I fell straight to sleep then woke and realised I hadn't cleaned my teeth," I said, holding a bone-dry toothbrush I'd snatched from the sink.

He frowned. "Oh, I heard a noise. I thought it was you."

I gave a small, forced laugh. "These floors creak all the time; it probably was when I walked into the bathroom."

I hadn't left the bathroom, keeping most of my body shielded by the heavy oak door. I wasn't sure why I wanted that barrier, but I was glad of it. I didn't want Ronan to see my shaking hands or my trembling legs.

He nodded swiftly. "I'm sorry to disturb you," he said and started to back from the room.

"Are you okay, Ronan?" I asked, wondering if he'd mention Carol's visit.

"Sure. I was catching up with some paperwork and thought... well, if you're okay, I'll let you get back to bed. Goodnight, Lizzie."

"I thought I heard someone outside, or maybe downstairs earlier," I said, probing.

"No, it might have been me on the phone. I was catching up with Rich."

He lied to me. I smiled as he backed from the room and closed the door but not before giving me a broad smile, one that would have caused those little flutters in my stomach just a few hours prior.

I felt so sad, so down, as I sat on the edge of the bed. I could have accepted him telling me that he'd had a conversation with Carol. I could have understood what he'd said. To have lied made me feel even shittier than if he'd been honest.

His words swirled around my mind. *'She is staff. Nothing more.'* He had spat the words such was his annoyance at her questioning.

I wondered why Carol was so interested in me and what she meant by *all the affairs*. He had told me that he hadn't been unfaithful to her. I sighed and picked up my phone. I wanted to speak to Joe, but after seeing the time, I decided to wait.

I tossed and turned in a once very comfortable bed, finding every non-existent lump to rest on. I felt like the main character from *The Princess and the Pea*, more so when I gave in and climbed from the bed. I turned on the bedside lamp and inspected the taught crisp cotton sheet.

For the first time, I felt awkward. I wanted to head down to make myself a hot drink but felt...like *staff* rather than a guest. I sat on the edge of the bed and listened. I couldn't hear any noises at all. *Even staff would be allowed to make a drink*, I thought, defiantly.

I left the bedroom, making sure to creep along the hallway and past Ronan's bedroom. I tiptoed down the stairs and then made my way to the kitchen. I stood in the semi-darkness while the kettle boiled.

"He doesnae mean harm wi' his words, yer ken," I heard.

I screeched, holding one hand over my racing heart and another over my mouth as I spun around.

Charlie stood by the door. He walked in, and I noticed his big toe poking out through a hole in his woollen sock. Why the fuck I was concentrating on his big toe was beyond me. He pulled out a chair and sat. He waved his hand to the teapot, and I stared at him.

"I'll have one if you're making," he said.

I grabbed the teapot from the table and opened the lid; it was ready with teabags for the morning brew, so I filled it and pulled out the chair opposite him.

Curiosity was getting the better of me. "What do you mean?" I asked as I poured his tea in a mug. I waited while he spooned four sugars in and then stirred.

"I saw you. You heard him, and that vampire," he said. It seemed a rather articulate statement from someone I couldn't understand just a few days ago. "He'll have told her that so she leaves you alone. He fell in love after her, and she destroyed that. He won't want that for you. You need to hang on in there," he said before raising his mug, pushing back the chair and walking away.

I was left sitting there wondering what the fuck I was supposed to do.

I wrapped a blanket around my shoulders as the cold started to seep into me. Should I leave and go back to London, or stay a little longer? I didn't want to just be *staff* but it was clear that perhaps there wasn't to be a relationship, despite what had been said in the beginning. That day, however, I'd felt excited by something. I hadn't felt that way in years, and I mean, *years*. The house was a project I could really get my teeth into and who knew, maybe it would look good on my non-existent CV? In fact, I chuckled, it would be the only thing on my CV since I'd never officially held down a job.

I topped up my mug with fresh tea and a splash of milk. I needed to stop being silly and accept a friendship with Ronan, and get on with the job.

I climbed the stairs and walked the hallway. Ronan's bedroom door was open; it hadn't been when I'd passed before. I hesitated, wondering if he was in there or not. Whether I should knock and see if he wanted a cup of tea. Before I could make a decision, he stepped from the room. He wore just a pair of shorts and his nipples were like bullets. I wanted to place the hand that had cupped the mug over them for fear they'd snap off in the cold.

"Shit," he said, startled.

"Are you okay? I went to make tea, did I disturb you?" I asked.

He stared at me. "No, I thought I heard someone talking. Voices echo around this old house."

"They sure do, Ronan. Now, would you like some tea, the pot is still half full?" I replied, raising my eyebrows at the same time.

He sighed, and his shoulders sagged. "Is it too late to talk?" he asked.

I didn't care what time it was—if he and his frozen nips wanted to spend some time with me, I was up for it. That was until I dragged my pre-menopausal-hadn't-had-sex-in-an-age mind back to the fact he hadn't been particularly kind about me.

"It's never too late," I said. "You might want to put some clothes on, though. I could hang my coat from your nipples," I said, speaking out loud something that should have stayed as a thought.

Ronan laughed, covered his nipples with his palms and walked down the hall and stairs and back to the kitchen. I followed.

I sat and wrapped the blanket around me; he sat opposite, thankfully with a throw over his shoulders so his toned and rather lovely torso didn't further distract me. I poured him some tea.

"Carol is obsessed with money. Before Mum died, she kept coming around, pretending to visit even though she hated my mum and even though she'd remarried because she believes she's entitled to more. We divorced years ago; she got nearly everything I had back then. It's not enough, though. I met another woman a few years ago, and Carol fucking haunted her. We had to call the police at one point, but this was before the new stalking laws. She took photos of her all the time, called her work telling lies, and since Demi was a teacher, it caused all sorts of problems. I didn't want her to think there was even a friendship between us."

I nodded. "So, it's not the murderer in *you* I need to worry about. Joe didn't give me any hints of what to do with a psychotic ex-wife. I might have to Google that."

Ronan was unsure, initially, whether to laugh or not. I smiled sweetly, not giving him a hint either way. Eventually, he gave in. The corners of his mouth crinkled, and he let out a relieved laugh.

"It wasn't nice to hear what you said. And yes, I *did* hear. I'm a woman of a certain age, Ronan, one that has been through a shit couple of years *and* one that might like the opportunity to release that anger and frustration. You don't need to *protect* me from anyone. Also, I'm not staff, you don't pay me, and you haven't offered me a contract. If you want me to just be *staff* have that contract and a salary idea ready tomorrow. If you want me as a friend, to help you, then from now that's what you'll refer to me as, regardless of what your ex thinks."

I held his gaze. I was done with being kind and nice and understanding. Ronan reached across as if to shake my hand, something quite formal, and disappointment flooded me. Instead of the shake, however, he just held my hand and rested both on the tabletop.

"I'm sorry. It was totally the wrong thing to say, and it won't happen again. I highly doubt she believed me anyway."

I fixed him with a stern stare. "Now, *affairs*, plural?"

He shook his head. "Lies, plural, you'll hear many. I had every intention of leaving Carol, and when I tried, she'd blackmail me to stay. She told me she had cancer, Lizzie. Who does that? She told me she was pregnant, many times, and each time lost the child but would never go to a consultant or hospital. I stopped believing her. I didn't love her, but I felt obliged to stay, and I felt sorry for her, which is terrible."

"What happened to Demi?" I asked.

"That's a longer story, for another day?" There was a pleading tone to his voice.

"Okay, no more talk about it, for now. Can we do one thing tomorrow?" I asked. Ronan nodded without even knowing what I wanted. I gestured across the kitchen. "Can we get this fucking Aga fixed?"

He laughed. "I fear it needs replacing. I don't think it's worked for years. However, tomorrow, you can have the task of finding us an engineer to see if it *can* be rescued. Or we replace it. This kitchen needs an Aga, for sure. And the boiler needs a service too."

Ronan held my hand as we carried our mugs of tea from the kitchen. The hallway was warmer, but even there, I could see my breath when I exhaled. I shivered all the way up the stairs.

"What we can't do is upgrade all the heating in one go, the house would suffer from it, it wasn't designed for central heating."

I understood his point. "I don't think it would hurt to at least light some fires in some of the rooms. Those books in the library are curling from damp. The house needs to dry out," I said as if I had any clue on such a historic building.

He cringed. "Then we need to add a chimney sweep to the list for tomorrow. I doubt they've been tended to in years, either."

We paused outside Ronan's bedroom. "I *am* sorry, Lizzie," he said.

I nodded. "Just know, I'm not a child, and I don't want to be lied to or mucked around. It's already transpired you and Joe had a conversation you failed to include me in so, no more, yes?"

He gave me a wink and clinked his mug against mine. "Agreed."

There was a moment of awkwardness as he didn't want to walk into his room, and I didn't want to leave.

I huffed. "Goodnight," I said, and I turned.

Although itching to look back because I hadn't heard the floorboards creak indicating he'd entered his bedroom, I didn't. Instead, I walked into mine and closed the door. I then punched the air and hissed out a 'yes.' Childish, I know, and I wasn't sure what I'd won, other than to state that he needed to make a decision as to whether I was staff or not.

I deflated—what if he chose staff?

CHAPTER TWELVE

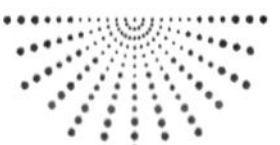

I spent most of the following day spending Ronan's money, which was quite exciting and also terrifying. I made notes of three of everything and everybody, then checked in with him before I bought or scheduled. It got to the point that he snapped at me, telling me he trusted me not to spend every penny he had and that the credit card had a limit anyway. I chuckled as I organised for an Aga specialist to attend the following day, and a chimney sweep for that afternoon. I bought wooden crates and packaging for the pictures, and I also googled abstract art. It seemed there might have been a market for it. I decided that I might select the better ones and take them to a gallery. I was sure that Joe would have a contact, so I emailed him to ask. His reply came quickly:

Of course I have a contact in the art world. I have contacts in *every* world, my darling. Now, let me get this straight… Ronan's mum rolled around on the floor, naked, and in paint? She set up a camera to photograph herself doing that? Mmm, maybe we need to visit that BDSM club. I think it might be more suited there ;)

I laughed at his comment. He had ended his email saying that he would let me know who best to *pitch the nudes* to. I wouldn't tell Ronan until I actually had something to tell, of course.

"Maggie, I've got someone coming to look at the Aga tomorrow. What do you think? Will it work again?" I asked as I sat munching on a sandwich.

"Oh, it would be magnificent if it did. I remember baking bread and cakes and pies in that. It would heat this room and half the house in its day. It hasn't worked for such a long time, though. Charlie tried to fix it, but Verity didn't seem to care. It runs on oil, and that's not something she was keen on," Maggie said.

"What about the boiler? Where is it?"

"Outside, in the courtyard, there's a fuel tank and the boiler. It works; it's just not man enough for the whole house. We had a delivery of fuel just a week ago but, other than Charlie tinkering, that boiler hasn't had a service in years."

"Do you know anyone locally? Or maybe the Aga man can do the boiler while he's here," I said.

Maggie shrugged her shoulders. "I used to have a file of who did what, maintenance and all that, but it went out the window to be honest. I should say, it's so nice to get on top of all those things again. It would be wonderful to see this old house back up to scratch."

I hadn't thought of the tasks that she would have done in the past. As housekeeper I didn't think that scheduling maintenance would have been up to her, but I didn't want to step on toes, either.

"It would be nice, wouldn't it? Together we can get this wreck sorted and then it's got to be so much easier," I said.

When I returned to the library—a room where I'd cleaned the windows, bashed the curtains to release some of the dust before removing them for professional cleaning, dusted as far as I could reach and had Charlie light the fire—I was ready to roll again.

I found a glazier to come and quote for the cracked windows, and a window cleaner with extendable poles to clean the outside. As enthused as I was, so were Maggie and Charlie. It was as if we were all breathing a little life into the house *and* into each other. They had decided they were going to take a room at a time, starting at the bottom and working up. Each would have a thorough clean and notes made of what needed to be repaired. There was a lot that Charlie could do himself with the tools he said he had, but I asked him to make a note of what he needed.

"I think we ought to set a budget," I said, as I sat with Ronan. The estimates and scheduled spend was mounting up.

He winced when he saw my sheet of paper. "I do think we need to get the house in order before we tackle the outside, and before we think about any money-making enterprises," he said. I didn't disagree. I wanted to get cracking with the film set idea. I'd found a forum of homeowners and the fees were staggering.

"There's plenty Maggie and Charlie can do, and to be honest, there was always plenty they could have done but haven't. I don't know why. It doesn't matter, but I had an idea you might not totally like," I said, cryptically.

I had heard back from Joe that a friend of his might be interested in the *artwork.* I had taken a couple of photographs and emailed them. He'd replied—among the *ha ha ha's*—that he would forward them on. But it was the email I'd received just an hour prior to sitting with Ronan that had me excited:

Babe, you're never going to believe this, but my friend is pissing himself over those photos, and I don't mean in the weak bladder sense. He loves them! Can you imagine that? All we ever needed to do in art class was roll around naked, and we could have earned millions! You'll need to get some

down here for him to look at, but he seems willing to exhibit and sell, if that's what actually happens.

I read the email—omitting the pissing part—aloud to Ronan.

He gasped. "No way would someone want to buy those," he said, his eyes wide.

"Ronan, look at this." I turned the laptop around so he could see the enlarged version of the photograph that I had sent Joe.

Splashes of vibrant colour filled the screen. Although there was no order to the image it was striking. The more I looked at it, the more joyous it had become and then to discover the naked form of Verity in the middle was a bonus. The concept had certainly grown on me.

I added, "There's a fellow, I forget his name, and he might be Scottish, but he paints animals using streaks of colour like this, and he's really successful." I was exaggerating my art knowledge when all I'd seen was an advert for a print on Facebook.

"Seriously?" Ronan asked. I nodded. "Well, I guess it won't hurt to show them to him. Do you think Joe might keep it from Rich for the moment? He had a real thing about what our mum did, and if he knows she's going to be plastered on a wall in London somewhere, he might freak. He does, at the moment, still own half of all this."

I fired back a quick email to Joe knowing full well it was fruitless. Joe had the biggest mouth and was the worst gossip I'd ever known.

"As soon as the packing material arrives, we'll take some down to London and see if we can't raise some funds that way," I said. "And if they are sought after, what better way than to exhibit them here."

I laughed as I thought of limp dick and saggy tits, as I'd named them, out in the campsite with the cream of the art world perhaps in a marquee on the lawn sipping Pimms and admiring the photographs and paintings.

"Just dinnae want nae earthers here," I heard. Charlie had walked in with a basket of logs ready to stack by the blazing fire.

"You need to tell me again about these earthers," I said. Ronan coughed, choking on the sip of tea he had just taken. He waved his arm, but Charlie ignored him.

"They pump the trees," he said—or at least that's what I thought he'd said. He'd gone back to a harsh Scottish accent interspersed with Gaelic. "And they pump the ground, dig holes all over the place, they do, like fucking moles."

He walked from the room, and it descended into silence.

Ronan, thankfully, translated. "Pump, means have sex."

I nodded, not that I actually needed it clarified; it was quite obvious what Charlie meant. Yet again, silence descended.

"Bohemian," both Ronan and I said at the same time and then burst into laughter. I nodded. Of course there were would be *earth sexers* on this palatial Scottish mansion with its deer, and gatehouses, and naked artists.

When we had calmed down, I said, "They electrocute moles, don't they?" I was sure I'd read somewhere that it was an effective method of pest control.

He was trying to remain calm and pursed his lips. "I have absolutely no idea." Then he frowned, probably wondering why on earth I'd mentioned that.

I lost all train of thought and concentration. "I think I might need a little fresh air. The chimney sweep will be here shortly. I might take a walk down to the gate and back."

"Wait for me. I could do with getting all thoughts of *earth sexers* out of my mind as well."

I still had the coat and the boots that I'd borrowed, but I was going to need some thicker socks. I'd doubled up but had only brought a couple of pairs, and my jeans alone weren't stopping my skin from pimpling with cold and chafing on the denim.

"I might need to find a town for some new clothes, and I need to check in with my bank soon," I said.

He nodded. "We can head into town later if you want a change of scenery. I can't promise Harrods, but there are some pretty good shops for hiking and wet weather gear."

It sounded perfect, and I decided it might be nice to get an idea of the local town. We were going to need their support if we were to put on any events at the house.

"I forgot," I said as we left the front door. "What do you *call* this?" I said, waving my arm and walking backwards, gesturing up at the house.

"*A wonderful Heritage Castle* so the council call it," Ronan replied.

Although there were no traditional turrets or those slitty windows for arrow firing, I could see where the *castle* might come into the description.

We walked down to the gate, and I tried my hardest to push one but failed. "Maybe you should consider having these gates repaired as well." It was half open and very firmly stuck.

He scratched his chin and chewed on his lip. "Add that to the list for Charlie. I'm sure they could just do with a clean up, repaint, and a little oiling. Although they used to be electric when I was a kid. Dad wanted security. Mum believed that everyone should enjoy the property and the grounds. I agree, in part with her, but a little privacy would be nice," he said. "Follow me."

We strode along the lane a little way. The only sounds were my feet slopping around in the wellies, and slapping on the tarmac road as if I was overly heavy-footed.

We followed the boundary wall until we came to a small cottage. It was picture perfect or could have been. There was a hole in the roof, broken glass in the windowpanes, and I could see where plants had grown over the front porch. I sighed at its neglect. Joe would have a coronary at all the properties in a dilapidated state.

Ronan pushed through the creaking gate. "I used to live here for a while."

We walked around the side to the rear of the property, and I cupped my eyes to peer through the glass in a back window. I saw another range cooker, a newer version to the one in the main house, albeit much smaller. The kitchen, although dated, looked cosy, and I could imagine a sofa at one end of the room and a couple of dogs in a basket in front of the range.

"It looks lovely, Ronan, but why is everything so rundown? This could have been rented out, bringing in an income to the estate," I said, conscious that I sounded scolding.

He shrugged almost in defeat. "My mum just wasn't that way. She wasn't commercial at all. She lived frugally, and she still had enough money to keep doing what she did. She didn't die with millions in the bank; in fact, most of it will go to the government when it's all finalised. I don't know—she just didn't think the same way as us." He sighed.

"Is renting something you'd consider?" I asked.

"For sure. There are four cottages that we own, and an apartment in town. Maybe, instead of the naked spa, we might turn those gatehouses into holiday lets, or long-term rentals as well? Less work and regular income. I have to think about the times I won't be here," he said.

I hadn't thought of him not living in the house. I guess I assumed he would. I turned to walk back to the path and found myself crossed legged and very firmly stuck in the mud.

"Fuck," I growled. I knew I was going to fall. I could see it before it happened, and I knew there was absolutely nothing I could do about it.

Ronan decided to help. He leapt forward and managed to grab one arm as I swiftly descended. I face-planted in the mud, and I didn't stop there. Both feet left the oversized wellies standing proud and facing the window I had been looking into. I rolled to my back.

"Oh…" Ronan said as he placed his hands under my armpits. I wasn't sure he was going to lift me. "Ooof," he said, as he did.

I curled my feet up, not wanting to put them in the mud while Ronan held me at arm's length, getting redder and redder with the exertion.

"Put me on the path!" I shouted, wincing at the pain in my poor pits.

"I'm stuck," he said.

"Put me back in my boots then!"

"I'm fucking stuck," he repeated.

I hung in the air on ever-shaking arms and looked down. I guessed the weight of him holding me had managed to cause his wellies to sink ankle deep in mud that sucked like a professional whore.

"Lizzie…"

He didn't finish his sentence before he dropped me on my arse with no warning to extend my legs. My feet touched the mud, and Ronan fell forwards. His arms landed either side of me, and I closed my eyes as if it would save the bump on the head I was sure was about to happen.

I opened one eye to see his face just a couple of inches from me. "Oh my fucking God," I said, and then laughed. "I'm going to pee!"

He joined in with the laughter, which made it worse. I was guffawing so hard I fell backwards. “Mud angels,” I screamed, waving my arms around.

Ronan was on all fours, part way up my body, and when I’d stopped laughing and looked at him, my stomach flipped.

For a moment, he was quiet. “We need to get out of this mud,” he said eventually, and I nodded. He managed to stand and release his boots. He grabbed mine and then reached down for me, and I scrambled to my feet.

“Oh, Lizzie,” Ronan said, he started to laugh again. We didn’t stop laughing as I walked in just my socks back to the house.

We met the chimney sweep on the drive. “What the…?”

“Mud,” was all I could manage.

He grinned. “I can see that.”

Maggie came to the door, to greet the chimney sweep but gasped when she saw us. “Oh my Lord. Whatever happened?”

“Mud,” was all I managed, again. I could feel the tears of laughter roll down my cheeks, and I imagined they had created a nice clear track through the dirt.

“She needs hosing doon,” Charlie said. I was being stared at by the three of them, and that made me laugh harder.

“At least go round the back,” Maggie said, and I noticed she had, for once, mopped down the front hall floor. Trouble was, *going round the back* was another ten-minute hike in soggy socks and a chill wind.

Ronan wrapped his arm around my shoulders. Despite the fact I did have a coat, it was my face—a head covered in wet muddy hair—my hands and feet that were cold. I wasn’t about to complain, though. When we reached the courtyard, he ran ahead and grabbed another pair of boots. They stunk, and I made him put his hands in them in case they contained a nest of toe-eating spiders. I even jumped on the front to be sure. When I was confident I wasn't going to be munched on, I slipped them on. Not ideal, but they gave me something clean to enter the kitchen in.

"You might as well strip here," Ronan said. I stared at him. He clarified, "Take your socks and jeans off, and the coat, Maggie can wash them."

"I'm not walking around in my knickers. The chimney sweep is here," I hissed.

I hadn't cared that he would see my pants, and I struggled to remember if I was wearing my big girl Tena pants or the pack of Brazilian ones from Marks & Spencer that I didn't know which way round they went. They were either an oversized thong or had a skinny front.

"Wrap a blanket around yourself," he said, grabbing one from the chair.

As he held it out with one hand, he unbuttoned his jeans with the other. I grabbed the blanket and turned my back. Not because I thought he might prefer the sight of my arse, I didn't want to see his… Well, you know.

Anyway, I flicked off the wellies and peeled off my socks and jeans. Thankfully, the coat was near my knees, and it gave me time to peer at my knickers. I breathed a sigh of relief, whatever ones they were, they were pink and pretty, and they covered my *hooha*. I gave a subtle feel just to make sure nothing was escaping the sides of the material before I pulled off the coat and wrapped myself in the blanket in mere seconds.

I gathered up my clothes, and his jeans and boxers, blushing at the thought of his nakedness under his blanket and dumped them in the linen basket. I wouldn't expect Maggie to wash my clothes, but I would need some help with the ancient washing machine.

"Tea?" Ronan said.

"I need—"

"You need to sit and warm from the inside before you have a bath, you'll get chilblains," he said, all authoritative-like.

I'd never had chilblains, but the word was scary enough to make me sit in my jumper and knickers and wait for tea. I was glad I did. The blanket that Ronan had around his waist was dragging on the floor, and a couple of times he'd tread on it, and it pulled loose, showing off part of his backside. I'd only seen Joe and Harry's, and neither was as tight as the one in front of me. I pretended to be digging out dirt from under my nails when he turned and placed the filled teapot on the table. I grabbed mugs from the centre and poured as he sat.

"What a fucking day," he said, as he pulled his mug towards him. "Lizzie, if you could see yourself…" He chuckled as he raised his mug to his lips.

I had suspected my face would have mud on it. I could feel the tightness to my skin as it had dried, although I could never have imagined exactly how much but I discovered after I'd drunk my tea and headed to my bathroom. The bath would take too long to draw, so I opted for the shower. I'd need to wash my hair anyway. I reached in to turn the handle hoping, by the time I'd removed my jumper and knickers, the water might be running warm.

I then faced the mirror and screeched. I could see my eyes and my mouth, obviously. I could see the two clean tracks down my cheeks, but I couldn't see any more skin. My whole face was covered in dried and cracked mud. I looked like a beauty victim with the worst facemask. Scary. I dragged the jumper over my head, feeling the crackle of the dried mud in my hair, and wrenched down my knickers. I left them all lying in a pile on the floor with the blanket, and I climbed into the shower. The water was warmish—not enough to stop me shivering—as I washed and rewashed my hair. By the time it got to conditioning, I was standing under a cold stream. I rinsed as best I could with chattering teeth and then turned it off. I wrapped a towel around my body and one around my head, and I sat at the antique dressing table to look at myself in the slightly distorted and coloured mirror. My cheeks were rosy, and my eyes were shining. Maybe there were some special minerals in the mud. Perhaps we shouldn't immediately ditch the naked spa idea. I plastered on some moisturiser, flicked a little mascara over my stubby eyelashes and dressed. I was back down in the library that was doubling up as our office in no time.

"What do you think?" Maggie said. She held some red brocade material over the threadbare sofa.

"I like it," I said running my hand over the material feeling its softness.

"I think I could re-cover these myself. I found this material in one of the attic rooms; there are reels of material up there. We might be able to do some curtains as well."

"I think the colour is perfect for in here," I said as I glanced around picturing how it might look.

The room had wooden panelling to one side, broken only by the floor-to-ceiling French doors. The opposite wall held the bookcase, which was the length and height of the room. Some of the books were behind glass and some exposed. I'd wondered whether to make a list of some and see if there was anything of value gathering dust there. I didn't want to come across as someone who was looking for everything to sell, but I wanted Ronan to know he had options. If there was a rare book or two, was it insured?

"Can you help me get the sewing machine down?" Maggie asked. "Charlie has gone to cut down some trees."

"Cut down…"

"If we're going to have fires all the time, we're going to need lots of wood and Ronan is still with the chimney sweep, although I made him put some trousers on," she said.

I laughed as we made our way up the stairs and along the hall. There was a further staircase at one end that took us up to more rooms that clearly hadn't been opened up for years. In one, alongside an old Singer sewing machine was a crib and the most stunning dappled grey rocking horse. I had a romantic idea that Ronan had slept in that crib or rode that horse but judging by the age and decline of both, it could also have been Verity herself.

"I'm so glad you're here," Maggie said. I was sure she'd said that before. "I used to cry when another room got shut off because it fell apart."

"It's a stunning house. Ronan has to sort things with Rich, but he'd love to keep it going," I said, hoping I wasn't divulging something not true.

"Now there's a pest if ever I saw one." Maggie shook her head as she spoke.

I lifted the sewing machine and made my way to the door, frowning at her as I passed.

My confusion must have been evident as she continued, "Rich was trouble as a child, a teenager, and then an adult. Bled his mum dry, he did. It's why half the rooms got shut off sometimes. She couldn't afford to keep it all going after bailing him out time and time again."

What Maggie had said had differed slightly from Ronan, but I wasn't going to nit-pick the details. I suspected Verity did bail out Rich, but I also believed she had no thoughts about money, no regard for it, which, in one way, was an enviable position to be in. We carried the sewing machine down to the kitchen where it was dusted off. Maggie expertly threaded some cotton, and we tested it on a tea towel. It produced a neat line of stitches, so the re-covering of the sofa and some new curtains were planned. I made notes while she measured because I had no idea how to work out width and depth and height and whatever.

“We’ve got a venison stew in the oven for dinner,” she said, somewhat randomly.

“It smells lovely already,” I replied.

“I’ll tell you because some townies don’t like to eat venison.” She rolled her eyes.

“I’ve eaten it before. Is it from here?” I asked. She nodded.

I wasn’t daft. I knew where my meat came from. Living in London had its advantages in that every corner had an organic-free-range-gluten-free-know-its-name butchers, bakers, coffee shop and every other thing artisan. And we had the French market and fuck knows what they were selling, but it was often delicious. It was a sales thing, obviously. But it did also mean that we ate some wonderful meat with stickers from stately homes; not see-through meat that should have come from a chicken twice my height, such was the size of breasts, filled with more pharmaceuticals than Pfizer had.

“Who shoots them?” I asked, remembering the man I’d seen in the courtyard but never seen since.

“Charlie and Ronan, mainly. Manuel, he was Verity’s *friend…*” Maggie even did the quotation mark fingers, and I stifled a laugh —who did that anymore? “He’s the *part-time* estate manager, when he gets off his arse.” She did it again! However, I got the distinct impression she wasn’t a fan.

“I think I saw him, Manuel you say?” I asked.

“I don’t know if that’s his real name.” She leaned towards me—not that there was anyone else in the room—and whispered, “He’s a gigig.”

I stared at her. “A what?” I asked.

She waved her hand around as if it would make things clearer. “You know… A gigi…whatsit.”

I wasn’t sure how I kept not only a straight face but stayed put on my chair when she crooked her arms at the elbows, closed her fists, and thrust her hips back and forwards.

I pursed my lips trying to compose myself. “Gigolo?”

“That’s what I said. He’s probably from Wales,” she spat. At that, I did laugh.

She grinned, clearly enjoying the gossip. “I think he fakes that accent. He hasn’t got a clue about estate management, but Verity took him on. He lives in one of the cottages.” She took the pad and pen from my hands, collected the material, and headed back to the kitchen.

“You look bemused,” I heard. When my eyes came into focus, I noticed Ronan standing in the doorway.

“Maggie, gigolos, and curtains,” I said, turning back to my makeshift desk.

“Ah, Manuel. I haven’t introduced you yet.” He strode into the room and smiled as if it was perfectly normal to have a gigolo called Manuel, who was probably from Wales, living in a cottage on his estate.

Ronan sat and told me that all the chimneys had been done, I nodded, expecting to hear something more about the gigolo from Wales. Nothing. Perhaps Maggie had been right, and Manuel was Verity’s lover. That could very well be why Ronan didn’t want to talk about it and why he seemed to have kept his distance.

For the rest of the day, we went through the pictures and photographs. We selected what our untrained eye thought were the better ones. When the packaging arrived, we would box up what we thought should stay behind and take the others to London.

❧

Dinner was delicious. Maggie was an outstanding chef and, I felt, completely wasted at the house. She could have a restaurant in the city. Instead, and in addition to her role as housekeeper, she'd been making tea and sandwiches for the nude artists that frequented one weekend a month from spring to autumn, weather dependent, of course.

I'd followed Ronan to a cellar of wine prior to dinner, and he'd selected a couple of bottles. After helping Maggie clear the dishes and adding a new dishwasher to the list of essentials, Ronan and I settled back in the library with the bottles of red.

I don't think we intended to drink them both, but with the ambience created by the open fire and the dust free room, we both curled up on the decrepit sofa, one at each end, and we chatted.

We spoke about childhood, and I began to realise one thing; all the money, the big house and the acres of land, the horses and dogs, and deer and shotguns didn't make for a wonderful upbringing at all. Ronan had been—and I got the impression still *was*—exceptionally lonely.

"Dad was always either working, in the States, or fucking one of his many mistresses," he told me, adding a bitter laugh and another slug of his wine.

I looked at my glass. I was on my second refill but only just. One bottle was empty and the other about to be as Ronan shook the bottle to get every last drop into his glass. "I'll go and get another," he said, and although not slurring, his accent was more prominent.

"No need. I've had enough," I said. I didn't insult him by telling him that I thought he had as well. I hated when people did that. It was his hangover—his choice.

"I haven't," he said as he placed his glass on the coffee table and stood.

"Do you want me to come with you?" I asked, conscious of the fact he could fall down the stone stairs.

"You're too nice, Lizzie. I thought that the moment I met you. You're funny and kind, and I think it's easy to take advantage of you. That makes me sad," he said as he walked across the room.

I stayed in my seat.

I wasn't sure what he meant by any of his comments and hoped that it was just the drink. If he thought I was easy to take advantage of, was that what he was doing? Was he telling me, actually *informing* me, that *he* was taking advantage?

"Can someone be too nice?" I whispered to his retreating back.

Ronan had the capability to give whiplash. I was glad that I'd started to hold back a little. Thankfully, my heart still had that layer of protective bubble wrap that kept me conscious of further hurt.

I gave him five minutes before I went to find him. He was slumped in a chair in the kitchen having partly made a pot of tea instead of making it to the cellar for more wine.

I finished off making the tea and then nudged him awake. "How about we get you to bed?"

"That's a nice offer. I'll take you up on that," he said, with a laugh.

"Let me rephrase. How about I help *you* get into your *own* bed alone?"

"Shame, but a drunken fumble probably won't enhance our friendship, will it?" His laugh made me smile.

"No, and I'm pretty sure that Joe had instructed me never to sleep, or fumble, with anyone even slightly tipsy."

"Good ol' Joe. Did he tell you never to make a cup of tea for a drunken man?"

"No, that was my mother. Let's get you upstairs, and then I'll bring you up a cup."

Ronan wasn't drunk enough that he couldn't make the stairs, but he was a little wobbly, and the last thing I wanted to do was clean up blood after he'd cracked his skull on the stone floor once he'd fallen down them. Also, the beautiful carpet on the treads could get ruined.

I walked behind him up the stairs, not that I would've been able to hold him should he have fallen backwards. I slowed as we reached the landing and watched him weave his way down the hall to his bedroom. Once he had entered I went back down. I picked up the glasses and empty bottles from the library and then worried about the fire.

I decided, stupidly, water was the best way to douse it. I wasn't sure it was a good idea to leave it going overnight. I grabbed a filled jug of water from the kitchen and threw it into the fire. It spat, hissed, cursed me, I was sure, but more importantly, it smoked. I ran to close the library door to stop the smoke escaping and then to the French doors. I rattled, tugged, called it a fucker before it finally opened and I could waft the smoke out.

The curtains, I knew, were going to be replaced, so I wasn't worried about grabbing one and using it to wave fresh air around. By the time I thought the fogginess had cleared, I was freezing. I managed to close the doors and, satisfied the fire had died down, I headed back to the kitchen.

The Aga specialist was visiting the following day, and as I looked at the contraption, I hoped that he would be able to fix it. I could imagine putting a 'real' kettle on the hob and waiting for it to whistle.

I poured the tea and carried two mugs up the stairs, hesitating outside Ronan's bedroom door. I couldn't knock; I didn't have a free hand, so, called out instead. He didn't reply. I used my foot to push the door open a little and then stifled a laugh.

Ronan was lying naked, on his back and sporting a very impressive hard on. I left his tea on the bedside table and, after another study of his cock, left the room. I had placed my tea on my bedside cabinet when I realised I couldn't leave him that way. He'd freeze his balls off, so I walked back. He hadn't moved, obviously, and even though I was sure he was dead to the world, I still tiptoed around.

I wasn't strong enough to roll him and pull the duvet from underneath so scanned the room for blankets. I pulled open his wardrobe hoping to find some there. On the top shelf was a spare duvet. Although without a cover, it would keep him warm. I pulled at it. As it slid from the shelf, a framed photograph fell to the floor, and the glass shattered on impact.

"Shit," I whispered, and then stared at Ronan.

His cock twitched, and I wasn't sure if that was because he was waking. He mumbled and moaned. I crouched down to pick up the broken glass when I heard him moan again. I turned my head and stretched my neck up to see over the end of the bed.

I gasped.

Ronan had his hand around his cock and was stroking slowly.

"Oh, God," I muttered, and ducked down further. He wouldn't have seen me where I was, but he would notice the open wardrobe door.

"Oh, God," I whispered again as he moaned a little louder.

I wanted to cover my ears at the sound of slapping skin when his *sleepwank* got vigorous. I tried to sing in my head and the only, bizarrely, song that came to mind was *The Wheels on the Bus*. There was no way I wanted that running on constant in my head.

"Oh, God," I hissed, yet again.

He mumbled, but I couldn't make out what he'd said. I wasn't sure I wanted to, either.

I used my foot to push the wardrobe door as closed as I could and shifted to my knees. I piled the glass and scooted it under the bed for safety and then picked up the photograph that had fallen. As Ronan wanked in his sleep, and I was praying he *was* asleep, I stared at the image of him with the most beautiful smile directed at a redheaded woman. If love was visual, it was there in that image. She wasn't his ex-wife, so I could only assume it was the one after. A tear pricked at one eye. I couldn't ever recall, not even in my wedding album, a photograph of a man looking at me the way he looked at her.

Ronan mumbled, skin was slapping skin, and I was crouched behind the end of the bed hoping he'd come soon and fall into his drunken coma so I could leave. I sighed and covered my ears again when the bed started to rock and bounce against me. I was being jolted forwards and back, but I couldn't move out of the way, I'd be seen. I had no choice but to endure the pounding.

Then it all stilled. I held my breath, hoping he was done. I counted to sixty and knowing one minute had passed, I gently peered over the edge of the bed. He was still on his back, and his cock was flaccid although his hand was still wrapped around it.

I grabbed the duvet and crawled around the side of the bed that his head was facing away from. When I'd got halfway along the length of the bed, I paused to listen. The only sound was his heavy breaths. I rose and quickly threw the duvet over him and then ran. It wasn't until I was back in my room that I realised I still carried the photograph.

I placed it on my bed as I closed the curtains and then undressed, exchanging clothes for my PJs. I picked up the photograph and then climbed under the duvet. I turned it over in my hands and noticed writing on the back of the frame.

No matter what, I'll always love you, Demi. There could never be another that will come close.

I could only assume it was written by Ronan. I opened the drawer of the bedside cabinet and placed it in. I'd put it back in the wardrobe the next day.

I didn't sleep well at all that night. I dozed and woke, tossed and turned. I checked my phone and played a word game, wishing I had a sleeping tablet to hand. I'd been given a low dose prescription from the doctor when I first found myself single. I'd rarely taken them and wondered if they'd even be in date.

It was early hours when I'd finally fallen into a deep sleep.

CHAPTER THIRTEEN

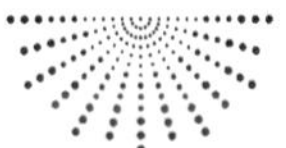

"Good morning," I heard. I opened one eye, partly.

Ronan was standing beside the bed with a mug in his hand. He placed it on the bedside cabinet, and I shot upwards into a sitting position. I had closed the drawer, hadn't I?

I looked over to check and hid the relieved sigh.

"Thank you," I said, picking up the tea and wondering why no one knocked on a bedroom door in this house. "You seem bright this morning," I added.

"Did you cover me over last night?" he asked.

I shook my head as I sipped, and he frowned. "I must have been wasted. I don't remember doing it myself."

"I wouldn't have said you were wasted, but you sure weren't totally sober."

"Anyway, the Aga man is downstairs, you'll be pleased to know he thinks he can restore it, and I got a text to say the packing crates are being delivered at eleven fifty-seven precisely," he said.

"That's great news about both." I was hoping that, after he'd finished with his news, he'd depart the room.

No matter what he said or did, my eyes focused on his hand, knowing where it had been the previous evening.

"I'll let you get dressed. See you downstairs?"

I nodded and used sipping my tea as an excuse not to continue the conversation.

Once Ronan had left, I threw back the duvet and ran for the bathroom. The only reason I ran was so my feet didn't linger on the cold floor. I needed to pee and clean my teeth. I couldn't face a shower. I dressed and brushed my hair and then reached inside the drawer for the photograph. Just as I grabbed it, I heard voices in the hallway. Ronan was instructing Charlie on some repairs. I placed the frame back in the drawer; I could hardly wander into Ronan's bedroom with Charlie watching.

❧

I listened to the Aga man talking to Ronan; listening was about all I could do. Like Charlie, when he wanted, the man spoke so fast and with such a strong accent that I struggled to understand him. Judging by the smiles, however, I thought the conversation was a positive one. That was until he sat and wrote a quote. I winced at the four figures, but Ronan didn't seem to be overly worried. Obviously, I had no idea what an Aga would cost if replaced, and I did have to smile when Ronan shook his hand, and they set a date for work to commence.

I decided to help Maggie with some washing. She seemed to have a stack of linen that she'd taken off beds in rooms that hadn't been used in years. They were stiff with dust. We took them out to the courtyard, shook them well for fear of clogging the machine, and then carried them into one of the small buildings where Maggie loaded one of two industrial sized washing machines.

"Why the industrial machines?" I asked. It seemed overkill for the amount of residents in the house.

"We used to have a ton of guests back in the day," she said.

"Ladies," I heard in a heavy foreign accent, and I turned.

Manuel held his hand out. His black hair and startling blue eyes did not confirm his heritage. I knew some Italians had blue eyes, but thought it highly possible he did have some Spanish in him.

"Hello, I'm Lizzie," I said, taking his hand.

He shook lightly, limply. "I'm sorry not to have met you before now. We need to do accounts, yes?"

I wracked my brain for who he reminded me of and the only thing that sprung to mind was a character from the TV show, *Benidorm*. Like Maggie, I wasn't entirely convinced on the accent.

"I offered to tidy up the office and get the files in order so they might make some sense to Ronan," I said.

He chuckled. "Yes, make sense to Ronan." I thought his comment a little disingenuous.

"Since he has to ensure the survival of the estate, or put everyone out of work, it might help to know exactly where he stands, financially, don't you think?"

He had no answer for me, and I felt an instant dislike to him. I was firmly on Maggie's side that he was nothing more than a gigolo coming to the end of a free ride.

Manuel—and I didn't for one minute believe that to be his name—flounced from the washroom.

"What a big prick," I said, picking another sheet from the basket.

"I saw him naked once—you'd never use those words where he was concerned." Maggie waggled her pinkie at me.

For a moment, I had no idea what she meant, but then it dawned on me, and my eyes grew wide. I knew they had because the cold hit my eyeballs and they watered.

"You saw him naked?"

She grinned. "Everyone is naked here at some point."

"You and…" I could not bring myself to ask if Charlie was ever naked.

She placed her hand over her heart in feigned shock. "No, not us, we don't do that art thing. But *he* was one of the models. It's how he met Verity, and then she seemed to want to keep him around."

"Maybe it might be time for Ronan to rectify that. I mean, if he isn't an estate manager, what's the point of him now?"

Maggie shrugged her shoulders. "And I bet his name is Mick," she added.

We had loaded more sheets into the second of the two washing machines, placed the woollen blankets to one side, and piled the duvet covers up ready for a second load. We headed back into the kitchen.

"Mick from Wales," Maggie said, and then chuckled.

"Who's Mick?" Ronan asked, a frown of confusion crumpling his brow.

"Manuel, we bet his name is Mick," I replied with a giggle.

Ronan's features clouded. It seemed perhaps Mick-stroke-Manuel wasn't up for discussion. Maggie raised her eyebrows at me, and I folded my lips inside my mouth as if to keep them shut. The rumble of a truck on the drive saved us from any further chat.

"It's the crates I think," I said, looking out the window.

Ronan and I walked to the front door to meet the delivery. Sure enough, five large wooden crates, a couple of large poster tubes, and bubble wrap were unloaded and carried into the *art room*. I'd never packed art before and thought the bubble wrap to be the best material for each piece, then we could stack a few in each crate. I hadn't thought far enough ahead to know how we would then move the crates from the room to wherever they would end up, of course.

We spent the rest of the afternoon sorting through the paintings and photographs. The more we did, the more I realised, even with my basic knowledge of what constituted art, they really were rather good. Ronan thought otherwise.

I brushed dust from my jeans. "We're going to need a trolley of some kind. And somewhere warm to store them."

"I was thinking about that. I'm going to let Manual go because we can't get in that office and get the paperwork, he keeps blocking me."

"What do you mean, blocking you?"

"It's always *mañana* with him."

I placed my hands on my hips. "You own the place, Ronan. We're done here so let's go and do it. He can't physically block you from the room."

Ronan scratched his chin. "I was hoping he'd work with us. There's a lot I don't know about estate management."

"Then right now you're on a par with him. I doubt he knows anything about it, either. Google will be our best friend," I said, smiling at him. How hard could it be, honestly?

I also wondered why Ronan was so hesitant where Mick…*Manuel* was concerned.

I grabbed a couple of black sacks from the kitchen, and we walked to the estate office. Manuel was sitting behind a desk with his booted feet on it and papers were scattered everywhere. He had his eyes closed.

"Come to start clearing this office," I called out, in an attempt to wake him.

He startled. "What you mean?" he asked, in pigeon English.

"She means, we have come to start work in this office. We need to make some sense of accounts for the estate and this, apparently, is where they are," Ronan said, slowly.

Manuel dragged his feet from the desk, scattering more papers, which he made no attempt to pick up. Then he stood and stomped from the room.

"Have you seen Benidorm?" I asked as he passed me.

He scowled. "Huh?"

"Benidorm, the TV show?"

He made a face like a snarling dog. "No, why would I?" he said, and I noticed the slight slip of the accent.

"No reason, I just thought, being Spanish, you might have liked it."

He didn't answer but continued his walk across the courtyard to the dog kennels.

"Is he responsible for the dog breeding as well?" I asked Ronan.

"No, we have a local farmer do that. We don't farm any of our land anymore—we rent it all out. Somewhere in here should be all those details."

I was a little surprised at how far 'off the ball' Ronan had taken his eyes. He was a businessman, yet this business, which he had always stood to inherit, was a mess. I didn't voice that, of course.

I picked up the scattered papers and gathered everything on the desk into one neat pile. I wiped down the seat behind and then dragged another to the front. We sat.

“First, we need to separate out all these papers in some sort of order. If we find one relating to the land, we put it here,” I said, tapping the desk. “The dogs can go here.” I found a pad of yellow Post-Its and wrote on each before sticking it to the desk so Ronan wouldn’t forget.

“You start with that lot, and I’ll start with the filing cabinet. Then we’ll put it all in date order and decide what needs to be kept and what can be binned.”

“This is going to take days,” he said despondently.

“I know, but once we’ve done this, you’ll know exactly where you stand.”

As I rifled through the filing cabinet, I found bills for the house as well as the estate. It seemed good ol’ *Manuel* was in charge of everything.

A thought had begun to germinate in my brain, so I asked, “Do you think Manuel believed he’d be a recipient in your mum’s will?”

“Yes, I’m sure he did. Why?”

“Look at this,” I said, handing him a bank statement.

Although the statement was old and screwed up, the account belonged to Manuel, and I was sad to see it was Manuel and not Mick, but the entries shouldn’t have been there in my opinion.

Ronan stared intently at the paper. “That’s the butcher we sell the venison to. And that is one of the tenant farmers,” he said.

“Manuel appears to have been stealing from the business. I wonder if your mum knew?”

He shrugged his shoulders. “The first thing I need to do is ring these people. I doubt they had any idea what was going on.”

“What we’ll do is send a letter to everyone explaining that you are taking over the estate management until a suitable replacement can be found, and in the meantime you want all payments to go into a new account. You also need to find your real bank accounts and see what’s going in there. I can’t believe your bank wouldn’t have already been in touch.”

“They have. I had a meeting with the new bank manager. The accounts are in credit, so I wasn’t overly worried. Some money is going in there, obviously, but not all I guess.”

We worked in silence for a little while with just the sounds of shuffling paper until we had five piles on the desk and an empty filing cabinet. Ronan had started to write a list of the businesses that were associated with the estate and we made new files for those. We then started on the remaining pages.

“A lot of this is junk mail and rubbish, to be honest,” I said, throwing some letters offering Costco membership.

“I can’t believe how little I know about this place,” Ronan said with a deep sigh.

“The thought had crossed my mind,” I said, gently.

“I guess I haven’t spent enough time here. And therein lies the problem. I don’t know if I want to live here full time, but I also hate the thought of these houses being *holiday homes*. I don’t want to sell it, either.” He sighed in frustration. “I really need to make my mind up. Rich is going to start pushing soon for his money.”

“Probate takes a while anyway, doesn’t it?”

“There was a will and a trust in place, so it should all be fairly straight forward. I haven’t heard from the solicitors for a few days, I’ll chase them up.”

By the time my back was aching from leaning over and my shoulder hurt from stretching from desk to filing cabinet, we had sorted everything into the correct piles. We were no clearer to understanding what was earning and what wasn't, of course. That was stage two and for Ronan to deal with.

"Why don't you call your accountants? They must have the latest figures," I said.

"I have all those, but they don't show it all. As we've discovered, not everything went through the books. What the accounts show as profitable might be overshadowed by another area of business. And I don't particularly want to start highlighting income that hasn't been declared. The fucking tax bill I've got coming is going to hurt enough," he groaned.

I didn't really know enough about inheritance tax to help other than something like that should have been sorted years ago. In one way, I could envy Verity her life in as much as she didn't appear to have a care in the world, but I also wondered how she'd feel to know only one of her children was now in the unenviable position of having to make sense of the mess she'd left.

Dogs howled outside the room, and I guessed Manuel was back from his walk.

Ronan stood. "I think I'll confront Manuel now."

"I'll leave you to it. I'll go and make a late lunch—we haven't eaten. Do you fancy a sandwich?"

He nodded, and I left the room as he called Manuel. The fake Spaniard sneered at me as he walked past, and he actually gave me the shudders. I wondered what on earth Verity saw in the man; her vibrancy would have been overshadowed by his coldness.

I made a couple of sandwiches and wrapped Ronan's in foil, then sat with my mobile at the kitchen table and decided to give Joe a call.

"Hi, how're things in freezing Scotland?" he asked when he answered.

"Freezing. I didn't pack very well," I replied with a light laugh.

I told him about the house, the paintings, the naked art sessions in the woods and how disappointed I was that Manuel wasn't, in fact, Mick, even though I doubted his Spanish origins. Joe told me that he'd sold a house to my ex.

"I'm pleased for him...*them*," I said, trying to muster up the 'pleased.'

"I wanted to tell you because he's splashed it all over social media," Joe said.

"I haven't been on social media for yonks, and I deleted him as a friend anyway," I replied.

"You can still see things. There's a photograph of him shaking my hand in the hall once the deal was done. I didn't exactly get a say in whether I wanted my picture taken, and I'm pissed off it's on social media as well."

Joe was a social media whore. He spent more time on Facebook and Twitter than any bored teenager. I highly doubted he was pissed off but trying to make me feel better about it.

I smiled. "It's perfectly okay, Joe. Honestly, I think everyone needs to believe me when I say I really *am* pleased for them, and I don't care if they plaster photographs all over London."

"That's great; they did invite me to their housewarming. I hope you don't mind. I said yes only because they're inviting all their neighbours and it might be good for business."

"Of course I don't mind." The stab to my betrayed heart had caused my breath to catch in my throat.

"Are you okay?" I could hear the concern in his voice.

"Yes, sorry, a piece of my sandwich went down the wrong

hole, couldn't breathe there for a moment. Oh, hold on, I think Ronan needs me…" I pulled the phone away from my ear for a few seconds. "Joe, I have to go. I'll call you back later?"

"Sure, and it was great to hear from you. I miss you, you know? When are you coming home? I might have some nice properties for you to look at."

"Soon, and I miss you, too. Email me the details. I really need to start thinking about somewhere to live."

I disconnected the call after saying goodbye and placed my phone down. I felt a hand on my shoulder as a tear left my eye and dripped onto the wooden table.

"Your sandwich is there," I said, as Ronan took the seat beside me.

"Why are you crying?"

"I choked on a piece of—"

"You didn't. I was standing by the door."

"Joe just told me my ex bought a million-and-whatever pound property and he's going to their housewarming, for business reasons mind, and it seems everyone is moving on, but I'm stuck going round the same circle," I said without taking a breath. "He's also emailing me some property details, so I guess I need to think about buying a house." I wiped my eyes on the back of my sleeve and stood. "Anyway, enough about that. What happened?"

"I told Manuel he had a week to clear his things from the cottage and that he has lost his job. If he goes quietly, I won't get the police involved in his theft."

I widened my eyes, impressed by Ronan's firm handling of things. "Oh, what did he say?"

“He called me a prick, a wanker, a tosser, and a loser.” He laughed, not that I thought he should have. I bristled in anger on his behalf. “Then he told me my mum gave the best blow jobs and liked taking it up the arse.”

I spat my tea across the table. “What did you say to that?” I asked after gathering my composure.

“I know.”

“*You know*?”

He shrugged. “Yeah, I just said, I know.”

I frowned.

He exhaled a deep sadness-filled sigh, betraying his earlier laughter. “I *don't* know, obviously, but it stumped him enough to have him shut up. Now he's wondering what I meant by it I guess.”

“What happens now?”

“Now, I have to find a replacement. And I've called all those that were paying him. They didn't question when he just gave them new bank details and are very much apologetic.”

“Well, that's a good job done, I guess.”

“What's up with the gigolo?” Maggie asked as she walked into the kitchen.

“He got fired for stealing money from us,” Ronan said, not holding back the details.

Her eyes were wide. “He did *what*?”

Ronan told her what we'd found in the office.

She folded her arms across her chest. “Well, I think you've been too generous with him,” she said.

“Where is the cottage he lives in?” I asked.

"Further down the lane from the one you face planted in the mud at. There's a row of three. He has one, and the other two are empty."

"When did you last make sure they were all secure? He could be renting them out as well as diverting income."

Maggie rubbed her hands together. "Let's go and check. I could do with getting out for ten minutes."

The three of us piled into a Land Rover—different to the one we'd driven in before that stunk of wet dogs—and Ronan drove us to the cottages. We were half expecting to see Manuel but thankfully didn't. Instead, we made our way to the middle one. Maggie had a key, and she opened the front door. The cottage was absolutely gorgeous, the kind I'd expect to see on a twee programme about country living or read about in a book. It was the kind of cottage I'd love to live in if it could be transplanted to Kent. The front door opened into a hallway with a brick inlaid floor. There was a wooden staircase up and two doors off. The first led us to the living room with its log burner raised on a brick plinth. The wooden floorboards were in need of a sanding and varnish, and there was a lighter patch in the middle where a rug had sat for years. Beams crisscrossed the walls. The living room ran into a dining area, which then led sideways into the kitchen. I was surprised at the size; the cottage was a little tardis. Every now and then, as we walked around, I smelt something sweet.

"Can you smell that?" I asked. Ronan shook his head, but Maggie frowned.

"Almonds," she said. I wasn't sure what an almond smelled like so couldn't confirm.

"I think this is a wonderful cottage. Why aren't they rented out?"

I asked.

“There aren’t that many people around here, to be honest. Those that are, live closer to town,” Ronan said.

“What about a holiday let then?” I asked.

“If I can find the right manager then, yes, in the summer we get a lot of tourists, especially around the loch.”

I loved the way his accent came into force when he said, ‘loch.’ He practically spat the word.

I left the room and walked up the stairs to find two decent sized bedrooms and a bathroom. The smell, however, became stronger. As I looked around one room, I noticed a light. It filtered through a gap between the ceiling and the wall. I headed back out of the room and looked up.

“Is there a loft?” I shouted downstairs.

“I imagine so,” Ronan called back.

I found the loft hatch in the second bedroom. I also found, rather conveniently, a stick with a hook specifically designed to open the hatch, which I did, and then pulled down the metal ladder.

“What are you doing?” I heard.

“Checking the loft. There’s a light on,” I said.

“Don’t go up there on your own,” he said, as I was halfway up. “And if you ignore that, don’t step between the beams.”

“Oh my fucking Lord!” I exclaimed, and then immediately stepped between the beams.

I felt the floor give way, my foot continued in a downward motion, and the scrape against my skin most categorically told me I’d gone through the floor, or ceiling, or both, or whatever it was called.

“What the…?” I heard.

"I fell through the floor, but, oh fuck, Ronan, there's a drug factory up here," I shouted. I felt Ronan push my foot as if to propel me back through the hole I had created.

I dragged my foot back up and balanced on a beam while Ronan climbed the ladder.

"What's going on up there?" Maggie shouted.

"Someone has a cannabis farm going on," I replied.

"Can you keep your voices down?" Ronan asked, grumpily.

"There is no one here to hear us," Maggie said.

"Oh fuck," Ronan uttered, reaching for his phone.

"What are you doing?" I asked.

"Calling the police."

"Don't, we could sell this. This shit goes for thousands," I said. I was, of course, joking. I had no idea what cannabis sold for.

Ronan hadn't fallen for the joke. He stared at me through narrowed eyes and screwed up his nose. It was as if he was seeing me for the very first time and wasn't impressed.

I rolled my eyes and slapped his chest playfully. "I was kidding, call the police." As he did, I noticed a hole in the wall that would have divided the loft from the neighbour. More lights, more plants, and a stronger smell was on the other side.

"Manuel is a right little drug dealer," I said, with a laugh.

"I don't know why you're laughing," Ronan snapped. Sometimes I thought he'd had a humour bypass, but I realised, it *was* serious. He owned the cottages that the drug factory had been set up in.

I felt my cheeks heating. "I'm sorry. Did you tell them about Manuel?"

"No, I just said we climbed into a loft, and it's full of drugs."

"What do they look like?" Maggie asked.

"Green plants," I replied.

I heard her muttering and was sure it was, "Oh, dear."

"Maggie, is there anything you want to tell us?" Ronan asked flatly.

"Well, he told me they were herbs, good for the old folk," she said. Although I couldn't see her, I could imagine her wringing her hands.

"Maggie?" I said. I had managed to keep to the beam and had crouched down to look out of the loft hatch as Ronan descended the ladder.

Her brow was crumpled, and her nostrils flared. "Manuel said they were herbs and good for the joints. He told me to put them in the cakes." If she continued to wring her hands, she'd have no skin left, I thought.

"What cakes?" I said, but started to giggle. I had an idea which ones she meant.

"The art group," she almost whispered.

I raised my eyebrows, despite the fact it was no surprise. "The naked art group? No wonder they were able to prance around the woods without clothes on a freezing day." I could barely get the words out such was my mirth.

Maggie started to laugh with me.

"It's not funny," Ronan said. "You could have killed them."

That made us laugh harder. "Oh, Lord, do you think I'll go to prison?" she asked, spluttering the words.

"I need to pee," I said, swinging my bum out of the loft hatch. I fumbled around, finding the treads on the ladder while still laughing.

"Oh, those poor pensioners," Maggie said, forgetting she was one herself.

That was it. I was halfway down the ladder and needed to cross my legs so tight. I held on while Ronan was trying to *assist.* I was laughing too hard to speak and tell him to stop pulling at my legs, for two reasons. First, if he parted them, pee would leak, and second, he was grabbing hold of the broken skin from when I stepped through the ceiling.

I tried to shake him off. "I need to pee, seriously. Stop pulling my leg, or I'll piss all over you!"

Maggie fell to the floor, and I wasn't sure if she was having a heart attack or if it was because she was laughing so much. At least it meant Ronan let go of my leg to help her. I jumped down and rushed to the bathroom, grateful my bladder held until.

"Oh, bollocks," I whispered. No loo paper.

I'd hovered anyway, so decided to shake. Twerking wasn't something I'd ever done and was most certainly something I was totally shite at. However, I shook as much as I could and then pulled my knickers and jeans up. I'd have to change when I got back.

It was half an hour later that the police arrived. I opened the front door and was immediately greeted by a drug dog that stuck his, or her, nose straight between my thighs. The thing sneezed!

"That will teach you," I said, patting its head and then chastising myself for petting a working dog.

I followed the police back up the stairs and into the bedroom where Maggie started to babble away about cakes and naked pensioners, Ronan was shaking his head with exasperation, and the police were climbing the ladder to the loft.

"We're going to need you to leave," I heard. I was happy about that.

I grabbed Maggie's arm and dragged her to the stairs. I looked over my shoulder and stage-whispered. "She has dementia."

Ronan groaned out loud before waving his arm furiously for me to leave. The policeman was simply frowning at us.

We left Ronan giving whatever details were needed to the policeman, and it was quite exciting to see three police cars in the lane. One chap was on his walkie-talkie ordering up a van, or so I thought I heard. I guessed they'd need to remove the plants and they were hardly likely to fit in one of the cars.

"Do you think we're in trouble?" Maggie said, with a worried expression as I helped her into the front seat of the Land Rover.

"Yes, I imagine they'll come by later to arrest you," I replied.

She gaped, and I laughed. "If you stop telling them you make cakes for the naked OAPs I think we'll be fine."

"Oh, Lizzie, I don't think I've laughed as much in years. Ronan sure needs to get that rod out of his arse," she said.

We were still chuckling, much to his disgust, when Ronan climbed behind the steering wheel. He didn't speak as we drove back.

"What's going to happen?" Maggie asked him as he parked up.

"They'll remove all the plants and then arrest Manuel, they said."

"If he decided to do a runner, where would he go?" I asked as I climbed out.

"I have no idea. I never really knew him, and I could fucking kick myself for that now."

"Ronan, this isn't your fault. And it was rather funny," I said, smiling at him and trying to lighten the mood a little.

He scowled at me. "I didn't think so. I think it's just another load of shit on an already loaded plate for me."

He walked into the house and Maggie and I stood still. "Is he okay, do you think?" she asked.

"I have no idea. Is he normally this…stiff?" I asked.

"No, well certainly not before…" Maggie didn't finish her sentence.

"Before I came here?" I asked, gently.

"I don't think it has anything to do with you, honestly. He's off, grieving; maybe it's finally hit him. He hasn't cried at all, Lizzie," Maggie said, concern lacing her words.

"Maybe. Anyway, we can't just stand out here."

Ronan was nowhere to be seen. I assumed he had headed back to the office. I wondered if the pressure was getting too much for him, and maybe I wasn't as much help as he was hoping. I decided to go and find him.

He wasn't in the estate office or the kennels. I looked in the washroom and the shed where he kept tractors and quad bikes. It was too chilly to take a walk around the gardens, so I headed back in and upstairs to find some layers. As I walked into my bedroom, I screeched.

Ronan walked out at the same time as I pushed the door open. "Why is this in the bedside drawer?" he asked, aggressively, waving around the photograph of him and Demi.

I was stumped as to what to say. "Why were you rifling around my drawer?" I said, regretting it immediately.

"It's *my* drawer, Lizzie. Please leave my things alone," he said, and then stomped from the room, not giving me a chance to respond.

In fact, he brushed past my shoulder like he would a man in a bar that had annoyed him. I stood, open-mouthed, watching him walk to his bedroom.

"How fucking dare you," I whispered.

My voice cracked, though. How on earth could I tell him how I ended up with the photograph? My cheeks coloured just at the thought. I wasn't sure what to do and was pleased to have the ping from my phone as a distraction. I walked to the bedside cabinet to see the drawer still open. There was nothing of mine in that drawer—my book and e-reader were on the top with my phone. I picked it up to see an email from the art dealer that Joe had introduced to me. He was looking forward to meeting us and was excited to see what we would bring.

After Ronan's tantrum, I wasn't sure it would be an 'us.'

The more I stood there, the more cross I became. I left the bedroom and walked down the hall to Ronan's. As I approached, my nerve failed me; more so when I glanced in through the crack of the door, and he was lying on the bed with the photograph on his chest. I wasn't sure if he was awake or not. I should have barged in and woken him. I should have told him what an arse he was being. I did neither of those things. I carried on down to the art room, and I packed the images I knew I would take to London the following day. Bollocks to Ronan, but I wasn't going to let Joe down.

I headed back to my room and packed my suitcase.

CHAPTER FOURTEEN

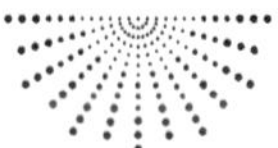

I had Charlie run me to the train station early the following morning. Ronan hadn't surfaced; he hadn't joined us for dinner the previous evening, either. He had dismissed Maggie when she'd taken him a snack and hot chocolate.

"I'm not running away. I genuinely have to get these pictures to the art dealer," I said to Maggie as she wrapped a scarf around my neck as if I were a child.

"But you have your suitcase," she said.

"Yes, I have stuff in there I need back home: my hairdryer, makeup and whatnots."

I was being honest. I didn't care that Ronan was being a prat; I wasn't running away early in the morning because I was upset, although I *was* still very upset. I'd googled the trains and preferred that method of travel to sitting in a hostile environment with him anyway. I had my books, I would buy some snacks, and I had pre-booked a first class seat. I could have flown, but I didn't relish the taxi fare from the airport *or* trying to work out which coach to get home.

"I'll call once I've arrived home," I said, having handed Maggie my mobile so she could plug in her number.

The old Land Rover rattled its way into town and the station.

"He doesnae mean any'hin by it, yer ken," Charlie said. I'd now gathered that he wasn't referring to *me* as ken. He simply meant 'you know'.

"That's the second time you've said that in his defence, Charlie." I felt I had a better grasp of his accent in the week I'd been in his company.

Charlie shrugged his shoulders. "He doesnae, that's all. He needs to grieve."

"I'm sure he does. Maybe you could tell him that?"

"It's the anniversary, yer ken?" Charlie said as he unloaded the suitcase.

"Anniversary?"

"Of her death…Demi…she died. Did he no' tell you that?"

No, he hadn't. It might explain why he was upset that I had her photograph, but it didn't explain why he felt the need to be so rude.

"He didn't tell me that. Still, it doesn't excuse how rude he was to me," I explained.

"No, he doesnae know how to express himself. It was his mother, see? She had all the expression and the boys? Well, they brought themselves up. Me and Mags, we didnae do a good job in that."

I reached across and patted his arm fondly. "Charlie, don't ever think that. If they had to bring themselves up, you two were the best people to have around for guidance. No one is to blame for rudeness other than the one offering it," I said.

Charlie smiled, toothlessly, as he handed me my suitcase.

I smiled back at him. "Thank you. Remind Maggie that I'll call and that I'll let Ronan know what happens with these pictures."

With a wave over his shoulder, Charlie left. I walked to the nearest Costa to grab a decent cup of coffee and some snacks, and then headed for my platform. I was quite excited to board the train, I hadn't ridden one in years. There were a couple of changes to navigate before my arrival in London, and the journey was estimated to take a little over eight hours, but it was comfortable, and I could relax.

I read, I slept on and off, and I drank too many cups of coffee and ate awful food from the trolley that came up and down the aisle pushed by a pleasant young girl. I was sure I'd end up with a dodgy belly, and that was the last thing I wanted on a train, but hunger took precedence. I took walks, mostly to the loo, which, for a train, was clean and roomy. The first class section was pretty empty. I saw the tops of two heads in the carriage; both looked to belong to men.

I ached when we finally pulled into Euston. My back was stiff from sitting so long, and I had a banging headache but put that down to too much coffee, although I suspected the eight hours of thoughts about Ronan had something to do with it too. I was actually looking forward to some quiet reflection in my flat when the taxi finally deposited me there.

Joe had texted, he wanted to come over for a catch-up, but I put him off until the following day. I asked him to accompany me to the art dealer, as I had no idea what to say or do and knew he could wing it way better than I could. That evening, I wanted to sink into my sofa with a bottle of wine, a Chinese takeout, and watch crap TV.

As I opened the front door, I was met by one of the downstairs neighbours. An elderly woman that I'd often smiled at, bade a good morning, but never taken the chance to get to know. I felt bad about that.

"Ah, Lizzie, there you are," she said as if she had been waiting for me.

"What can I do for you…?" I paused realising although she knew my name. I didn't know hers.

"It's Danny's cat. I don't suppose you have a key to his flat?" she asked.

I stared at her. "Danny's cat?"

"Yes, Pat. I have him in my flat, and I wondered if you had a key. I could pop him back home. He loves coming for a visit, but last time, when Danny was away, he never went home, and I wasn't worried because…well, Danny wasn't home, but I don't think I should be feeding him, should I?" she rambled on.

I frowned, trying to make sense of her words. "Can we back up just a little? When Danny was away, Pat stayed with you?" Danny had only been away once, and *I* was meant to be feeding Pat who, possibly, was stuffed…or maybe not.

"Yes, Danny didn't ask for me to look after Pat, but he climbs down the back of the building, and I have a little window open. He comes in regularly."

"How does he get out of Danny's flat?" I asked.

"I don't know, maybe Danny has a window open as well. Anyway, do you have a key or not? I know sometimes neighbours have keys. I can pop Pat back in the apartment before Danny gets home."

"I don't. I'm sorry. Is Danny not in?" I asked.

"No, I haven't heard anyone coming in. I'll hang on to him for a little longer. I've got a little cooked chicken he can finish off," she said with a broad smile.

I returned her smile. She hardly left the flat, and if Pat was a little comfort for her, then it was better he climbed out of Danny's than staying there alone all day. As I climbed the stairs to my floor, I started to laugh.

"Oh God," I whispered to myself as I remembered that I'd thought Danny was playing a prank with the stuffed cat.

"Hold the door," I heard, and I turned to see Danny rushing up the stairs with Pat in his arms.

I held the door so he could walk through. "You're back then?" he asked.

"No, this is a mirage or a hallucination," I said, chuckling.

"Ha ha. Anyway, it appears Pat has been cheating on me with Mrs Dingle downstairs."

"Is that her name?" I asked.

"No idea, but it seems to suit her, and she answers to it. Did you notice him getting out when you fed him?"

"No, I admit, I didn't see him much at all, to be honest. So, he could have been cheating on both of us with Mrs Dingle."

"Will you hold him for me while I check all the windows?"

I held up both hands, one showing a suitcase in it, and the other showing the picture tube.

He rolled his eyes. "After you've deposited those, obviously. I don't want to put him down in case he legs it. The cheeky fucker lets me think he's old and infirm. I might have to rename him Spider Cat."

We walked along to my door, which I opened. I left the suitcase and picture tube just inside my flat and then followed Danny to his door. He handed me Pat, who wriggled and stared at me with slitty eyes, obviously weighing me up, or blaming me for having to decamp to Mrs Dingle because I hadn't actually fed him beyond discovering the stuffed version. The look he gave, if he could talk, would be to inform that he was telling on me. I refused to look at him any more.

I followed Danny from room to room, which wasn't long since there were only four in total. It was in the bathroom that I noticed a small window in the shower that was propped open.

"Do you always leave that open?" I asked.

"Yes, because the extractor isn't man enough, and I worry about mould. I didn't think he'd be able to climb that high." Danny reached up to close it.

"You could just make sure the shower door is shut, I doubt he'll get over that. But, how far is the drop? Surely he would hurt himself," I said.

"I don't know. I've never been in the garden, have you?"

"No, to be honest."

We decided to take a look. I placed Pat on the sofa where he hissed at me before curling up. We left the flat and made our way down the stairs, all the while, Danny talked about the bloody cat. It was how wonderful Pat was, Pat this, Pat that, he gave an account of every day of the cat's life and a tally of how many animals Pat brought in as presents. I shuddered at the memory of the drawer of 'presents' minus their innards and awaiting stuffing. Perhaps Danny was so attached to Pat that he thought he'd make toys of his kills?

I remembered then that I thought Danny very odd.

I rushed down the remaining stairs and power-walked to the back door. It was locked, and I fumbled with my keys, wondering if I had one. I tried a couple, and eventually one opened it, so we walked into the communal garden. It was lovely, and I wondered why I'd never taken the time to sit on the patio in the metal furniture with a cup of tea or meet Mrs Dingle for a chat. I vowed to rectify those things. We looked up and calculated which was the bathroom window. Halfway down was a lintel that stood proud of the brick to create a ledge. Pat could have landed on that, and then if he jumped again, he'd reach a canopy over Mrs Dingle's living room window.

"Easy escape, but dangerous. Why don't you see if you can put in a cat flat somewhere?" I asked.

"I'm not staying here long enough, to be honest," Danny said, as we walked back inside.

"Oh, that's a shame," I replied, not knowing for one minute *why* I'd think it a shame seeing as I didn't like the guy.

"Yeah, it seems that I'm about to be made redundant." His tone of voice made me feel sorry for him.

"I'm sorry to hear that. What a nuisance, can you find another job locally?" I struggled to remember what he did for a living.

"Even if I did, the firm pay my rent. I'm not likely to get a job that will cover the rental for this place. I don't know yet what redundancy package I'm entitled to," he said, as we reached our floor.

"I'd have a word with Joe. Surely it would be better to have a constant lower rent than an empty property." I wasn't sure why I was trying to help. Danny had been nothing short of rude since we'd first met.

"Maybe. It's a nice place, and I get on with the neighbours," he said, with a wink.

I smiled back. "Well, mystery solved with Pat anyway. I'll see you around," I said, as I unlocked my front door.

I thought I heard him reply, and I was sure the word dinner was mentioned, but I pretended not to. I didn't want dinner with

Danny. In that half hour, he had been pleasant, and I had made a mistake about the prank stuffed cat, but he'd been rude on two other occasions, so I'd convinced myself.

I was still miffed over Ronan. I didn't want the distraction of Danny or Joe even. I was more than happy to wallow in my own pity for the evening. I also had a ton of washing to do, removal of the yeti coat I'd developed while in Scotland for warmth, and I was sure I would soon be sporting a monobrow.

I took a long bath, which resembled a dog clipping parlour by the time I'd gotten out—it took the same length of time to clean it as it had to soak in it—and I headed to the bedroom for some more pampering.

I moisturised, brushed my hair, plucked my eyebrows, and that one stray hair on my chin that refused to give up despite my constant plucking. You'd think, if you plucked enough, you'd manage to remove the follicle and the hair wouldn't grow back. Isn't that what happened to old ladies? I was sure that I read that somewhere. Or perhaps chin hair, or hair that appeared anywhere it shouldn't, was made of much sturdier stuff.

Take pubic hair, for example. I parted my legs and looked at the meagre offering covering my hooha. I gasped as I caught a stray grey.

"What the fuck…?" I grabbed the tweezers. That sucker wasn't staying, not that anyone had, or would be, looking at my hooha anytime soon. Still, it wasn't staying.

Once the offending stray grey was gone, I decided that perhaps a trim up was in order. I had a little electric trimmer specifically for hoohas that I'd bought years ago. I couldn't remember where, but I rifled through drawers until I found it. I propped one foot on the bed and gave myself a little shave. Except, I hadn't thought to put the guard on the blades. What should have been a little trim up ending up resembling a nineteen-fifties kid's haircut to get rid of lice. I had clumps of hair in places, bald in others. I had short bits, long bits, and bloody bits.

"Oh, fuck," I said aloud and wondered just how many times a day I said the F word.

I rushed into the bathroom and wet a flannel under the cold tap. I held it to my hooha and hoped it would stem the blood from nicked skin. I'd have to shave the lot off. I rubbed some shower gel, wincing as it stung the open wounds and used a Bic to give myself a Hollywood Hooha.

I began to chuckle. It was quite liberating to be hairless down there. I patted myself dry and then decided to look in the mirror. In my imagination, I wasn't fifty-years-old. I didn't feel it; I didn't think I acted it. I didn't believe I looked it until I saw my wrinkled old hooha. It hit me then: I'd missed hooha care off my daily moisturising regime. Not that I could recall ever being told to add it, of course. I checked my arms; I didn't have bingo wings or old lady spots. I didn't have that many wrinkles or saggy skin on the back of my hands.

But I did have baggy fanny flaps.

I grabbed some body moisturiser and read the back, wondering if it was okay for hoohas. It didn't say it wasn't, so I slathered some on. I'd overdose on moisturiser in the hopes my baggy flaps would tighten up a little.

Of course, I wasn't delusional enough to know I could reverse fifty years of neglect, but I was that woman who read every fashion magazine, knowing the skin couldn't absorb all the crap they recommended—we were not made of sponge and even if we were, we'd oversaturate one day—and try it. I had thousands of pounds worth of miracle creams in my bathroom cupboard.

I walked, a little bow-legged back to the bedroom and grabbed my fleecy PJs. I called for a takeaway and opened a bottle of wine while I waited. Twenty minutes later, I was dishing up noodles with sweet and sour chicken and salivating over *Outlander*.

I slept well that night. There was no tiptoeing to avoid frostbite to the soles of my feet, no wondering if the pipes had frozen or if there would be hot water for a bath or shower. I felt like I was back in civilization. I loved Scotland. I loved the house. I loved hot water on demand, heating, and take outs more.

CHAPTER FIFTEEN

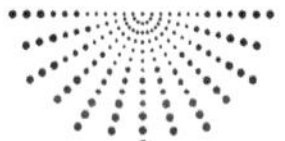

I hadn't heard from Ronan, and that disappointed me. He knew it was the day of the appointment and, okay, I could have hung around a little later to speak to him before I left for the station, but then I would have missed my train, so I convinced myself.

"Oh, look at you," Joe said, as I let him in the apartment.

I wore a cream suit with a black silk shirt. I thought a professional approach would be needed. Joe was in jeans and a sloppy T-shirt that didn't smell too fresh.

"Did you go home last night?" I asked, sniffing him.

He cringed. "No, does it show?"

I snorted. "Yes, you stink. There's some deodorant in the bathroom. Go and spray some over you."

He laughed as he did just that.

We left the apartment, and I hailed a taxi. Joe had the address for an exclusive art gallery in Soho.

"So, what happened in Scotland?" he asked.

"First, I'm annoyed that you and Ronan had a conversation about me, without including me in that. I thought he was asking me because he liked me, not because you had told him I might be good staff," I said.

"*Good staff?*"

I waved an annoyed hand. "Staff, great at doing admin, whatever it was you said."

Joe turned a little diva on me. "I'll tell you what I said. Ronan was worrying about trying to do it all himself. I said he should speak to you because you are brilliant at organisation, that's all. I thought if the two of you worked together, it might spark something."

I hummed, not entirely convinced. I then told him most of what happened, right to the point of leaving.

"Hold on, he was doing what?" Joe asked, stifling a laugh.

"Wanking, and I had to hide at the foot of the bed with the bloody photograph of his dead best love."

"Oh, my God," he said. The taxi driver frowned at me in the rear view mirror.

"What would you have done?" I asked the driver. If he wanted to listen in, he could add his opinion.

"Same as you, love. Except I might have left the photograph there and when he asked who covered him over, deny all knowledge of it. He would think he did it when he was drunk."

"Yes, well, I didn't think that much about it," I snapped, annoyed I hadn't done just that.

"You just wanted to see his willy," Joe said. Both he and the taxi driver convulsed in laughter.

"You watch the road, and no, I didn't want to see his *willy.*" I scoffed. "Who uses that word nowadays, anyway?"

"So have you spoken to him at all?" Joe asked.

"No, he lost his phone, remember? He had to get a new number, and I don't have it."

"And he won't have yours, either, I bet," Joe added.

I hadn't thought about that. "I have Maggie's, so once we've seen this art chap, I'll call her." I settled back into my seat while we fought the mid-morning traffic.

❧

The stark white walls, floor, and ceiling were blinding and the macabre images of *Old woman in throes of death,* as the label claimed, did nothing to enhance the premises. I wasn't sure whether the pile of screwed up paper in the corner was meant to be an exhibit or something waiting to go in the bin. A gentleman held a phone to his ear, and he waved us over with a beaming smile as he finished his call.

When he finally did, he greeted us. "Joe, my friend, how are you? And this must be Lizzie?" he asked.

He held me at arm's length as one would a child they hadn't seen in ten years. Then he kissed both cheeks. I had an urge to wipe where he'd left slobber and hoped he'd hurry up and do the same to Joe. I grabbed a tissue from my bag in preparation.

As he turned to Joe, I dabbed at my face, but the stickiness of his lips stayed. I was convinced he must have had some gloss or at least a balm coating his lips.

"Lizzie, this is Dave," Joe said, since Dave hadn't introduced himself.

The man with the tweed suit, waistcoat, and cravat looked the least like a Dave. I'd have expected a Henry as his name.

"So, you have something for me to look at?" he asked, eagerly getting to the point.

I handed him the tube, and he walked to what resembled a pasting table. He rolled out the two pictures I'd brought. One was a photograph, the other a painting. He used weights to hold down the corners, mumbling about them being rolled up. I glanced at Joe, who wagged his finger in a mock *telling off.*

He hummed, arrhed, walked around, paused with his finger on his lips, and walked some more. Walked away, returned, cocked his head as if a different angle might produce a different image. He peered close and then stepped back. The whole process was done in silence and must have taken a good ten minutes. Eventually, he turned to Joe and smiled. Joe pointed to me.

"I love them, Lizzie," he said, finally turning to address me.

"That's great to hear," I replied, now stumped because I had no idea what to say next.

"Would you exhibit with a view to selling them?" Joe asked. I praised Joe in my head.

"I would like to, yes. Would the artist consent to an opening?"

"She's dead—"

Before I could finish my sentence, he interrupted. "Oh, that's even better."

I gaped at him.

"I didn't mean that to sound so cold, but buyers love a dead artist," he added, making his initial statement sound even worse.

"I'm sure Lizzie, and I will attend on her behalf. Now, how will this work?" Joe asked.

Dave went on to explain that he'd have a brochure made, at our expense, of course, he'd expect ten images to display and that he would take forty per cent of the sale.

"That's too much," I said, not knowing if it was or not. "Thirty per cent and you cover the brochure costs."

He placed two fingers against his sticky lips and tapped as if in deep thought. I sighed. I was an ardent shopper, and I knew the negotiation tactics he was attempting to employ.

He removed the fingers from his lips and held out his hand. "Deal," he said. I was reluctant to take his hand but thought it rude not to, so afterwards I discretely wiped the stickiness away.

"Fantastic," Joe added. I wasn't sure it was a word I'd use. We needed Ronan's permission before any of it happened.

"What price do you think you could achieve?" I asked.

We were back to the sticky lip fingering, the staring, walking around, and deep breaths.

"That photograph should fetch around fifteen hundred to two thousand pounds. The painting? A little more. I'd like to think we could get about five thousand for that. We have to remember, this is an unknown artist, but we have the fact she's dead, so there will be no more," he said.

Again, I had no idea if that was a good estimation or not, but I tried not to show any excitement, the photograph was only A4 sized, and the ones back at the house were larger.

"I'm going to need to check my diary, but if we're to proceed, I'll need those other paintings and photographs for framing, and maybe cleaning…" he rambled on, turning his attention back to Joe. "Two weeks good for you?" he asked, and I was finally brought back into the conversation.

"You're asking if you could have ten of those in two weeks?" I repeated to be sure that was what he had said.

“Yes, two weeks. Then we’ll organise the opening for a month after. I’ll confirm available dates,” he said.

I nodded, trying to appear like I knew what was going on. “That sounds fine. I look forward to hearing from you.”

After asking for a receipt and receiving a surprised look from Dave, Joe and I left the two pictures with him and, with the receipt, started to walk to a taxi rank.

“Well, that went great. Can you believe that shit is worth that kind of money?” Joe asked as we arrived.

We climbed into a cab and gave an address for an Italian restaurant we liked. A bottle of prosecco and some lunch was required.

“Maybe we should have touted the pictures around. He seemed too keen,” I said.

“Yes, but how many pictures are there? You said there were loads, so we sell this lot, and that might create a massive demand for Ronan to be able to sell them direct.”

Joe wasn’t just a pretty face. “I’ll email him all that when we get the dates,” I said.

“Surely you’ll see him before that, won’t you?”

“I don’t know. He’s not the easiest of person to work with, to be honest, and he’s so up and down at the moment. I think he needs to take some time to grieve for his loss before tackling the mess that estate is in.”

It was a massive cop-out, I knew, but it was an excuse I was sticking with, and I was actually proud of myself for coming up with it off the cuff. The truth was that I had no idea what to do. I liked Ronan, more than just a friend, and that was never going to be reciprocated. Perhaps I needed to get used to that before I returned.

"Anyway, you'll never guess what I discovered last night," I said, and then went on to tell Joe about Pat the cat and Danny being made redundant.

"Oh my God, you could have starved Pat if Mrs Dingle hadn't fed him. And there's not much I can do with the rent—it's what the owner wants to charge. Why are you so concerned about him all of a sudden?"

"I'm not. I feel bad about Pat and who wouldn't feel bad for someone about to lose their job?"

"Not me. Now, over lunch I have some amazing properties for you to look at. I forgot to email the details to you."

"You're not that much of an arsehole, so stop pretending to be," I said.

Joe laughed as we left the taxi, and we walked arm in arm into the bistro.

We celebrated with a bottle of prosecco and ate a lovely lunch of seared prawns in a lemon and garlic sauce—delicious and messy. Joe then brought up his emails on his phone to show me two properties he'd found in Kent. I found it tough to read all the details on such a small screen, but I loved both.

"Can you make appointments to view them?" I asked.

"Of course. They're being sold by someone I know, so I'm hoping that connection will go in our favour. She knows that I'll be aware of the exact value and what she's earning out of it."

"Lovely. I'm quite keen to find somewhere permanent and get my things out of storage. Those fees are building up."

"I can organise that tomorrow if you like. It's the only free day I have for a couple of weeks."

I nodded as I took a mouthful of prawn. As much as I'd loved the flat, I was keen to have my own place, to settle and start to rebuild my life.

Later that evening, I texted Maggie and asked for an email address for Ronan. I told her that it had been a success at the gallery and that I'd speak to her soon. She replied pretty quickly, and I wondered if Ronan had been with her when she received my text. I wasn't sure she'd know his email address off the top of her head.

I typed up all that had happened, keeping it straight to the point. I did ask how he was, and I left it that he would confirm if he wanted to go ahead and that perhaps he might like to select the photographs and paintings. I was happy to receive them if he wanted to courier them down. I went to bed waiting for a reply from him.

CHAPTER SIXTEEN

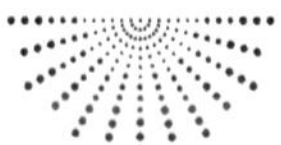

Joe texted me to say he was outside. It was a rare day that he drove a car even though he had two stored in a garage that he paid an extortionate rent on around the corner. That day he'd brought the mini. I loved the little red car. It was a classic Mini Cooper, and he'd had a plan to race it through Italy once. The door creaked when I opened it, and I slid onto the hard leather seat, then leaned over and gave Joe a kiss to his cheek.

"I love this car. You will leave it to me when you die, won't you?" I asked.

"Well, I don't plan on dying anytime soon, and since we're the same age, there's nothing to say you won't go before me," he said with a smirk and looking slightly distracted as he navigated into the London traffic.

From where we were, getting to the Blackwall Tunnel would be the longest part of the journey. It wasn't miles in distance to hit Kent; it was just the volume of traffic on roads barely capable of containing it that slowed us up. Eventually, we hit the motorway, and the scenery started to change from prison-grey coloured buildings to green and brown fields.

"I think I've got Mum to agree to a home. I've found a wonderful one in Sevenoaks that I honestly believe she'll love," Joe said.

"How is she doing?" I felt guilty for not keeping up on her health.

"She's deteriorating, but she still knows who I am. I just hope she has a heart attack or a massive stroke before the dementia gets too bad. I'd hate for her not to recognise me."

I understood where he was coming from. My nan had dementia, and it used to kill my mum whenever we visited, and she'd have to explain who she was each time. I reached over and squeezed his hand.

"Where are we off to first?" I asked as I turned the heating up a little.

"The three-bed cottage in Halfmead. It's not too far from a motorway, and you're also close to the international station. You can go one way for London or the other to Paris and beyond," he said, with a laugh. I wasn't sure what was funny.

It was another half an hour before we turned into a country lane with high banks and trees either side. We continued down this lane slowly.

"It should, if the satnav is right, be on our left somewhere," Joe said. "Here." He slammed on the brakes causing me to jolt forward.

There was a low brick wall and on one column, before a wooden gate, was a small plaque with the house name. Joe must have had amazing eyes, the plaque was so worn, even parked beside it, it wasn't clear.

"Is someone going to meet us?" I asked.

"Yes, although I suspect they're not here yet. We're about ten minutes early. Go and open the gate," he said.

"Won't the owners be here?"

"No, it's vacant. A probate sale."

"No one died here, did they?" I asked.

"Not that I'm aware of, now get out and open the gate. If a tractor comes, I'll be blocking the road."

I opened the car door and looked out; I didn't want to step in a puddle of mud. I tested the ground and finding it firm enough, I climbed from the car with a huff. Those low down seats weren't that easy to get out of. I opened the wooden gate and waited until Joe drove in. I left it open and walked the driveway to the cottage. I stopped about halfway and looked. It was chocolate box and, from the outside anyway, perfect. The cottage was rendered cream with wooden sash windows that I knew would need replacing and a thatched roof. On top of the roof was the tradesman's mark, a fox chasing a rabbit. The straw looked patchy in places and obviously due for renewal.

Joe climbed from the car. "What do you think?" he called out.

I sighed dreamily. "It's lovely, Joe. Needs some work, but beautiful."

I walked back to the car and opened the door to grab my jacket and put it on before we walked around the side of the property. To the rear, there was a stone patio and then lawn. The garden was large and contained a handful of fruit trees. Beyond the garden were acres and acres of farmland. To one side was more farmland and to the other, the garden of the neighbouring property, although the property itself was shielded by trees.

We peered through the kitchen window. "It's a renovation project, obviously," Joe said.

"Obviously," I replied, staring at a range of units that must have dated from the nineteen-fifties. There was a dresser, painted white with duck egg blue doors, and I remembered a similar one standing in my nan's kitchen.

I did love the size of the garden. Having lived in London all my life, garden space was at a premium, and although I had a garden when I lived in the marital home, it was more a courtyard. I stared down towards the bottom where the range of fruit trees stood, wondering if I'd need a ride on mower. Or maybe a gardener.

The sound of a car heading up the driveway prompted us to walk back to the front of the property. A woman in heels that immediately sunk into the ground climbed from a smart and impractical white sports car.

"Bollocks," she said, then looked up and smiled at us. "Sorry, be with you in a mo." She reached into the car and pulled out some wellies, slipped them on, and then joined us.

"Joe, and you must be Lizzie?" she said, reaching out with her hand.

I shook it and was pleased that she addressed me first. It was clear that although Joe and Judy, as she introduced herself as, knew each other professionally, they didn't have a friendship. Joe in business mode always made me smile. Even his tone of voice was different.

"Did you manage to look out back?" she asked.

"Only briefly, we got here just a few minutes ago ourselves," I replied.

"Let's get in, shall we? Joe, did I explain it was a probate sale?" she asked, and then a conversation ensued between them about the complications of such things. All I knew was that it meant someone had died, and the 'estate' was selling the property.

Judy produced a large old-fashioned key, and after a little jiggle and a kick to the front door, it opened. We were in a fairly large square hallway with the most wonderful ceramic tiled floor. An open staircase was to one side, and there were three doors off.

"We have a downstairs loo, but, as you can guess, there's a fair bit of renovation to do here. Joe told me that you'd be up for a project." I wasn't sure where Joe had gotten that information.

"We have a nice sized living room with open fire and through the end door, the kitchen."

We walked into the living room first, and I fell in love. Like the cottage in Scotland, this had beams across the wall and ceiling, a brick chimney with a grate and hearth. Although someone had put shelves in the alcoves, I could already picture the room stripped of the ghastly wallpaper, the brickwork cleaned, and the fire roaring.

"Is there any other form of heating?" I asked, not noticing a radiator.

"No, putting that in and updating the electrics would probably be the first investments I'd make. The lady that lived here had done so her whole life. There's a lot of history in these beams."

"Is the house listed?" Joe asked.

"No, thankfully, so there is a huge amount of potential, and of course, the price does reflect the level of work required."

I popped my head into the downstairs loo and was surprised at the size. It wasn't as awful as I was expecting; the traditional old lady style avocado coloured toilet and sink were still in place, and, hopefully, useable. The kitchen was larger than I'd first glimpsed with another open fireplace. I could imagine stylish new units with a seating area at one end of the room. I also thought it might be possible to knock right the way through and make it one very large space. The fact that I was planning suggested I was interested, and I chuckled. I didn't want to get ahead of myself.

Upstairs there were three bedrooms and a bathroom, which obviously came from the same shop as the avocado loo downstairs. The walls were a dirty green, and it had a carpet that I didn't want to walk on, but it wasn't a bad size. There were two okay-sized bedrooms and one small.

Judy said, "I'd consider, and I think it would give more value, in making this a two bedroomed with en-suite to both and a dressing room to the main bedroom."

"I thought it was cause for shooting to get rid of a bedroom," I said, laughing at Joe's wide eyes. In London, a box room was worth thousands, if not tens of thousands, in value.

"Out here, it wouldn't reduce the value at all. Of course, the more bedrooms you have, the better, but you should be looking to resell this to potentially management-level London workers who have a short drive to the fast track train. They don't care about an empty room; they want the mod cons."

She had a point. More people were moving from London into its neighbouring counties and with a train just a short drive away that would have me in London in under twenty minutes. What she was saying made sense.

Judy added, "Of course, if you wanted to, you could extend. If I were buying this house to live in any length of time, I certainly would."

"Lots of potential," I said, as I made my way back down.

We didn't bother with the backdoor; it appeared that Judy didn't have a key, so we walked around the side.

"Not only do you have this, but the field beyond also belongs to this property. However, it has been, and continues to be rented out to the local farmer. It provides a small annual income, but more importantly, you get your logs for free, and he's a brilliant handyman," she said. "Easy on the eye as well," she added, with a chuckle.

I rammed my elbow into Joe's side to shut him up in advance of any cougar comments.

"I like it. I'm not sure about the level of work needed. But... there's something about this property. It reminds me of one I visited in Scotland recently," I said.

We decided to follow Judy to the second property, which was the other end of the village. We drove through the centre with its green, church, and importantly, a pub. There were a couple of local shops, a butcher and a baker, and I thought I saw a small café.

"This is gorgeous," Joe said. "And an hour's drive from me! I could come for weekends. Imagine sitting on the green with a pint watching the cricket."

"I don't like cricket *or* pints, but yes to weekends and gin and tonics. So, honestly, what did you think of that property?"

"It's overpriced, and Judy knows that. The problem with a probate sale is if we're only just out of probate the owners want the most they can get, as time goes on, the prices tend to drop because they just want their money. It needs a good one hundred thousand spent on it, and I'm not convinced that you'll make much back if you sold within three years. I also don't go along with what she said about getting rid of a bedroom. It has potential, for sure, but we'd need at least eighty grand off that price. I think we'll see that still for sale in six months time."

The second property we approached was, again, set back from the road but completely different.

"Wow," I said, as we came to a stop.

In front of me was a black wooden barn conversion. The central portion of the barn was floor-to-ceiling glass on both floors, and I spotted a galleried landing with a couple of sofa's looking down on us. Excitement bubbled inside me.

We followed Judy into the central hallway, and I looked up at the eaves and those beams that I was beginning to yearn for. To one side was the living room, and I was thrilled to see an open fire. There was a central staircase and to the other side, the downstairs loo and smaller living room—the snug as Judy called it. We walked through the hallway to the kitchen diner. The back of the house opened up to a terrace via folding doors. I tried to keep my excitement in check. I didn't want to tip Judy off to how much I loved the property. All thoughts of the renovation project went out the window. The barn was perfectly to my taste with its off-white painted walls, oak beams, stone floor, and modern kitchen and bathrooms.

"Heating?" I said, not seeing any radiators, again.

"Under floor," Judy said. I slipped off a shoe to feel the warmth.

The upstairs had the three required bedrooms, one master with an en-suite and dressing room, and a family bathroom. I could move straight in. I walked around on my own, leaving Joe and Judy talking shop. For the second time since I'd become single, I felt positive about something. And I felt at home.

There was a lovely garden beyond the terrace, and like the previous property, fields to all three sides.

"How much is this one?" I asked.

"Five hundred and sixty-five," Judy replied.

"Any movement on that?" Joe asked. I wasn't sure that I wanted to negotiate. I would have gotten my bank to transfer the money that day if I could.

"There is, it's a divorce," she said. "The wife doesn't want to leave, but he wants the money." She sighed and shrugged her shoulder as if it was an inconvenience. I bristled.

"Is she getting half of this?" I asked.

Judy shook her head. "I have no idea."

"Do you think you could ask her to speak with me?" I asked.

Judy frowned, and Joe sighed, knowing exactly what I wanted to know.

"I love this property, it's perfect, but before I make an offer I'd like to speak to the owner," I said.

Judy pulled her mobile from her pocket and dialled. When the call was answered she explained that a potential buyer wanted to ask a question. I guessed she'd received the required permission because she handed the phone to me. I took it and walked away for privacy.

"Hi, my name is Lizzie, and I wanted to say, I love your home and, being newly divorced myself, I understand how hard this is for you."

"Thank you. I appreciate that. I can't stay, and I can't buy him out, but the one thing I did say to Judy is only the best person can buy the house. I guess that's pretty dumb really," she said, with a chuckle.

"Do you mind if I ask you a really personal question?"

"I guess that depends what you're about to ask," she replied.

"Are you getting half of the equity from this sale or half of everything? I guess that's what I want to know." It was a super cheeky question but important to me.

She hesitated before answering. "He has agreed to give me three quarters of the property and half of all joint assets. I put my heart into converting that barn, and he recognises that. I also have to house his child."

"Thank you for your honesty. I'm going to offer the full asking price," I said. She didn't answer, but I heard a sharp intake of breath.

She thanked me in a voice that cracked with emotion. I said my goodbye and was sure that we would meet before everything was finalised. I'd want a second visit to measure up for *things*. I walked back to Joe and Judy and handed her the mobile.

"Full asking price, but I also want a quick turnaround," I informed her.

"Lizzie—" I knew that Joe would caution me and want to get a better price, but I could afford it, and I wanted to help that woman.

I held up my hand. "Full asking price. I'm a cash buyer, and I'll instruct my lawyer this afternoon to get cracking."

Judy tried to conceal her joy, and Joe was shaking his head. "Lizzie, this house, as Judy knows, is overpriced by about fifty thousand," he said. He would have done his research, of course.

"That may well be the case, but that's my offer. Shall we decide which bedroom is yours when you visit?"

Judy walked out to her car to call her office, and we toured the barn again. The more time I spent in there, the more settled I felt. I could physically feel the weight being removed from my shoulders, the frown lines starting to ease out.

I couldn't move the smile from face. "I love it here, Joe. I feel totally at home, and I don't even have a thing of mine around me."

"I know how you feel. It just has that *something* when you walk in, doesn't it?"

I nodded and actually felt sad when it was time for us to leave. I didn't want to push the owner out, but I did want a quick turnaround.

Before we left, I gripped Joe's arm. "Oh my God, Joe. I just bought my very first house!" I wanted to do a dance and clap my hands. I wanted to run from room to room and plan where my furniture would go. "We can't stay here any longer really, can we?" I asked.

Joe laughed and threaded his arm through mine. "Let's go and visit the local pub," he said.

We left Judy, who promised to email me later that day, and drove to the pub. It was midweek and midday. The pub was empty save for two elderly gentlemen who nodded as we walked in. They sat on stools at the bar and beside them, on a third stool, was a dog.

While I had a large glass of wine, Joe toasted me with a pint of Coke. We chatted about the house and my impulse decision. I had no idea about the area, but I wasn't far from a motorway or train station. I'd google when I got home…I felt like I was betraying the barn when I thought of the flat as home.

"Have you heard from Ronan?" Joe asked. I was thankful for the sip of wine I'd just taken as I shook my head. I didn't want to talk about him.

I still hadn't received a reply to the email I'd sent, and I was beginning to get pissed off. Maggie had texted a couple of times, asking how I was and when I was returning. She made me laugh with anecdotes of saggy tits and her husband, limp dick. It seemed that they might have been charged with keeping the art meeting going. They had set up a 'clean up' party, Maggie said. With Charlie's help, they were *tarting up* the glamping area. Saggy tits—and I really should have stopped calling her that—was looking forward to my return as well, according to Maggie.

"So, everyone is missing me, except him," I said, breaking my vow not to talk about him.

Joe's gaze was filled with pity. "I don't know what to say. I wish I hadn't recommended you to help him, but I thought he really liked you and it would be a good opportunity to spend time together."

I sighed. "I don't want you to feel bad. I'm pissed off at his silence, but I also understand his grief. I've been there. I'm wondering if I'm just an easy target, Joe." I took a sip of my wine as a wave of sadness washed over me.

"You're not, Lizzie, and we're not having a pity party here, okay?"

Joe wasn't necessarily one who dealt well with emotion. It was often because he held himself so tightly, protecting his heart like a suit of armour, that when someone close had a flip out, he didn't cope.

"Anyway, we need to get back," I said, draining my wine.

Joe smiled, and I was sure it was because he was pleased I was dropping the subject. I guessed it made him feel awkward.

We chatted on the way back about the barn, how excited I was, and the possible art exhibition. If Ronan didn't reply, I'd have to get Maggie to deal with it, assuming he would still want to sell the art, of course.

I waved to Joe after he'd dropped me off, with a promise to let him know what Judy said when she made contact.

"Hi. You look happy today," I heard. Danny came through the main front door just behind me.

"I just bought a house, well, a barn conversion in Kent," I said, still excited, but wishing I hadn't told him. I didn't want him to know too much of my personal business.

"That sounds great. I've always fancied a conversion of some sort. You'll have to invite me over for dinner when you move in," he said, opening the stairwell door.

I stood, expecting him to let me walk through first, but we collided as he barged through.

"Excuse me," I said, obviously not sarcastic enough when he smiled in return.

Danny walked up the stairs in front of me, as there wasn't the room to walk side by side, not that I would have wanted to. I had to admit to myself, despite his crass and rude manner, he did have a nice bum. Tight buttocks in tight jeans wiggled in front of me as he took each step.

"How's Pat?" I asked, I wasn't remotely interested in the pest; it was more for something to say.

"Ah, he's not too well. I dread the day he dies, to be honest. I've had him years."

"Be a shame, I guess."

He looked over his shoulder at me. "You might like to take him with you to your new barn, Lizzie. He'll be great at getting rid of the mice." I wished he would just hurry up the stairs.

I gave a snide smile. "I'm a dog person myself. I also don't intend to have mice."

"That's a shame. I'm not sure what's going to happen to Pat if I have to move."

For someone who was so much in love with his cat, he seemed quick to try to palm him off. "What about Mrs Dingle? She'd love him," I offered as we reached the top.

"I could speak to her, I guess." As before, he pushed through the door in front of me, this time letting it slam in my face. He didn't even say goodbye as he opened his flat door and walked in. I heard him call Pat as he shut it behind him.

"What a prick," I said, to myself of course.

I picked up the mail the postman had shoved through the letterbox and marvelled that he'd bothered to walk the stairs. Often he just threw it on the floor in the main hall. It contained a couple of bills, some junk mail, and a handwritten envelope. I recognised the handwriting and left it on the hall table. I wasn't sure that I wanted to read what it said. My ex-husband had my mobile number, if it was important, he could call, and I suspected it was nothing more than a new address card. I sat at the kitchen table and laid the bills to one side. Instead, while I waited for the kettle to boil, I flipped through the junk mail.

I chuckled as something caught my eye. It was a rubber slimming suit, similar to a wet suit but designed to make you sweat off the pounds. The accolades were amazing. One woman had lost half her original body weight in the catsuit. I left the junk mail on the table with the bills and made my tea. I checked my phone regularly for any communication from either Ronan or Judy. I received neither, but I had a text from Maggie:

Just checking in. Charlie had a fun day with Saggy Tits, and he made a list of repairs for the cottages. They are going up for rental. We are interviewing for a new estate manager next week. Hopefully, you'll get to meet him as well. Mags xx

I sighed and giggled at the same time. We'd have to stop calling Saggy Tits that and find out her name. She was a nice old dear, and it was pretty insulting of us, even if we did mean it with fondness. I felt a pang of sadness at Maggie's text. I missed her, and even Charlie if I was honest, and I'd only really known them a short while. I missed Ronan, but I couldn't get past how horrible he'd made me feel. My ego was bruised enough; I didn't need his kicking me to the kerb added to that. I texted back:

Hey, Mags, great to hear from you. All good here, I bought a house! I'm so excited. I'll send you some pictures. I did email Ronan, but I haven't heard back. Maybe you could ask him what he wants to do about the exhibition? If he doesn't want to go ahead, I really need to let Dave know. I'm glad Charlie had a good day, and we need to find out Saggy Tits' real name! Will speak soon. Xx

I didn't mention anything about returning to Scotland. I wasn't sure if I'd be welcome if I just turned up. It was up to Ronan what happened next.

CHAPTER SEVENTEEN

I surveyed the coffee table and giggled. One empty bottle of wine and another slowly joining it were sat side by side. It was a nice wine that I'd popped out earlier to buy from a local convenience store known for its bin-ends at reasonable prices. I hadn't eaten, that was the problem. It had been two days since I'd sent the text message to Maggie. I'd had replies from Judy that I'd passed on to my solicitor, but nothing from Ronan.

"Aw, fuck him," I said, waving my half-full glass around.

Next to the wine was a parcel that I was yet to open. I hadn't told anyone about the contents for fear of being called out as the sucker that I clearly was. I had practised what I'd say; I'd simply repeat some of the accolades and pretend to know the lady that lost half her body weight. I chuckled again as I placed the glass on the table.

I picked up the box and walked to the bedroom. I slowly stripped off—the slowness was so I didn't topple over—and unpacked the rubber catsuit, as I'd renamed it, from the box. I could do with losing a few pounds, and if it was as easy as sitting in a rubber suit while watching the telly, I was up for that. It saved the embarrassment of the gym or the blasted Pilates class that I'd never returned to.

I made sure to pee, just in case, and I stood naked as I read the instructions. I was to put the suit on, obviously, for an hour a day and carry on as normal.

As normal!

I guessed I could do my housework, but unless I could fit clothes over the top, there was no *carrying on as normal* in a rubber catsuit.

If I thought getting Spanx on was hard enough, the suit topped that. I tugged and folded, rolled and grunted with exertion. After twenty minutes I got the suit to my waist. Already I could feel my legs pulsing and was worried the circulation was cut off.

I decided talcum powder would aid getting it over my already perspiring chest. A plume of talc wafted around me as I squirted. I was sure some actually hit my skin, but with my wine goggles on, I wasn't sure. Everything around was a haze anyway. However, the top part of the suit slid up. I then had to reach around the back to pull on the piece of material attached to the zip. At the point the zip reached my neck the bloody piece of material came away in my hand. I threw it down and shrugged, not for one minute understanding the consequence of that.

When I unpacked the hood with his slits for eyes and nose, and a perfect circle cut out for my mouth, I began to wonder what on earth I'd bought. I creaked as I moved, the tightness of the suit made my arms hang away from my body, and I walked as if I'd pissed myself.

"I just have to watch a movie for an hour," I said aloud.

A rubber catsuit on a leather sofa, more specifically, the *noises* that were produced as I tried to sit and get comfortable made me howl once again. With tears running down my cheeks, I grabbed my phone to take a selfie.

Joe, look! I bought this fat suit thing. It will make me sweat off pounds. Don't I look cool? Ha ha ha

I deleted the text before I sent it, realising, even through the wine fuzzed brain, it was a stupid idea. Joe would more than surely show the image to everyone he knew. I loved him, but I didn't trust him.

I wasn't sure how long I'd sat. I'd watched part of a movie, and when the commercials started, I realised how hot I felt. My cheeks were burning, and I began to feel very uncomfortable. Not that I'd ever had a panic attack in the past, but I could feel my heart racing, and I became agitated. I stood and tried to pull the rubber away from my throat. It moved a little but not enough to waft any air down. I reached around my neck to the zipper, and although I could touch it, I couldn't push it down, and my arms were just not flexible enough to reach *up* my back to grab it.

"Oh fuck," I whispered, anxiously. I looked around the room hoping that a hook on a stick would miraculously materialise.

I had thought that if I took a shower it might loosen it, but then images of a shrink-wrapped piece of meat came to mind. What if the hot water caused it to tighten? A cold shower then, at least it would cool me down. It did the opposite. With my head freezing, my body temperature was creeping up. I grabbed a towel and tried to dry myself off.

It appeared that water was causing the catsuit to shrink, or my body was starting to swell under the pressure. A thought popped into my head: if the swelling had nowhere to go, I'd soon have feet the size of dinner plates or cheeks like a hamster storing food. I started to laugh, and then the worst thing happened. I needed to pee, *really* bad.

I managed that cross-legged walk back to the bathroom with an idea of what to do. A wine-fuelled idea that was genius. I grabbed a pair of scissors and cut a hole between my legs taking great care to suck in as much as I could to avoid a nasty nip on the hooha.

I fell on the toilet and the relief of being able to pee made me sigh. The trouble was, when I fell on to the loo, I also dropped the scissors behind it. Even without the restriction of the suit, I would never be able to angle myself enough to reach behind. Whoever had designed the bathroom had never had to use it, clearly. The loo was positioned between a wall and the sink unit. There was barely enough room to get a mop around the back, let alone my arm.

"I need help," I said.

Had I not drunk nearly two bottles of wine, I would have managed the situation, and I most certainly would not have been considering walking from the bathroom, grabbing a towel to put around my waist and cover my exposed bald hooha, then heading to my front door. I knew Danny was home because I'd spied him through my spy hole when he'd returned earlier. I didn't like him, and I knew he'd make fun of me, but all I needed was someone to lower the zipper.

I froze as I heard a knock on my door. It wasn't as if I could even check my watch for the time—it was stuck up my arm and under the rubber sleeve. I knew it was late, though. I put my eye to the spy hole, and all I could see were flowers.

"Who's there?" I called out.

I highly doubted it was Danny, he'd never have the foresight to present flowers for any reason, and I sort of hoped it might be Mrs Dingle, not that she had any reason to bring me flowers, either.

"Lizzie, can you open the door? It's me, Ronan. I'm…can you open the door?"

I froze, for a second time, and the panic set in. What was he doing at my apartment door with flowers at that time of night?

I didn't have a choice. "Ronan, I need help," I called out.

"Lizzie? What's wrong? Open the door," he shouted with an extremely worried edge to his voice, before pounding on it.

I grabbed the key to unlock and pulled back the bolts. As I pulled, he pushed, and I tumbled backwards landing on my arse. Thank fuck the towel stayed put.

"What the…?"

I held out my hand. "Don't laugh at me." The suit was so tight, I thought I'd never get up from the floor.

His smirk was getting broader. "What are you wearing?" he said.

I started to cry. "It's supposed to make me lose weight, but I drank wine, and then I got stuck and I dropped the scissors, and you've been so fucking horrible because you didn't know that you were wanking and all I did was try to cover you over when the photograph fell…"

He frowned and shook his head. "Lizzie, pause, take a breath. I got *some* of that, some I hope I misheard. First, we need to get you out of your…gimp suit…you look like you're about to explode."

I sniffed back the snot leaking from my nostrils. "Don't take the piss out of me."

I was an ugly crier, always had been. In fifty years, I could never just daintily dab the corner of my eye and have perfect makeup left. Oh, no. I had mascara dripping off my chin, my lips and eyelids would be swollen, my nose would be red and running, and if I really got going, got to the wailing stage, I'd make faces as if someone had shoved a colonoscopy tube up my arse without lubricant or warning.

"Hey, Lizzie. I'm so sorry. Let's get you out of this and then we can talk," he said, gently. He turned me around and tugged on the zip. It was firmly stuck, glued in place by the mush that had once been talc and sweat.

"The scissors fell down the back of the loo, and I can't reach them," I said, still sniffing and hiccupping.

Ronan walked into the kitchen and returned with a knife. I screwed my eyes closed in preparation for being massacred while he cut down the line of the zip. As the garment parted, and my body fell into its natural size, I sighed. It was better than the tight-bra-off-after-tits-had-been-in-scaffold-all-day sigh. It was better than the got-the-fucking-Spanx-bodysuit-off sigh.

"What is that?" Ronan asked, sniffing his hands.

I looked down to see white gunge all over me. It resembled… No, I wasn't going there.

"Talcum powder," I said, and then rushed into the bathroom. I managed to get the suit off to just below my arse.

I lowered the loo lid and sat, no matter what I did, I couldn't peel the fucking legs from my skin.

I wanted to sob again. "Ronan," I called out sounding completely defeated.

"Yes?"

"I need help."

I grabbed the nearest towel and wrapped it around my upper body and nether region bits. When he came into the bathroom, it was all I could do to lift one leg. He crouched in front of me.

"Lizzie, if I pull you're going to slide right off that toilet. I need you to hold onto something."

There was absolutely nothing for me to hold onto, not while also holding the towel.

"We might have to do this in the bedroom," he said. I didn't want to, but I nodded.

I penguin-walked to the bed and sat. I wrapped one hand around the headboard post, and the other held the towel shut. Ronan grabbed the sides of the suit and pulled.

Instead of the suit sliding off my legs, as we'd both hoped, what actually happened was my body flew in the air the towel parted to show off my 'Hollywood' hooha. I let go of the headboard to grab whatever part of the towel I could and at that moment I was pulled to the floor. I wasn't just pulled to the floor. I landed heavily on my bare arse, and Ronan kept pulling me across the room until I felt like I'd left a trail of skin behind me.

"Carpet burns!" I shouted as he managed to get the suit to my ankles. There was no way it was going beyond those; they had swollen to the size of melons.

"Stay there," he said. It wasn't like I was going anywhere. I had a sore arse and a rubber suit around my feet.

He came back with the knife and cut the thing from me. I brought my knees to my chest, let my forehead rest on them and cried again. I was beyond the point that I cared what he could and couldn't see. I cried a little more when he sat and wrapped his arms around me.

"Hey, come on now. In the morning we're going to laugh like mad about this," he said.

I nodded because I believed we would. "Thank you," I said, looking up at him.

He had sat to my side. "Do you need anything for your backside?"

"I think I can manage. I do need a shower, though."

"I'll go and make some tea. I drove all the way here, and I'm starving," he said with a laugh.

"You'll find some stuff in the fridge," I replied, leaving him to walk to the kitchen.

I took a shower, careful to inspect the graze on my bum. In one way, I was quite pleased to have a carpet burn; it had been many, *many* years since I'd had one. In another, as I started to sober up, the embarrassment hit me, and I was mortified knowing, every time I sat for the next couple of days, I'd remember. I picked some moisturiser to slather on and then my PJs.

Ronan was eating a sandwich at the kitchen table. The flowers lay on the sideboard in the hall.

I picked them up as I passed. "Are these for me?"

He lowered his gaze for a moment. "An apology, and I know, they don't go anywhere near how much I need to apologise to you," he said as he stood. He took the flowers and wrapped his arms around me. "I'm so sorry," he whispered into my wet hair. The tingle returned.

"Let me make some tea. I think I need it," I said.

He returned to his sandwich, and I made two teas. I was surprised at how quickly I'd sobered up, yet knew in the morning, I'd probably have a banging headache as well as a sore arse. I placed his mug in front of him and then took a seat opposite.

I winced as I sat.

"What are you doing here?" I asked. "Not that I'm not pleased to see you, though." I quickly added.

He laughed gently. "I imagine you're only pleased to see me because I got you out of your gimp suit."

"Will you stop calling it that? It was a sweat suit, a cheap one, obviously. Now, answer my question." I smiled to soften my words.

He took a deep breath in. “Charlie tore a strip off me for not telling you everything. And he had every right to. I was upset because it was the anniversary of Demi’s death. You want to know why I hate my ex so much? She caused that death. She drove her car at Demi’s when she was drunk and high on her medication. Demi swerved and hit a telegraph pole, then rolled down a bank. She died.”

For a few seconds, I was mute with shock. “Why wasn’t your ex arrested for murder?” I whispered.

Despondency overshadowed his features. “Because there were no witnesses.”

“How do you know she did it then?”

He fixed me with an anger-filled gaze, his nostrils flared. “Because she told me. I went to the police, and she called me a liar. I never told you the whole truth, Lizzie because I still find it hard to process. She told the police that I’d hit her, tried to strangle her. I’ve never laid a hand on her, but I wanted to.” He clenched his teeth. “Oh, God, I wanted to put my hands around her throat when she stood laughing at my tears. That’s why I hate her. That’s why I tried to keep you away from her. That’s why I distanced myself from you because I didn’t want to risk you. That’s why, when I found the photograph broken, it all became too much for me. I didn’t get out of bed for days, not until Charlie threatened to *tan my arse* if I didn’t pull myself together.”

My heart squeezed for his pain. “I don’t know what to say.”

“Say nothing for now, please. I’m sorry.”

“Have you been home?” I asked. I remembered him saying he had driven straight to me from Scotland.

“No, not yet. I wanted to see you first. I have the photos and paintings in the car,” he said.

My heart sank. “So you came here to give me the pictures?”

"No, Lizzie, I came here to ask you to forgive me for acting like a complete dick and getting it all so very wrong."

I wasn't sure what part he had got wrong, but I agreed that he had acted like a dick. I yawned, the evening catching up on me.

"Blimey, it's nearly two in the morning," I said, finally looking at my watch.

"I should go," he said.

"You can always stay here," I offered then quickly added, "The sofa is really comfortable."

"That would be good, thank you. I don't think I could stomach the drive, you've exhausted me already," he said, giving me a gorgeous smile.

"You really upset me, Ronan," I said, as I stood.

His smile turned to a sad one, and he nodded. "I know. Tomorrow… erm… can we go over what you said when I first got here?"

I could feel my cheeks colour. "No, you know exactly what I said. I only wanted to cover you up so you didn't get cold, and then I had to hide while you… Anyway, you've embarrassed yourself, I've done the same—we're quits," I said, and held out my hand.

He took hold of it and instead of the shake I was expecting, he pulled me into a hug.

"Thank you," he said.

I backed away and mumbled that I'd get some bed linen for him. By the time I had returned, he had kicked off his shoes and was stretched out on the sofa. I handed him a pillow and a duvet, then wished him a good night.

❧

I woke just a couple of hours later with a raging thirst. At first, I was disorientated and lay still, wondering what the noise was that I could hear. The evening slowly came back to me, and I wanted to groan out loud. I could hear the gentle snores of Ronan in the living room. I slid from my bed and winced as the scabs on my butt cheek rubbed against my PJs. Desperate for a glass of water, I left the bedroom and padded quietly to the kitchen where I opened the fridge to get a bottle. I didn't want to disturb my guest with the noise of the tap running or the kitchen light, so I stood in the dark with just the light of appliances to illuminate me.

"It there one for me?" I heard, just as I was about to take a mouthful of water.

"Oh, sweet Jesus," I said, as cold water poured over my chin, up my nose, and down my chest.

I grabbed a tea towel to soak it up before my nipples stood out like coat hooks. Ronan laughed, and I heard him walk up behind me. His bare feet slapped against the tiled floor.

"You scared the life out of me," I said.

He reached in and took a bottle himself. "Can't sleep?" he asked.

"I was thirsty. What time is it?"

"Five-ish, I think. Are you hungry?"

I stared at him. "I've had, what, three hours sleep? I'm grumpy, for sure."

"Get dressed," he said.

"For what?"

"Come on, live dangerously, get dressed." He had that smile that sent messages from my brain straight to my hooha and livened up the butterflies in my stomach on the way.

"I can't go out, look at my hair," I said, grabbing handfuls of it.

"So put a hat on. Go, get dressed, or I'll throw you over my shoulder as you are."

A standoff ensued. I stared at him; he returned that. Neither of us blinked, and in my head, I could hear the music that played on every western movie when a duel was about to start. He took a step towards me; I took one to the side. He raised his eyebrows; I did the same. I raised him a smirk. He countered that by puffing up his chest and rolling up his sleeves. I salivated at the sight of his muscled and tattooed forearms; it was the distraction he wanted. He lunged, I screamed, he grabbed me, and in a flash, I was hanging over his shoulder holding on to his belt and looking at a tight buttock.

I grabbed one cheek, digging my nails into his jean-clad flesh and laughing maniacally.

He walked me into the bedroom, and none too gently laid me on the bed. "You grabbed my arse," he said. I continued to laugh. "You. Grabbed. My. Arse. Should I be offended?" His lips twitched.

He walked to my dressing table and opened a drawer. I scrambled from the bed as he pulled out a pair of knickers and threw them at me. He opened another and grabbed a bra.

"They don't match," I said, still laughing. He grabbed the bra from me and replaced it with another.

He walked to my wardrobe and opened it. He pulled a pair of jeans and a jumper from the shelves. I caught them as he threw them over his shoulder. I rushed into the bathroom and dressed. When I returned, he was sitting on the bed with my hairbrush. He parted his legs and waved to the floor. I frowned but knelt between them.

He brushed my hair.

A shudder rolled over me like a wave at his touch. It was so gentle and to have my hair brushed by anyone other than my hairdresser was…odd, but not. It felt like the most natural thing in the world to have him behind me, but somewhere in my brain, I countered that it shouldn't. I barely knew him. I wanted to punch him when he bashed me on the top of my head with the back of the brush.

"Oww, that hurts," I said, as I rose and turned to him.

"Come on. Breakfast."

He grabbed my hand and as he dragged me to the front door, I snatched my keys from the hallway table. I stuffed them in my jeans pocket as we left the flat and quietly made our way downstairs. He continued to hold my hand as we rounded the corner to find his car on a permit-only parking bay and with something stuck to the windscreen.

"You got a ticket," I said, my breath condensing in the cold air. I shivered realising I didn't have a coat or socks on my Converse-clad feet.

"No shit, Sherlock," he said. I giggled as he opened the door of the Range Rover he still had on rental.

"You're going to have to give this back soon," I said, as I slipped into the luxurious leather seats.

"No, this one is mine," he replied as he closed the door.

He turned up the heating as the car idled and then he drove. We crossed London to Brick Lane in the East End. We pulled up opposite the busiest bakers I'd ever seen. Cab drivers were queuing, there were people dressed to party, but with heels in hands and sensible flip flops on their feet, there were businessmen on their way to an early start.

"Best bagels you'll ever eat," he said, as he turned the car off. "Wait here."

I stayed in the car while he hopped out and crossed the road. I watched as he jumped the queue and high-fived a man behind the counter. He was served immediately and without paying, and then he was back in the car. He reached into the brown paper bag and handed me a smoked salmon and cream cheese bagel. The dough was still warm, the salmon had the most wonderful oak flavour as if smoked over old wine barrels, and the cream cheese melted in my mouth.

"Mmm," I said, grabbing a tissue to dab my mouth. "That is gorgeous."

"We supply the salmon," he said, taking a bite of his bagel.

"No way! From the loch?" I asked.

He laughed. "No, there's a river that runs through the land, we fish them, although never on a Sunday." He laughed, but I wasn't sure what was funny. I frowned at him. "One of those silly laws, no salmon fishing on a Sunday," he clarified.

I finished my bagel and fished in the bag to see if there was another.

"Still hungry?" he asked.

I nodded. "I'm trying to lose some weight, remember? So, even if there was another, I shouldn't eat it."

"Lizzie, you're perfect as you are," he said, as he wiped his mouth.

I startled as someone knocked on the window. Ronan lowered the glass, and two takeout cups were passed through.

"Man, thank you," Ronan said, grabbing them. Another paper bag was handed over.

Ronan had a quick chat, and the guy left. He held aloft the paper bag. "Now, if you eat this, are you going to do something as stupid as you did last night?" he said.

I laughed as I reached out to snatch the bag from his hands. I looked to see two doughnuts. I took one out and swapped him the tea for the bag.

“Oh, we’re going to be neighbours, sort of,” he said, sipping his tea.

“Sort of neighbours?” I wondered if Danny was moving out soon.

“I bought the renovation property.”

I stared at him. “How did you know about that?”

“Joe knows I like to dabble in property, so when you decided on the barn, he sent me the details.”

“Oh, okay. Is it somewhere you’ll live?” I asked.

Inside, I was mildly annoyed. Joe had known how upset I had been with Ronan’s silence, yet they seemed to be having yet more cosy chats behind my back. Of course, Joe could be friends with whomever he chose, but I would have hoped *my* friendship with him would have been worth more than a small commission for finding a buyer for a property.

“I don’t know, I guess. It depends on how it rebuilds. I don’t live that far away from your barn anyway,” he said. “As the crow flies, it’s probably only three miles. Maybe you’d like to come for dinner tonight? Stay over. I ought to return the favour,” he added.

“That would be nice, but I should tell you, I’d be absolutely no good at getting you out of a *gimp suit*.”

He laughed. “No gimp suits in my house.”

He screwed up the paper bags and placed his tea in the cup holder. He then started the car, and as the London traffic began to get busier, he drove back to my flat.

“We need to get the pictures over to the gallery,” I said.

"Here's a plan. Why don't you grab an overnight bag, and we'll drive to my place. We can take a walk, I'll show you the area, and then we can chill out before dinner. Tomorrow, we can drop the paintings off to the gallery."

With only three hours sleep, I would have rather climbed back into bed, but I liked him. I wanted to spend time with him, so I nodded. He parked in the same spot that he'd received the parking fine without a care and we walked to the flat.

I gathered an overnight bag and filled it with items I thought I might need. I kicked off my Converse and pulled on some socks. I then sat at the dressing table, redid my hair and applied some makeup. I found my walking boots and placed them in a plastic carrier bag—they still had mud on the soles from the last time I'd worn them.

I picked up my handbag, making sure I had my purse, phone, spare knickers and panty liners, all the usual things required for a daytime bag. Then I was ready.

❧

The journey to Ronan's house wasn't any longer than Joe and I had taken to view the barn. I suggested that we might drive past so I could show him. He took a lane to divert from the route, and after weaving through another couple, we exited onto the village green. For a moment I was stumped, but Ronan seemed to know the way. We slowed as we came up along the barn.

"I just walked in and immediately fell in love," I said as I stared from the car window.

"I felt the same when I bought my cottage. I think you always know when it's the right house for you," he said.

I hadn't wanted to ask him what he intended to do now he had the house in Scotland as well. He had indicated he wasn't someone that agreed with those that owned property and only holidayed in their manor houses, or castles, or whatever it was they had.

"She's divorcing her husband," I said, quietly.

"I heard. Is that why you offered the full asking price?"

"It was. Harry was okay when our divorce proceedings started, but once his solicitor got involved it all changed. I never wanted half of everything, just enough to let me buy a house and live comfortably. I got a little more than I was expecting, but I'm not complaining," I said, with a laugh.

"That's the first time you've mentioned him by name," Ronan said.

I turned to him. "I don't want to dwell on the past anymore. There's no need for me to be bitter. I feel sad, desperately sad that my marriage was a lie, but I do believe he *loved* me—he just couldn't live the lie any longer. One day, he woke up, and he broke down and told me he'd been gay all his life. He'd had sex with other men during our marriage."

"I'm not entirely sure I'd be as forgiving as you're being."

"I thought long about why I don't hate him. I went through a period where I didn't want to speak his name, but…I guess since everything was finalised just before we left for Scotland, I feel as sorry for him as I do for myself with all the wasted years."

When we thought we had sat for long enough before we'd be deemed suspicious, we moved on.

"I really like it, Lizzie," he said, as he used their drive to turn around.

"I think I'm going to be happy there. Now I know a 'sort of' neighbour, I won't feel so isolated. It's amazing how quickly the friends disappear when you're a single woman."

We continued through the village on a different route until we arrived at Ronan's cottage. As we pulled to a halt outside, I smiled. The cottage, similar in style to the renovation project, wasn't what I expected at all. I guess, having been in the Scottish castle with its vast rooms and dereliction, to step into a pristine, chocolate box cottage was so different. Ronan had to duck to walk through the front door, which opened straight into a living room with a log burner in one corner.

"This is so lovely," I said as I placed my overnight bag at the bottom of the wooden staircase.

I followed Ronan through the living room to a kitchen diner. Beyond that was a large sunroom with another log burner and seemed to be the place he spent the most amount of time. I noticed a newspaper still open on one sofa, although a few weeks old, and a cup that Alexander Flemming would've been proud of. I picked up the cup and took it out to the kitchen.

"I think this needs throwing," I said, handing it to him.

"I'm sure it will wash up okay," he replied with a laugh.

"Remind me not to drink from it then."

Ronan was making a pot of coffee. "Take a seat. This will take a few minutes."

I settled into the corner of the sofa, which was surprisingly comfortable, and looked out to his garden. Although a little messy inside, the garden was immaculate. I wondered who tended it for him. The borders were neat, and the lawn had recently been mowed. Perfect stripes led the eye down to a hedge and the fields beyond. It was quiet and peaceful, like the barn, and there was a good feeling about the place that I imagined, after the chaotic upbringing Ronan had, would be a haven for him. I could smell the coffee brewing; hear the bubbling as it was pushed through the machine. I heard the rattle of coffee cups on saucers…

What is that noise? I thought. At least I thought I'd thought it and not spoken it out loud.

It was only then that I realised I'd fallen asleep. A noise had woken me, and when I opened my eyes, I saw Ronan at the other end of the sofa. He had stretched out with his feet on a stool. His T-shirt had risen a little, showing a trail of hair leading under the waistband of his jeans. On the floor was his coffee cup. He looked so peaceful, with a small smile on his face, I wondered what he was dreaming about and prayed it wasn't the same as the last time I'd seen him asleep. I chuckled as I stretched my legs out and stood.

I reached down to pick up his cup and headed to the kitchen. I remade the coffee, and while I waited for it to brew, I stood at the windows looking out. I heard Ronan shuffle on the sofa, and I looked over.

"Hey," he said, pushing himself into a sitting position.

"I'm making a fresh coffee. I hope you don't mind," I said.

"Of course I don't mind. Did I tell you that you snore?"

"You did, once before, if I remember. That's very gentlemanly of you to point it out, of course," I replied with a smirk.

"I was about to say, I believe in honesty, but I'm not sure I'm in a position to state that, am I?" he replied with a chuckle.

"I concur, now, how do you take your coffee?"

I poured him the black coffee with one sugar that he'd requested and returned to the sofa.

"This is a lovely cottage, but not what I was expecting," I said.

"What were you expecting?"

"I don't know to be honest. I think, having lived all those years in Scotland in that vast house, I guess I didn't expect something as cosy."

“I think it’s because of all those years rambling around in those vast spaces with nothing to do and no one to do it with is the exact reason I wanted *cosy,*” he replied.

“I like space. I need to have natural light, which is one of the reasons I wanted out of London to be honest. I can’t seem to bear the noise and fumes. I want to see the stars and not have them obscured by light pollution. I think I need a period of peacefulness.”

“Will you come back up with me after we drop the pictures off?” he asked.

“I’m not sure, Ronan. I was never sure why I was invited in the first place. I thought we were friends, then it seemed I was staff, and then somewhere in between until I wasn’t anything.”

“You’ve never been nothing, Lizzie,” he almost whispered. “I got it all very wrong, and I’ve apologised, and I’ll keep on apologising if needed. I would like you to join me for a few reasons, the main ones being, I like your company, even if you do snore, get stuck in mud, and wear a gimp suit. You’re the first person I’ve met that sees beyond the romance of a castle in Scotland to the practicalities of what the fuck to do with it. I can’t do it on my own, more importantly, I don’t want to.”

“I’ll need to be back when my house purchase goes through,” I replied.

“I’ll help you move.”

“Bring me up to speed while I decide.”

Ronan told me that the police had arrested Manuel, whose real name, sadly wasn’t Mick but most certainly was Derek. I burst into laughter. It was a perfect name for him, and yet again I was reminded of characters from the TV show, *Benidorm.* All the cannabis plants had been removed, much to Maggie’s dismay, and the builders were in blocking up the hole in the loft as well as updating the three cottages. They were going to be let out, although he hadn't decided if he'd try for long term or holidays yet.

The art group had been told they could stay. Ronan couldn't bring himself to remove that last piece of his mother, but the glamping site would be updated. Saggy Tits, whose real name I had learned was Petal, was in charge of forming an organised group that would pay a monthly fee to go some way towards the upkeep. I was pleased to hear that. Although it had been most disingenuous of me to refer to her as saggy tits, I just couldn't seem to remove the name and replace it with Petal.

"The Aga works, and Maggie made bread in it. We have constant hot water but not quite constant heating yet," Ronan said.

"Well, that's it then. You've sold it to me, again. I'll need to go home and get more clothes, obviously."

"Thanks, Lizzie. And I am sorry about everything. I'm so fucking anal when it comes to friendships. I don't know what to do for the best sometimes."

I smiled. I would have preferred him to use the word *relationships,* but I'd take friendship since that's all it was likely to be.

"Now, how about a walk?"

I slipped on my walking boots, wrapped a scarf around my neck, and pulled on my coat. Ronan did the same, and we left the cottage by the back door. We crossed the garden to a small gate I hadn't notice at the side of the property and then walked down the lane.

"Wrong side," Ronan mumbled as he grabbed my shoulders and pushed me closer to the hedgerow.

"Doesn't matter what side if a car comes," I said, laughing.

"I was brought up a gentleman, Lizzie. I need to get back in touch with him."

We talked as we walked. Well, *he* talked because we were walking slightly uphill and I wasn't able to talk, walk, and breathe all at the same time. I did puff out a complaint about how unfit I was.

"Petal wants to get the yoga class going again. You could join that," he said.

"Please tell me they do that dressed."

He laughed and then shook his head.

"Do they arrive naked?" I asked. I didn't recall seeing piles of clothes anywhere.

"No, there's a gate and car park they come in. Not that I've sat and watched, but I imagine they get undressed there and leave their stuff in the car. They bring essentials, like towels and stuff, and that all stays in the tents."

I wasn't taking too much notice of where we walked, but we seemed to be doing a circular route crossing an open field and were about to head into a wooded area. I always found woods spooky, more so in the day. There was a silence that I found eerie. We walked a well-worn path that was littered with fallen leaves. The smell of rich earth wafted as we stepped through them. I collected a few conkers; their shiny brown outer shell reflected the light. Conker brown was always a colour I strived to achieve at the hairdressers, never quite getting there. I popped the conker in my pocket, intending to show the hairdresser next time I had an appointment.

Ronan and I chatted about our childhoods, our parents, and he had to laugh and place his hands on his knees to catch his breath when I told him my parents were swingers.

"Please, let me meet them one day," he said breathlessly.

"Are you kidding me? They won't come on to you, you're too young, and we'd have to go to Spain, they won't come here. But, no. You can't."

"So what happens if you remarry? Won't your dad be walking you down the aisle again?"

"I don't think I'll ever remarry, and if I did, it would be on a beach somewhere, or a field or… I know you said you don't want weddings in the house, but what about by the loch?"

I hadn't visited *his* loch, but as the talk of weddings progressed, I had a vision of a wedding party on the grass with the loch in the background. It could be so romantic.

"Midges," he said.

"Huh?"

"What is Scotland famous for? Except tattooed good looking men in skirts and haggis? Midges. There's one month of the year where only the tourists venture near the lochs, but the fuckers are around most of the summer."

I hadn't listened beyond *tattooed good looking men in skirts*. Ronan snapped his fingers in front of my face. "Lizzie?"

"Sorry, I got stuck at the men in skirts thing. Do you have a kilt?"

"Of course I have a kilt. I'll wear it next week. I'm sure we can find an occasion." He laughed as he spoke.

"Are you…" I gestured to his nether regions. "Underneath?" I whispered.

Ronan leaned closer. "There's no one around to hear you," he whispered back. I liked that he was so close, and maybe it was because it came off the back of men in skirts, but my heart missed a couple of beats.

"Well?"

"How about we wait, and I'll show you. It's not like you haven't seen my dick already," he said, rather too loudly for my liking.

My cheeks flamed so much I was sure smoke would seep from the top of my head.

“Oh, come on, it must have been funny,” he said, bumping my shoulder before we continued to walk.

“It was mortifying. I was hiding, Ronan, on the floor at the bottom of your bed. I was singing in my head and covering my ears so I didn’t hear you. No, funny isn’t a word that springs to mind,” I replied.

For the second time he had to stop because he was laughing so hard.

When he was done, he slung his arm over my shoulder, and we walked together. We must have been out for about an hour when we emerged from the woods into a lane, and again, Ronan positioned me close to the hedge. He removed his arm from my shoulders, and I missed it. As we rounded a corner, his cottage came into view.

“Where is mine from here?” I asked.

“You’re the other side of that wood. I guess you could walk it. I can’t imagine it would take that long.”

“I don’t think I’d walk through woods on my own, not even in the middle of the day,” I said.

“You’ll have to get yourself a car.”

“I haven’t driven in so many years. I might need lessons.”

“When we get to Scotland, I’ll take you out in the Land Rover. You’d have to do something spectacular to smash that up,” he said.

We arrived back at the cottage, and while Ronan filled the log burner with kindling, ready for a fire, I headed to the kitchen and opened the fridge to see long life milk. I screwed my nose in mock disgust at the 'fake' milk. Still, it would have to do for my drink.

"You know you invited me to dinner? You don't actually have anything in your fridge. What did you plan we could eat?" I shouted.

I shrieked as I felt him immediately behind me. His breath ghosted the back of my neck as he peeked over my shoulder.

"Hmm, maybe we'll have to eat out," he said. "Or get a Chinese delivered, whatever you choose."

"I think you probably owe me dinner out actually," I said, wanting to step back but not being able to. I wanted to close the fridge. I wasn't sure if my erect nipples were from the cold or him being too close.

I stepped back, feeling his chest against my back, and I pressed myself into him as I squeezed the fridge door past me and closed it. I turned, and still, he stood in the same position.

I stared at him. His gaze travelled over my face coming to rest on my lips, and I bit down on my tongue so it didn't poke out and run over them in any kind of involuntary suggestive manner. He reached up and tucked a piece of hair around the back of my ear.

"I'm glad you've forgiven me," he said.

"I don't know that I have, yet."

He leaned just little forward, and I closed my eyes. The hand that had tucked the hair away cupped my chin. I felt his breath on my skin as he turned my face slightly and gently kissed my cheek. I smiled and opened my eyes. Was he flirting with me? I hadn't had a man flirt with me for years. He sure was giving me mixed signals.

Ronan ran his hand over his chin and then he smiled. He stepped back and made coffee. I wanted to grab hold of him, pin him to the fucking counter, and kiss him. Of course, I'd never do that.

Instead, I sat in the living room in front of the log burner and waited for him to return.

"How about an early dinner since I don't have anything in for lunch either?" he said, bringing the coffee and some biscuits through.

"Sounds good to me. You didn't really think this, *invite me for dinner and sleepover* thing through, did you?"

He laughed. "No. I'm actually trying to remember the last time I did the dinner and sleepover thing, and it has to be a few years now. I'm pretty much winging it here," he said.

I raised my cup to him. "Same."

It was nice just to sit and chat some more with him. He told me about his work. He told me that from an early age, he had decided he wanted to be his own boss. When he had finished his business degree, he persuaded his mum to loan him some money, and he'd invested in a bar with a couple of friends. The bar had failed, but he'd learned some valuable lessons. One was to never trust anyone in business. His mum loaned him some more, and he bought the bar at a fraction of the price the group of friends had to pay initially. He worked day and night, turned it around, and sold it for a profit, paying his mum back for both loans. And so it went on. He bought some property, renovated and sold. He bought a couple of vintage vehicles, had them repaired and then sold for a profit. It seemed that he could turn his hand to most things.

"So this project that you initially wanted to speak to Joe about, what is that one?"

"It's a small boutique hotel with a spa. I'm not sure it's something I wanted to be involved in, but I loved the property. It's too large to be a house, so I thought I'd get it up and running and then sell it."

"I don't know why Joe doesn't get involved in interior design;

he'd be amazing at it. His eye for detail is unbelievable. I know when he sells property, he sometimes has the homeowner redecorate and refurnish."

"So I heard. I saw what he did at the bar and thought he might be interested in the hotel project. So far he's come up with some great ideas. But that's a long term project, there's a lot of building work to be done first."

"Do you have your own builders?"

"I contract most of it out, but I'm pretty handy at building most things."

The thought of a shirtless Ronan with dirty hands, and a sweaty torso as he built walls flashed through my mind. Maybe all the images I was having of Ronan were because I was hungry, or tired, or both. I grabbed a couple of biscuits.

"Oh, fuck," I said, using two fingers to try to scoop the broken biscuit from the coffee before it turned to mush, scolding myself in the process.

"Give it here," he said. He took my mug, and I sucked my fingers into my mouth to soothe them. I heard him take in a breath as he watched.

"Burned them," I said, colouring again and waving two fingers in the air at him.

He went to tip it away and make a fresh cup. "Can I have tea?" I called out. Too much coffee would have me awake all night with palpitations.

The thought of Ronan, naked from the waist up, repairing a wall in one of his many fields wearing a kilt and work boots, was more likely to keep me awake with palpations than all the coffee off the Blue Mountain.

"I seem to remember that it might be my turn to ask a question," he said when he returned.

I couldn't remember whose turn it was, but I settled back to wait for it.

"When was the last time you had sex?"

I stared, open-mouthed. He stared back at me. I blinked a few times and then closed my mouth. I probably opened it again, gaping at him.

"Well?" he demanded with a cheeky glint in his eye.

"I'm not going to answer that!" I stuttered.

"Why? You said we got to ask any question we wanted," he replied with a smirk.

"I don't recall saying that at all." I wanted to laugh, but his smile was testing my need to be outraged.

"It was definitely something like that. So, you're not going to answer? Mmm, interesting." He tapped his chin.

"There's nothing *interesting* about not answering a question."

"Come on, Lizzie, you watched me wanking," he said.

I gasped, knowing my cheeks would flame at the memory I was desperately trying to suppress. "I did not *watch*…forget it. Over two years ago if you really must know. I'm not exactly keeping a diary of it and if you want to know more, then the last time I had a smear I was advised I was at that age where I should think about lubricant and I had vaginal atrophy."

Ronan laughed.

I took a deep breath in. "My turn," I said as a slow grin spread on my face because I knew he wouldn't want to answer my question.

"Who were you dreaming of when you were—"

"You," he said, interrupting me. "I haven't had sex in about a year, but I've wanked more in the past month than I did as a teenager."

"I don't..." I started to say that I didn't know what to say, and I genuinely didn't.

He scooted up the sofa so he was closer. "Have I embarrassed you?"

"Yes, a little. That was rather intimate for *friends*. Don't you think?"

"Well, I'd hoped that maybe we might be more than just friends."

I closed my eyes and sighed deeply. "You give me whiplash, Ronan," I said, quietly.

He laughed, but I detected a slight edge of embarrassment to it. "I give myself whiplash. I don't know how to do this anymore."

I turned sideways and reached forward with both arms. I grabbed two handfuls of his T-shirt and pulled him to me. I kissed him. It was tentative at first, unsure. That was until he placed his hands either side of my head and gripped my hair. He leaned into me, and I settled back against the arm of the sofa. He took charge then. His tongue swept over mine, and his kiss became more desperate. I could hear his, or it could have been mine, breathing becoming more rapid. I could feel his grip tighten in my hair, and the pull caused my core to tighten. A banging on the front door stopped him.

He pulled his head away slightly. He stared at me as we both listened. The knock came again.

"Bollocks," he whispered. "Let's ignore it."

"You can't, the curtains are open, and we're in full view. In fact, there's an elderly lady looking through right now," I whispered.

"That'll be Mrs Sharpe. Wait right there. Don't move, will you?"

He pushed himself off me, and I straightened up. While standing facing me, he adjusted his hard cock to a more comfortable position.

"Put a jumper around your waist, or something," I whispered, as she knocked again.

"She's as blind as a bat. She won't be looking at my cock, trust me."

He strode to the front door and opened it. A breeze blew through.

"Ronan, I'm sorry to trouble you. I wasn't sure you were in. I can't get my boiler going, and I've no logs," she said.

He invited her in.

"Oh, you have company. I'm so sorry. I'll go, and it's no matter."

"It is a matter. Now, this is Lizzie. Lizzie, Mrs Sharpe lives opposite, just up the lane. Tell me what happened to the boiler," he said, turning his attention back to her.

"It just stopped yesterday. I tried to call a plumber, but I couldn't get anyone to come out. I've waited all day for someone, and they called, they can't make it now. I was getting worried because the temperature is going to drop. I've got a plug-in heater, but it's not warm enough."

"Mrs Sharpe, why didn't you call me yesterday?" he asked.

"Because I didn't want to trouble you, I knew you were in Scotland dealing with your loss."

I stood up, subtly readjusting my top. "I've got a good idea. Why don't I make Mrs Sharpe a nice cup of tea, and you take some logs up for her?"

"I don't want to trouble you," she repeated, but the subtle shake to her hands and the watery eyes suggested otherwise.

"Let me get my shoes on, and a jumper, and I'll run a wheelbarrow full of logs over. Give me your keys, Mrs Sharpe. I'll put the heater in your bedroom and get the fire going in the living room, how's that? I'll also call someone to get here tomorrow morning and repair the boiler." He reached for his mobile as he spoke.

Ronan left and Mrs Sharpe followed me to the kitchen. "I'm so sorry," she said.

"Please, don't apologise. You should have come over earlier," I said. I hated the thought she could have been sitting there freezing. It was cold out and, as she said, the temperature was due to drop. I made her a cup of tea, and she wrapped her hands around it for warmth.

"He's always on the go, but every time he's home, he makes sure I'm okay. Ever since my Matthew died, Ronan has made sure to check on me."

"That's lovely to know, Mrs Sharpe. How long were you married?" I asked as we sat at the kitchen table.

"Sixty years, Lizzie. We fell in love a few years before that, of course."

The smile on her face as she recalled those years was wonderful to see. She told me about her husband and some of the many trips abroad they had taken. She was a well-travelled woman who didn't seem to miss those days. I guessed her memories were enough to keep her going.

She had finished her tea when Ronan walked back into the cottage. "You've got a fire lit, and the heater is in your bedroom. I found a couple of blankets that I've put on your bed just in case it doesn't warm up enough. There's a pile of logs beside the fire that should keep you going tonight. I'll be over first thing in the morning to relight it. How's that?" he asked.

She stood and placed her hands on his forearms. "Thank you so much." She turned to me. "You've got yourself a wonderful human being here, Lizzie. Hang on to him."

Ronan walked her back to her cottage, and I thought on her words. I'd like the opportunity to hang on to him, but somehow, I wasn't sure how a relationship would work. I was soon to live in Kent, he had a cottage a village over, but the majority of his time would need to be spent in Scotland.

I decided to take my overnight bag upstairs. I wasn't sure what time we would be eating out, but I wondered if Ronan wouldn't mind me taking a bath. I climbed the stairs to find three doors off a landing. I loved that the floor was uneven, tilting to one side. I opened the first door to find the bathroom. I was pleased to see a roll top, claw-footed bath under the window. There was a separate shower in the corner. The second door I opened would have been a spare bedroom, I imagined, except it just held wardrobes. Ronan was using it as a dressing room. The third room was, obviously, the bedroom. A large bed stood against the back wall facing the windows. Other than two bedside tables with lamps, there was nothing else in the room.

I wondered where I would have been expected to sleep on our *sleepover*. I smiled as I placed my bag on the bed. If it was separately; he was taking the sofa. I grabbed my toiletry bag and pulled my hair into a high ponytail. I didn't want to get it wet.

I walked back to the bathroom and ran the bath. I sat on the edge, wafting my hand through the water, testing it, and laughing as I remembered the dog shampoo. I had thought to pack some bubble bath in my bag this time, so I poured a little in as I heard the front door open and close.

"Lizzie?" I heard.

I turned off the taps. "I ran the bath. Is that okay?" I called down.

"Of course it is. Do you want a glass of wine before we go out?"

"That would be nice, thank you. I won't be long."

I stripped and climbed in the bath. I had just lowered my shoulders under the bubbles, thankfully, when he walked in. He sat on the edge of the bath and handed me my wine.

"Shouldn't you knock?" I asked.

"In my own bathroom?" He smirked back. "Do you want me to? I can't see anything, which is a shame."

I laughed and reached for the wine. "I don't get you sometimes."

He shrugged. "There's not much to get, I guess. Like we've said, neither of us has dated in a long time who knows what we're supposed to be doing. Is there dating etiquette I've missed?"

"Walking in on your *date* in the bath before there's any…Well, that might be a no-no," I said.

I regretted the words. I saw his lips twitch, and his eyebrows rise. "Before there's any, what, Lizzie?" he asked.

"You haven't seen me naked," I said.

"Then you most certainly have one up on me, don't you?" He reached in and pulled the plug while taking my glass from me.

I screeched and laughed. "I haven't washed yet!"

I fumbled trying to re-plug the bath. I grabbed the flannel from the side as the water became lower than my boobs and covered them. "This is so unfair," I said, laughing.

"It is. I'm sorry." He reached in and re-plugged the bath.

I sat forward, not caring that the flannel fell, and took my glass of wine from him. I sipped from it and rested back, not caring that my tits were on show. For a fifty-year-old, they were still fairly pert.

"Shall I tell you a secret?" he said. I wasn't sure I wanted to know but nodded anyway.

"When I had to cut you out of your gimp suit, I saw it all anyway."

I let my head fall back to the edge of the bath, and I closed my eyes while I groaned. It didn't help that he laughed.

"I thought I'd have a little trim up, although why I bothered, I don't know, and I found a feminine shaver, but I didn't realise I had to put a guard thing on it."

"So you gave yourself a buzz cut?" he said, trying hard not to laugh.

"Yes, and then when I started, I could hardly stick the hair back on, so I had to shave the whole lot off, and now it itches like I have a bloody venereal disease. I've been trying to subtly scratch my hooha all day."

That was it. The noise that erupted from Ronan startled me into a sitting position. He fell to the floor, and I jumped out of the bath, slipping as water sloshed over the wooden planks. Ronan was lying on his back; his hands held his stomach and red wine had spilled everywhere. I crouched down, completely naked, beside him in a panic.

"Ronan!" I shouted.

He couldn't catch his breath. I placed my hands on his chest and pummelled. He opened his mouth and sucked in air, and then he laughed. He made strange noises, and I wasn't sure what he was trying to say. Eventually, I understood.

"Hooha!" he said, screaming the word. He was still lying on his back, still laughing to the point tears were running down his cheeks.

"You bastard!" I said, but his laughter was infectious. I sat back on my heels. "Are you taking the piss out of me?" I asked.

"Not you, just your hooha," he said in a screechy, high-pitched voice.

"Well, you're lying in a pool of water and wine," I said as if that was even remotely comparable.

He reached out as if asking me to pull him up. I took his hands, stupidly. Before I could take a breath, he had pulled me forward, and I fell onto him. He wrapped his arms around me, and his lips were on mine. His moan made me kiss him back as feverishly. His arms tightened around me, and one hand slid down to my arse. He squeezed. Just as earlier, instead of a knock on the front door, his mobile started to ring. It not only rang but also vibrated against the wood floor he was lying on. We tried to ignore it, but even after it cut off, it started again. I pulled my head away and let my forehead fall to his chest.

"Fucking hell," he said. He raised his hips, and I felt his erection press against me as he pulled the phone from his pocket.

"Mrs Sharpe, are you okay?" he asked. I slid to one side, wincing as my knees hit the wooden floor.

Ronan sat up and gave me a wink. "Okay, we'll be as quick as we can," he said.

He disconnected the call and stood. He reached down and helped me to my feet then pulled me into his arms.

"You are gorgeous, and I can tell you now, when we get back from dinner, the phone is off, the door is locked and nothing is going to stop me making love to you."

I looked up at him in surprise.

"That's okay, isn't it?" he said, hesitation laced his voice.

"That's perfectly okay by me, but…" I stepped back, suddenly very conscious that I was naked. It didn't occur to me that nakedness wasn't an issue for him at all.

He reached to cup my chin and lift my head. 'But, what, Lizzie?" he asked, gently.

"I haven't done this in a long time."

"Neither have I. Hopefully, it will be like riding a bike, never forgotten," he said, and then chuckled. "Now, a log has fallen off the fire, and although it's not about to burn down her house, Mrs Sharpe is worried about the scorched carpet. Let's get ready, go to her, then the pub for dinner."

I leaned up on tiptoes and kissed him briefly. "Give me five minutes," I said.

I walked back to the bedroom with him following, and although my hands itched to cover my arse, I kept them firmly by my side.

"I can't believe we've seen each other naked the way we have. And with the lights on!"

He stopped walking. "Lizzie, every light in this bedroom is going to be blazing so I can see each inch of you and every expression that crosses your face." That tingle was like an electrical current connecting my ears, my brain, and then flowing straight to my hooha.

I watched as he pulled his T-shirt over his head. "Do me one favour?" I looked at him. "Please, don't say hooha again." I threw a cushion at him as he laughed again.

I dressed in jeans with a white shirt. I brushed my hair. I grabbed my makeup bag and, although I'd never taken that long to apply my *face*, I was done in a couple of minutes. In fact, I was pulling on my boots before Ronan had even finished buckling his belt. I could have kicked myself. I had been concentrating on getting ready, and I hadn't taken the time to admire his naked form, again.

We were in his Range Rover within twenty minutes of the call.

CHAPTER EIGHTEEN

Mrs Sharpe was tearful, and I didn't think we should run in, sort out the fallen log, and then rush off. I agreed to the cup of tea that she offered us. She was clearly very lonely and seemed to me, to be overly-disturbed by the loss of her boiler. Ronan explained that he had arranged for someone he knew to visit the following morning. He made her a flask of tea and took that up to her bedroom. He suggested that, if she were anxious with the fire, he'd put it out, and that maybe she could read in bed. He even offered to carry her television up so she could watch her soaps. She decided on a book.

I helped her upstairs, but she waved any further help away. I made sure that she had her telephone beside her bed and she promised she would call if she needed us.

Ronan locked up and we, finally, headed off to the pub.

"I'm sorry about all the *interruptions*," he said as he held open the car door.

"I think she's a lovely lady. It's nice that you do a lot for her," I said.

"I like her. I don't mind helping her, to be honest. But I do think that she might need a little more help than I can give. She seems to be getting anxious a lot, scared in the evenings, even though she knows I'm just a walk away. It worries me that she has no one when I'm in Scotland."

As Ronan didn't have a pub near him, we drove to the pub that would soon be my local. It was still early, a family was sitting at one table and an elderly couple at another. We chose a bottle of wine and to sit on a couple of leather chairs around a coffee table next to the fire. We were told by a friendly bar lady that we didn't need to book a table and just to give her a wave when we were ready. She handed us two menus to browse.

I felt awkward, and I wasn't sure why. I guessed the two kisses that we had shared had been pretty spontaneous, but there we were, drinking wine, having a meal, knowing how the evening would end. My stomach tightened with nerves. I felt like we were making small talk, there wasn't the natural flow to our previous conversations.

Ronan reached over and took my hand. "What's wrong, Lizzie?"

"I feel nervous all of a sudden," I said, with a smile deciding to be honest.

"Does it make it better if I say I feel the same?"

"A little." I smiled. "What is it when you get to this age? It's not like we haven't done this before, even if it was so long ago."

"When did you date someone last?" he asked.

"You are my first, no…second. I dated my husband when I was fifteen and married him soon after."

"Then it's pretty okay to be nervous, isn't it?"

"Can I tell you a secret?" I took a large gulp of my wine waiting on his answer. He nodded, keeping eye contact with me.

"I haven't had an orgasm in over ten years. I've faked many, though."

He didn't reply immediately, and he took a sip of his wine before speaking. "Can I ask one favour of you? Don't fake anything with me, please. You might not orgasm; I might not get it right. I think we're going to be like a pair of fumbling teenagers, even though this conversation already has me hard as stone. If you don't, it's okay, we just keep going until you do." He finished with a wink.

"I think I do need to move off this conversation and onto safer ground," I said, laughing more with embarrassment than humour.

I vaguely remembered a time back in the day when I'd go out with Harry, and we knew we'd be at it like rabbits before we even got in the front door, and it was exciting. I wondered why I didn't have that level of excitement. It was fear that had started to run through me. I remembered the nurse and the lubricant comment, how I'd shaved all my hair, and now I had nothing more than stubble. What if I needed to pee? I felt my hands start to shake.

"Let's order, shall we?" he said. "And, Lizzie, nothing needs to happen at all."

I gave him my order of steak and chunky chips with a side salad, and he opted for the same. I watched him at the bar—how casual and friendly he was while he placed our order. Regardless of how off he had been with me over Demi's photograph, he was a very personable man. It seemed that he could talk to anyone. I texted Joe:

Help. I'm going to have sex, and I'm bloody terrified!

His reply was super quick

You're about to have sex? What, right now? Get off the fucking phone and get to it ha ha. Seriously, what are you

terrified about? And I'm assuming you're consenting to the sex, of course. If you're not just reply with an X, and I'll call the police!

I replied:

Of course I'm consenting. I don't know. It's been a while!

Oh, babe. You'll be fine. Trust me. Who are you with anyway?

I couldn't remember if I'd told him that Ronan had returned or not. We'd both been so busy the past couple of days that we hadn't caught up, so there was no time like the present:

Ronan. I'm in the pub near my new house. He lives just a couple of miles away.

Joe:

I know. That's why I thought it would be nice to show you those properties. Just call me Cupid. Now get off the phone and go and have fun xxx

I didn't answer him, and I wasn't sure if, yet again, his interference was welcomed or not. He had always been the master manipulator, but I hadn't fallen for it in the past. Perhaps, subconsciously, I wanted his interference. I shook my head and sighed as I replaced my phone.

"Is that sigh something I should be worried about?" I looked up to see Ronan standing beside me. He held out his hand. "We can sit at our table."

"No, I just texted Joe. Did you know that he deliberately showed me those cottages so that we would live close?"

Ronan frowned and then laughed. "No, I didn't. Playing at matchmaker was he?"

"I guess so." I gathered my bag and took his hand. I was going to chill, relax, not overthink anything, and just enjoy his company.

I tried, I really did. I ate my meal, we talked, and we laughed as he told me some funny stories from his renovation projects. We drank coffee, and then he paid, refusing my offer of half the bill. He took my hand, and that's when I quietened. I don't think I spoke on the journey back to his cottage at all.

He parked the car, and for a moment, we just sat.

"Nothing needs to happen, Lizzie," he whispered.

"I know. Can we go in, please?"

He opened his door, and I waited until he'd done the same to mine. Yet again, he took my hand, and we walked into the cottage. He didn't stop—he continued straight up the stairs and to his bedroom. He stood in front of me, in silence, and he stared. He took a deep breath in and exhaled slowly, and I found myself mirroring that. He placed a hand on the side of my head, and his fingers threaded through my hair. I watched his tongue gently wet his lower lip, and that was it for me.

My stomach clenched, and I could feel my clitoris throb. I took the step forward, as I reached up to place my arms around his neck, and I kissed him. I led all the way. Which, I guess, was what he'd been waiting for.

His hand tightened in my hair, and he pressed his body into mine. His other arm wrapped around me, holding me tight. A feeling of security, of belonging, washed over me. I wanted to shed a tear and kick myself for being worried. Everything we did was in sync, our heartbeats, our breaths, even when we changed head position. It all flowed as if we were just meant to be.

When he pulled his head away, I missed the sensation of his tongue, his lips covering mine. I missed his taste and the sound of him dragging in air through his nose.

He reached to the buttons of my shirt and undid them, but before he slid my shirt from my shoulders, he looked at me with a slight frown. I nodded, and he gently smiled. I undid the button and zipper of my jeans wriggling them past my hips until they fell to the floor. I continued to undress myself until I was, once again, standing naked in front of him. I watched as he scanned my body before pulling off his T-shirt and slipping out of his jeans himself.

When he picked me up and laid me on the bed, then climbed on beside me, all earlier nerves vaporised. I was completely in the moment with him. He did exactly what he'd promised. He took it slowly—he kissed every inch of my body, stroked and pleasured me in ways I'd never been pleasured before, and I realised something. No one had ever made love to me before. Harry's lies, his deceit, had always held him back from giving me what Ronan had.

And as for not having an orgasm for ten years? I made up for it.

CHAPTER NINETEEN

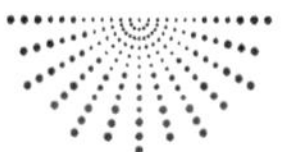

I turned as sunlight hit my closed eyelids. I could feel Ronan in the bed beside me, and I smiled as I recalled the previous evening. I wasn't sure of the time, but the light streaming in through the window was enough to tell me it had probably gone past the time I'd normally surface.

"Hey, beautiful," I heard, and I finally opened my eyes. Ronan was lying on his side, facing me.

"What time is it?" I asked.

"Just gone eight. It's still early."

I stretched, surprised at the ache I felt. "I think I might exchange Pilates for sex," I said.

"As long as I get to be teacher," he replied, laughing.

"Teacher? Do you think I need lessons?" A moment of panic washed over me.

He rolled his eyes and placed a kiss on my nose. "No, far from it. I just meant you have a teacher in Pilates…it was a joke."

"I ache a little."

"That's a good thing, isn't it?"

I wanted to kiss him, but I was also conscious of where my, and his for that matter, mouth had been. I wasn't sure it would be the most pleasant of morning breath.

"Shall I make you a cup of tea?" I asked.

"You're my guest. Wait here."

I watched as he climbed from the bed in all his naked glory and left the room. He returned ten minutes later with two cups, one in each hand. He placed one on his bedside table and one on mine. I shuffled into a sitting position and reached for it while he climbed back under the duvet.

"Are you okay?" he asked, as I sipped my tea.

I smiled at him. "I'm better than okay, although I'm also sad."

He looked a little alarmed. "Why?"

"Because what you did, *we* did, was amazing, and I realised, some of what I felt…well, that was a first for me. I guess, I'm not explaining this very well at all, but I think that was the first time someone actually made love *to* me. I don't know if you understand what I mean or not."

I felt a tear leave the corner of my eye and quickly swiped it away.

His gaze was filled with such sincerity. "I think I do, and I'm sorry that it's taken this long for you to feel that. I'm also honoured and flattered that it was me."

There was such openness and honesty in his words and expression. I could have fallen further in love with him there and then, knowing that would have been a stupid idea. I suppressed it. Ronan wasn't looking for love—I got that. I assumed we had a *relationship* of sorts, though.

What did the youngsters call it? Hooking up? That wasn't for me. I wasn't up for sex without dinner or a movie. I knew that much. Joe had many a *fuck-buddy*, and I'd shake my head at that because I knew, no matter what he'd said, he was also looking for love.

"What are you thinking?" he asked.

I sighed. "Nothing, honestly. I don't know if *enjoyed* is the right word, but I really enjoyed last night." I laughed to shake the melancholy from me. "Maybe it's just post-sex blues. Is there such a thing?" I asked.

"I have no idea, but I know a cure for it."

He took the cup from my hand and pulled me to him. I didn't care that I, or he, hadn't cleaned our teeth. I didn't care that my hooha probably had a slight odour of latex from the condom he'd used. I cared only what his hands, his fingers, and his tongue were doing as he slid under the covers, grabbed my hips, and pulled me down.

I let go of all my inhibitions, and I screamed out his name. I took pleasure, and I didn't feel selfish about it. I instigated, took charge, told him what I wanted, and when. I submitted and followed his requests. I came alive under his touch.

I felt, I smelled, I tasted.

I dared to dream that I could have this, *him*, for a while at least.

❧

The bath water was cooling when I climbed out. I felt a little sore between my legs, and when I stood in front of the full-length mirror, I gasped.

"You bastard," I whispered, and then giggled.

Just above my hooha was a bite mark, a love bite right on my fanny. I checked my neck and any obvious places to make sure I was clear of his branding. I dressed and then joined him downstairs. I didn't mention the love bite. I wasn't sure I wanted reminding of it myself. Ronan had laid out some toast, jam, and marmalade. He held his mobile to his ear, and he smiled when he saw me. His wet hair was standing up in all directions. He'd showered earlier and run a towel over his head. He wore trousers but was yet to put on his shirt. My eyes widened when he turned, and I saw the claw marks down his back.

I inspected my nails to be sure there was no sign of evidence. The last thing I wanted was to eat my toast and have his skin sticking to it. I wanted to laugh at the absurdity of that. I'd sucked his cock—I was sure a little of his back skin in my mouth wasn't anywhere near as bad. I could feel myself colouring at the thought of what I'd done. I slathered on some marmalade for something to do and to have my brain return to safe ground.

"That's great news, Mrs Sharpe. No, you don't need to worry about the invoice, I'll sort it out with Pete first, then I'll come and see you about it another day."

He was leaning against the kitchen counter watching me. "That's okay, okay, speak soon," he said, then disconnected the call. "Her boiler was repaired this morning."

"That's good, was she happy?" I asked as he came to sit beside me.

"More than. Now, do we need to arrange an appointment with this Dave fella?"

"I emailed him yesterday, he said to give him a call when we're half an hour away, and he'll be there," I said.

I wanted to say more, but Ronan had picked up my hand and sucked one of my fingers into his mouth. He then licked the remaining marmalade from a second finger. I hadn't realised I'd spilled any.

I watched with amusement. “Remind me to cover myself in this if that’s what happens with a small spillage.”

“Mmm, food play, I like the sound of that,” he replied with a minuscule upwards flick of his brows.

I coughed, choking a little on some toast that hadn’t quite been swallowed. I sipped my tea as he patted my back and laughed.

He kissed my temple and then rose. I watched him pull on the white shirt that hung over the back of a chair—he buttoned it, undid his trousers, and I was aware he hadn’t worn boxers to tuck it in. He rolled up the sleeves a little before he placed a waistcoat over it.

While he cleared the dishes, I rushed back upstairs to clean my teeth and gather my overnight bag. I’d already stripped the bed, despite Ronan’s protests that he could do it when he returned, and I looked longingly at it as I passed. I was back down as he was tying his shoelaces. He took the bag from me, and we left the cottage.

“How long will it take us to get to Soho?” I asked as he punched in the address to his satnav.

“Just over an hour, according to this. I haven’t driven to Soho in years, so I’ve no idea if that’s accurate.”

He backed from the driveway, and we started the journey. I enjoyed my time with Ronan while he was driving to Scotland, and I enjoyed my time while we were on the motorway to London. I didn’t enjoy the way he morphed from calm and in control, to something that resembled a black cab driver. He flipped the finger at tooting horns, even when he was in the wrong lane. He pulled out into traffic when he shouldn’t have, and he dared a lorry to take out the side of his rather nice Range Rover when he was in a bus lane, illegally.

“City driving isn’t your thing, is it?” I asked when we eventually pulled up on yellow lines outside the gallery.

"Can you tell?"

"There was a hint every now and again, more so when you called someone a *fuckwit,*" I said.

Ronan laughed. "I'm sorry. I haven't driven in town for such a long time. But we made it in one piece."

"Just about!"

Dave was standing at the front door, and I wondered if we were going to have a *fashion-off.* He, too, wore a shirt—although his sleeves were not rolled up—and a waistcoat. He had added a bow tie to his, whereas Ronan had his collar undone. Both wore the same coloured trousers. He waved when he saw me, and I climbed from the car, narrowly avoiding a dick on a pushbike who gave me the finger as he wobbled past on the wrong side of the road.

I introduced Ronan to Dave, and they shook hands. I let them walk to the back of the car where they unloaded some poorly wrapped pictures. I could see Dave wincing at the sight of loose bubble wrap and newspaper dividing the paintings. They were carried in and placed on the pasting table.

Dave did the same things he did when I first met him. He tapped his lips, walked around, back and forth, contemplating. He then decided he wanted them all. Paperwork was exchanged and despite Dave's attempts at keeping us there for a celebratory drink, he was told that we had important business back in Scotland that needed our urgent attention. We were back in the car an hour after parking, with a ticket to add to a collection I could see in the glove box.

"You do pay those, don't you?" I asked.

He grinned. "Of course I do, I think."

I shook my head. I'd make a point to get them from the car and check. "Now, your apartment?" he said.

"Yes, okay." I wasn't sure that I'd said I would accompany him back to Scotland but, I had no plans until the sale of the barn went through, so no reason to hang around.

"Oh, I didn't tell you," I said, I then proceeded to tell him about Pat the cat being real. "I also feel a little sorry for Danny. He's about to lose his job, which means he'll have to move."

"Didn't you say he was rude to you on more than one occasion?"

"Yes, but that doesn't mean that I can't feel sorry for him," I said, as we approached the building.

Ronan parked, and we headed in. We were halfway up the stairs when Danny came through the door from our floor.

"Lizzie! It's good to see you. I have a huge favour to ask," he said, as he bounded down the stairs.

He completely ignored Ronan who placed his arm around my shoulders. He stood and smiled at me.

"Well?" I asked.

"Huh?"

"What's the favour you need to ask?"

"Oh, right, yes. I just wondered if you'd give Mrs Dingle my flat key. She's going to look after Pat because I have a job interview in Manchester. I'll be away overnight. She's not in."

"Why don't you put the key through her letterbox?" Ronan asked.

"Because…" Danny rolled his eyes dramatically, and I bristled. "She nailed shut her letterbox because she was sick of getting everyone's post."

I knew that, on occasions, the postman couldn't be arsed to walk to our flats, so left everything in the hallway, but I wasn't aware that she'd been receiving it all.

"I'm going to be leaving for Scotland shortly," I said.

"I called Mrs Dingle. She's on her way back, but I'll miss my train if I don't go now."

"How long is she going to be?" I asked.

"Twenty minutes, max, she said."

I held out my hand, it would take that time to get packed, and Danny dropped his key into my palm.

He gave me a smile. "Thanks, Lizzie," he said and then continued to bound down the stairs.

Ronan stared at me. "What?" I said.

"You're too nice sometimes."

I shrugged my shoulders. "Maybe I am, but I'd rather be nice than not," I said, with a smile.

We continued to walk to my flat door. "By the time I pack, she should be back. Now, how long am I likely to be with you?"

"As long as you like," he replied as we entered, and my heart fluttered a little.

Ronan emptied the fridge of any perishables for me. He filled the bin bag and walked it to the bin store while I packed a suitcase. I remembered how unprepared I was the last time with the weather, and we were another couple of weeks towards winter. I packed what I thought would be suitable and added an extra couple of jumpers. When I sat on the suitcase to squash it enough to be able to zip it up, I realised, with the holdall I'd filled, I'd nearly emptied my wardrobe. I grabbed my diary to check what hair appointments I'd need to cancel. I thought I'd find one locally to Ronan. I dragged the suitcase to the hallway and returned for the holdall.

As I walked into the bedroom, I felt an arm grab me from

behind. I squealed as I was pulled backwards and laughed as I fell onto the bed.

"Ooof!" Ronan exaggerated his pain as I landed on him.

"Aw, did I hurt you?" I said, wriggling so that I was lying on top of him.

He wrapped his arms around me. "I have a feeling you might," he said quietly.

I wasn't entirely sure what he meant. I didn't reply. Instead, I just kissed him.

I rested my head on his shoulder and felt such contentment. The knot that niggled constantly in my shoulder seemed to have melted away—the ache I used to feel in my lower back had been forgotten about. I placed my hands on his chest and pushed myself up.

"I think twenty minutes must have passed by now," I said. I continued to push up until I slid off and was standing.

"We can stay here for a little longer," Ronan said, adjusting his cock to a more comfortable position.

"Let me run down and give Mrs Dingle the key," I said.

I left him and bounded down the stairs. I knocked on Mrs Dingle's door and received no answer. I checked my watch. It had been nearly half an hour since Danny had left. I knocked again. When I received no answer the second time, I tried jiggling the letterbox. It was firmly closed.

"Oh, for fuck's sake," I said. I opened the main front door and looked both ways up the road. There was no sign of her.

I knocked on the door opposite, not knowing the name of the occupants but hoping they might recognise me as a neighbour. There was no answer there, either. I peered through the letterbox, hoping to see someone. I cursed again because the flat looked empty.

I walked back up for my mobile.

"All done?" Ronan asked.

"There's no one in," I said. I rifled through my handbag to find my phone. I dialled Joe.

"Hi, are you busy?" I asked when he answered.

"I'm at a property, but I have a minute. The *potentials* are having a wander around by themselves. What's up? I thought you were off to Scotland sexing."

"Sexing? What on earth is that?" I laughed. "I have a problem. I agreed to take Danny's keys to give to Mrs Dingle in number one, but she isn't in, and I don't know what to do."

"Mrs who?"

"That's what Danny calls her. Anyway, I need to give her the keys; she's nailed her letterbox shut because she was fed up with the postman, so I can't even pop them through. No one is in number two, and I need to leave."

"Why do you keep agreeing to things Danny asks?" he said.

"I know, I know. Can you help me? Someone has to feed the bloody cat."

"Tell you what, you feed the cat now, make sure he has water and whatever. I won't be home until tonight, so I'll pop down and get the key from yours. She must be home by then."

"Okay, I'll leave his key on my hallway table. Thank you, love you, and remember, Ronan invited you up to visit. You can come and see the nudist camp," I said, with a laugh.

"I'll be up next week. I've moved some appointments. Go and feed the fucking cat, and I'll call you tonight."

I relayed the conversation to Ronan, and together we walked to Danny's. There was no need for the two of us, but the last time we'd been in there, there had been a dead cat and handcuffs. Ronan wanted to see if it had changed any.

"I'm not sure we should be snooping," I said, as I headed to the kitchen and he, to the bedroom.

"Oh come on, you know you want to. I'm only going to see if the dead cat is still on his bed."

It was wrong. I knew it was, but for some reason, I tiptoed to the bedroom. Danny had left me in the shit so, in my mind, it was fair dues. Ronan opened the door and looked in—he quickly pulled it shut.

"What?" I asked. "What's in there?"

"You don't want to see," he said. I bloody well did.

I pushed past him and opened the door. "What the fuck…?"

Lying on the bed was a blow-up doll. A doll with no clothes on, a mouth shaped like an O and with her legs parted. I stepped close to look.

"She has hooha hair!" I said, astonished.

Ronan covered his mouth to suppress the laughter. Why we thought we had to sneak and be quiet, I had no idea.

I stepped even closer. "That's disgusting."

The dead cat was in its position between the pillows. The handcuffs were still there, and a thought ran through me.

"You don't think he handcuffs it, do you?" I said, turning to Ronan.

He couldn't speak for laughing.

"She's got scuff marks on her wrists," I said, pointing to it.

He still couldn't speak for laughing. I was beginning to giggle as well.

"We need to get out of here. You didn't let the cat in, did you? He might puncture it," I said.

I couldn't get a word of sense from Ronan. I tutted and pushed past him. I pursed my lips to suck in air and call for Pat. I heard a thump as if he'd jumped down from somewhere and discovered him padding across the living room floor. I walked into the kitchen to find his food bowls. I wasn't going to bother with the litter tray, assuming Danny would have cleaned it that morning anyway. I washed the bowl, and placed some food in it, topped up his biscuits and gave him fresh water. All the while, he sat on the kitchen table and stared at me with his devil eyes. I wasn't sure a cat should be sitting on the kitchen table, although I didn't believe, judging by the death and plastic on his bed, Danny was particularly worried about hygiene.

However, I picked up a magazine and prodded Pat. He stared at me some more. I prodded him again. He didn't flinch.

"Blink, you bastard," I said. He neither answered me, obviously, nor blinked. I'd never thought to question whether a cat blinks or not. "I hope your eyeballs dry up."

"Interesting reading," Ronan said, taking the magazine from my hands. He showed me the cover of two naked men in a rather compromising position.

I grabbed it from his hands to take a closer look and also wondered if I might book an eye appointment.

"Oh," I said. One naked man was bent over the back of the sofa, and the other was behind him.

He most certainly wasn't scratching his back because his friend had an itch. A thought hit me, and I threw down the magazine. That startled Pat who jumped from the kitchen table.

"He could be using that to…" I screwed up my eyes and immediately ran the hot tap. I squirted washing up liquid on my hands and thoroughly washed them.

“Your friend certainly has some strange habits. How old is this Mrs Dingle?” Ronan asked finally gaining his composure.

“Ancient. He left a dead cat out for me, a blow-up sex doll for her, yeah, I think strange is a good word to describe him.”

I just didn’t get Danny at all. If Mrs Dingle thought Pat was in the bedroom, she’d search for him, just as I had and found the stuffed cat. Why on earth would he leave that out, if not as a prank? Except, it wasn’t funny. Well, it wasn’t funny to me, although Ronan kept *leaking* the odd chuckle.

We left the flat, and I locked up. I placed the keys, as promised, on my hallway table and took one last look around the flat. When it came time for me to move, most of what I had would fit in a van, and I could have the removal company deliver my things from storage. There would be some items I’d need to buy. I didn’t empty my home of *all* the contents, just one of everything that was doubled up, and my personal items.

It was going to be a long drive to Scotland, and I offered for us to stay at the flat and leave early the following morning, but despite the fact we would arrive late at night, Ronan was keen to get going.

“Maybe you can give me driving lessons, a refresher, when we get there so I can share the driving with you,” I said, as I settled into the car.

“I don’t mind driving, to be honest. I guess I do so much of it,” he replied.

It wasn’t long before we hit the motorway and to break up the monotony Ronan flicked through the radio channels until he came to a quiz show. We alternated with the answers, playing against each other and his knowledge was immense. Not only was he up on current affairs, something I had no interest in, his understanding of world politics was impressive. We debated the benefits, and non-benefits, of European and other worldwide leaders, deciding we were pretty much, politically, on the same page. He told me of some of the countries he had visited. How he'd taken a year out and travelled to Brazil, sailed part of the Amazon, got sick in Indonesia while on an orang-utan conservation programme and nearly died. He'd scuba-dived the Great Barrier Reef, and eaten bugs in Africa while building homes.

"I wish I'd done some of that. Now I look back, and I wonder what my life would have been like had I not married so young. I always dreamed of travelling. I remember having a list of countries that I wanted to visit. I don't think I've been to *one* of them. Harry's idea of a wonderful holiday was a cruise around the Med. We did that year in and year out to the point I rarely got off the boat, I'd seen the sites so many times."

"Nothing stopping you having an adult gap year. It's all the rage," he said.

"Yeah, I can just about get myself from my flat to the gym with only taking a wrong turn once."

"I don't know why you don't consider it. It's enriching. I can say that. I learned more about *me* and about life in general in that one year than I have in all my years on this planet. Seriously, there are companies that will organise an adult gap year for you if you don't want to do it yourself," he said, with a smile.

As much as I loved his enthusiasm for travel and the adventures he'd undertaken, it was another reminder that what we had wasn't permanent. I hid the sadness.

"It might be nice to take a long holiday on land somewhere," I said, not really knowing what more to say.

"I can't do beach holidays. I have to be active," he said, as he indicated to pull into the services. "Need diesel, do you need to pee?"

"I'll squeeze one out, I'm sure," I said, at which he laughed. "Strange things happen to our bladders when we hit fifty. They grow their own mind. One minute, no pee, seconds later, busting to go. Laugh, you leak. Sneeze, you leak. It's why I keep a spare pair of knickers in my bag," I said, laughing with him.

Chat about spare knickers reminded me that I needed to stock up on some panty liners. While Ronan filled up the car, I browsed the meagre offerings and wondered if we should head around the main service area and hope they had a chemist. I kept a watch on him, and when he slotted the nozzle back into the pump, I headed to the counter and paid. I exited just as he entered.

"I've paid," I said.

"Okay. I'll get some cash and give it back," he replied.

"I don't want it back. Now, do you think we could go to the main service area? I need some bits from a chemist."

"Sure, which reminds me…" He didn't finish his sentence, and we walked back to the car dodging the puddles of diesel that I felt should have been sanded over at least.

We drove around to the main part, and Ronan walked with me to the chemist. We separated at the aisles, and I was thankful, I didn't really want him helping me choose panty liners. I grabbed my usual, doubling up in case I couldn't buy them in town, and headed for the counter. Just as the cashier was about to ring up my purchases, I heard Ronan call out to wait.

"Can you add these?" he asked the cashier and planted two twenty pound notes in my hand.

I looked at what he'd added to the counter and wanted to shrink. Condoms, various tubes of lubricant, a cock ring, and some liquid that was meant to prolong orgasm, so the label said. I turned to see him gone.

"Bastard," I whispered, and the cashier, without batting an eyelid, rang up the purchases.

"Would you like a bag? Five pence." I nodded, what did she think I was going to do with it all? It would hardly fit in my little bag, and I had no intention of parading around with a cock ring in my hand.

"He can bloody well pay for my panty liners," I mumbled to myself.

"Sorry, I didn't catch that, was there anything else you needed?" the cashier asked.

"No, I think we have enough for now," said the reappearing Ronan.

I paid for the items but refused to carry the bag. Ronan laughed as he swung it around, proud of its contents.

"That was mean," I said. "And what's with the cock ring?"

"Never used one, saw it, thought it might be fun," he said with a shrug of his shoulders.

"I'm not taking any drugs," I said, huffing my way over to Costa to grab us some takeout coffee.

"It's hardly illegal or dangerous if it's sold in Boots and made by Durex, is it?" he said, rather too loudly for my liking.

I bought two coffees and handed him one. He leaned forward and kissed my temple in thanks. We walked back to the car and continued our journey.

❧

It was dark when I was woken by my stomach grumbling. We were off the motorway, but I wasn't sure exactly where. I straightened myself in the seat.

"Did I fall asleep?" I asked, knowing full well I had but that always seemed the right thing to ask.

“No, you’ve been riveting company. Told me all about your sexual fantasies, which was interesting,” he replied. He hadn’t taken his eyes off the road.

“Ha ha. Where are we?”

“We’ve just gone past Oban, so about another half an hour and we’ll be home. Maggie has left some food for us in the kitchen.”

“I never asked, do they live in the house as well?”

“Sort of, there are a couple of annexes attached. I’ll show you. I need to open the window a little to get some fresh air to wake me up. Are you okay with that?”

“Of course.” I hadn’t thought that he might be tired and cursed myself, again, for not getting my driving skills up to scratch.

The blast of icy air soon changed my mind. I reached around to the rear seats and grabbed Ronan’s coat, wrapped it around myself and breathed in deep to capture his scent.

“I can shut this,” he said.

“No, I’m snug now.”

We continued the rest of the journey in silence until we came to the gates. Ronan pushed a button mounted on the dashboard and the gates started to swing open.

“Had those fixed,” he said with a smile and clearly pleased with himself.

“One thing off the list,” I replied.

The drive to the house had the same effect as the very first time I approached. The gravel road with fields either side led the eye perfectly to the grey stone building with its two turrets and Saltire flag blowing in the breeze.

“Do you lower that when you’re not home?” I joked.

"Always good to be proud of your heritage," he said, with a smile.

"Is probate all done now?" I asked as we came to a stop.

"Yep, and Rich has been paid off. So, Lizzie, I can officially welcome you to *my* home."

I smiled at him as he left the car and ran around to open my door. "I'm pleased for you," I said, taking his hand so he could help me down.

We walked to the boot and unloaded the suitcase and bags. A light had been left on over the front door, and the minute I stepped through, the house felt different. There was warmness. I could feel that some love was being injected back into the old place. I left my bags by the stairs and followed Ronan to the kitchen.

"Blimey, the Aga's working well," I said. The warmth in the kitchen was ten degrees higher than the vast hallway we'd just walked through.

"It works a bloody treat. The repairman was most impressed. He recalled his dad installing it years ago!"

"No way. How amazing that he was able to fix it."

"Yeah. He even took some photographs to display on his website. What we're now doing is having the enamel repaired as well."

The cream Aga had some digs and dents, some chips in corners, but to me, that added to the charm. I could still smell the bread that Maggie had made, and I hoped that when I lifted the tea towel covering something on the kitchen table, I'd find some. Ronan opened the fridge to find a plate of cheese, and I put the kettle on to boil. With the tea made, we sat at the table, and I sliced off some bread.

"This smells delicious," I said, cutting some cheese and scooping a spoonful of homemade pickle onto my plate.

I savoured the bread and cheese while making too many ridiculous noises of appreciation for Maggie and the Aga. When I was done eating, I stretched and yawned.

"Bedtime," Ronan said. We cleared the plates, and a moment of doubt hit me.

Would I be sleeping alone in the same room I'd stayed in before? Ronan carried my suitcase up, and he walked past the bedroom I assumed to be his, and to the one I'd used, with the en-suite bathroom. He placed the suitcase on a small table beside the wardrobe and kicked off his shoes. He flopped on the bed and patted the space beside him.

"This is actually my bedroom so, do you mind if I share it with you?" he asked.

"Why did you give me your bedroom? I would have been comfortable anywhere," I said, sitting on the edge of the bed.

"Because this one has a functioning bathroom. The room I slept in, which was Rich's, doesn't."

"Why was…" I didn't want to finish the sentence that was on my mind, which was to ask why Demi's photograph was in *Rich's* bedroom and not Ronan's. "Why don't I go and clean my teeth?" I said.

I was halfway through scrubbing my teeth when shirtless Ronan walked into the bathroom. He unzipped his trousers and peed. He smiled at me as he did, and I shook my head. In all my years of marriage, Harry never once shared a bathroom with me. In fact, we had completely separate rooms; separate bedrooms as well towards the end. He blamed his snoring and bad back on needing to sleep alone, which, of course, was an all-out lie. Ronan finished his pee and flushed. He left his trousers undone but, thankfully, did tuck his cock away. He stood beside me at the sink while he washed his hands. It seemed the most natural thing in the world.

"Fuck it, toothbrush," he said. He left the room and shortly returned to do his own teeth.

By the time he was done, I was under the duvet.

He slid in beside me. "Pyjama's?" He laughed.

"A vest top and shorts, not exactly a onesie," I replied. "You never know, there might be a fire, and we'll need to get out quick."

He snuggled in beside me and placed his hand on my stomach. He ran it up, dragging the vest top with him.

"Easy to get off, I see," he said. I raised my arms above my head so he could do just that.

❧

I was awake, but I refused to open my eyes. I heard the footsteps across the floor, and the clonk as a cup was placed on the bedside cabinet, the footsteps around the bed, and another clonk.

"Thanks, Mags," Ronan murmured, as he shuffled beside me.

I refused to acknowledge the tea, Maggie, or the fact she had walked in to see Ronan and me in bed together. Regardless, I was sure the colour of my cheeks would give me away.

A minute or so later, I felt Ronan lean towards me. "She's gone, you can open your eyes now," he whispered.

I laughed and slapped his thigh. "We need a lock," he said before I could.

"I'm so embarrassed," I said, sitting up and reaching for my tea.

"About being in bed with me?" he asked, there was a tone of surprise in his voice.

"God, no. About being *caught* in bed with you."

"How old are you?" he asked, laughing.

"Not the point. Funny how she knew to bring both cups in," I said.

"She probably went to the other bedroom first. Or maybe she heard you screaming my name," he said, with a wink.

I gasped at the thought as panic washed over me. "I did not! Oh God, how thin, or thick, are these walls?"

"I'm joking. But you did. The walls are thick enough, and their annexe is the complete other end of this monster," he said, referring to the house.

I showered—and it was wonderful to have the constant hot water—and then dressed while Ronan did the same. I made the bed, wondering if it smelled of sex and resisted the urge to sniff his pillow.

I was tying my laces when he walked into the room with a towel around his waist. "All my clothes are in the other room," he said.

"I'll see you downstairs," I replied, gathering the two mugs and deciding to brave Maggie on my own.

She was in the kitchen, and once again, the smell of bread made my mouth water. It was as if she was in overdrive. There were pies lined up on a counter ready for baking.

"Good morning," I said, as I walked in.

"And a good morning to you. What time did you both get here?" she asked.

"It was late. That bread you left out was delicious. I've never known how to make bread."

"I'll teach you. Now, all those pies need to go in. The art group are gathering today."

"Surely not in this weather?" I asked, looking through at the rain and mist outside.

"Even in this weather. It's not *that* cold outside," she said.

"It's fucking freezing," I heard. Ronan walked into the kitchen and, as was his way, kissed my temple.

"You're getting soft. Too many months down south," Maggie said, although she pronounced *south* as *sooth*. She laughed at her own wit.

"Honestly, will the arty lot be okay?" I asked.

"They have a fire—they have shelter. They get too into their art to notice the weather, and we can take them some nice warm pies for lunch," she said.

I wasn't sure I wanted to walk around people in the nuddy handing out pieces of pie. But I did want to speak to Saggy…*Petal!* I wanted her input on a permanent structure for days when the weather was less favourable for being naked.

"I dinnae want them earth lovers digging holes. I turned my ankle," I heard.

Charlie walked in, accompanied by a dog. A lovely dog with big brown eyes, a tongue lolling from his mouth, and a very wiggly tail. I stroked his head as he sat beside me.

"You need to tell me where these earth lovers are," I said.

The room quietened. Maggie started to giggle, and Charlie smirked. "Maybe I'll show yous after ma chores," he said with a wink.

I looked at Ronan, who smiled. "I'll come, too, Charlie," he said, but I fully suspected he knew exactly where they were.

Ronan left with Charlie to help with maintenance work in the courtyard; some of the old buildings needed roof repairs before the winter took hold. I helped Maggie with some cooking. I learned that her pies were well liked that the pub, which I knew to be part of the estate, and some locals bought them from her. She showed me a tin where she kept the money, insisting that it went towards household items that needed to be paid for in cash.

I held up my hands in protest. "Maggie, it has nothing to do with me," I said.

"I don't know. Our Ronan is pretty keen on you. I don't know the last time he had anyone *stay over* with him," she said, doing that blasted quote thing with her fingers.

"Surely Demi stayed here?" I said, fishing.

"No. Obviously, he had the cottage as well, even when he was single. Before being married to the piranha, he never brought women back here. I know he was worried what people thought of his mum, but he used to say to me that the house was a special place, and he never wanted it tarnished with bad memories." She winked at me.

"I think it's more likely he just grew out of that thought. He is mid-fifties," I said.

"Mid-forties," she corrected me. "Unless I lost ten years somewhere," she added with a laugh.

I was sure he'd told me he was mid-fifties, and I wracked my brain to remember when. Had I just assumed he was older than me?

I shrugged as nonchalantly as possible. "Mid-forties, I can't remember what he said to be honest," I replied to get myself out of the situation.

We worked in silence for a little while, and I pondered on what I felt about dating—if that was what I was doing—a younger man. I had never been the one to worry about an age gap unless it was huge.

"That's them all done, now for tea," Maggie said as I loaded the last of the pies in the oven. There was a rack of them cooling, and the smell was certainly making my mouth water.

"I don't think you're going to be any good for my figure," I said, with a laugh.

"Och, get away with you, you skinny wee mare. Now, apple or cherry?" she asked, waving a knife over the fruit pies.

I could never resist a cherry pie, so settled on that one. I made tea, she laid two plates on the table, and I fell in love with Maggie and her cherry pies.

Later, Maggie heaved a large metal tea urn from a cupboard and instructed me to fill a plastic crate with cups and sauces, a couple of teapots, milk jugs, four litres of milk, filled sugar pots and spoons. I added small dessert plates and forks, a pack of napkins and a tablecloth.

I carried the plastic crate, and she carried the urn and balanced a box of tea bags on the top. Outside the back door was a quad bike. I placed the crate in a large basket that was attached to the end of the seat and Maggie placed the urn beside and a container of water that had been left by the bike. She expertly wrapped a piece of tarpaulin and two bungee cords around the lot to secure it.

"Hop on," she said. I stared at her as she cocked her leg over the seat. She patted behind her, and I climbed on, although with some trepidation.

"Have you driven this before?" I asked as she stalled it.

"Of course, hold on."

We finally got going and bounced along a track through the woods. What Maggie hadn't mentioned was the mud that got kicked up off the wheels and splattered us. I could hear her maniacal laughter over the roar of the engine. The way she hunched over the handlebars you'd think we were speeding along, in fact, I was sure I could have jogged quicker. All she needed was a leather hat with earflaps and a pair of goggles, and she could have walked off the set of an old comedy show. We were going so slowly, I didn't feel the need to hold on at all. However, sitting up meant I took the brunt of the mudslinging. Maybe that was why she crouched.

Whatever it was we hit had us both jolt forward, the quad bounced up and over until it slipped backwards when the engine stalled.

"Are you okay?" she asked, as we came to a halt.

"Yes, what happened?"

"I think we got stuck."

I looked down to notice the back wheels in a rut. The muddy water came halfway up.

"We're going to have to push it out," she said, also looking down.

I translated that to mean *I* was going to have to push it out. I slid one leg off and leapt as far over the rut as I could. I didn't want to land smack in the middle of the water and ruin my walking boots. I landed with a splosh and wanted to cry. A townie's walking boots were a precious thing, not really bought to wear in wet weather, mud, or when pushing quad bikes from holes.

"You know, if you gave it some welly it would drive out," I said. Surely those bikes were designed to drive in and out of holes and mud.

"What do you mean?" she asked.

"Just open the throttle and drive it out." I so wished I hadn't recommended that, or at least asked Maggie to wait a moment so I could move out of the way.

I didn't ask, and I didn't move in time. Before I could blink, or even close my mouth, I was showered by the contents of the rut. Muddy water sprayed over me. It dripped from my nose, my fringe was plastered to my forehead, and all I could do was spit and then spit some more to get rid of the grit from my mouth.

"Oh, my. Oh, my," I heard. I hadn't wanted to open my eyes for fear of them being polluted. I rubbed at them as much as I could and then opened.

Maggie sat there with both hands over her mouth. "Oh, my," she repeated.

"I'm driving," was all I said.

I walked to the quad bike, and Maggie shuffled back. I slung my leg over like a pro and shot off so fast she was nearly deposited off the back. She screeched and then laughed as we roared down the track to the campsite. All I wanted to do was dump the tea and pies and get back to the house for a bath. The damp was seeping through my clothes, and the cold was biting into my bones.

I came to an abrupt halt, and Maggie headbutted my back. She laughed again, mumbling something that had the word *roller-coaster* in it. In front of me was the elderly couple, still naked, but with wellies on, and Eric, bless him, had on a pink woollen knitted hat, the exact same as the tea cosy my nan knitted one time for me. His dick was nowhere to be seen, but his ball sack hung down by his knobbly knees.

"Lizzie, how nice to see you…are you muddy, dear? Whatever happened?" Petal asked peering closer at me. I guessed, going naked also meant forgoing glasses.

"Never mind, we have tea and pie for you all," I said.

Maggie unhooked the crate and urn, and we carried it to the main yurt. I didn't want to look to see what was slapping behind me. Inside the yurt was another couple, much younger, in fact, I would have put them at mid-twenties. He was sitting cross-legged, pinching his fingertips with his eyes closed, and she was painting him. And I mean, painting *him.* Blobs of paint were dabbed onto his skin as he hummed.

I placed the crate on a large table and then turned to Maggie. I held up the cord of the urn, waving the plug. As if on cue, what sounded like a mini jet engine fired up.

"Generator," she said, taking the plug from me and crawling under the table.

I didn't speak after that. I laid out the tablecloth, put cups on saucers, cut pie and dished up while the urn gurgled.

"I *am* sorry," Maggie said, and I felt awful. At that moment, her voice was small, and I realised that she was worried that I was cross.

I gave her a smile despite the muddy water having dried and cracked on my face. "Oh, Mags, it's okay, honestly. I do need to get back, though. I'm getting really cold."

Petal shuffled into the yurt with Eric in tow. "Lizzie, this is awfully nice of you, isn't it, Eric?" she shouted his name only. He nodded his head.

"We'll need to leave you to clear up, if that's okay? Lizzie is rather cold," Maggie said.

"You should get those wet clothes off," I heard. I turned to see the painted man standing now, and wished to fucking God I hadn't.

I heard Maggie take in a sharp breath, and she nudged me on the arm. She didn't need to; it wasn't hard to miss the rigid cock that stood proud. I had no idea how long it was, but it waggled around like a sword about to duel. I felt a little pee leak out from the internal howling with laughter that was going on. The only reason I couldn't reply was because my jaw was clamped so tight to stop the hysteria about to erupt from me. I raised my hand as if to speak, but couldn't.

"She's not feeling well," Maggie said.

That was it. I had to leave. I ran from the yurt with Maggie running after me. Eric asking what was going on, and Petal was telling him we had just *witnessed* Antonio's cock.

"Oh my God," I said, as I skidded to an abrupt halt, causing Maggie to collide with my back, and pushing us both into a pile of freshly turned over mud. In front of us was a woman with her arms wrapped around a tree. She, obviously, was naked but she'd dug a little trench, a moat filled with more muddy water.

"What is she doing?" I asked, quietly. "No, don't tell me, I think I have a good idea."

I turned on my heels and navigated around the moat back to the quad. I got on the front, and without a word, Maggie climbed on behind, and I drove us back. It wasn't quite breakneck speed, but we got back in a quarter of the time it had taken us to arrive. I pulled into the courtyard and waited for Maggie to climb off. She was still laughing at our encounter, to the extent that Charlie and Ronan walked out of one of the outbuildings to see what was going on. Both stood still and stared at me.

"What the…?"

I held up my hand to stop Ronan's question.

"Don't ask, just…don't ask. I saw a man being painted who had the largest cock I think I've ever seen, and I've seen that Photo-shopped one that went around Facebook. I saw a woman kissing a tree… Kissing. A. Tree," I repeated, and I think that was more for my own clarity than anything else. "She had built a moat around her and her tree. Saggy tits and limp dick were lovely, although Eric wore a woollen hat and both had wellies on. It was surreal, and I think I just need a bath to warm up. Maggie, you can explain how I came to look like this."

With that, I stomped off, not caring that laughter sounded behind me. "Oh, and someone needs to go back and pick up all the dirty crockery," I shouted as I kicked off my boots and walked into the warmth of the kitchen.

I was soaking in the bath with real bubbles that time and my eyes closed when I felt Ronan run his finger down my cheek. I opened my eyes to see him kneeling beside me.

He smiled, and I started to laugh. The more he just smiled, the more I convulsed and became worried I might waterboard myself again. I clung on the sides and howled with laughter.

I tried to speak. "You should have seen his…his…oh my God, his co…" I just couldn't get my words out coherently. "And she was…tongue in a hole in the tree…" That was it, at that thought, I knew I had to get out. I was either going to piss myself in the bath—and I didn't fancy washing in pissy water—or drown.

I reached out to him. "Help…" Thankfully, he understood. He leaned in, placed his hands under my armpits, and he lifted me, as one would do a child. I swung my legs over the bath and stood while he wrapped me in a fluffy white towel. He watched as I peed, and I really didn't care about that. With tears still streaming down my cheeks, he guided me to the bedroom where I sat, not caring what got wet, on a chaise that was probably hundreds of years old.

In the end, I had to put my head between my knees for fear of fainting from lack of oxygen. It had been hard to catch a breath between laughing. Even though he wasn't there, and I doubted he understood a word I'd said, Ronan laughed along with me. When I was done, when all the chuckles, giggles, guffaws, and screeching had been expelled, I slumped back with utter exhaustion. Who knew something so funny could be so draining?

"Now, do you want to start at the beginning?" he asked.

I waved my hand like I was swatting a swarm of wasps away. I shook my head and closed my eyes. I took some deep breaths in until finally, I was calm again.

"I can't, not yet."

Ronan stood. He carried me to the bed and laid me down. I was still wrapped in the towel, and instead of slipping under the duvet, he placed a woollen blanket over me. It was surprisingly warm, and I was thankful for it. Ronan climbed on the bed, and I curled into him. Every now and then, as I thought back, I emitted a little chuckle, and he would match it.

"Did I tell you my mum was bohemian?" he whispered.

I wanted to roar again, but I refused. I clamped my mouth and nodded instead.

Oh yes, she, and the whole place, was a throwback to Woodstock, I thought. I drifted into sleep.

CHAPTER TWENTY

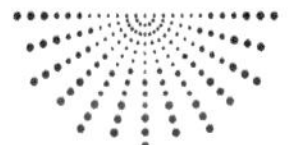

I could hear a crackle, and the smell of burning logs jolted me awake. Ronan was crouched by the open fire in the bedroom that he'd lit to warm the room. I looked out of the window to see darkness, although that didn't give me a clue what time of day it was. The nights rolled in super early in that part of Scotland, an hour earlier than down south, I was sure.

"Hey," I said, pushing myself into a sitting position.

He stood and walked over. "I molested you while you slept. I hope you don't mind," he said, with not a hint of a smirk on his face.

"That's okay, just as long as you didn't bite my…you know, like you did before. That wasn't a nice thing to do," I said, crossing my arms over my chest in mock indignation.

"I wondered if you'd notice. It wasn't intentional, a spur of the moment thing."

"Yes, well, don't do it again," I said.

“No, ma’am. Now, you missed lunch, but dinner will be in an hour. I can bring something up, and we can eat here if you want?”

“No, you shouldn’t have let me sleep so long. Poor Maggie would have been left with all the clearing up,” I said, pushing the blanket off me.

“Charlie did all that. I don’t think Mags could stomach *Big Cock*, as she now calls him, by herself.”

I started to chuckle, thankful the earlier hysteria didn’t return.

“I hope you earn well out of that art group,” I said, swinging my legs over the side of the bed.

“Not much, but it was my mother’s project so, I guess it’s a legacy to her.”

I smiled at him. “It’s a good thing to do. They seem to enjoy themselves, although I wonder if you should add some form of anti-bacterial soap to the bathrooms you need to install.”

He frowned. “I wasn’t aware I was installing a new bathroom block.”

“Stops them shitting in the woods, or wherever naked artists go. I told you, we’re going to make a business out of that,” I said, with a laugh. I was still up for the idea of the naked spa, which reminded me of something.

While I got dressed, I asked Ronan about the hotel Joe was advising on. I was sure that Joe had promised me a weekend there.

“It’s on hold at the moment. I think my priorities need to be here for now.”

I understood what he meant. If he could get on top of the house and its associated businesses then he’d be free to get back to his other activities.

"Maggie said there was an estate manager starting…or did she say you were interviewing? I can't remember now." I finished dressing and slipped my feet into my Converse.

"Yes, I've got a couple of people lined up for interviews. I've also got a couple of students from the farming college that I'm going to take on as part of their course. A little like work experience, I assume."

"That sounds interesting."

Ronan told me that although a lot of the land was rented out to tenant farmers, there was the deer population to deal with —I didn't want to get too involved in that conversation—the salmon fishing, stone walling, and general maintenance that had gone to pot while under the care of Manuel. He said the next project for him and Charlie had been the felling of some trees, but before they could do that, they needed to reorganise the log shed. The new logs would have to go towards the back to season. He asked me if I wouldn't mind working on the estate office.

We had gone through paperwork, there was still a lot to be archived, and the room needed a complete refurb before it could be called a workable space. I looked forward to the task. Although there was so much to deal with, a plan was being formulated which gave Ronan some direction. All that was needed was the funding for it all.

"So what do you earn from the puppies?" I asked as we sat around the kitchen table eating the most delicious steak and onion pie, mash potatoes, and vegetables.

"Those ones, when they're ready to leave Mum should fetch about three to four thousand pounds each," Ronan said. He looked to Charlie for confirmation and received a nod.

"You're kidding me? That much?"

"They're from good stock. A pup recently sold for over fifteen thousand—not one of ours, sadly."

I had no idea that a good sheepdog was worth that much money, but then I remembered an old TV show when I was young, and the work that went into a dog was enormous. If it was an award-winning dog, the price could triple.

I knew there to be seven pups, and although that would bring in a nice sum, once the care and vet bills and all the other things associated with puppy breeding were taken into account, the profit would be swallowed up in an instant. Ronan had agreed, though, that the funds from the puppies would be used for the art retreat and it was my job to source the best quality log cabins and yurts for the cheapest price. Ronan and Charlie could do the groundwork, and he decided he would call upon his contractors to spend some time on the project as well. If it was going to be done, it was going to be done well, although a project simply in memory of Verity.

While I had been back home, he'd drawn up some plans, and I had to ask if he'd actually drawn them, they were as close to an architects spec as I'd seen. He showed a tarmac road leading from one of the gates to a car parking area. From there, a path led into the woods and to the existing clearing. He had a log cabin for socialising, with a kitchen area and log-burning stove. A second cabin needed to contain toilets and showers, with a space for lockers for personal items. There would be seven yurts, and he'd estimated that we only needed three new, two existing ones were beyond repair, and the rest could be worked on. He'd certainly thought it through.

"You're not going to do all that while they're here, are you?" I had images of builders and tree kissers not quite mixing well.

"No, they don't come back until spring now," Charlie said. "Unless the tree lover gets lonely, then she might sneak in every now and again."

"Each to their own, I guess."

I couldn't understand why anyone would be in love with a tree, and I was curious, but not enough to seek her out and ask. I didn't want to put her in a position of having to explain. She was comfortable with what she was doing, and she was with a group of people that obviously understood her.

CHAPTER TWENTY-ONE

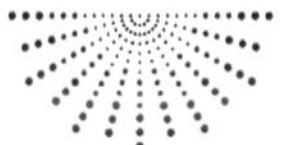

For the next few days, we were busy and it was nice to watch Ronan in the workshop from the estate office window. He wore jeans that fitted into his work boots. Some days he had a T-shirt on, even though the weather was abysmal, and sawdust would be stuck to his muscular arms. Other days he wore a long waxed coat with rain running down his forehead. All days, he got more and more sexy. I'd been surrounded by the suited dicks from the city for many years, but there was something about a man willing to get his hands dirty, able to create and repair and mend, to carve a little figurine into a wooden tent pole that only we'd know about, that had my heart fluttering.

"Do you have plasters in here?" he asked, coming into the office.

"I do, actually. I restocked the first aid kit as I wasn't sure what capabilities you had around a chainsaw."

I left the desk to reach for the first aid box on a cleaned and repainted shelf. The whole room had been dusted, swept, washed, and repainted. It was a nice place to work. I had removed some pictures of Ronan's dad with horses and replaced them with others of deer and dogs and cattle from the farm.

Ronan held out his hand. His palm was scuffed, and a blister had formed. There were smears of blood from scratches. Nothing serious, but I suspected he wanted the blister covered. He washed his hand under the cold tap in the yard and dried it on his dirty jeans.

"That's healthy," I said, squirting some antibacterial spray on his palm.

"Fuck, that stings."

"Don't be a wuss. Now, do you want the plaster over that blister?" I asked. He nodded.

When I'd patched him up, I patted his arse and gave him a wink. "You're certainly brightening my view with all your manly goings on over there," I said.

He laughed. "Manly goings on?"

"You remind me of a Diet Coke advert, all sexy and sweaty. Shame Charlie's over there with you."

"Well now, Lizzie, Charlie doesn't see too well, and this office has a lockable door." He stalked towards me as I replaced the first aid box. "You can play nurse."

I laughed as I was pinned to the cold stone wall.

"I diagnose a serious case of *notenoughsexsyndrome*," I said.

"Oh, no. Is there a cure?" he asked dramatically, clearly enjoying our little game, as he ran his hands up my sides, scrunching my jumper up with them. I shivered as the cold air hit my skin.

"I think there might well be. Let me think…"

"While you do that, I want to kiss those lips of yours."

My heart missed several beats, and butterflies danced in my

stomach. He reached behind my back, and I felt the scratch to my skin of calloused hands that had been working. I deepened the kiss, wanting to feel him closer to me. He pushed one of his legs between mine, and I was getting so worked up I could have dry humped him.

I slipped my hands under his jacket and around his body, holding him tight as his tongue explored my mouth, as mine tasted him. I could feel muscles move under his jumper as he twisted his body into mine, needing that closeness. He removed his hands from my skin and held my head instead. I moaned and curled my hands into fists, bunching his T-shirt in them. That moan spurred him on. He pressed harder into me; I could feel his cock, hard and straining against his jeans. My body started to hum, static coursed over my skin, and he took the air from my lungs as he claimed my mouth, holding my head so tight as if he owned me. At that moment, I wished he did.

"I need to fuck you so badly," he whispered as he pulled his head away. His hot breath fanned over my face.

I captured his lip between my teeth, biting gently, sucking and licking. His moan was all I needed to hear. I pulled my head back and silently slid away from him. I walked to the door and locked it, placing my back against the wood and out of sight from anyone walking past. Smiling, I kicked off my boots, undid my jeans and slid them, and my knickers, to my feet. Before I had righted myself, he was there, his jeans undone and his cock in his hand. He grabbed one thigh and raised my leg. I hooked my arms around his neck, and he lifted me. I wrapped my legs around his waist, and he did what he'd said he needed to do.

❧

I returned from the rather unpleasant outside loo after cleaning myself up. It reminded me of my nan's old council house before they installed a bathroom. Ronan was leaning against the desk.

He smiled as I walked in, reached out to grab my hands and pulled me to him.

"We didn't use a condom, are you okay with that?" he asked.

"I'm fine, I'm hardly likely to get pregnant at my age, and I'm assuming you don't have any nasty diseases Joe hasn't yet warned me about," I said, with a laugh.

"Good, and no, I haven't. Have you?" he teased.

"Would it comfort you to know I had a full health screening when Harry left me, and I found out he'd been sleeping with her. I'm healthier than a virgin, according to the nurse. Although I will take great delight in telling her she was wrong about the lubricant need."

I had started to surprise myself with how forward I was. How unashamed I'd become in talking about sex and demanding what I wanted.

"Sleeping with *her*?" Ronan said, and it occurred to me I had never told him the full story.

"He ran off with a drag queen. And not just any old drag queen, one over six feet tall who used to be a sailor in the Navy."

Before he could even smirk, I started to laugh. I wasn't sure exactly when the hurt had stopped. When it didn't actually bother me to speak his name and to even remember *some* times with fondness. In fact, I'd decided, I would even send them a *New Home* card. Ronan joined in the laughter.

"Oh, Lizzie. If I didn't know it was all true, I'd never believe the half of it." He kissed my nose. "Now that you have distracted me for all of…" he consulted his watch, "Bollocks, that was only like half an hour. I'll have to owe you. Now that you've distracted me for *all* that time, I have to get back to work."

I watched him walk back to the workshop and Charlie shook his head while laughing. I wasn't sure what Ronan had said, but I didn't care, either. It was with a smile that I sat back behind the desk and continued to archive all the old accounts and file all current tax year items. The accountant was visiting later that week to go through the receipts. I was sure there could be a saving made if Ronan would use an online accounting programme. I knew Joe used one for all his expenses, and it never seemed to be that difficult. Maybe, when he visited, he could help me set it up.

I sat back in my chair, and a small pang of doubt hit me. I was thinking as if I was going to be around for a while when I knew that not to be the case. I had a house purchase going through hopefully, and Ronan, at some point, would need to get back to his businesses. Being in Scotland was romantic and wonderful and it was a delight to spend time with him, Maggie, and Charlie, but it was like being on holiday, and I knew it would come to an end.

I had two choices: I could take what was on offer and enjoy myself, or I could continue to protect my nearly-healed heart and never experience life. The thought of not spending time with Ronan made my chest hurt. I had fallen for him; there was no doubt about that. I'd never say anything, of course. I also knew I'd take whatever was available for the time being and worry about the heartache when it came.

An hour or so passed when I heard a tap on the window. Ronan beckoned to me. Rain dripped from the rim of the hat he wore. At first, I shook my head, but he tapped and beckoned again, so I walked to the door.

"What?" I asked.

"Come and see what we've done. We need your approval it seems."

"It's pissing down," I complained.

"So? It rains a lot in Scotland, get used to it. There are coats and hats on the hook."

...get used to it. I wouldn't think too much into what he'd said. But I did rush to grab a long coat and a hat. I found some gloves and slipped them on as well.

"Jump on," Ronan said. He sat astride one of the quad bikes that pulled a trailer of wooden posts. I climbed on behind, making sure to tuck my coat under my backside.

When we came to the clearing that had originally housed a few tents, some bunting, a moat around a tree, and bare patches of earth, I sucked in a breath. In just a couple of days, it had been transformed.

Five yurts of various sizes stood in a circle around an area filled with bark chippings. In the middle of the area was a large fire pit. Benches made from logs were scattered around, and I could see the new path, again made from log edging and filled with bark leading through the woods. To one side were two areas marked out and a bloody big hole.

"What's that for?" I asked.

"Septic tank will go in there, and we'll need some sort of container to store water for the showers. I'm thinking of a rain-water system since we have that in abundance."

"That's every ecological," I replied.

"Goes with the ethos of what this is all about, I guess. I hadn't thought of it in that way—it's just the cheapest option," he laughed.

I tucked my arm through his. "You know, I think your mum would be so proud of you for doing this. You know, if she was anything like you, I would have loved her."

He didn't speak for a while. "Thank you. You have a lot of the same qualities. Both very caring and maybe a little too forgiving."

I shrugged my shoulders. I didn't mind those qualities at all.

"Has Petal seen this?" I asked.

"Not yet. I'll invite her back when it's all done, and she can give her opinion. She's appointed herself unelected chairperson for the art group and will be collecting subs, as she calls them, each month to contribute."

"At least if it can stand on its own two feet, it would be good." I wasn't sure what the art group cost other than teas and coffees, cakes, and snacks. They bought the food they barbequed, the art supplies, and easels.

"I think we'll have this done in another week. You know, I haven't been this enthusiastic about the place since I was a kid. Thank you for that."

I wasn't sure what I'd done other than to give ideas, but if it helped, I was happy. We unloaded the wooden poles, and we climbed back on the quad and drove. Instead of heading to the house, Ronan took a different direction. We powered on through the rain for a little while until we came to a clearing. Ahead of me, I could see the loch and beyond that, mountains and forests. Ronan slowed, and we took a path that led to a wooden structure and an old jetty. I was guessing it was a boathouse of some sort. He stopped the bike, and I slid off. I walked to the beginning of the jetty, not sure how safe the structure was.

"When I was a kid, I spent all summer here, just jumping off and swimming; if the weather was good enough, obviously. I fished, repaired this jetty, and we sailed our boats."

When *I* was a kid, I played penny up the wall at the council flats I lived in and dodged the drunks and the druggies that sat in the copse in the middle of my urban jungle. I felt a connection to Ronan that made me believe we were similar, yet our upbringing was worlds apart.

"I bet it was idyllic," I said.

"I did it more to get away from my parents. All they did was fight. It was a depressing house to live in, which is why my mother ended up with mental health issues, I'm sure."

I never asked Ronan how his mother had died. I doubted it was old age; she might have only been in her mid to late sixties. But there was something in the deep breath and the long sigh that made me reluctant to pry. It was too personal.

He opened the door to the boathouse, and I saw two old small sailing boats moored side by side. One had a hull of green water that had clearly sat there for a long time. There was a mezzanine floor, and I could imagine summer nights lying on blankets and listening to the sounds of the loch.

"This would make an amazing property, Ronan," I said, remembering an episode of Grand Designs where the owners fixed up an abandoned lifeboat station.

"I often thought about doing that. When I moved into one of the cottages with… Well, when things got tough, this was my sanctuary. No budget for it right now, but it could be a project for another day."

"How are the cottages coming along?" I asked as we walked back to the bike.

"Builders will be finished in a day or so, then it's just decorating, furnishing and we're ready to advertise for next spring. I guess we need some sort of website, really."

With all the plans Ronan had, I was starting to think that his life was going to be permanently in Scotland. Although an easy journey back down south: a flight, train, or the long drive he so enjoyed, would have him back in Kent frequently, there was a lot to oversee at the estate. Unless he got a cracking team to run the place and could afford their wages, of course, he was going to find himself having to make a decision on where to live at some point. I suspected the estate was going to consume a lot of his time, and I wondered if he was aware of that.

We took a slower drive back, a different route, and it reminded to me ask Ronan to take me around the whole estate. We could pack a picnic, and I could get to see just how vast it really was. I knew Charlie would go out to fix fences or walls and he'd be gone all day. In my head, I was picturing acres of land divided up into small parcels with sheep and cattle.

We came to a halt, and Ronan turned to me. He had his fingers to his lips, and then he pointed. I followed his gaze. Standing between some trees was a stag—a huge beast with antlers that would have been the length of my arm. He must have spotted us, or at least smelled our scent as he looked our way. Not overly fazed, he cocked one leg and waited.

"Isn't he beautiful?" Ronan whispered.

"He is. I don't think I've ever seen a stag in the wild. Seen plenty of girls, nothing like him, though. You're not going to shoot him, are you?"

Ronan laughed. "No, he has sired some fantastic meat; he can live a little longer. Anyway, the season has finished."

I hoped he was joking about the *live a little longer,* and I hoped he was serious about the season being over. I wasn't dumb. I knew where my meat came from. I ate mainly free range, but I was also a hypocrite in that I didn't want to witness that.

"I'm gutted I don't have my camera, we don't get many pictures of him. Charlie named him Ruairidh. It means royal and with red hair. If you got close to him, you'd see is coat is chestnut red."

"Does it make you sad to know he might get culled?" I asked.

"No, because when that time comes, he'll be wanting it. He'll be old or sick, or injured to the point he might not survive. We cull the hinds, and some of the males, but never the dominant ones. We have to, Lizzie, to ensure their survival. They would eat their way through this land, and all neighbouring lands in no time and then have nothing left if their numbers weren't kept in check. It's not nice, and we don't turn it into an *event,* but it's all part of land management."

"When did you learn to shoot?" I asked as he started up the bike and the stag moved on.

"I don't remember how old I was. Charlie taught me when I was kid. I guess I had my first gun when I was a teenager. Pigeons, birds, deer obviously, rabbit. We eat everything we shoot. Or we sell it to the butcher. I'll teach you if you like?"

It didn't pass me by that it was yet another thing that Charlie had taught him, and I began to realise how fractured his relationship with his father had been. I wondered if he'd been in touch since Verity's death but didn't want to ask.

We pulled into the courtyard as Charlie was wandering out with a puppy in his hands.

"What do you have there?" Ronan asked.

"Broken leg, I think. Waiting on the vet, but I think he needs to be away from the others," he replied.

The puppy was yelping, and I could hear the howl of Mum from the kennels. Charlie nestled the puppy in some straw just outside the bars where Mum could poke her nose through and still sniff him.

"I wonder how that happened," I mused.

"I don't know. It's odd. He has a couple of puncture wounds as well. I think we move them inside, Ronan. Maybe something tried to take him."

"*Something*?" I asked.

"A fox or a wild dog maybe. Doug, the farmer next field over, reported a wildcat sighting, but I think he had too much whisky in his belly," Charlie answered.

Ronan chuckled with him. "Let us know when the vet arrives."

He parked the quad bike in the workshop and took my hand. We walked into the kitchen to the smell of yet more baking.

"Taste," Maggie said, shoving what looked like the rock cakes of my youth in my hand. It was hot, and I bounced it from palm to palm to cool it down.

I took a bite, and it melted in my mouth. It was doughy and sweet with currants and pieces of something slightly sour. I looked at it and picked out a piece of the red fruit.

"Redcurrants," she said, "I thought I'd experiment."

I gave her a thumbs-up as I took another bite.

"I'm going to grab a shower and get out of these clothes," Ronan said.

"I'll do the same… not at the same time as Ronan, of course… after you've…" I said.

Maggie laughed, and Ronan grabbed my hand to drag me from the kitchen while I finished the rock cake.

"Do you have wildcats here? I thought they were pretty much extinct," I said, as we climbed the stairs.

"They nearly are. I've never known one to come so close to us, though. I guess if it's hungry enough, but to take a pup? I don't know."

Ronan stripped out of his clothes and left them in a pile on the floor. His jeans still had sawdust over them, and his T-shirt was filthy. He was a messy guy, not that it was my place to point that out to him. While I waited, I removed my clothes. I sat with my dressing gown around me wondering if I ought to shave my legs yet. My hooha hair had started to grow back, and I was dismayed to see some greys. I inspected just as Ronan walked back into the bedroom.

"Want me to do that for you?" he said, startling me.

"I was checking how many grey hairs I have," I said, quickly removing my hand.

"Why are women so fascinated with all that stuff?"

"Because, often, men make us so self-conscious."

I walked past him into the bathroom and hung my dressing gown on the back of the door. As I stepped into the shower, I heard a car come up the drive. Ronan shouted that he'd be down with Charlie, and I guessed the vet had arrived.

I showered quickly, surprised to note that I must have acclimatised to the Scottish weather, as I hadn't felt as chilled that day as I had before. Often, when I got in the shower and my skin reddened, it reminded me of how much I needed to warm up. I dressed in a clean jumper and jeans and pulled some fluffy socks on. I would ask Maggie if I could accompany her into town, I wanted to buy my own wellies and not have to rely on the spider homes of unknown occupants from the boot room. There was no telling whose feet had been in those, and I swear one had mice in it.

I walked down and met her in the kitchen. "Can I come into town next time you go? I need some wellies. My walking boots are really not up to actual walking off-road in," I said.

"Of course, I'm heading there tomorrow. Got that lot to take in, so you can help me."

On the counter, were two blue plastic crates filled with pies. She had been super busy since the Aga had come back to life.

"There's a carcass outside we need to take as well," she added.

"I thought Ronan said hunting season was over."

"It is. That one was road kill. Nothing goes to waste here," she replied, and then laughed at the look on my face. I was such a townie!

"Anyway, I need some wellies, and I thought I might get a rain-coat that fits and doesn't have bugs in the pockets. I could also do with some new books. I'm nearly finished with that one you want to read."

"Oh, yes, I'd forgotten about that. We'll pick up some Viagra while we're there," she said, with a wink.

"Maybe I won't lend you the book. Be aware, I'm told, according to the author's page on Facebook, babies were conceived after reading that book." It was my turn to laugh at the look on her face.

Charlie and Ronan walked in as we were laughing.

"What's funny?" Charlie asked.

"Lizzie has a rude book she's reading. She's going to lend it to me, but it might make me pregnant," Maggie said, as she started to put vegetables in pots.

"A rude book, huh?" Ronan said, nuzzling the side of my neck.

"It's a book, an erotic romance, and it's a great read. It's not all about sex…well, it is, but there's a story to it as well," I said, protecting my book fiercely. "How's the pup?" I asked to change the subject.

Charlie pursed his lips. He nodded before he spoke, and it seemed as if he'd thought through his answer and just given himself permission to speak. "Broken leg, as I guessed. Something tried to drag him through the bars. Seems Mum might have had a go, as she had a cut to her nose. Anyway, I've moved them to a safer place."

"What will happen to the pup?" I asked.

"We'll have to see if we can find a home for him. He cannae be a working dog now," Charlie replied with a sigh.

"I'll take him," I blurted out. I'd never owned a dog before, but I was going to miss company when I moved into the barn. "I'll pay all the vet bills if he can stay here until I go home."

"Those collies don't always make great pets, Lizzie," Maggie said with concern. "They need a lot of work."

"If his leg heals well enough, it'll give me an incentive to get out and walk," I said. "I'm happy to pay for him."

"Lizzie, if you want him, you can have him. He's not going to be worth anything as a working dog," Ronan said, and I smiled my thanks.

"What did the vet do, Charlie?" I asked.

"He strapped his leg but was reluctant to take him from his mum. He doesn't seem to be in any pain, so it's wound management and waiting until the bone sets. He might be crippled, so we don't know how well he'll walk," he replied.

I nodded in determination. "I know, and if he can't walk too far, that's fine by me as well."

"Looks like you got yourself a dog," Ronan said. "Have you ever owned one?"

"Nope, and I'll do puppy training and whatever when I get home."

I saw him frown at my words, but I wasn't sure what it was I'd said to cause that. Maybe collies didn't do well in puppy school.

"Maggie and I are going into town tomorrow. Is there a pet store?" I began to get excited.

"I think maybe you should wait until we know what the future holds for the wee pup," Charlie said.

Dinner was served, and talk of the estate continued. It seemed that was the time of day that Charlie caught Ronan up on everything that had been happening, and he even had some good news.

"So, I was talking to the college, about those kids, and it seems they are short on accommodation," he said.

"Student accommodation!" I said, excitedly.

"Not sure. Too messy, parties every night, trashing the place..." Ronan countered.

"Farming students? They're not rock stars," I said.

Charlie pointed out, "Not students. The teachers or whatever they call them. They can't get good teachers because there's nowhere to live."

"Now that sounds better. I can do teachers," Ronan replied.

Ronan told Maggie and Charlie that we would clear up. Maggie liked to watch her soaps in the evening, so both retired to their annexe. I promised her that I'd have the book for her in the morning. I only had a chapter to go, and I intended to finish it that night.

"Do you want a glass of wine?" Ronan asked.

"Yes, please. That would be nice. I'm just going to get my book."

I left him to head to the cellar, and I rushed upstairs to grab the paperback. I chuckled all the way back down as I thought of Maggie reading it. I'd told her it was super sexy, but I wasn't sure if she believed me. I left it on the sofa while I stacked some logs on the already lit fire. I heard Ronan come in and the clink of glasses being placed on the coffee table.

"So, let's see what's so great about this book," he said, as he picked it up, and I winced as he fanned the pages like a croupier would a deck of cards.

He stopped and started to read out loud. I knew the scene he was about to stumble upon, and I coloured with the thought. I sat and picked up my wine as he read. His accent and the sultriness of his voice, as he read out a particularly erotic scene, was beginning to arouse me.

“Wow, does this get you hot because it’s sure affecting me,” he said as he continued to read.

“You reading it is getting me hot,” I said, chuckling.

“Is my Scottish accent getting your hooha all excited?” he asked, completely exaggerating it.

He placed the book down and shuffled up the sofa. I laughed as he closed in on me. He said something that was completely foreign. I placed my wine glass on the floor.

“What did you say?” I said, wriggling as he pulled on my jean pockets to slide me down the sofa. By the time he got to answer, I was stretched out, and he was lying on top of me.

“It’s Gaelic, the real language of my home country.” He dipped his head to kiss me.

“What did it mean?” I asked, as his lips brushed over mine and followed my jawline to my ear.

“Tha gaol agam ort.”

I guessed I wasn’t getting a translation, and by then I was pretty much distracted anyway. We made out like a pair of teenagers, kissing, teasing, and I laughed when Ronan suggested a break for wine before we attempt to get to third base. What he really meant was that he had a cramp.

I straightened myself back up and curled my feet underneath me. I’d had more sex in the past few days than I’d had in years. It wouldn’t hurt to give my hooha a little rest. Ronan thought that hysterical. I picked up my book, and he read the newspaper. It was nice just to sit with him, drink wine, listen to the fire, and sigh as I turned the last page of my book. I closed it and just rested one hand on the top. It was a classic love story, with a lot of heat thrown in.

I loved a good fictional love story because, until Ronan, I'd never had that passion. Until Ronan, I believed it only existed between the pages of my books.

I looked over at him as he concentrated on the financial section. In profile, he had a strong jawline, and his dark brown eyes and hair gave the illusion that he was European, French maybe. He had that straight nose, regal looking. He didn't resemble the picture I'd seen of his father and, of course, I hadn't seen any of his mum without being covered in paint.

The fire had started to die down, and a chill descended on the room. I ran my hand up Ronan's arm. "I'm going to head up," I said.

"I'll clear this away, and then I'll be up, okay?"

I nodded. As I walked up the stairs and watched him turn off lights, for a moment, it felt like we were a *real* couple living together. The fire in the bedroom was low, but I knew we wouldn't add any more logs; there was enough heat to take the chill off the room. I sat on the edge of the bed and pulled off my socks, I slipped out of my jeans and knickers, and then pulled my jumper over my head, and by the time I was removing my bra, Ronan was in the bedroom. He smiled at me as he walked to the bathroom. I heard him pee; he never shut a door even when he was using the loo. I guessed it was a man thing; many a time I'd walk in on Joe sitting and playing some game on his phone.

When I heard the tap run, I joined him to clean my teeth. I stood beside him, naked, and when he was done, he kissed the back of my neck. I shivered at his touch.

I climbed into the bed and snuggled into his side. He wrapped one arm around me, and I heard him sigh with contentment. I felt my stomach grumble a little, and I shifted to get comfortable. The rumble moved from my stomach.

"Oh," I said, and then let out a fart. I buried my head into his chest in absolute embarrassment.

“Jesus, Lizzie, you sound like an old sailor,” he said, laughing.

“I’m sorry. I tried to hold it in,” I replied, laughing myself.

He tightened his arm around me. “Well, I’m glad you feel comfortable to let it out, and thank fuck you don’t stink. That would have been embarrassing.”

I was still chuckling when I fell asleep.

CHAPTER TWENTY-TWO

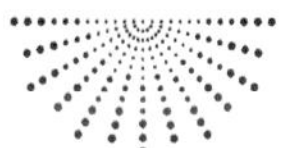

I'd received a text message from Joe delaying his trip up to see us. I decided to give him a call as his message was a little cryptic. I was dressed and about to head down for breakfast, although Ronan had already been up for ages. I didn't know what it was about Scotland in the winter, but I was more tired than ever. I put it down to not having as much sunlight at that time of year, and not having the streetlights to give false daylight for longer hours than was real. I dialled Joe's number as I left the bedroom.

"Hi, I got your text. Is everything okay?" I asked when he answered.

"I'm more than okay. Your neighbour? Phwoar," he said, and then laughed.

"My neighbour? Have you been drinking?" I asked.

"Danny," he said.

"I know who Danny is but...*phwoar*? Are you sure?"

“We’ve had a couple of dates. Lizzie, I could fall for him.”

I was stunned into silence. I had reached the kitchen, and I guessed something in my expression must have alerted Ronan to walk towards me. He mouthed, asking me if I was okay, and I nodded.

“Are you there?” Joe asked.

“Yes, sorry, I was a little shocked there, Joe. Are we talking about the same person, the jerk who lives opposite me, with a dead cat and a blow-up doll and…?” I was about to state that he had a gay wank mag on the kitchen table that I’d used to assault Pat with.

“Is he bi?” I asked.

“I guess so. Does it matter?” Joe was getting defensive. I needed to back off a little.

“No, of course not. I don’t think I’d go as far as a *phwoar,* but if you’re happy, and he isn’t taking the piss out of you, then I’m glad.”

I was guessing by that point, Ronan had got the gist of what I was saying.

“What?” he mouthed silently. I shrugged my shoulders.

“So, Danny and I have decided to spend a couple of days in the Cotswolds to see how we get on. I know it’s quick, but we have a real connection.”

“I’m thrilled for you, Joe, I really am. The Cotswolds are lovely. You have a great time, won’t you?”

There wasn’t much else to say other than goodbye, and I disconnected the call.

“Wow, so *dead-cat-blow-up-doll-and-gay-wank-mag-guy* is dating Joe?” Ronan said.

"Yep. They're going to the Cotswolds." I hadn't anything else to add, really.

Ronan laughed. "Rich *will* be upset."

"Maybe you should tell him. It might make him get his finger out of his own arse."

Maggie spat her tea across the kitchen table.

"Who's gay?" Charlie asked.

"Everyone by the sounds of it," Maggie said.

At that, the sip of tea I'd just taken was expelled through my nose. "I'm not going to think about it. I hope they go, it's awful, and Joe comes home and… That was terrible of me, wasn't it?" I was shocked that I could actually think that way.

No matter what my experience with Danny was, if Joe was happy, then it should be good with me. However, Joe had his own house, bought and paid for, and a successful business. Danny was about to be made redundant and lose his rented flat. Was I being too cynical?

"Are they both coming here to visit?" Ronan asked.

"No, Joe has delayed. To be honest, I doubt he'll come at all now he's off to the Cotswolds, and I know he has some appointments coming up with his mum, so he won't have time. He's dealing with my house as well, although that should be straight forward. I'm a cash buyer, and there's no chain."

"How long did they tell you it would take?" he asked.

"Eight weeks but I'm expecting twelve. The survey hasn't been done yet, which reminds me…"

I texted Joe to make sure he chased up the surveyor that he'd lined up before he headed off on his jaunt. Although I was more than happy to do it myself, Joe seemed reluctant to pass over the details. I just put that down to his control freak nature, and his, 'I know best,' attitude. He sent me a thumbs-up in reply. I sent him another text wishing him a wonderful trip and to take loads of photographs for me.

Ronan texted Rich to tell him Joe was in love with another man and we were all so pleased about that. I thought that to be more bitchy than my comments about Joe and Danny's relationship, so I was pleased to been usurped in the 'shit friend/relation' department. However, I wasn't sure I wanted Joe to end up with Rich either. He'd played Joe along like a good one for a long time.

"Relationships, huh?" I said, shaking my head and buttering some toast.

"Yep, who'd have one?" Ronan replied with a laugh.

My stomach knotted.

❧

Maggie and I left for town. She drove the old Land Rover, and I was quite grateful for the fact it was old. I had to hold the door closed because the latch was broken. I wondered how roadworthy or legal the vehicle was but was assured there were no police locally. That didn't comfort me. The reason I was grateful, however, was that Maggie didn't seem to have any 'spatial' awareness. More specifically, she didn't seem to understand width. The road was wider than the vehicle and straight. I could see for miles, yet she hugged the hedge at my side, the side where the door didn't shut, and I was hanging on to it in the hopes it didn't catch a branch and fling open, with me still clinging to it.

"You know, I might have lived in a city, but even I know you could move over to the centre of the road in a county lane," I said and winced at the screech as another branch gouged the side of the motor. I was sure every tree and hedge would have a green paint stripe along it.

She didn't appear to hear over the sound of the jet engine under the bonnet. The Land Rover was a real utility vehicle without any mod cons, least of all any form of soundproofing between the engine and the passengers. And I was sure I could see daylight through a hole in the footwell.

What the Land Rover was great for was parking. In the sense that she could abandon the vehicle anywhere and we'd never know if it had been hit. Every panel had a dent. She wrenched up the handbrake so hard that I knew it would take two hands to release when it was time, and turned off the engine.

"I love this old thing," she said, patting the dash.

"I think it loves you, too," I said, praying that it did so we'd get home in one piece.

"I remember when this was bought new. These things go on for years. Anyway, if you walk up the high street, you'll see a horsey shop. They'll have your wellies. There are a couple of nice clothes stores as well. How about we meet in the cafe for a coffee in…" she looked at her watch, "Half an hour? That gives me time to unload all this and chat."

"Let me help you unload first," I said.

She waved me off. "My girl will be out in a minute," she said.

I hadn't thought about Maggie and Charlie having children. Not that there had been cause to mention it, of course. As if on cue, a stunning redhead walked from the bakers. She didn't resemble either, but her smile when she saw us was broad.

"Maggie," she said, holding out her arms for a hug.

"Lizzie, this is one of my kids. One of many that Charlie and I fostered over the years. Angie, this is Lizzie. She's Ronan's friend." I wanted to catch the hands that did the 'quote marks' before she even raised them. The emphasis on the word *friend* alerted me to the fact they were coming.

"Oh, Ronan's *friend*," Angie said, thankfully forgoing the quote marks. She held out her hand. "Ignore Maggie. She does love to embarrass us all at times."

I shook her hand and there was something about her smile and her demeanour that made me sure she was a kind person.

"Lizzie needs wellies, so I'm sending her up to Greg's," Maggie said. I hoped Greg was the owner of the horse store rather than a cheap bakery.

"You'll find plenty there. Tell him Maggie sent you. He was one of her boys as well. Might give you a discount, although I doubt it," Angie said, with a laugh.

I left them to unload the pies and walked up the high street. People smiled and bade me a good morning, as they stood and chatted, discussed the news and the weather. Some I could understand, some had such heavy accents, but I thought my ears were getting attuned to it. I even found myself, at times, replicating how certain words were said.

I found the shop I was looking for. It wasn't hard as I tripped over a stack of colourful plastic feed buckets that were set on the pavement outside the shop window. Once I'd righted them, a little bell rang as I opened the door.

"Lizzie? Come on in," I heard. I looked to see a man up a ladder hanging a horse rug over a rack. "Angie rang to say you were on your way. Wellies you're after, is it?"

Greg climbed down the ladder, and he took me aback. I don't know what I expected, but he had a beauty that no man should have and that every woman would be jealous of. What held my gaze were his piercing blue eyes. It took me a moment to realise that he'd held out a hand for me to shake. I, eventually, took it.

“I’m doing the ‘London thing’ with the shake, but I understand we’re practically family so we should hug,” he said, with a laugh. I took a step back, and out of arms’ reach, just in case he wasn’t joking.

“You don’t sound Scottish,” I said, not sure if I was insulting or not.

“I left here as soon as I could. I’ve lived all over the world. I guess I have a mishmash of an accent.”

“But you came back,” I said.

“There’s something about this town that will always hold a piece of your heart. And when you’re ready to settle, you’ll come back to grab it.”

It was a profound statement from someone about my age, I guessed. I hoped that he had settled. He had a pleasant smile, mischievous eyes, and a tone of voice that cajoled, but something made me feel uneasy around him.

“That was very deep,” I said.

He placed his hands over his heart. “As deep as the ocean I am.” He laughed. “Anyway, you’re after some wellies, I hear?”

“Yes. I have walking boots, but they’re not man enough for the estate,” I said.

Greg led me to another room of clothing. There were jodhpurs, leather riding boots, Hunter’s Wellingtons, kiddie wellies, jackets and coats, jumpers and hats, gloves and scarves. Everything the modern and fashion-conscious horse owner could need.

“How about you have a look around, and I’ll finish putting those rugs away,” he offered.

I nodded my thanks. I was drawn to some thick woollen socks, the kind a nanna would knit. I expected them to itch, but they were as soft as cotton. I picked up a couple of pairs. I was also drawn to the purple wellies but thought them too *I'm-from-London-and-I've-never-stepped-in-cow-shit-before* so opted for a traditional green pair. I tried them on and, deciding they fitted, placed them on a chair. I added the socks and a gorgeous cream jumper—the kind of Aran knitwear I used to see in seventies knitting patterns or on adverts for Norwegian hand cream.

"How are you doing in there?" I heard.

"Good, I'm just going to try on a coat," I said, picking up a waxed one.

"You'll be all *countrified* before you know it," came the reply, and I prickled a little at that.

There were a lot of townies that never took the time to venture into the countryside and yet had an opinion on country life. I wasn't one of them. I relished my time, as a child, in a caravan on a farm in Kent. Then, when I was a little older, the chalet on the beach in Cornwall. We could never afford to travel abroad when I was a child. In fact, the first flight I took was to Benidorm with my parents in my early teens. I hated it, they loved it, and it was where they retired to. There were only so many nights I could sit and watch Sticky Vicky pull items from her vagina in the guise of entertainment. I shuddered at the memory, still, each to their own.

The coat I had on was a perfect fit, and I loved how many pockets it had. I'd lose everything in them, of course, but it was going on my pile. It would be perfect for dog walking in the winter when I got home as well. I tried on a hat, added a pair of gloves and a scarf, and I was ready to pay.

Greg rang up my purchases, and I handed over my debit card.

"So, Ronan's *friend*," he said, over-emphasising the word, and I wondered why the fuck everyone felt the need to say it.

"Yes, his *friend*."

Greg laughed, and I wasn't sure what was so funny. "Since you're just friends, if you fancy a night out, I put my number on the receipt," he said, handing me three large bags.

I wasn't sure how to reply initially. "Err, thanks." I took my bags and left the shop.

Maggie was right, there were a couple of lovely clothes shops on the opposite side of the road, and I browsed through the window. I slowly walked back down, taking note of the chemist, the bakers, the butcher, a fishmonger and the fruit and veg shop all with colourful displays of produce making me think there would be no need for a supermarket in the area. Maggie had told me there was one in a purpose-built retail park a mile or so away if it was needed.

I met Maggie in the café and plonked my bags down under the table. I took a look around. "This is a gorgeous place," I said.

There were tables set with floral tablecloths and china cups and saucers. Little silver spoons were laid beside them and in the centre of the table were small glass jars with fresh flowers. We ordered a coffee each, and I detailed all my purchases.

"I didn't realise you fostered," I said.

"Yes. It started by accident really. We had a tree surgeon working on the estate, and he had his young son with him all the time. Mum had run off, sadly. Anyway, it was just too much for Dad to manage. Verity helped, offering accommodation for free, but there were still bills to be paid and the job he had meant he needed to travel. So we offered to look after Aaron. Charlie and I enjoyed doing it, so we signed up as foster parents. We've had about thirty children over the years. Some stay for a little while, respite for the parents for whatever reason, and some for longer."

"When did you stop?"

"We lived in one of the cottages, but when Verity started to—she sort of lost her mind for a while—we decided to move into the annexe to be closer for the boys. We fostered for a little longer, we had Angie and Greg at the time, but we needed to also look after Ronan and Rich, so we gave it up."

"What happened to Angie and Greg?" I asked.

"Angie was sixteen, she was given accommodation, and Greg, who was fifteen, nearly sixteen at the time, moved to a relative's, an aunt."

"I thought about fostering a while ago, but my ex-husband wouldn't have any of it."

"Why didn't you have your own kids, if that's not too personal a question?" she asked.

"Not too personal at all. Harry couldn't, and although we were candidates for donor sperm, we just never seemed to have the time for it."

I didn't add that Harry and I had many a conversation about it, and I'd never questioned his hesitancy or his *reasons* to wait until the following year. By the time I realised he was never going to be ready, it was too late for me. I didn't want to be an *old* mum. I made myself believe that I could never have had a strong enough urge because it was better than acknowledging I'd been manipulated by my husband.

I owned *wine goggles* where everything looked rosy after a couple of glasses, and I also had *Ronan goggles*. Maybe the empathy that he thought I had was because of how he made me feel. When I wasn't with him, my fondness for my ex dissolved.

If I delved too deep into my feelings for Ronan, I also saw the heartache that was to follow.

"I know Charlie said to wait, but is there a pet store here? I want to get a collar, and I didn't think to look in the horse shop."

"There is a feed merchant on the way home. I'm sure they would have dog things. I know Charlie has come home with a couple of beds from there. We can call in on the way back."

I smiled in thanks, and we continued to chat and drink our coffee. We argued over who was to pay. She won, and I vowed to get the next one.

The feed merchant's had a wide selection of pet products, and I picked up a small blue collar with a metal tag. I'd get the tag engraved when I settled on a name. I knew the puppies would be weaned soon, so I picked up a couple of bowls and a bed. I also threw in some towels embroidered with dogs. I'd remembered a programme on the TV once where the dog trainer recommended running a towel over mum to help newly homed pups settle. Pleased with those purchases, I added them to the back seat with my others, and we continued on home.

On the drive was a glazier's van, and I could see a man replacing some glass in the library windows. Charlie was behind, repainting the frames even though I thought the weather was too cold. Surely it wouldn't dry, and in the morning there would just be a white line where it had run over the grey brick and puddled on the gravel floor. I kept my thoughts to myself, of course.

I took my purchases to the bedroom while Maggie headed off to the kitchen. I decided to text Ronan, not knowing where he was:

Hey, I'm back with new wellies and a coat, among other things.

He replied:

I'm at the cottages, walk on up in your new coat and wellies, among other things.

I chuckled at his reply and decided I would. I pulled on the warm woollen socks and carried the wellies and coat downstairs.

"I'm going to meet Ronan," I said, as I poked my head through the kitchen door.

"Have fun," Maggie replied.

Having spent a few minutes trying to find an exit button on the newly repaired gates, I eventually started my journey up the lane. It wasn't far, we'd walked it before, but I hadn't realised how uphill it was. I puffed and panted my way only to nearly end up in the hedge as a car sped past me. I shouted after it and then panicked when it stopped. I had nowhere to go, and I certainly wasn't going to turn around. I watched the reverse lights come on, and I stood tall. The car reversed until it was alongside me—had it been an inch closer its mirror would have hit me.

"I'm so sorry. I didn't see you until it was too late," I heard. I leaned down and baulked. Sitting in the driver's seat was Ronan's ex-wife.

"For someone who lives here, who drives these lanes regularly, I would have hoped that you might have thought about your speed," I said, not backing down.

"Oh, it's you… I said I was sorry. Now I've been suitably chastised, can I go?"

"You chose to stop and reverse, but yes, you can go." I stood and stepped as close to the hedge as I could.

She drove off but noticeably slower. A thought came to my mind. Ronan believed she had been instrumental in the death of Demi. Nothing had been proven, of course, and he could, in his grief, have it very wrong, but this road was a straight lane, and there is no way I couldn't be seen. I looked down to my hands and noticed they were shaking.

"Stop being stupid," I said to myself, and I carried on walking.

I could see the three cottages ahead, and I could also see the car slow. Carol nearly came to a halt, and Ronan stood and stared at her with his arms crossed over his chest. She obviously thought better of stopping, as her wheels spun on the old tarmac kicking up dust and stones, causing Ronan to turn his back as a shield. I wanted to curse her.

"Nice boots!" he said, with a smile as I got closer.

"Thank you. Did she say anything to you?"

"No, why?"

"She nearly ran me off the road—we had words."

He reached into his pocket for his mobile. "She nearly…*what*?"

"What are you doing?"

"Calling her," he replied.

"And then she knows you, and I are bothered. Put the phone down. Why have you still got her number anyway?" I asked, regretting that question immediately. "Sorry, it's none of my business. Just don't call. I told her to slow down, she apologised, end of matter."

He replaced the phone in his pocket and didn't answer my question.

He reached out to wrap me in his arms. "Are you sure you're okay?"

I melted a little. "I was a bit shaken, to be honest. I don't do confrontation normally. It was that, *give someone the finger and then they reverse*. I could hardly run anywhere, so I told her off."

Ronan laughed at my comments. "I'm glad you're okay, but I *will* have words with her, Lizzie. Now, come on in, let me show you what we've done."

He led me to the first cottage; the one Manuel had lived in. It was completely transformed. A wall between the kitchen diner and the living room had been removed, making it one large L-shaped space. Patio doors had been installed in the back, and the light that poured into the rooms was blinding. The white walls reflected that, and the cream carpet warmed the room. I made a point to only walk on the plastic that had been laid to keep the carpet clean and followed the room to the kitchen.

"It's lovely, Ronan," I said.

The kitchen was fully fitted with stainless steel appliances, ready for someone to move straight in.

"The other two are the same, and Charlie was right, I contacted the college, and I've got two of these rented out for a year already."

"To students?"

"No, lecturers. I've got a tenancy agreement sorted with them, deposits, and one month up front. All I've got left is a little snagging, and then they can move in."

I smiled—his enthusiasm was contagious. "That's great news. I'm pleased for you. What about the estate manager position?"

"I was thinking I might hang on to that myself for the moment. I've some students starting as soon as the Christmas break is over. We've done without a *real* estate manager for so long, I want to take my time over employing the right person, and I don't know that there are the funds just yet."

I nodded in agreement although I wasn't sure I agreed. It meant he was staying put for sure.

"What about your cottage?"

"I don't know, yet. I often lock it up for periods of time." He seemed quick to change the subject. "Anyway, come and look at the view."

We walked out into the small fenced garden that had a stone patio, and the rest was laid to lawn. The view was amazing though. To one side was the house and to the rear were fields of heather and fir trees, and then beyond those were the snow-topped mountains.

"Can you ski there?" I asked.

"Yes, although most people go to Aviemore which is east of us. I'll take you over there for the weekend if you ski," he said.

"I don't, but I've always wanted to learn."

"I'll teach you," he replied, taking my hand in his.

We returned to the cottage and out of the front door. He left the keys with the builder that was in and out of the third cottage and walked back to the house with me.

"We'll have a frost tomorrow," he said, as he looked up at the sky.

I followed his gaze, but all I saw were clouds. "How can you tell?" I asked, still staring upwards.

He chuckled. "The weatherman said on the radio."

I whacked him playfully. "Oh, honestly, I thought you could tell," I said, laughing along with him. "I met Angie and Greg today."

"Did you? How was she?"

"Very cheerful," I answered, immediately noting he hadn't asked after Greg.

"She's a sweetheart. Now, I thought we might go out for dinner, what do you think?"

"I'd love to, thank you." Ronan should have got a gold star for the diversions in conversation. Seeing as he didn't want to talk further about them, I told him, "I bought a new jumper. I could wear that."

He turned to me and scooped me into his arms, nuzzling my

neck. "Do that, then I can molest you in the car on the way home. A little layby loving," he said with a playful nibble.

"Layby loving?" I laughed out loud as he turned and pushed the numbers to instruct the gate to open.

With a glint in his eye, he said, "You must have made out in a car before?"

I felt my cheeks colouring. "No, I don't think I have," I replied quietly.

He didn't respond, and I wasn't sure that he got the tone in my voice. I was glad. I didn't want to have to explain that something as silly as a teenage fumble in a car had bypassed me. It was as if that should have been a rite of passage, but I'd missed out.

Ronan grabbed a sandwich, and we headed out to see how the pup was doing. Charlie had been monitoring him and told us that he'd be up on his feet and trying to have a walk around but, of course, with his leg strapped up, it was hard. The vet had said two to four weeks, and the break would be healed, and until then, we had no idea *how* he would walk. I picked him up, and he licked my chin as Ronan sat in the straw and stroked Mum's head. She had been out in the run for exercise, and he picked mud from her fur. Now her babies were hungry and suckling as if it were their last meal.

"I'll have to think of a name for you, little one," I said, kissing his nose and then putting him back on his mother's teat.

Ronan had work to catch up on, and I wanted to finish logging and documenting all the paperwork. We sat either side of the desk and worked in silence. It was comfortable. I could get used to being in his company, whether we were talking, laughing, or just being.

It was dark, and there was a low-lying mist when we travelled to the pub. I much preferred the comfort of Ronan's Range Rover to the old Land Rover, and I made him laugh with my detailed description of the journey I'd taken with Maggie. We arrived at the pub, and instead of sitting in the bar, we were shown through to the restaurant at the back. I hadn't noticed the restaurant the last time we'd been there. I shuddered as I remembered the encounter with his ex-wife.

The menu wasn't extensive but the selection, for a local pub off the tourist track, was amazing. I chose buffalo steak and read where it had been reared, which, of course, was locally. Ronan was able to detail the supplier of everything on the menu, and although the estate owned the pub, he hadn't had a hand in running it for a few years. We both decided to skip starters after I'd seen the dessert menu; my mouth started to water immediately.

The conversation turned to my impending house purchase, and Ronan commented on how excited I seemed.

"I can't wait. I had a lovely house, and I know that's not the most important thing about life, but if I'm going to grow old on my own, I'd rather do it in comfort," I said, and then laughed. Ronan didn't join in, or rather, he did eventually, but it seemed forced.

Once our meal was eaten, we continued to sit and chat. He told me stories of his childhood, and I was further reminded of how different our lives had been.

"How often was your dad around?" I asked as I sipped my coffee.

He shrugged. "I don't really remember. He came and went, fucked around, beat my mum, I beat him, and then I left. I didn't see him for years. I refused to. I refused to see my mum because she kept forgiving him, and I couldn't stand to see that anymore."

"Oh, I'm so sorry, Ronan." I wasn't sure what I could say that would comfort him.

He shook his head. "It's okay. It's why Rich hates me, I guess.

He was left to pick up the pieces when I walked, but I'd protected him for all the years before. One day, I got a call from my mum. She was in pieces, telling me that Dad had finally left. I thought she would be pleased, Lizzie. He'd beat her regularly, yet she cried and begged him to stay. I didn't understand."

Pain crossed his features, and I saw him swallow hard. He averted his gaze and sipped on his wine. I let him be, not wanting him to dwell on any more painful memories. Before I could change the subject, it was done for us.

"Hi, Lizzie," I heard. I looked up to see Greg with a broad smile.

"Oh, hi," I replied.

"Did the boots fit okay?" he asked.

"Yes, thank you. I tried them on at the shop, remember?" I wasn't sure where he was trying to take the conversation, but it wasn't hard to see Ronan become agitated.

"Ronan and I are talking," I said, hoping that he'd understand the conversation didn't include him.

"I can see. How are you, Ronan?" Greg asked. "Haven't seen you in ages."

"Very well, thanks for asking." Ronan's reply was curt.

Greg chuckled. "Well, Lizzie, if you fancy that drink we talked about, you've got my number," he said, he then raised his pint glass to us and walked off.

Ronan mumbled under his breath.

"You don't like him, I take it?" I asked.

"It doesn't matter whether I do or don't, does it? Shall we go?"

I reached for my bag and to get my purse. "I'd like to pay for this evening if you don't mind?" I said, offering a smile.

"I do mind. They'll send an invoice." His tone of voice was

clipped, laced with an annoyance that seemed to have sprung from nowhere.

I blinked rapidly a few times and held back my retort, confused by the change in him. He'd been sad when he talked about his mum and dad but the Ronan sitting, or rather standing, and waiting for me to join him, wasn't pleasant. I'd met this one just the once before, and I wasn't keen.

I stood and walked to the front door. I didn't wait for him to jump around me to open it, I did it myself, and I let it slam in his face. I stood by the car, pretending to fumble in my handbag and waited until I heard the beep of the fob unlocking the doors. I wrenched on the handle and climbed in, then made a point to fuss with my seatbelt, so as not to just be sitting looking stonily ahead. Not that it mattered, Ronan started the engine, and we drove back in silence. The only time I thought he was about to speak was while we waited for the gates to open. From the corner of my eye, I caught him half turn towards me. Then he seemed to change his mind. I sighed and shook my head. I was out of the car and walking up the stone steps to the front door before he'd climbed out himself.

"Fucking whiplash," I whispered into the dark hallway. I carried on up the stairs to the bedroom.

I was standing in front of a long mirror brushing out my hair when he came in. I stared at his reflection. He walked straight to me and without speaking, wrapped his arms around me.

He rested his chin on my shoulder and looked at my reflection. "Don't date Greg, please?" he whispered.

I scowled in disbelief. "Why *ever* would you think I would?"

"Because he said—"

"He wrote his number on the receipt. He didn't *give it to me*. I haven't given him *any* indication that I would like to date him, and he hasn't asked. He offered to take me for a drink, which could mean as friends, although I have no idea because there wasn't even a conversation about it."

"I misunderstood," he replied.

"You did, and then you acted like a child. If I wanted temper tantrums and foot stomping I'd date Joe!"

"He and I don't get on," he said quietly.

"I can see that. You don't have to tell me why, of course, but give me some credit, and some respect, in future," I said, a little gentler than I had spoken before.

"He was the one Carol cheated with."

"Ah, that's awkward." I wasn't sure what to say, really.

"He was pissed off that he had to leave Maggie and Charlie so they could look after Rich and me. It wasn't our decision, and from what Maggie said, he only had a few months left with them before he would have been out of fostering." Ronan sighed still holding me and still looking at my reflecting in the mirror. "When he was an adult, he came back and started an affair, out of spite, I believe."

"I'm sorry that all happened to you," I said. I was sorry for him. I also thought that he had a lot of baggage that he would do well to lose, not for my sake, but for his.

"Is it worth hanging on to that anger still? Doesn't that give him the edge over you?" I asked gently.

"When I went to the police to tell them what Carol had said about Demi's car crash, he turned up and said that she was with him that night. I know that wasn't true, but I can't prove anything. So, is it worth hanging on to? Maybe—for Demi's sake. And yes, it most certainly does give them an edge over me, I guess."

I couldn't imagine what it must have been like for him. To have had that second chance ripped away from him so brutally. I also believed that anyone he fell in love with—if he were capable of doing so again—would always be in her shadow. I felt sorry for him, *and* for me.

"I think that we shouldn't bother to visit that pub again," I said, giving him a smile. I wanted to brush the evening under the carpet.

❧

Later that night, I was wide awake and watching Ronan sleep beside me. His long eyelashes rested on the skin under his eyes, and his dark brown hair was partly standing up in places. He lay on his back, and his chest rose slowly as he breathed in and out.

I envied Demi; I think that she was the one that had the best of him. Carol hadn't a clue what she had, and I had the one with the cracked heart that was lightly papered over. That's assuming I actually *had* him at all. I couldn't make him out. He was jealous of Greg, and I understood why: he was insecure in relationships because of his past—weren't we all?—and I wasn't sure I was the right person to be able to help him move on. I didn't think that he thought that deeply about our relationship for it to have any meaning or to start the healing process. I wanted to cry at that thought.

I slipped from the bed and pulled on my PJs, wrapped a robe around myself and shivered with the cold. I found my slippers and placed my feet in them, then quietly left the room.

I sat at the kitchen table and reflected. There was only five years difference between Ronan and me, yet, there were times when that felt like more. In a way, he acted much younger than his years. It was obvious he was considerably hurt and continued to be, by Carol's betrayal, and possible lies, and also the death of Demi. However, the way he harboured those and the way he allowed that to distort even the slightest misunderstanding into something of magnitude wasn't in my nature. I was trying to be patient, but it was hard work, coupled with not knowing if there was even a serious relationship between us.

I sat in the semi-darkness wrapped in the warmth from the Aga. I could still smell bread and pies that had been cooked the previous day, and I knew that I would miss the house when it was time to leave for good. Although I hadn't known Maggie and Charlie for long, only visited the house a couple of times, I knew that they, and it, would leave a lasting impression on me. Even Saggy Tits—and I chuckled at what had become a term of endearment—would forever be one of many fond memories.

I took a deep breath in and came to a conclusion. I was getting close to the barn becoming mine. I could do with being back in London to pack up my flat and spend some time going through what I had in storage; selling off, or donating what I didn't want, and generally preparing for the move. In other words, until I could figure Ronan out, or until *Ronan* could figure Ronan out, I was running away. I would give him the respect *I* so demanded, though, and tell him that I was needed back home.

❧

The following afternoon, I decided to take a walk. I wanted to clear my head and get my thoughts in order. Ronan offered to accompany me, but I declined. I cited hormones or some other shit that meant men often backed off immediately, not Ronan, though.

"Why do I get the impression that it's more than that? If you want to spend some time alone, you can just say," he said.

"I want to spend some time alone."

His eyes widened and, regardless of what he'd said, he clearly wasn't expecting that.

"Ronan, there are times I love your company. There are times, like last night, like the day you found the photograph and *pounced* on me before you even gave me a chance to explain, when I know, I'll never be able to compete with the demons in your head, or with Demi," I finished quietly. "And it shouldn't be a competition."

He didn't speak, and I wondered if those were words he'd heard before. They didn't seem to come as a surprise.

I pulled on my new coat and placed the hat on my head. I also took his hand in mine and squeezed. "I'm just taking a walk, that's all," I added.

I left the house through the back door and wondered if I'd find my way to the gatehouse and back. I thought it would probably take an hour. I checked my pocket to make sure I had my phone just in case. There were wide tracks that wove through the woods. Those tracks all went somewhere, so I decided I'd follow in the direction I believed was correct.

It was nice to listen to the birds and to breathe in the cold air. The sun streamed through the bare branches of the trees, and I kept to the centre of the tracks where tyres hadn't churned up the earth. I paused as I spotted a deer in front of me and pulled out my phone to take a photograph. She looked at me as I snapped away. I zoomed in and could see her nostrils flare as she tested my scent. Something startled her, and she bolted away. I stood looking in the direction that her head had swung to but saw nothing, and I continued to walk.

My nose was cold, and I was having to wipe it frequently, but I was enjoying myself. The solitude gave me time to think.

I meant every word I'd said to Ronan. Until he dealt with his grief, for both Demi and his mother, any potential partner of his would forever be walking on eggshells and that wasn't something I was prepared to do. I could accommodate baggage. I had a fucking trunk load myself, but I had put aside my hurt ready to embrace another relationship, and I didn't believe that Ronan had.

Thoughts whirled around my head, and the walk wasn't exactly clearing them, nor was it putting them in any real order. There was a small part of my mind telling me to pack up, get back home so I could sort out my flat and prepare for my move. There was another part that didn't want to. I'd fallen for Ronan, I knew that, and maybe I was a sucker for punishment hanging around while I knew that my feelings wouldn't be returned.

I decided I needed half an hour of no thoughts. I'd taken a meditation class once, just the once, I remember falling asleep and being woken after everyone had left with drool down my cheek. I never went back, obviously. I did recall a technique to empty my mind. I tried, and it sort of worked. Instead of Ronan, I had the words, 'empty my mind' floating around my head. I chuckled and decided to sing to myself instead.

Now, I don't profess to be anywhere near what most would call a singer. I scream in the shower, and when doing housework, that's it. I was neither, but I was alone. Just as I was about to open my mouth, I saw all the birds from one tree squawk and fly away. It was followed by an eerie silence. I stood and looked around me. I checked my watch and was shocked to see I had been walking for over two hours. If I had been on the right path for the gatehouse, I should have arrived by then. I heard male voices, and I was about to call out when instinct told me to keep quiet. I darted into the tree line and waited.

From the trees opposite came two men, both were dressed as if about to tackle some insurgents in the Middle East. They were camouflaged from head to toe. I covered my mouth to stifle a nervous giggle. One had green and black paint over his face, and the other had a balaclava that was rolled up under his nose to expose his mouth. Maybe breathing through that wool wasn't pleasant. Both, however, carried shotguns.

Neither had dogs, there wasn't a gun carrier thingy between

them, and they sure didn't look like they were meant to be there. Maggie had told me that Ronan and Charlie shot the deer that went to market, but they didn't hold organised shoots. *Poachers*. They had to be poachers. I fumbled around for my phone and pressed the video. I doubted they could be easily identified but who knew. As they started to walk my way, I zoomed in to get the best headshots I could. They were blurry, and it was more because my hand was shaking than having a poor camera.

I watched as they paused and then turned to face back the way they'd come. I covered my mouth as a deer—it could have been the one I saw earlier—crossed the path. I watched as they slowly lowered to their knees, and one raised his gun.

"Please run," I whispered. The deer didn't seem to be overly fazed.

I couldn't stand there and watch. It wasn't because I didn't want to see a deer shot, although I didn't, it was because I didn't believe they had the right to.

"What are you doing?" I shouted. I must have startled the one with the gun, a shot rang off, and I screamed, the deer ran.

"What the fuck are you doing?" I shouted again, fear making me a little more brazen than I should have been.

Neither answered me as I stepped from around the tree. "I've photographed you. I've forward that to the police, just now," I lied, holding my phone up as evidence.

Both stood. One turned and took a couple of steps towards me. I held my ground, but I was convinced he'd see my legs shake. I was sure I would piss myself if he took another step. His friend grabbed his arm and dragged him in the other direction.

"Go on, run," I shouted, as they did.

I stumbled back to the tree and leaned against is. "Oh, fuck," I said, realisation hitting me. I turned to walk back the way I came, holding my phone aloft when I realised I didn't have one bar of signal.

I started to run, which wasn't the easiest in wellies and a long coat that wrapped around my legs. I felt like I was wading in treacle as my boots became heavy with attached mud. I soon tired and came back to a walk. As I did, my foot slipped down into a hole, and I twisted my ankle. I cried out as heat was immediately followed by ice-cold pain. Tears sprang to my eyes, and I fell. I landed heavily on my hip, jarring my shoulder as I reached out and locked my arm to save myself.

"Oh, fuck," I said, pushing myself into a sitting position.

I could feel the boot tighten around my ankle and knew it was swelling badly. I managed to push myself into a kneeling position, all the while still holding my mud-covered phone. I got to my feet and knew instantly I was in trouble. I couldn't put any weight on my left foot. I dragged it to the edge of the track, using a tree to support myself. I started to cry, and it was only then that I noticed the weak winter sun was beginning to lower. Dark clouds were rolling in on the horizon. All I needed was a crack of lightning and the clap of thunder, and I'd be screwed.

The pain was taking my breath away. I tried to suck in large gulps of air and closed my eyes to focus on my body and try to ignore the pain. I realised very quickly that was all rubbish. The more I tried to meditate, the more the pain in my ankle reminded me I'd been an idiot.

I checked my phone again. The signal was flipping between zero and one bar. I thought I might be able to get out a text.

Ronan, I came across some poachers. I scared them off, but I fell. I've twisted my ankle I think, and I can't walk. I don't know where I am. I thought I was heading to the gatehouse, but I walked over an hour, and I didn't see it. I don't know what to do.

Before I could press send, the signal went. I tried but received an exclamation mark indicating it hadn't sent. I knew I had to move. I reached out to the next tree and hopped, and then again. Where the gap between trees was too large, I dragged my leg, causing such excruciating pain that I screamed out loud. I began to wonder if I'd broken it.

I heard a beep, and I wept with relief as I saw the message logged as sent. I had no idea how many tracks there were that ran through the woods, but I suspected that there wouldn't be many. I knew the one to the glamping art area was narrower, maybe that would give him a clue. I typed out a second text.

The track I'm on is wide with tyre marks, not the same one to the glamping area.

It didn't send, and it was as I looked at my phone, I started to panic. I had five per cent battery. I hardly used my mobile, so I was notorious for letting the battery run down. Joe used to moan constantly at me. He wanted me to upgrade, blaming my short battery life on my ancient handset and telling me about a gazillion newer versions. At that moment, I wished that I'd listened to him.

I knew I had to keep moving. I hadn't deviated off the track, so it was a straight route back, but it was how far I'd get before that black cloud deposited whatever it was harbouring and my ankle gave up. The tightness of the boot was adding to the painful swelling, and I believed I'd have to cut it off.

The already low temperature dropped further, and the black cloud that had been tracking me decided to make my day even worse. Big fat droplets of rain pelted down around me. I checked my phone to see a black screen, and I placed it in my pocket. I sobbed as I trudged on until I wasn't watching and tripped again. I fell, and all I could do was to drag myself until I rested against a tree. I tried to slide off the boot, thinking it might ease the pain, but it was firmly stuck. I pulled my knees up into my coat, making sure to cover myself. All I could then do was wait. I knew I'd be found. I just wasn't sure how long it would take.

I rested my head back on the tree, confident the brim of the hat was wide enough to keep my face mostly dry, but the splash back when the cold raindrops hit my arms stung like little pinpricks. I'd stopped crying but had started to shiver as the cold was seeping into my bones. I gently sang to myself, not caring whether I was in tune or not. And when I didn't want to sing anymore, I sat in silence, straining my ears for any sound of rescue. I couldn't hear the birds anymore, but I could hear the gentle rustle of the last remaining leaves and the bushes as the breeze started to pick up.

I wasn't surprised when darkness crept over me. I watched it. Looking down the track, I could see the sun set and as it did, it dragged its weak rays with it. The light was chased off by the night. I felt despondent and incredibly stupid. I'd stomped off, doing a *Greta Garbo* and stating that I wanted to be alone, and I hadn't thought to check my phone had enough battery, or to even tell someone where I was heading to *be* alone. Other than the rain hitting the ground, there were no other sounds, and I started to get spooked.

I closed my eyes, not wanting to see if anything nasty was creeping up on me. In my mind, the wood was awash with axe murderers and poachers that wanted to shoot me.

I wasn't sure how long I'd sat for. My body was stiff with the cold. I'd gone beyond shivering and even for a townie with central heating and never having experienced the cold, I knew that was dangerous. I needed to move, but I just couldn't get myself up. I was beyond crying—the tears were frozen in their ducts. I believed that when I raised my head, I could hear the crack of frozen bones moving. I needed to move, even if that meant crawling. I had to start making my way back on the track. I began to doubt that Ronan had received the message. I didn't think it would take so long to find me. I pressed against the tree to give me some leverage to stand.

As before, I stumbled from tree to tree. The driving rain blurred my vision, and it wasn't long before even the moonlight I'd been able to navigate by, deserted me. I stood for a while, letting my eyes adjust to my ever-darkening surroundings and whimpered with fear, cold, and desperation. I thought I'd made good strides. I thought I'd taken step after step, but I wasn't sure. I fell again, that time, through sheer exhaustion.

❧

I screamed. The pain that ripped through me made me heave. I felt hands on me, and I was turned. I threw up. I was sure I could hear Maggie gently talking to me. My face was wiped, and then it was back to nothing but warmth and darkness.

❧

I opened my eyes to a room that was subtly lit with green light. I shuffled and realised I was on a bed. I turned my head to see machines; the green light was emitted from them. The smell was clinical. I was in hospital. I used my hands to push myself into a sitting position. I was desperate to pee, so much that I had an ache in my stomach. When my eyes adjusted to the dim light, I saw Ronan slumped in a chair in the corner of the room. His jeans were dirty. He had removed his boots, and I could see his brown socks. He wore a blue woollen jumper that had risen slightly above the waistband of his jeans. I coughed, not to wake him, but because my throat was sore. He didn't stir. I sighed. In the movies or my erotic novels, the hero would have woken—or not even been asleep in the first place—and would have leapt from their chair to be beside the heroine's side. Not Ronan. He did shift, but that was to break wind.

'For fuck's sake," I whispered, trying to swing my legs over the side of the bed. That was when I realised one was in plaster.

I fumbled around for a nurse call button and pressed. Ronan snuffled and shifted again. I wanted to throw something at him.

"Hi, you're awake," the nurse said, whispering.

"I need to pee," I said, not bothering to whisper. I was the one in need, not Ronan.

"I don't think we can let you out of bed just now, so I'll grab a pan, okay?"

I nodded and waited while she left the room. I looked at him, and the more I did, the more I saw the dishevelled hair and the mud on his face and hands. He hadn't taken the time to clean himself up at all, which was probably why he had no boots on.

"He's been here all night. We couldn't get him to leave, so we gave up and let him stay," the nurse whispered when she returned.

I gripped the sides of the bed and lifted my arse. It wasn't how I wanted to pee, but it was the only choice I was given. She slid the plastic pan under, and I held myself in a horizontal squat that killed every single muscle in my thighs and stomach to the point that peeing was difficult.

"You can rest down," she said.

"Yeah, and then it will tip over, and I'll be lying in my own…"

"Hey, you're awake," I heard.

"Oh, fuck."

"Okay, so now we need to clean you up," the nurse said with a laugh.

Ronan had startled me, and as I'd turned to look, one arse cheek had slid off the pan, and it had tipped mid-flow. Having a fifty-year-old bladder wasn't anywhere near the same as a twenty-year-old. There was no stopping mid-flow; there was no pelvic floor control at all. I continue to pee over the bed.

Ronan stood and, in complete ignorance that I had just peed the bed, walked over. He took one of my hands in his and leaned down.

His soft lips covered mine. "Jesus, Lizzie. I was so fucking scared," he whispered, and his voice was hoarse.

"I texted," I said.

"I know. I'd left my phone on charge in the kitchen. We had started to get worried about you. Charlie and I searched locally and then Maggie saw my phone and checked for messages. I kept ringing, but yours was off," he said quietly.

I started to cry, and the nurse removed the pan.

"Oh, you were…" he said as he glanced down.

"Yes, now shut up, please." I continued to cry.

Ronan leaned over me, kissed my lips again, and then my eyelids. "Hey, you're safe now." He brushed my fringe from my forehead and then kissed it.

"If you can give us a minute, please," the nurse said.

"Yes…sorry…of course…I'll call Maggie," he said and then slipped on the polished floor as he scuttled from the room.

"He's a sweetheart, isn't he?" she said, as she rolled me and whipped out all the bed linen in an instant.

She had me washed, redressed in another fetching arse-exposing hospital gown—what on earth was the point of those things—and a clean sheet back on the bed before he returned. He came in with two takeout cups of coffee. The nurse left after telling me that she'd rustle up some toast.

"Are you hungry?" he asked.

"Starving."

"Here, have this, and I'll see what's in the vending machine," he replied, handing me a cup.

"Ronan, it's fine, just sit with me, please?"

He pulled up the chair and took my hand again. "You scared the living daylights out of me," he said. His gaze held mine.

"I scared the living daylights out of myself."

"I want to say, don't do that again, but I let you go, and I could kick myself for that," he said, his voice was full of remorse.

"I'm fifty-years-old—a big girl. I wanted to take a walk, and it was my fault not to check my phone." I started to cry again and thought it was just pure relief. "So, what happened?" I asked.

"Charlie and I had been out on the bikes, searching in different directions. Maggie called through to Charlie, and he came and found me. We took the logging route. I found you face down and semi-conscious. You were flown here. You've broken your ankle, but I think you might have known that. They knocked you out so they could straighten it. But they were more concerned you might be suffering from hypothermia."

"I stopped shivering, and then knew I was in trouble," I whispered. "What time is it?" I looked out the window to see the sun starting to rise.

He looked at his watch. "Just coming up to seven, in the morning," he said.

I was taken into the hospital the previous evening, and I must have slept the whole night, thanks to the residual anaesthetic effects. I was grateful for it. I had flashbacks to feeling so cold and being wrapped in something akin to foil. I had no recollection of being flown, and I think I would have enjoyed that experience.

"Joe is here," he said.

"With Danny?"

"No, on his own."

We fell silent for a while. I rested back, and he ran his thumb over the hand he was still holding. It was a comfort, and I started to doze. That was until the nurse reappeared with an anaemic looking piece of toast and a cup of tea that was more like hot milk.

"I don't think I can drink that," I said, placing the tea to one side, but I nibbled on the toast. It quelled the nausea a little.

"I'm sorry, Lizzie. This is all my fault."

"I tripped, that's not your fault."

"You wouldn't have been there had I not had my head up my arse. You're right, though. I need to take some time to grieve and get my shit together. Joe is going to take you home," he said, bowing his head and avoiding my gaze.

I reached over to him and placed my hand on the side of his face. "I think that's a wise thing to do, Ronan. You need to let go of the past before you even stand a chance at happiness."

He simply nodded. "Maybe, in a few…" he started.

"No time limit, Ronan. Don't put a time on it. You need to take however long it will take. There's one thing I need you to do for me…" I started to cry again. "You need to go now." My voice cracked, and although he didn't look up at me, he nodded.

He stood and raised my hand to kiss my knuckles. "Goodbye, Lizzie," he said.

I didn't reply, I wasn't able to, but I watched him walk, with slumped shoulders, to the door and leave without a backward glance.

❧

"Hey, what's all this?" I heard.

I looked up to see Joe walk in. Ronan had been gone an hour or so, and I was still crying. The doctor had been in, checked me over, and told me I was fit to leave, although I wasn't sure he realised I was leaving for London.

"I'm ready to go home, they said. But I don't have any clothes here," I whimpered.

Joe held up a small holdall. "He packed my bags?" I asked.

"Maggie put this together, I believe. She left a note in there as well. Come on, let's get you dressed and home."

"I fell for him, and I shouldn't have," I said, quietly.

A nurse helped me dress. Joe insisted on pushing the wheelchair I'd been told I had to exit the hospital in. I laid the crutches over my lap; careful not to take out the legs of everyone we passed. Joe pushed me towards a sleek, silver Audi.

"I hired it. I thought it might be more comfortable for the journey home," he said, sadly.

I nodded. "I'll have Maggie courier down my other things. Thank you for coming to get me. I know it's a long drive."

"I flew up last night, stayed at the castle. Fuck me, Lizzie, what a place. Needs an overhaul, I told Ronan that, but, boy, it was impressive." He settled me into the car, but I tuned out. I wasn't interested in his enthusiasm for Ronan's house. I just wanted to get home and lick my wounds.

I slept on and off. We stopped at the services twice so Joe could grab coffee and refuel. He helped me hobble to the disabled toilet and offered to come in, but I assured him I could pull my own trousers and knickers down, even while balancing on a plaster cast foot. I walked back out to meet Joe, who had two coffees and some sandwiches. We sat in the car, and I devoured a dry, unappetising sandwich, and drank the coffee. We did that mostly in silence.

❧

It was dark when Joe escorted me from the Audi and Danny met us at the door. Each took a side of me and they helped me to my flat. I was in my fleecy PJs, and Danny had made tea. He seemed different. Gone was the cockiness. Instead, he was full of concern for me. He made me smile by calling Ronan a cock and telling me that he'd never liked him, despite only meeting him once or twice. Maybe he wasn't all bad. Perhaps I had him completely wrong. There certainly seemed to be so many sides to him, but the one I liked the most was the one that gave Joe such a look of love that my heart missed a beat on their behalf.

"I'll leave you to get settled. Joe, I'll see you later, yes?" Danny asked, and the earnest look in his face made me smile.

"Yes, I'll be over later," Joe replied, and for once he seemed a little reserved, shy even.

I lay on the bed, and Joe fussed with pillows so I was comfortable. I had a flask and a mug of tea, a couple of books, and a new mobile that was fully charged. I picked it up.

"All your numbers are on there," he said, as he sat beside me.

"How?"

"The cloud, my lovely. Anyway, tomorrow, we debrief."

"Before you go, what's going on with you and Danny?" I asked.

"Oh, Lizzie. I don't know what happened. I just…I connected with him in a way I've never done before."

"He's bi?"

"No. He's full-on gay. The woman you saw him with was just a friend. He told me that he'd pretended they'd…whatever." He waved his hand dismissively. "He has a strange sense of humour. I'll agree with you on that. But, Lizzie, when you get to know him, like, really get to know him, he's absolutely nothing like you think."

I glared at him in disbelief. "He has a dead cat…"

"Pat's brother. He thought Pat was mourning so much he stuffed him, or whatever they call it. That's why he lays it on the bed so Pat can snuggle up against it."

I went to speak, and Joe held his hands up. "I know, it's fucking weird, and I told him that." He shrugged his shoulders.

I felt my eyelids begin to droop.

"I'm going to leave you now, but I'll be back in the morning, okay? We've got a lot to sort out, your new house being one."

I wasn't sure I heard him leave the flat. I'd snuggled down, felt my body sink into the mattress, and I slept.

CHAPTER TWENTY-THREE

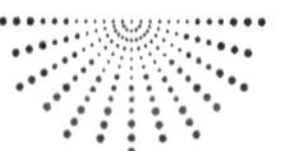

Breaking my ankle was a blessing in disguise *and* the worse thing possible to have happened. Instead of spending the time packing up the flat and going through the items in storage, I simply employed the removal company to come and box my life up. However, that gave me many hours of thinking time. I missed Ronan, for all his faults. I missed Maggie and Charlie. The note that Maggie had left in my holdall had asked that I keep in touch, but I just couldn't at first. However, after a while, we started to text. After the initial 'how is he?' and the, 'he's struggling but agreed to speak to someone,' conversation, any further chat about Ronan was avoided.

I saw a side to Danny that I hadn't before, but I was still wary. I just wasn't convinced that someone could be so different to me than he was with Joe. I rarely had time alone with him, and I wondered if Joe made that deliberate so I couldn't *grill* him. He did, however, confess to his warped sense of humour over the blow-up doll but was mortified to know he'd left the gay wank mag lying around. He thought Mrs Dingle might not know what the doll was, and was grateful I'd removed the mag before she saw that. If I hadn't been so grumpy and irritated at the blasted cast on my leg, I might have also accepted that perhaps I'd had that humour bypass Danny suggested had happened.

"Let's raise our glasses," Joe said.

Danny, Joe, and I were sitting on the floor in the empty flat after the removal company had taken the last of my items. First thing in the morning, they were to be delivered to my new home. We weren't just celebrating my move, but Danny's as well. Joe had let slip, although I don't know why he'd want to keep it quiet, that he'd leased the flat to Danny.

I'd been thrilled at the speed the barn purchase had taken. I guessed no chain either side saved a lot of time. I revisited the house with Danny and Joe—they were a permanent item and therefore stuck together—the day before the money changed hands. Sally, the owner, was tearful but also excited to be moving on with her life. I wished her all the luck in the world and hoped that she had a good lawyer. She showed me how the alarm system worked, the appliances that were being left in the utility room, the ovens, and hob. We stood outside on the patio and drank a cup of tea. She sighed, wiped a tear, and then we left. She, to her new flat, and me, to my old one.

"To new beginnings," I said, finally raising mine.

Danny was moving into my old flat the following day. That night, I was to stay with Joe although Danny had offered his sofa. I'd pointed to my cast and explained that I wouldn't be sleeping on a sofa, and I most certainly wouldn't be sleeping in a bed with handcuffs and whatnots.

With our champagne drunk, they helped me to my feet, and I handed my glass to Danny. He took them to the sink, rinsed, and then left them on the drainer. I adjusted my crutches, and with Joe holding my handbag, I took one last look around before handing the key to Danny and then leaving.

"Are you sad?" Joe asked as I dabbed at my eyes.

"Yes, and no, of course. Thank you, Joe."

"For what?"

"For the loan of the flat, the job, even if you didn't really need to employ me, no rent for two years," I said, with a laugh.

"Ah, but you kept my investment property nice and clean. I could have had squatters in there," he replied.

He was the kindest person I knew and the one most likely to have the piss taken out of him. We walked, or rather, *he* walked, and I hobbled, down the road to his house.

"What's going to happen with you and Danny?" I asked.

"I don't know. He has job interviews lined up in London and Surrey. He has savings to live on, so he's insisting on paying rent. Lizzie, he's seriously intelligent, he has two degrees, so I don't think he'll be unemployed for too long. And, he told me, he has a whopping redundancy package to come."

"Are you happy?" I asked.

"I am. It's odd—how I feel about him is so very different to anyone else, including Rich, although I know now, it was just about the sex with him. Danny is different. Sure, he's strange, but aren't we all? Strange is good, right?"

"Strange can be good, yes. If you're happy, that's really all that matters." I smiled at him as we approached his front door.

I was emotionally exhausted and physically drained. Hopping, constantly, was bloody difficult, and if I didn't end up with some trace of stomach muscles by the end of the eight weeks I had to wear the thing, I was going to be mighty pissed off.

"I'm going to head to bed. I know it's early, but I need to lie down," I said.

Joe helped me to the bedroom and promised to return with a cup of tea a little later. I wasn't aware if he did bring me that tea.

Once I'd washed, changed into my PJs and climbed under the duvet in the spare room, I was gone. I woke a little before seven the following morning. I smiled—it was finally moving in day.

"Good morning, sunshine," Joe sang as he brought in a fresh cup of tea.

He theatrically swished open the curtains, and the winter sun streamed into the room.

"It's going to be a perfectly dry day," he said, waving his arm for some reason.

"That's handy. Nothing like moving furniture in the pissing down rain."

He sat at the edge of the bed. "Now, I don't want you to get all silly but, as soon as Danny is settled with a new job, I'm going to propose."

I nearly choked on my tea. It was the most unexpected thing I could have heard that morning. "Wow, you feel that deeply?"

"I do, and I believe he does as well."

"Have you actually asked him?"

"Of course," he said, snorting his words in a way that would suggest that was a big fat lie. "Sort of."

"Well, I'd be sure of how he feels before you do anything dramatic. Now, let me get dressed, and we can get over to the house."

I was dressed casually, and even though my stomach rumbled to remind me I'd eaten very little the previous day and it believed my throat had been cut, the three of us piled into Joe's little Mini.

"I need refresher driving lessons," I said, remembering that I was completely screwed for getting about now I wasn't up the road from Joe.

"You might just need to get behind the wheel. I'm sure you won't have lost it all," Joe said, not quite paying attention to me while he navigated the London traffic.

We chatted about my impending driving lessons and all the terrible things that could go wrong. Danny and Joe laughed, they finished each other's sentences, and I, rather shockingly, realised they were so similar. For as strange as Danny was, Joe was his equal. I chuckled. I remembered a time when he'd balanced a bucket of water on top of the door, ruining my new hairdo and soaking my carpet. I thought, not too fondly, of the time one Halloween, when he'd bashed on the back door of my house, covered in blood, with a knife in his side and real lamb's heart in his hands. It had been midnight, and I'd been hiding from all the trick or treaters that targeted my street. It was such a shock that I'd peed myself.

"What's funny?" Joe said, looking at me in the rear view mirror.

"I just remembered that Halloween when you turned up with a real heart in your hands," I said.

"A what?" Danny asked.

Joe recounted the story of how I'd peed myself in fright, and I laughed when Danny reprimanded him for such an awful prank.

"No different to you having me…wait, no, you didn't, did you?" I said, cryptically.

Danny turned in his seat. "Huh?"

"Lizzie thought Pat was dead on your bed, so she called Ronan to come and help her dispose of it. Ronan thought a person was dead on your bed and Lizzie was trying to dilute the body with bleach. I decided I wanted to see the dead cat, so I picked it up, it meowed, I dropped it, its eye fell out, and we had to glue it back together. And then we found out Pat was, in fact, alive and downstairs," Joe said, so matter of factly that I screamed with laughter from the rear seat.

Danny looked between us. "His eye fell out?"

"Yes, when fake Pat meowed, I dropped it, its eye fell out," Joe repeated.

For a moment I thought Danny was going to cry! The look that crossed his face was one of surprise, bordering on shock.

"Oh my God. You put his eye in the wrong way," he said, and then he laughed. He laughed so hard that we all joined in and Joe had to pull over onto the hard shoulder of the motorway.

"No, we put his eye in so he was looking left, or was it right. Anyway, he wasn't boss-eyed anymore," Joe said.

"You…thought…Oh my God. You thought I'd had you feed a dead cat?" Danny could hardly get the words out. All I could do was nod in return.

"And you did. You pretended to feed the dead cat, all the while Pat was downstairs!" He screeched the words out. "Oh, Lizzie! I fucking love you," he said.

Tears rolled down our cheeks, and my stomach hurt so badly.

"I thought you were pranking me. I was so annoyed with you," I said when I was calm enough to speak.

"I bet you were. That has to be the funniest thing ever. Pat, according to the vet, not my diagnosis, was depressed because his brother had died. I had the bright idea of using the tools my uncle had left me when he died—he was the taxidermist—to… well, keep Pat happy." Danny shrugged his shoulders. "Trust me. It's not something I'm going to do again. I need to get rid of all the *items* in the spare bedroom, but I just can't bring myself to throw them out."

By the time Danny had told us about his favourite uncle, we were closing in on the village. Just ahead, I could see the first of two lorries that contained all my things. I was as much looking forward to reuniting and reacquainting myself with my life, as I was moving in.

Boxes had been labelled with the appropriate room the items had been taken from. I just had to tell the removal company which of the three bedrooms the ‘bedroom’ boxes had to be stored in. I opted to have them all placed in one, and I’d spend some time going through each one. There wasn’t as much as I’d originally thought. I had a sofa that was minuscule in the large living room, and a wooden dining table that looked completely out of place in the high-tech and modern kitchen. My bed fitted in, simply because it was a plain divan with a cream headboard.

It took only the morning to have the two lorries unloaded and off they went. Joe, Danny, and I started to unpack. We dealt with the kitchen first—that was the easiest. There was a large utility room, which I was thankful for because it proved to be a useful storage room for the empty boxes and packing material.

Danny headed off to find us something to eat, returning with two carrier bags of food from a supermarket he’d been directed to. I appreciated his thought. I was also pleased to know the supermarket delivered to my house.

My house. It seemed strange to use those words after so long. I took pictures that I sent to Maggie and was rewarded with *oohhs* and *aahhs*.

By the time the sun had set, we had some semblance of normality. What we hadn’t managed to unpack was stored behind closed doors.

“We need to get going,” Joe said, checking his watch.

“Thank you so much for helping me,” I replied, hugging them both.

I waved them off, and for the first time in a while, I was alone. I closed the door softly, and I just hobbled around, room to room, smiling. I loved the barn, and I immediately felt at home. I found a stack of logs in a small shed down the side of the house, and I lit the log burner. I sat on my sofa with a couple of wall lights on, and I sipped on wine. I raised my glass to my new life.

❧

It took two full days to unpack every box and then rebox half of it. I had wedding photos and wondered why I'd decided to keep them. I didn't want them, yet couldn't bring myself to throw them away. I was left with four boxes that would need to be moved to the loft or the shed, and three boxes of items to be sent to the charity shop. I'd taken a taxi to Tesco and stumbled around with crutches and a shopping cart. Eventually, the Wi-Fi was reconnected, and I could order online. I stocked up on all the heavy items, bulk buying where possible, as I knew, until I sorted out a car, I wasn't going to be attempting a shop on crutches again. I praised modern life when I was able to register for the doctors online, found a new dentist, discovered there was a beauty parlour in the village and made an account with a milkman. Country living seemed to make me keen to recycle more and cut down on my plastic use.

I had kept busy for the first week and then started to grow a little bored. It was the plaster cast that was keeping me confined. The weather wasn't good enough to venture out into the garden, I was afraid of slipping over, my toes were only covered by a sock, and there was so bloody little I could do on crutches. I abandoned the crutches when I was indoors, sure that bones knitted pretty quickly, and I wasn't harming my ankle by walking on the plaster cast by that point.

By the end of the fourth week, I was going nuts. Joe and Danny visited a lot, they stayed over, and it was wonderful to have their company, but I was lonely and hadn't realised just how much I would be. I knew it was because I was restricted. Once that cast was off, I could walk to the green, and join the various clubs I'd been given leaflets about. I could drive to the supermarket, to

London, and further out into Kent.

While I was confined, I thought more and more about Ronan.

Maggie and I had taken to calling each other, and I was always delighted to hear from her. She told me they had a new estate manager, the cottages were rented out, the students had been out and about, and the log cabin was finished for the art group. I could picture the spaces as she spoke about them. We still avoided talking about Ronan.

When it came time for the cast to come off, I was as excited as a child in a sweetshop. I declined the offer of keeping the cast and ignored the advice that I would be weak on that side. I slid too quickly from the bed I'd been laying on and stumbled sideways. The one thing I was over the moon about was being able to scratch my very hairy leg.

"Fuck me, you look like a yeti," Joe had said as he watched the cast come off. "And it stinks!"

There was an unpleasant odour, and I was looking forward to getting into the bath as soon as I got home.

"Lizzie, can we talk about Christmas?" he said, as we climbed back into his car so he could drive me home.

"Yes! I meant to tell you. I think I might visit my mum and dad, do you mind?" I asked.

I saw the relief in his face, and he blew out the breath he had been holding. "Oh, right, of course. Your mum and dad?"

"I know. I haven't seen them in ages, but they're getting on. They wanted me to come."

It was an out and out lie but judging by the look on Joe's face, the perfect response to his question. Danny had let slip a couple of weeks back that he thought he and Joe were spending Christmas with his parents. They were desperate to meet Joe, by all accounts. Joe knew I'd be alone, and that would cause him anxiety. We'd spent the past couple of Christmases together.

"If you're sure," Joe said. "Maybe we'll head up to Danny's parents then," he added.

I smiled as we continued on our way home. It was one month to Christmas, and I was looking forward to decorating a tree in my living room—to sit with just the twinkling lights for company. I wasn't worried about spending the day on my own at all. In fact, I was quite looking forward to it. I would cook. I would sit at the table to eat and drink wine. I would watch the Queen's speech, maybe doze a little, and I would sit with a blanket and more wine and cry at a soppy movie. I could walk to the pub. I could join the church choir on the green and listen to them singing carols. I could wrap up warm and take a walk through the woods—it would remind me of Ronan. I wasn't sure, but maybe it was the same wood that connected our villages.

"Here you are," Joe said as we pulled on to my drive.

Joe seemed anxious to get going, and I knew it was only to avoid the rush hour traffic.

I leaned over to kiss his cheek. "My new car comes tomorrow," I said.

I had finally bought a second hand car from the local dealership, even though I hadn't even test-driven it. The sales team thought I was mad, and many offered to take me out in their vehicles for practice. I had my *lessons* booked with the landlord of the pub.

"Fantastic! I wish I were going to be here to see it. Will you send me pics?"

I laughed and nodded. "It might be a pic of Harold in a bush," I replied.

"Harold?" he enquired as I climbed out.

"Yes, Harold the Honda." I waved as he reversed out and immediately took a call on my mobile.

"Hey, are you around? Fancy a glass of wine?" I heard.

I'd struck up a friendship with Jake, the landlord. I think he would've liked for that friendship to develop into more, but I'd been honest with him from the beginning. I wasn't ready for that. My heart was still tender. I did, however, enjoy his company.

"Give me five?" I said.

I rushed in, slid off the yoga pants and washed and shaved my one leg. I pulled on some jeans and boots, and it was an utter relief to be able to walk normally—if still a little wobbly. I grabbed my coat, made sure my phone was charged, and that the torch that lived permanently in my pocket hadn't run out of battery life. Then I set off for the short walk to the village green and the pub.

"Lizzie, how are you?" I heard. "No crutches?" another called out.

The locals greeted me and offered a drink, and a stool was pulled out for me. I was welcomed, and it felt wonderful. I chatted to Pam and Del, who kept me entertained with stories of their time owning a bar in Spain. I was the youngest of the group, but it was hard to tell. They were so active, always encouraging me to join their walking group, monthly dinner club, wine tasting, and gardening club. I intended to join all at some point. I accepted the glass of red from Jake and smiled at him. He had been widowed some years ago, and I was very fond of him, but not enough to take our friendship beyond that.

It was a couple of hours later that I decided to walk back. I was accompanied by Pam and Del most of the way before they branched off to their lane. Del, bless him, although I wasn't sure any neighbours would bless him, shouted until he knew I was back at my front door. I laughed as I inserted the key and switched off the alarm.

Being in the barn always brought a smile to my lips. It was tinged with sadness, but that was lessening with each passing day. I found that I had been able to laugh about something that had happened with Ronan instead of having that pang of hurt. Later, as I lay in bed, I whispered a little message to him, wishing him well and hoping that he'd have a peaceful Christmas.

CHAPTER TWENTY-FOUR

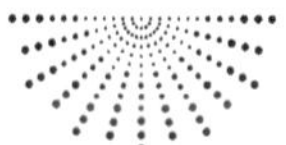

Harold the Honda had been standing proudly on the drive for a couple of days, and Jake jangled the keys in his hand.

“You reverse out. I’m not doing that. Then we’ll drive to the supermarket, and I’ll go round the car park,” I said.

“You drove perfectly okay yesterday,” he replied.

“I know, but that was in *your* car.”

The previous day, Jake had graciously, or stupidly, allowed me to drive his car around the pub car park, around the green, and then back. It was a journey that took all of about five minutes, and that was only because I’d stalled it twice.

“You are going to have to go backwards at some point.”

“Yes, but not onto the lane,” I said, looking up and down it and not seeing one car on the horizon.

Jake wasn’t moving. He stood, letting the keys hang from his finger by the passenger door.

I huffed and held up my hands. "Okay, but on your head be it if I crash," I said, grabbing the keys from his hand and stomping to the driver's side. He chuckled.

I turned the engine on and took two deep breaths, adjusted the mirror, the chair, the mirror again. I turned on the lights, the fog lights, and then the hazard lights. I cussed under my breath, and I readjusted everything back to how it was.

I was ready. I put the car into reverse, looked over my shoulder and drove, so very slowly, out onto the lane. I turned the steering wheel to miss the hedge, and when I was into a straight position, I put the car into drive, and off we went. I screeched a little in excitement but was also thanking my foresight that I'd bought an automatic and not a manual. The last thing I needed was to worry about changing gear. My hands gripped the steering wheel so hard—they were not coming off.

We arrived at the supermarket, and I drove around the car park and then, brazenly, I reverse-parked into a bay. I clapped with delight, and Jake laughed, then I drove us back to the pub.

"Are you sure you don't need me to come to your house?" he joked. "I mean, that's a huge driveway you need to navigate onto."

"You're so funny. Go. I'll be fine, but if you hear a crash, it was me," I said.

I shook a little as he got out, and I pulled back into the lane. I cursed as I heard the crack of a bush as it hit the wing mirror, but I made it back. I parked, got out, and laughed. I threw the car keys in the air, missed catching them, and then found myself on my knees and reaching under the car where the bloody things had decided to settle.

I winced as I stood; my ankle was still not back to full strength. I stood for a moment, just looking up at the house I'd lived in for nearly two months at that point. It seemed a lifetime ago that I'd moved in. The following day, I'd planned to decorate the front garden with Christmas lights—it was two weeks away, and I thought it a suitable time to start the celebrations. The pub was already decorated—half of the patrons loved it, half thought it too early still. I reminded them that some stores had Christmas items in from the end of October.

I put a lasagne in the oven and sat at the kitchen table to catch up with some emails. I'd completed my Christmas shopping online, and all parcels had already been delivered. I'd sent some parcels up to Maggie and included a couple of items for Ronan, just a book I thought he might like, a silly Christmas jumper, and a framed copy of the photograph of the deer that I'd taken. It was a fantastic picture—a complete fluke.

I planned to make arrangements with Jake, or maybe Pam and Del, to head to the local farm and collect a tree. The decorations I'd bought, stood in their boxes, in the corner of the living room, just waiting to be placed on it.

❧

I found that I loved driving. I went everywhere in my little car. I even ventured up to London to meet up with Joe and Danny for dinner and drinks before I 'flew out to Spain' and they left for Danny's parents.

It was the week of Christmas and it was chaotic. For the first time, I was glad I'd left London. Miserable people crowded on the streets, rushing in the rain to get to some place with sour faces. No one spoke; we barely got a grunt from the staff in the restaurant until it was time to pay. The prospect of a tip did wonders to activate the face muscles. Smiles were abundant; soon to be replaced with the sneer when the tip didn't appear to measure up to what they believed their service was worth.

"I'll call you on Christmas day, okay?" I said. Joe had been hesitant to talk about the approaching day, and I wondered if he knew I'd lied.

"You will have fun, won't you?" he asked.

"I most certainly will. Now, I need to get going. I think I've missed the traffic," I said.

I climbed in Harold the Honda, set the satnav to home and waved goodbye. I listened to the radio as I drove, never getting over sixty miles per hour by choice. I was sure the lorries sitting up Harold's arse weren't as happy as I was. I sang all the way home.

I'd showered and sat in the living room with my PJs on when the sweep of headlights flew across the window. It was unusual, and for a moment, I sat still trying to work out why. When I realised it meant a car had pulled onto my driveway, I stood. It was rare to have visitors in the evening, and I picked up my mobile and brought up Pam and Del's number. I didn't call, but I kept my finger hovering just in case. I heard a knock at the door but was worried about venturing into the hall, the front of the property was mostly glass. Whoever was out there, would see me, and I'd have no option but to open the door. I heard a second knock.

I stepped out into the hallway and then froze. It was raining, and he was standing there in a coat with a hat, holding a collie that was sporting a big red bow around his neck. I covered my mouth to hide the sob and felt tears sting at my eyes.

"Do you think you could open the door? It's pissing down," Ronan shouted. "Max is getting wet."

I laughed and rushed forward, then stepped back to let Ronan walk in. At first, neither of us spoke.

"Hi," he said quietly.

"Hi," I replied, equally as quiet.

"Max missed you," he said, raising the dog as if I couldn't see him.

I reached out and took Max from his arms. "Hello, Max," I said, as he licked my chin. He wiggled, and I placed him on the floor. He limped a little as he investigated.

"He'll always have the limp, and he might need an operation when he's a year old," Ronan said.

I nodded as I watched Max piss on the stone floor.

"I have things for him. A bed, and dog food, if you still want him," he said.

I looked up at Ronan. He'd lost weight, and he looked tired.

"Have you just driven down?" I asked.

"I have. I should have called but…" He didn't finish his sentence and looked so very unsure of what to say or do next.

"Would you like a glass of wine?" I offered.

Finally, he smiled. "That would be nice."

"How about you grab your… Max's things, and I'll get another glass."

Ronan walked back to the car and Max followed me to the kitchen. He sniffed around and bounced as I peeled off some kitchen roll to mop up his pee. He gave a little yelp and a wag of his tail. I noticed that when he did wag, his back leg would give way and he'd collapse to the floor.

"Poor Max," I said, picking him up.

"I wouldn't do that too often. He might expect it when he grows up," Ronan said with a grin.

He stood in the doorway with a holdall, a dog bed, and a carrier bag. He placed them all by the foot of the stairs and then removed his coat and hat. I walked to the downstairs loo to grab a hand towel. Even though he'd worn a hat, his face and hands were wet.

"I should have called, I'm sorry," he repeated.

"Ronan, I'm glad you didn't. I'm happy to see you."

He took a tentative step towards me. I met him in the middle. He began to raise his arms, and I didn't wait as I stepped into his embrace. He rested his chin on my head, and I both felt and heard the sigh that left his body. I could also feel the pounding of his heart.

"I was so nervous coming here," he whispered.

I pulled back to look up at him. "Why?"

"I wasn't sure of the reception I was going to get. I hurt you. I pushed you away. I hurt myself, and it's taken me this long to understand."

"How about we have a glass of wine and let's not talk about us, you can tell me what's been happening at the estate," I said, not mentioning that I knew most of it.

He smiled, and it caused my heart to miss a beat.

It wasn't that I didn't want to hear what he had to say—I just wasn't ready at that moment. I just wanted to be with him, to sit and listen to his voice and calm my racing heart.

We sat, Max, obviously exhausted by the journey, curled up on the bed I'd placed near the log burner. Ronan detailed everything that had happened at the estate. He seemed animated as he spoke, a little like the Ronan I'd first met.

We laughed as he told me about when the students first encountered the art group. Although the group were confined to the log cabin, Ronan told me, the students had stumbled across them when they'd taken a wrong turn. I laughed along with him, and it felt good. I told him about driving Harold the Honda and how Jake had helped me. He wanted to know about the people I'd met, and how I'd coped with the broken ankle. He frowned and bowed his head a little when I confessed to finding it hard during that time.

"I'm sorry, Lizzie. I know you've heard those words from me before, and I have no right to even imagine you could forgive me…"

I picked up his hand. "I don't have to forgive you because there's nothing to forgive. You were, still are I imagine, grieving. You needed to get your head straight," I said. I didn't want to ask if he'd done that—it had only been a couple of months.

"I know, and I'm not going to sit here and tell you that I have, but I made a start. I got some therapy. I'm still getting therapy, but I came to one startling conclusion…" He took a deep breath before he continued. "My life, even though troubled, was way less shit when you were in it, Lizzie."

"Way less shit, huh?" Inside, I was a mess. My stomach churned at his words and the way he looked, as if he had a big reveal for me, had my hand's shaking.

He smiled, and his eyes crinkled at the corners. "Yeah, way less. And those were totally the wrong words, but I'm terrified to tell you the truth." He paused and then sat up a little straighter, determination evident in his face. "I'm going to, though. Lizzie, I love you. I fell in love with you when I met you, and I fucked everything up time and time again. Yet, you still stood beside me. Until you didn't, and then I knew, I'd pushed too far. I have a habit of pushing people away, and I don't want to do that with you," he rambled.

I was dumbstruck. I replayed what he had said in my mind, praying I'd heard every single word correctly. More specifically, and I whispered the words as I recalled them, the fact that he loved me.

He took a deep breath. "I love you. I know I have a way to go before I'm not a dick, but I'd like to know if you and I could start again?"

I felt a very slight shake to the hand I was holding. It matched mine.

I leaned forward, and I kissed him, gently at first. When he wrapped his hand around the back of my head and pulled me further towards him—my heart started to pound. My stomach was a mass of flutters as we slid down into the arm of the sofa. He grabbed at my hair and moaned, and that sound reverberated through me. I was about to grind myself into him, such was my state of arousal, when I heard a yelp. I pulled my head back, not sure if that was Ronan.

Max was sat at the base of the sofa looking up at us. He wagged his tail and yelped again.

I laughed. “I think we need a little privacy, Max,” I said.

We held hands as we walked up the stairs, and I led him to my bedroom.

“I’ve missed you so much,” I whispered, as I stripped off my PJs.

We made love, and he told me that he loved me, again. I wanted to say it. I knew that I did, but I held back just a little. I needed to be sure he meant it. He whispered it again as I fell asleep in his arms, and I was sure that I heard him tell me three or four times more throughout the night.

❧

I was dressed and downstairs early the following morning. I didn’t want to wake up to dog mess and bless him, Max had held on until I opened the back door and he shot out through my legs. He peed, he sniffed, and he left a nice little deposit in the middle of the lawn, and then peed some more. I called him and was surprised that he immediately returned and sat at my feet looking up at me.

“Breakfast?” I said, to him.

"As long as it's you," I heard. Ronan walked up behind me, wrapped his arms around my waist and kissed the side of my neck.

"How about we eat…food…take Max for a walk, and then…" I turned in his arms. "We can make a decision about lunch and dinner."

Once breakfast was done, Ronan produced a lead and a plastic container of small poop bags. It seemed that Max had received some basic training as he bobbed along beside us. I heard a beep and waved as Jake slowed his car down. I leaned down and looked in the window.

"Hi, how are you?" he asked.

"Good, this is Ronan," I said.

"Ah," Jake smiled and nodded, understanding immediately that Ronan had been the reason that our relationship was a friendship only. He reached out to shake Ronan's hand. "It's nice to meet you. How about you both come to the pub tonight? It's the last dinner club this year," he said.

I looked at Ronan, who shrugged his shoulders. "It's up to you," he said.

"Thank you, Jake. Put us down for a table," I said.

I squeezed his arm as Jake gave me a kind smile. In another world, another time, I would have dated him, but I couldn't when all the time I knew my heart belonged to a Scottish man who was both frustrating and annoying, and sexy, and…

I watched Jake drive off and then turned to Ronan. "I assumed you were staying for more than one night," I said. I had noticed the suitcase through the rear window of his Range Rover.

"If you'll have me," he said.

I nodded. "I'd like to spend Christmas with you, Ronan. And

you, Max," I said to the little dog jumping up at my legs.

We continued our walk around the village green until we came to the hall. We paused and sat on the bench while I extended the lead to let Max have another pee and a sniff around.

"What the…?" I heard.

I turned to see Ronan pull a leaflet from the noticeboard of the village hall. I laughed as he read. "Limp Dicks and Saggy Tits Naked Gardeners. To raise funds for the Village Hall, come and join the photo shoot for the Naked Gardeners calendar. Tea and cake available." He looked at me. "Limp Dicks and…" he laughed.

"I thought it a bloody good title for our little fundraiser. Do you want to join in? I think we are missing a Mr December," I teased.

He re-pinned the leaflet and took my hand. We returned to my house and he took the key from me as I fumbled with the lock, then opened the door. Max was let off his lead, and he rushed to his water bowl and then flopped on his bed.

"Lunch?" I asked, with a smirk.

"Oh, yeah." Ronan took my hand and led me back up the stairs.

❧

Ronan stayed for Christmas, and then New Year as well. He got on well with Jake, who told me he approved and for that, I was grateful. We still, however, hadn't really had *that* talk. As snow started to fall one evening, I decided it was time.

"It's been so nice to have you here," I said.

Ronan turned sharply to me. "I think I can hear a *but* coming," he said warily.

"No, there isn't. I just need to know where, if anywhere, we're going with this." I held my breath for a moment.

Ronan placed his hands on either side of my face. He stared intently. "I love you, Lizzie. I've told you. I know what I want, but I don't want to put that on you. It has to be your decision."

"Maybe you could give me a hint as to what you want? It might actually make it easier for me, you know," I said.

He sat back and straightened as if about to give a speech. "I want us to live together, both here and in Scotland. I know it's a lot to ask. I will have to be in the two places until maybe one day we decide which one to settle in. I want... No, I *need* you by my side. I have a second chance here that I don't want to let go of. I loved Demi, but I love you more."

"You can't say—"

"I can, and I have. I'm not wasting words. I spent two months thinking of you, pining for you, as Maggie would say. Every day was torture, I felt like I couldn't breathe, and my heart hurt. I was devastated when Demi died, of course. But you telling me to leave felt so different. I can't explain, other than to say I didn't want it. I don't want to miss you anymore."

"When you say you want us to live together, where?" As much as I loved the idea, his previous behaviour left me a little cautious. I loved him, and I knew we'd end up together but the timing... I shook my head; spontaneity had taken over from my usual dithering on important matters.

"Wherever you want. Here, my cottage, a new house. I don't care as long as it's together."

"Here, Ronan, if that's okay. It's larger, and if I'm here and you're in Scotland, I'm not so isolated."

His smile started and didn't stop until he was beaming. "So that's a yes then?" he asked.

I threw myself into his arms. "It's a yes."

Ronan laughed, and Max jumped around, leaving a little trail of excited pee as he did. I texted Joe to give him my news, and I received a voice message that was simply a scream of happiness, so he had to translate. It made me laugh, although Max wasn't so sure, so he peed a little more.

Life was about to take a turn for the better, I was sure. I was happy to commute between Scotland and Kent. I loved both homes. In fact, I really didn't care where we ended up, as long as we ended up together.

"I've loved you from the beginning," I whispered, and I felt tears brim in my eyes.

"I'll rent my cottage out, and the new one when it's renovated. We're only ten minutes from Mrs Sharpe if she needs me," he rambled, excitedly making plans, and I started to laugh.

Ronan pulled me into a hug, and by the light of the log burner and the twinkling Christmas tree I watched the snow falling heavily outside the window, and we started to plan our future together.

CHAPTER TWENTY-FIVE

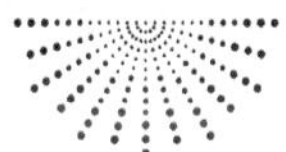

Readers, it's me, Tracie! I highjacked you and I'm sorry, but there is a reason for this. I need you to read this chapter…

So, I see you roll your eyes at Lizzie. Go on, admit it, you did! I hear you, also, muttering those words, 'never in a million years would she not know about being drugged!' You did, didn't you? Email me, tell me I'm correct. Shall I tell you how I know? Settle back, my lovelies, and let me tell you a short story.

I've said the same words myself. I've rolled my eyes until they ached.

Lizzie is my mum – bet you weren't expect that, were you?

Lizzie isn't my mum's name, of course, and this is a fictional story. BUT (caps for emphasis) a lot of what Lizzie has done was from memories of the same things my mother did. You need to understand why so you can stop rolling your eyes, you'll make them bleed ;)

My mum was fifteen-years-old when she met my dad (nearly sixteen, let's make it legal!). She had just turned seventeen when

I was born. She had a second child eighteen months later. She was a teenage mum living in a terraced house on a street in South-East London with other teenage mums. We had an amazing childhood, partly because my mum wasn't much out of being a child herself. Anyway, I digress…

When my mum turned fifty she divorced my dad and it hurt her, greatly. Now, my mum doesn't really do single. She's never been single. She dated one man and then, she finds herself wanting to date, wanting to meet someone new. But it's been fifty years, readers! The changes to how we lived and dated in that time were off the scale.

The things that Joe told Lizzie? Those were the things I told my mum. She didn't believe anyone would want to drug a fifty-year-old; I wasn't taking the chance. She didn't believe someone would want to assault a fifty-year-old; I wasn't taking the chance.

My mum hadn't done what most of us had. We dated, we met the arsehole and we had our heart broken, we met the nice guy and he wasn't exciting enough. We explored–she didn't, until she was fifty and single.

The second thing I want to bring to your attention. There are women like Lizzie, like my mum, that are very forgiving. I honestly believe that the older you become, the more tolerant, the more understanding, you are likely to be. My mum is way more forgiving that me. Just because *we* might have kicked Ronan to the kerb a while ago, doesn't mean it's wrong for another not to.

Forgiveness takes courage and strength.

That's all I want to tell you, readers, and I hope you'll forgive me for highjacking this ending.

If you enjoyed Limp Dicks & Saggy Tits, then can I

recommend A Virtual Affair to you? Although not a romcom, this book is very personal to me:

You can read A Virtual Affair as part of your Kindle Unlimited subscription…
http://mybook.to/AVirtualAffair

Love, Tracie, and the eternal teenager, her mother, Janet xx

ACKNOWLEDGMENTS

Thank you to Margreet Asslebergs from Rebel Edit & Design for yet another wonderful cover. I don't know how many it's been now!

I'd also like to give a huge thank you to my editor, Lisa Hobman, and proofreader, Claire Allmendinger from Bare Naked Words.

A big hug goes to the ladies in my team. These ladies give up their time to support and promote my books. Alison 'Awesome' Parkins, Karen Atkinson-Lingham, Ann Batty, Elaine Turner, Kerry-Ann Bell, Lou Hands, and Louise White – otherwise known as the Twisted Angels.

My amazing PA, Alison Parkins keeps me on the straight and narrow, she's the boss! So amazing, I call her Awesome Alison. You can contact her on AlisonParkinsPA@gmail.com

To all the wonderful bloggers that have been involved in promoting my books and joining tours, thank you and I appreciate your support. There are too many to name individually – you know who you are.

ABOUT THE AUTHOR

Tracie Podger currently lives in Kent, UK with her husband and a rather obnoxious cat called George. She's a Padi Scuba Diving Instructor with a passion for writing. Tracie has been fortunate to have dived some of the wonderful oceans of the world where she can indulge in another hobby, underwater photography. She likes getting up close and personal with sharks.

Tracie likes to write in different genres. Her Fallen Angel series and its accompanying books are mafia romance and full of suspense. A Virtual Affair, Letters to Lincoln and Jackson are angsty, contemporary romance, and Gabriel, A Deadly Sin and Harlot are thriller/suspense. The Facilitator & The Facilitator, part 2 are erotic romance.

Website:
www.TraciePodger.com
Email:
author@TraciePodger.Com
Facebook:
https://www.facebook.com/TraciePodgerAuthor/

Sign up for my newsletter and receive a copy of my novella, Evelyn: https://www.subscribepage.com/v8h1g0

ALSO BY TRACIE PODGER

Fallen Angel, Part 1

Fallen Angel, Part 2

Fallen Angel, Part 3

Fallen Angel, Part 4

Fallen Angel, Part 5

Fallen Angel, Part 6

The Fallen Angel Box Set

Evelyn - A novella to accompany the Fallen Angel Series

Rocco – A novella to accompany the Fallen Angel Series

Robert – To accompany the Fallen Angel Series

Travis – To accompany the Fallen Angel Series

Taylor & Mack – To accompany the Fallen Angel Series

Angelica – To accompany the Fallen Angel Series

A Virtual Affair – A standalone

Gabriel – A standalone

The Facilitator – A duet

The Facilitator, part 2 – A duet

A Deadly Sin – A standalone

Harlot – A standalone

Letters to Lincoln – A standalone

Jackson – A standalone

The Freedom Diamond – A novella

Limp Dicks & Saggy Tits – A standalone

www.ingramcontent.com/pod-product-compliance
Lightning Source LLC
Chambersburg PA
CBHW070542310726
48982CB00010B/1442/J

* 9 7 8 1 8 3 8 0 4 9 5 0 8 *